LOVE
MARRIAGE

MONICA ALI

LOVE MARRIAGE

virago

VIRAGO

First published in Great Britain in 2022 by Virago Press

1 3 5 7 9 10 8 6 4 2

A CIP catalogue record for this book
is available from the British Library.

Hardback ISBN 978-0-349-01548-4
C format ISBN 978-0-349-01549-1

Typeset in Garamond by M Rules
Printed and bound in Great Britain by
Clays Ltd, Elcograf S.p.A.

Papers used by Virago are from well-managed forests
and other responsible sources.

MIX
Paper from
responsible sources
FSC® C104740

Virago Press
An imprint of
Little, Brown Book Group
Carmelite House
50 Victoria Embankment
London EC4Y 0DZ

An Hachette UK Company
www.hachette.co.uk

www.virago.co.uk

Shumi
this one's for you

CHASTE

In the Ghorami household sex was never mentioned. If the television was on and a kissing-with-tongues scene threatened the chaste and cardamom-scented home, it was swiftly terminated by a flick of the black box. When Yasmin began her first period, her mother had slipped her a pack of Kotex Maxi pads and murmured instructions not to touch the Qu'ran. This was confusing because Yasmin never touched the Qu'ran anyway, except at the behest of her mother. But it also made sense because menstruation, as she had learned in a biology class, was linked to reproduction. And the dotted-line diagrams in the textbook were, surprisingly yet undeniably, linked to the actors who pushed their tongues into each other's mouths, thus ruining everyone's viewing pleasure.

Now, at the age of twenty-six, Yasmin knew all about sex. The human body had long since yielded its mysteries. She had slept with three men, and was engaged to be married to the third, Joe, a fellow doctor at St Barnabas hospital. Her parents, Shaokat and Anisah, liked Joe because as a doctor he was automatically suitable, and because everyone liked Joe, he was gifted that way. If Anisah longed for her daughter to marry a good Muslim boy it was an opinion she kept to herself.

1

Yasmin sat cross-legged on her bed, surrounded by medical texts, waiting to be called down for dinner. She should have been studying for yet another exam, but couldn't concentrate. Four books lay open to demonstrate a commitment that she was unable to put into effect. Instead, she leafed through a magazine she'd found discarded on the train. On the cover: Fake Split! Secret Reunion! She's a Wreck! The headlines referred to celebrities, all pictured, only one of whom Yasmin could identify. This dampened her enjoyment only marginally. She preferred, in any case, the stories about 'real people'. The one she had just finished was about a mother-of-three from Doncaster, who had recently discovered that her seven-year-old daughter was not her biological offspring, a mix-up having occurred at the hospital when she was born. The things people go through! And she, Yasmin, had nothing to worry about, and so much to be grateful for.

When tomorrow night was over she'd laugh at herself. It wouldn't be as bad as she imagined. Her parents would meet Joe's mother for the first time. They'd all eat dinner together at her house in Primrose Hill and discuss wedding plans and make polite conversation. Big deal.

The thought of her parents inside that discreetly sumptuous Georgian terrace induced a faint feeling of nausea. She swallowed it down.

Nothing embarrassing would happen. Fretting like this was stupid.

The bedroom door opened and Arif slid in. 'That is some bush,' he said, shaking his head.

She slipped the magazine under a book. 'Out,' she said. 'I'm working.'

His words slowly infiltrated. 'Out,' she said again.

Arif closed the door and leaned his boneless, insolent body against it. 'You know about it, yeah, the picture – like I was telling you, every article about her goes on about it – but I had to dig bare deep to find it. Wanna see, Apa?' He pulled his phone out of his jeans.

Yasmin had decided she wouldn't react, no matter what provocations her maladjusted little brother attempted. In spite of herself she recoiled, shrinking back on the bed as Arif brandished the phone. The last thing in the world she wanted to see was Harriet Sangster's private parts. She wondered, not for the first time, if Joe had seen the infamous photo of his mother, naked on her back with her legs split wide, head raised to stare, challenging and defiant, straight into the lens.

'It's a feminist photo,' she said, and her voice remained even. 'It was decades ago. You wouldn't understand. Stick with your porn. Stick with your hairless porn.' The photo was a rejoinder to the 'ladette culture' of the time. Yasmin hadn't seen it but she had read about it. In an age that deemed itself post-feminist, post-ideological, post-ironic, post-everything, Harriet had written about the dangers of the 'zero fucks' mentality, the intellectual poverty of the end-of-history attitude, the oxymoronic idiocy of the belief that it was uncool to believe in anything. Most of all she had written about what she saw as 'faux female empowerment': the girls-gone-wild trope of hard drinking and waxed-and-plucked sexuality that, as Harriet saw it, served male fantasies by way of soft-porn imagery in what were known as 'lads' mags'. Harriet had her own version of female liberation, including sexual freedom. Her version went against the zeitgeist. It had brought her attention, some of it far from positive. Despite that, or perhaps because of it, she had risen to a position of some prominence, and the photo was ancient history.

Arif smiled. 'What about Ma and Baba? Think they wanna see? Maybe they already saw. You know, Joe said I should come for the dinner tomorrow.'

'Get out now!' She picked the heaviest book off her bed.

Arif shrugged. 'You can't throw straight.'

3

'You little shit.' He'd probably seen the photo months ago. Since when did Arif have difficulty finding anything on the internet? He'd just been waiting, saving it up for maximum impact the day before the families met.

'Have you explained to Ma how it's, like, a feminist photo? She bought Harriet's book, right, the first one about all her lovers, all the men – and women – all very *feminist*. But I don't think Ma really got it. Because she was reading it, yeah, stood in the kitchen. Her face – you should've seen, Apa! She was stood over the bin, and her foot was on the pedal so the lid was open. And when she saw me, yeah, she let it drop. Into the rubbish. Like, well shamed and everything.'

He was laughing as she hurled the textbook, predictably badly, across the room, but he went out then and Yasmin jumped up and paced back and forth, trying to restore order to her thoughts.

BABA

By eight o'clock she was hungry. Standing outside the closed kitchen door, listening to the sizzle and clang, she debated whether to go in and help Ma or slip quietly back upstairs.

'Come, Mini,' her father called from the sitting room. He said Mini was her nickname but in fact no one else ever called her that. 'Sit with me.'

Baba didn't look up from his journal when Yasmin sat down on the sofa. 'Your mother is late with the food today because she has spent at least ten hours preparing shukto, alu dom, dal pakori, kachori and what have you. Every snack you can name, she has prepared. I told her fifty times we are attending a dinner not setting up a street-food stall, but does she take heed? This is what I have put up with all these years. The woman is stubborn as a mule.' He sighed and turned the page.

'Maybe we could just take a bit of each,' said Yasmin. But she knew there was no hope. They'd be dragging carrier bags stuffed with Tupperware boxes and metal tins, not presenting an elegant sampling plate of exotic delicacies. Harriet, of course, would be gracious enough to hide her amusement.

'I haven't heard this term before – "ghost surgeries".' Baba turned to Yasmin to see what she made of it. 'There's a whole article here about the number of American doctors getting sued for this. Would you like to know my opinion?'

She said that she would. A new pile of stuff had sprouted beneath the bay window. *Stuff* grew in this house like mushrooms in a damp dark wood. Boxes and bags of useless items that would end up in the garage or in the spare bedroom or foisted on neighbours who were too weak to resist a second-hand salad spinner pressed on them by Mrs Ghorami. Few of the whitewashed pebble-dashed semis in the street had escaped the overflow from 23 Beechwood Drive.

Baba removed his spectacles and considered. He had a habit, when thinking, of taking off his bifocals and folding them up, as if the truth could only be seen by looking in rather than out. He sat straight-backed on the wooden chair at the splintery pine dining table that served as his desk, with files and drawers stacked above and below. He had an office, the front room as it was always called, which had been kitted out with great ceremony some years ago when he became a partner in the GP practice at which he'd worked for the previous decade. The front room was lined with shelves that held science books and ring binders of journals. In the centre sat a large mahogany desk with leather and brass trimmings, and a forbidding black padded swivel chair. When Baba had an announcement to make, or when he delivered one of his lectures to Arif, about his lack of direction, his failure to grow up and take responsibility for his future, these interventions were staged in the front room. Otherwise, he preferred to sit in the living room and read at the table, and if he wished to watch the television he merely turned his chair around rather than submit to the comfort of the sofa or reclining armchair.

'It is a matter of consent, Mini,' he said, having concluded his deliberations. 'The patient must not only sign the form but his consent must be informed consent. If he does not know who will carry out the procedure then he is not truly informed.'

6

'Yes, Baba.' Yasmin knew he was looking for more from her. How could he fulfil the role of teacher if she did not adopt the position of student?

But she was mightily distracted. Her stomach broiled with a mixture of hunger and anxiety. For weeks she had been holding at bay – only just! – her fears about her parents meeting Harriet. The engulfing pressures of work had helped as had – to an extent – Joe's easy assurances. Harriet would not only be on best behaviour, she would be delighted and charmed. She loves you, of course, he said, but she's a bit disappointed you're not more Indian. Your parents are authentic enough to give her an orgasm.

She tried to put it out of her mind, but it hung around like next door's cat, whining and mewling on the windowsill. Now the day was almost upon her and she realised she'd been suppressing the wrong worries. Whatever Harriet really thought about Shaokat and Anisah would be cloaked by English manners and didn't even matter anyway. The English middle classes did not meddle in their children's matrimonial affairs. But Harriet Sangster threatened to bring – had already brought – sex into the Ghorami household, and she could not be neutered by a flick of the switch. What would ensue if, as had happened on Yasmin's first visit to Primrose Hill, she insisted on showing off her collection of Indian erotica? Or started on one of her pet topics, such as the cultural significance of pubic hair?

The image of Ma dropping Harriet's book into the kitchen bin made Yasmin clench her fists. She imagined a long silent drive home tomorrow night, Ma weeping softly in the passenger seat, Baba's eyes fixed on the road. She imagined him calling her into the front room, and standing before him as he sat in the black padded chair, wetting his lips as he always did when he had something important to say.

'This is a good one,' said Baba. 'Listen, and let's see if we can work it out together. A fifty-nine-year-old man presenting with fever, confusion, thrombocytopenia, rash and renal failure.'

Yasmin sat forward in a display of attentiveness. But her mind continued to rove. She was, she knew it, being ridiculous. Harriet would never behave like that. She would pride herself on her cultural sensitivity. That much was certain. And Baba would never forbid her to marry anyone, no matter what he thought about the prospective mother-in-law. As for Ma, well, as long as she was busy with wedding plans she would be happy. Ma was proud that her daughter was marrying the son of a famous writer, someone who had written not only books but also an opera, and plays that had been performed on the radio. She had said as much to Yasmin, and to the neighbours, and to relatives on three continents. It was only Arif and his needling that had made Yasmin so unreasonably anxious.

'The patient had been well until three days before admission,' Baba read aloud. He loved the *New England Journal of Medicine* case challenges, and they were his favourite father–daughter activity. 'Vomiting, diaphoresis and fatigue then set in ... By the time he was seen by emergency personnel he was non-verbal, unable to stand but able to respond to painful stimuli ... Come—' He broke off and motioned for her to come and read over his shoulder. 'There is a lot more information here.'

Yasmin stood by her father and tried to take it all in. *The blood pressure was 132/82 mm Hg, the pulse 110 beats per minute, the respiratory rate 26 breaths per minute, and the oxygen saturation 94% while he was breathing supplemental oxygen at 2 liters per minute by nasal cannula. The pupils were 3 mm and nonreactive. The skin was warm ...* She was unable to focus on more detail. Instead she kept glancing at Baba, seeing him as Harriet would see him tomorrow, the Indian doctor in his brown too-loose suit and too-wide tie. The way he sat, so erect and proper. Dignified, Yasmin thought. Had always thought. By the age of only fourteen he was the tallest man in his West Bengal village. And although, as Baba was fond of pointing out, starting at the age of forty on average a person loses half an inch a decade, at sixty he was every bit as tall as back then.

'Arif shouldn't come with us tomorrow night,' she said suddenly. 'Joe invited him to be polite but Harriet's only expecting three of us.'

Baba looked up at her and raised one thick white eyebrow. 'Are you concerned there won't be enough food? Your mother is intent on taking a two- to three-month supply.'

'No,' said Yasmin. 'It's . . . and also can't you stop her? And if Arif goes, he'll be . . . I don't know, you never know with him!'

'Don't get so excited, Mini. Arif will stay at home. But your mother will take what she has cooked because it is her way and it would be cruel to stop her.' He transferred his attention to the case study, and Yasmin experienced a twinge of shame.

Baba did not, on the whole, approve of excitement. Although it was to be tolerated in young children or the mentally infirm, it was otherwise a cause of reproof. His life was orderly. He worked, he studied his journals, ate his meals with his family, and occasionally drank a small measure of whisky from a ruby-red crystal tumbler that was kept with the whisky bottle in the top drawer of the mahogany desk. He watched the television news, documentaries about war-torn countries and the omnibus of *EastEnders* on Sundays with Anisah, who was a devout follower of many soaps. From time to time he gave his pronouncements, and whether they were about the domestic dramas or the state of the world they generally amounted to the same thing: to have a quiet and ordered life is to be fortunate indeed.

'Meningococcaemia?' ventured Yasmin, having read on. 'What do you think, Baba?'

Baba removed his glasses. 'I am looking forward to meeting

Mrs Sangster,' he said. 'It is a very happy occasion. My only daughter is getting married. The families are coming together for the first time. Nothing can spoil the evening, Mini. I hope you feel this too.'

Yasmin felt the hot itch of tears. She blinked and bit her bottom lip. It took a few moments before she could say, 'Thank you, Baba.'

He began to analyse the medical history out loud, and he thought that Yasmin's diagnosis bore some validity, due to the livedo pattern rash on the abdomen, but ultimately – for reasons he expounded upon – he considered thrombotic thrombocytopenic purpura to be the most likely cause.

While he talked, Yasmin nodded but scarcely listened. She felt a childlike comfort, as though her father had looked beneath the bed and assured her there were no monsters lurking below. Her father was looking forward to meeting Mrs Sangster. Of course he was! Harriet was respected and respectable. She was not some kind of porn star, as Arif tried his hardest to suggest. She wrote books on feminist theory and literature, lectured at two universities, and sat on the boards of at least three charities. The tightness in Yasmin's chest vanished, and she had a sensation of lightness (was also, perhaps, a touch light-headed from hunger) when she entered the kitchen, Ma having finally called them in to eat.

MA

Yasmin had never seen the kitchen tidy. And she had never seen it in such a state. Ma had wreaked a level of devastation that made Baba take an uncertain step backwards at the threshold. To his great credit, however, he pushed on and took his seat at the table without a word. The kitchen was Ma's domain and she ran it as she pleased.

'Too hot,' said Ma, the sweat gleaming on her high round cheeks. 'Rice and mix vegetable only tonight.' She turned down the radio. She always had it on for company.

'Excellent,' said Baba, who approved of plain food.

'Wow, Ma,' said Yasmin, gesturing at the steaming pans of curry and trays of deep-fried savouries, the condensation running down the window. 'You didn't have to do all that.'

'Yes,' said Ma, 'tomorrow there will be no time. I have to take Mr Hartley to Woolwich.'

'I meant—' Yasmin broke off. 'I meant it's fantastic. Thank you, Ma.'

Ma waggled her head in a way that meant *don't be silly* and also *look how much clearing up there is to do*. She could speak entire sentences by moving her head and using her eyes. She served Baba and Yasmin and filled a third plate for Arif,

11

although he had yet to appear. She wasn't hungry, she explained, because she'd been nibbling and tasting all day.

'Why can't the boy come downstairs without being told three times?' said Baba. 'Ah, here he is.'

Arif picked up his plate. 'I'll eat in my room, yeah. Cuz I got a load of work.'

'Sit down at the table,' said Baba. 'Tell me about this work while we eat.'

'Already told you,' said Arif. 'Developing an app.'

'A degree in sociology qualifies you to do this?' A sociology degree, in Shaokat's opinion, qualified his son for precisely nothing. The two years since Arif graduated had hardened rather than softened this view.

'Whatever,' said Arif, moving towards the door.

'Leave the plate on the table. You are too busy to eat.'

Arif hesitated. Yasmin knew he was weighing it up. He could ignore his father's quiet instructions and no more would be said about it. But on the first day of the following month he would find that his allowance had been halved, or even cut altogether. His pride or his pocket? Which would he save tonight?

'Nikuchi korechhe,' said Arif, under his breath. To hell with it all. He set the plate down and walked out.

'Don't take it up to him later,' Shaokat told his wife. 'Spoiling him does him no favours.'

Anisah tilted her head in assent and sat down, sighing heavily.

'Why are you taking Mr Hartley to Woolwich?' said Yasmin. Mr Hartley was the old man who lived next door. He had been ancient, as Yasmin remembered it, even when the Ghoramis had moved into the street, twenty years ago. Before that they had lived in a succession of rented flats and houses that all had some things in common. The traffic grumbled all night long and when you stepped out of the front door you were surrounded by people and smothered in petrol fumes. Baba always said you got more for your money living on a main road so Yasmin was surprised by the stillness here. *You know what this place is called?* Shaokat had asked his daughter as the removal men lugged crates and furniture. *Yes, Baba, Tatton Hill.* Baba shook his head and swept his arm in a gesture that encompassed the sleepy houses, the blinds half closed against the Saturday-morning sun; the shiny hedges and blank-faced garages; the grass verges and broad-shouldered trees lining the road. He spoke solemnly. *It is called our little piece of heaven on earth.*

'Taking him?' said Shaokat. 'If your mother learned to drive she could take him. She will go with him on the bus, although he knows the way better than she does.'

'Probably I am spoiling him,' said Ma. 'I am taking him to the man who sticks pins in him to cure the arthritis.'

'Acupuncture!' Baba snorted.

'He should put you in his will, Ma. You do more for him than his own children.' Mr Hartley's daughter and grandchildren lived somewhere in West London, and his son lived in Morden. Yet they visited only once or twice a year. Yasmin considered this shocking. It had been impressed upon her from birth that family came first, and the fact that the Ghoramis had little contact with their extended clan was merely a product of enforced circumstance.

'Will?' said Ma, looking shocked. 'Am I a vulture to eat his flesh and bone? And Mr Ackerman? I should feed on his carcass also?' Mr Ackerman lived at number 72 and was another beneficiary of Ma's social services. Mr Coombs, who lived in the bungalow on the corner, was especially partial to Ma's lamb biryani.

'No, you are an angel,' said Baba. 'If he leaves you his house you can set up a care home for all the lonely old white men.'

'Piffle-paffle,' said Ma.

*

13

'I can't choose,' said Ma, standing over two outfits laid out on her bed. 'The first impression is *so* important.' She had beckoned Yasmin into her bedroom.

Yasmin gazed down at a silk dress of stunningly florid design and hue, birds and flowers in turquoise, purple and lime green. Conceivably, with the aid of a team of stylists, a supermodel could pull it off. On Ma, who was short and cosy, it would be epically disastrous.

'Feel,' said Ma. She stroked the silk and fanned the skirt. 'Such beautiful material, and ten pounds only I paid at the British Heart Foundation shop.'

'The parakeets are very ... striking,' said Yasmin, her heart sinking at the prospect of introducing an eccentrically clad Anisah to the perpetually elegant Harriet.

'But this suit might be better for a first impression.' Ma moved on to her second choice, a brown skirt and jacket made of what appeared to be upholstery fabric, teamed with a white blouse that looked highly flammable.

If her parents walked in wearing his-and-hers brown suits with white shirts would Harriet be able to keep a straight face? Why couldn't Ma, after all these years, learn how to dress like a normal person? It wasn't hard. All she had to do was look around and copy everyone else.

'I don't know,' said Yasmin. 'I was wondering ... why don't you wear one of your saris? You always look amazing in a sari.'

'Oh, no,' said Ma. 'Mrs Sangster will think, This Yasmin-Ma is backwards. Why doesn't she adapt and integrate? This is why I say, first impression counts.'

Authentic enough to give her an orgasm. A sari would be the best choice, without a doubt. But what could she possibly say to Ma? Dress authentically tomorrow? Don't wear those embarrassing outfits? Even if she did it would make no difference. Ma had asked for her opinion, but Ma had a way of sweetly ignoring opinions if they were, in her view, the wrong ones. As Baba was fond of pointing out, she was the most gently stubborn person on the face of the earth.

'The dress, then,' said Yasmin.

'Clever girl!' cried Ma, as if Yasmin had passed a test. 'That's the one. Now, your father is worried I will say the wrong things tomorrow, so I have prepared. We will discuss wedding, and also weather. These two are definite. And I have read an article about the gender pay gap, also another about girls in science. These are suitable topics, if you are happy to agree?' She looked anxiously at her daughter.

Ma had been preparing and researching. She'd read Harriet's first book, or at least some of it before Arif had caught her in the act. She'd thought about what to say, what to wear. Yasmin wanted to say sorry, but for what exactly and how?

'Very suitable,' said Yasmin, which in the Ghorami household was high praise indeed.

ARIF

When she'd brushed her teeth and washed her face Yasmin decided to check on her brother. She wished he wouldn't insist on making life so hard for himself. Arif's door was ajar and the light was still on, but when Yasmin knocked and entered he wasn't there. The dirty plate on his desk suggested Ma had brought him his dinner despite Shaokat's injunction. Arif's dumbbells lay on the bed. That was the one thing to which he seemed seriously committed, bicep curls, which he'd stuck to every day since the age of sixteen. It had done him no good. His arms remained infuriatingly thin. His electric guitar was propped under the window. It had a broken string, but Arif never bothered to get it fixed, and sometimes he took it out with him saying he was going to 'band practice', which made Baba lift his bushy eyebrows and ask if the drummer had only one stick.

When Arif went out this late it meant he wouldn't be back until morning. Most likely he was with a girlfriend. He didn't mention these girlfriends to his parents but sometimes he said things to Yasmin about 'getting laid'.

She had seen him once in The Three Bells (their 'local') with a young woman whose blue-veined breasts wobbled with laughter as he leaned over and whispered in her ear. He hadn't introduced her when Yasmin left her friends to go over and say hello. Twice she'd seen him with another girl, who had bleach-brittle hair and an open smile. She'd introduced herself in the Costcutter as Lucy, 'as you'd guess', although Yasmin couldn't possibly, having never heard of her before. Arif had scowled and barely said a word, but the girl seemed not to notice, and the second time Yasmin ran into them Lucy-as-you'd-guess congratulated her warmly on her engagement, while Arif walked off mumbling about being late. Lateness was not usually something he minded about.

When Yasmin stayed over at Joe's house, which she did frequently, it was never mentioned at home. She was not expected to acknowledge it, nor was she required to deny it. Her absence was only mentioned in terms of nightshifts. Arif sometimes spoke of his own 'nightshifts', with a confected leer, but only to Yasmin, and out of earshot of Shaokat and Anisah. There was a don't ask, don't tell policy, which Yasmin interpreted as a courtesy extended by her parents, and which Arif saw as pathetic while simultaneously maintaining as much secrecy as possible.

Yasmin picked up the dirty plate, meaning to take it to the kitchen. She thought a moment and placed it back down. Arif didn't take kindly to anyone, even Ma, going in his room when he wasn't there.

Poor Arif.

In sixth months Yasmin would be married and gone, and Arif would be no further forward, would still be here trapped by adolescent defiance and dependence, strumming his broken-stringed guitar.

17

BRAIN EVENT

She prayed for bad traffic, roadworks, lane closures. They had left the house at five thirty, Baba insisted on it – rush hour, you never know, better not to take chances. He consulted the *A–Z*, cross-referenced his planned route with directions on Google Maps, and when they got in the car he plugged Harriet's address into the satnav.

There wasn't the slightest possibility of getting lost. And the dinner invitation was for half past seven. At this rate, flying north across the Thames as the traffic heading out of the city crawled south over Vauxhall Bridge, they'd be there an hour too early.

Yasmin sat on the back seat, wedged between bags and boxes of food.

'What to call Mrs Sangster?' said Ma, twisting around. She had teamed the birds-and-flowers dress with an orange wool scarf. Although she had oiled and coaxed her hair into a careful bun, the scarf kept catching on it. Black and grey tendrils floated free.

'Harriet,' said Yasmin. 'Joe calls her Harry. All her friends do.'

'Harry?' said Ma. 'No.' She moved her head in a manner that said she knew when she was having her leg pulled.

Any time you like, Harriet had said, just an informal family supper. Half past seven, but really don't stress, we'll see you when we see you. Joe lived with his mother because he'd grown tired of renting and because Harriet liked having him around. When she met him Yasmin thought of it as something they had in common: she lived with her parents too. Then he took her home and she didn't think of it that way any more. But when she, finally, after several months and many entreaties from Joe, took him to Tatton Hill to meet Baba and Ma, the fact that he lived at home with his mother seemed to work like a charm. It spoke volumes to them about their daughter's suitor – her first, as far as they knew – and their potential son-in-law.

Yasmin grabbed at the Tupperware tower as her father braked sharply behind a bus.

'You see how dangerous,' he said, 'and people aren't aware. On average one person is killed every three weeks by a bus in London. Not including those that die on board the bus itself.'

'Alhamdulillah, I have never seen anyone die on a bus,' said Ma, a frequenter of bus routes to Bromley, Norwood and Tooting, her favourite shopping areas. 'Mr Hartley choked on the 367, but he coughed and the sweet flew out of his throat into a baby pram. The lady was so angry . . . ' She talked on, explaining the whole sorry tale.

Please, prayed Yasmin silently, please don't let her talk too much this evening. She couldn't remember the last time she actually took out her prayer mat but when she prayed in her head she knew, she was almost sure, He was listening.

'Slips, trips and falls,' said Baba. 'The figures do not include choking or heart attacks – they could happen anywhere, the bus would be irrelevant.'

An English family would arrive at a quarter to eight. An Indian family would arrive any time after nine. Only the Ghoramis would turn up an entire anxious hour before they were expected.

Remember, Arif had said to her on the stairs, that dinner with Dr Shaw and his wife. He smiled his sloppy smile, and she wanted to slap it right off his face. I bet, he said, they remember it too.

Dr Shaw was the senior partner at the surgery, and when Shaokat had finally become a partner eleven years ago, a celebratory dinner was announced. The Ghoramis and the Shaws would dine together at La Grenouille, the finest restaurant in all of Tatton Hill.

Yasmin was surprised when she saw Dr Shaw. He was younger than Baba, and she had assumed he would be older. And the top four buttons of his baby-pink shirt were undone. He didn't look much like a doctor. His wife wore a short-sleeved black blouse and a pearl necklace and she did look like a doctor's wife, except one of her arms was missing. When she raised her right arm to wave at them, the stump of her left briefly popped out from the other sleeve. Arif started whispering in Yasmin's ear and she stamped on his foot to shut him up.

Dr Shaw, in return, was surprised to see Yasmin and Arif. He and his wife were seated at a table for four. It hadn't occurred to the Shaws that the children would come to a dinner for the father. It hadn't occurred to the Ghoramis that they would not.

The menu at La Grenouille was written in a looping cursive script that made the letters almost impossible to decipher. When they were finally seated, after what seemed to Yasmin an enormous commotion of apologies and explanations and re-arrangements of chairs and setting of places, she was relieved to be handed the heavy leather-clad menu so she could hide behind it. She stared at the tangled lettering but couldn't take anything in. She was distracted by Arif, seated next to her, again trying to whisper something. Ma said, 'Frog is on the menu? Restaurant's name is frog, isn't it? I know French people are eating, but I couldn't. I will be happy with anything else.' Yasmin cringed.

Ma's words were so obviously rehearsed. They were also, Yasmin realised, untrue: Ma only ate her own curries and regarded shop-bought meals, even sandwiches, with suspicion.

For what felt like hours but was possibly only a minute, Yasmin thought she had lost the ability to read. The individual letters became clearer but they swam and swirled, signifying nothing. It occurred to her that she may have suffered what her father would refer to as 'a brain event', brought on perhaps by the intensity of her shame.

'Well,' said Dr Shaw, 'how's everyone's French? Shall I translate?'

'I'll spend a penny for your thoughts,' said Anisah. She turned and patted her daughter's knee.

Yasmin pulled the lid off a Tupperware box and bit into a cauliflower pakora. Even cold it was good, deeply spiced, richly oiled, and yet with the magical lightness that only Ma could conjure out of the deep fat fryer.

'Penny for them,' she said. 'Spend a penny means go to the toilet.'

'No,' said Ma, 'I'll spend *ten* pennies. What is in your mind?'

Yasmin rummaged in the bag and pulled out another box. Ma never cared to have her English corrected. If she acquiesced it was without acknowledgement. More often she affirmed her rights by clinging to a word or phrase. Baba spoke English correctly. Too correctly. It made him sound foreign. He was thirty-one years old when he came so of course he was never going to sound exactly like an Englishman. Ma, Yasmin reminded herself, had moved to the UK at the age of twenty-six, the age Yasmin was now. If Yasmin, with her schoolgirl French, went to live in France, even decades later there would be phrases that caught her out. And Ma never had the advantage of work-ing, never developed friendships that went beyond neighbourly chats. At home her English sounded perfectly normal to Yasmin, but sometimes – like now – Yasmin heard her mother as she sounded to others, and though it was an unfair reaction she couldn't help it: it made her cringe.

'What is in your mind?' Ma repeated.

'Nothing,' said Yasmin, though her mind was on the rampage. Arif was pathetic, he needed to grow up. Why did this family have to have such a hideous car? Nobody in their right mind wanted to be seen in a Fiat Multipla, the ugliest car ever made, the bug-eyed, bulge-headed Elephant Man of motoring. What did Baba do with his money? Surely he could afford a better car than this. Would they stand on Harriet's doorstep carrying these plastic bags or leave them in the car and ask Joe to bring them in? Don't think about that dinner with the Shaws. That's exactly what Arif wanted. It had been years since she thought about it.

'Look,' said Ma, 'everyone is Arab here. It must be nice, living all together.'

They were driving up Edgware Road, and at last the traffic was moving at a respectable London crawl. A car horn blared, then another and another, a cacophonous contagion sweeping the lanes. Baba sighed and glanced at Yasmin in the rear-view mirror, seeking – she understood at once – to confirm three things: that the eruption of horns was unnecessary but was to be tolerated like all other inconveniences, that 'living all together' was a mistake that foreigners made, and that he had not fallen into that trap. His wife might not understand it, but Shaokat had made the best decision for his family. Yasmin looked away.

She would tell Joe all about dinner with the Shaws. Her parents had never spoken about it. Yasmin had never told her friends. That was what was wrong with her family: they never talked about anything. They weren't open like Harriet and Joe.

The car slowed and Yasmin realised they were on Harriet's street, her father looking for the house. Five minutes to seven. Not as bad as she'd feared.

'Mrs Sangster and Joe, only these two are living here? Very difficult without servants to manage a house like this,' said Ma. She, like Harriet, had grown up in a wealthy household. Only Harriet, however, had inherited family money. 'But it is only Joe and Mrs Sangster, no?'

'No,' said Yasmin. 'I mean, yes.' After the wedding it would only be Harriet. Joe and Yasmin had started looking for a flat already, and they'd move into it straight after the wedding even if there was building work to be done.

Baba parked the Multipla alongside Harriet's classic Jag and gleaming Range Rover. 'Very good,' he said. 'We are here,' he added, as if Yasmin doubted it. 'Well, shall we start to unload?'

Yasmin began gathering the bags.

'Now, wait, one thing – should I ask about the dowry before the dinner or afterwards?' He lifted his eyebrows to assure her he was joking.

'How much are you willing to give, to get me off your hands?' said Yasmin.

'Oh, no, Mini, it is they who have to pay dowry for my daughter. How much?' He pushed his spectacles up, so the thick black frames rested on his forehead while he performed the calculations. 'No, they cannot afford it. My daughter is priceless to me.'

PRIMROSE HILL

'I despise it,' said Harriet, with cool relish. 'Guilt is the most useless of all the emotions, the most pathetic, the most self-involved. Guilty about work, guilty about exercise, the environment, family, food, alcohol ... And the worst of all is liberal guilt, that shiny badge of righteousness worn with pride by the morally stunted. They didn't like *that* one bit! I thought, Yes, there's an article to be written and I should be the one to write it!'

'I'm amazed anyone comes to your salons,' said Joe. 'Do you think they'd feel guilty if they stayed at home?' He smiled at his mother and she wrinkled her nose at him.

'They come to be *stimulated*, darling. I poke them and they love it. And the hors d'oeuvres. Anyway, Shaokat, that's what I'm working on – an article about the horrors of liberal guilt, and I gave it a run round the block with my friends last week.'

Shaokat had enquired about Harriet's 'current projects and engagements'. It was a risky business. But Harriet, as promised, was on best behaviour. (No mention, thus far at least, of the book she was working on with a photographer friend: Harriet interviewing men about their relationship with their penis; the friend taking *de-eroticised* shots of the appendages.) They sat

at the kitchen table, eating Ma's offerings. Harriet had immediately determined they would replace the boring lasagne she
had in the oven (don't worry, Joe told Anisah, she didn't make
it, she has someone come in for all that). Anisah, blissed out by
the honour, sat quietly. She gazed around the vast and splendid
kitchen at the plate-glass doors that opened to the garden, the
sofas and rugs, the vaulting skylights and cushioned window
seats; the magnificent range cooker, breakfast bar and marble
countertops. Reheating and decanting the curries into china-
ware, she'd made herself at home amid the gleaming appliances
inside the workspace, and freely inspected the offshoot areas –
the larder, utility room, cloakroom, and the enclosed side porch
where shoes and boots lined up neatly next to the pretty stack
of firewood.

'This is very interesting,' said Shaokat. Yasmin fingered her
napkin. Why did he talk so slowly? It was painful to hear him.
'Tell me,' he went on, 'what is the horror, why is it so horrible?'

'I don't want to bore you,' cried Harriet, 'we're celebrating!'
She poured more wine into Shaokat's glass, although he had
hardly taken two sips. 'And there are wedding plans to discuss.'
She turned to Anisah and gave her plump hand a squeeze.
Without pause she continued, 'The liberal who feels guilty about
the social, political or economic order – global or local – who
knows that their comfort and ease depend on the blood, sweat
and tears of others, is the enemy of change in the world. You
know why?'

'We will in a minute,' said Joe. Yasmin adored the way he
teased Harriet. She rather envied it as well: Shaokat – she knew
this without needing to test it – would not tolerate such a thing;
and Ma was immune to all forms of irony.

'Hush, you revolting child,' said Harriet, rising. She was
sheathed, as usual, in something black and irreproachable.
When she paused to wrap her arms around Joe's neck and plant

a kiss on his head her triceps were advantageously displayed. 'Liberal guilt is the acknowledgement that the cushy number is just too damn good to give up. It says, Well I haven't actually done anything wrong, but I'm a good person so I feel bad. It's the by-product of an acceptance of the world as it is. I'll open another bottle of that Malbec so it can breathe.'

'I see,' said Shaokat, 'thank you for explaining this phenomenon.'

Every time he spoke Yasmin's hands began to tingle. Her palms had sweated all through the meal.

'No, thank *you*,' said Joe. He was seated next to Shaokat, and raised a glass to him. 'Thank you for coming. Thank you for bringing dinner and saving me from yet another lasagne. And most of all . . .' He looked almost shy as he glanced at Yasmin across the expanse of the blonde-oak table. He pushed his fringe out of his eyes. 'Thank you for accepting me into your family.'

Shaokat permitted himself a deep sip of wine and ran his tongue around his lips. Yasmin feared a lengthy oration was about to begin.

'No, it's worse than that,' said Harriet, swooping back fortuitously with the wine. 'It's not a harmless by-product. Liberal guilt facilitates the acceptance of the status quo because the guilt substitutes for action. It becomes the *action taken*, and therefore blocks any need to change anything at all. Useless. Worthless. Dangerous, in its own supine way.'

Anisah showed signs of stirring from her blissed-out trance. She gave a little cough and began to speak. 'If you do not do wrong things, you will not feel guilty. If you feel guilt and you do not know what wrongs you have done, then you must think quietly. This is something I practise. Sometimes my conscience is telling me, oh, you did not speak nicely to so-and-so, or you promised to visit so-and-so and you did not go.'

'Absolutely right,' said Yasmin, hoping she would stop there.

'Also,' said Anisah, 'I pray. God sees inside the heart, and if you have done wrong, and you sincerely pray, He takes the guilt and . . .' She made a discarding motion with her hand. 'Gone!'

'Preferable,' said Harriet. 'Enviable. Now that was delicious and thank you again, your cooking puts me to shame. I am replete.' She pushed her plate away but looked hungrily at Anisah. 'Would you please come to the next salon? We'd love to hear about your faith.'

'No!' said Joe, in mock horror. 'Don't let her get her claws into you. Harry, leave her alone!'

Yasmin felt all the alarm that Joe was merely pantomiming. She said nothing for fear of revealing it.

Harriet squeezed Anisah's hand again. 'That is a beautiful dress. You and I will do as we please without reference to our menfolk.'

'I am always consulting my husband.'

'Consulting, yes,' said Shaokat. 'Listening and abiding, a different matter.'

'Well, we haven't even talked about the wedding,' said Harriet. 'I have a few suggestions to make.'

'I'll clear the table,' said Yasmin. Of course Harriet had suggestions to make! It hadn't occurred to Yasmin to worry about Harriet taking over the wedding plans because she'd fixated on other worries – like Ma's outfit or the number of tiffin tins.

'I'll help,' said Joe, jumping up. 'Harry, hold the suggestions. Can't plan a wedding without the bride.'

'Your daughter tells me that yours was a love marriage,' said Harriet, who had not let go of Anisah's hand.

Ma waggled her head and smiled.

'The well-to-do Calcutta girl and the poor but clever village boy. A true romance, so I hear.' Harriet turned to Shaokat. 'A girl who merely listens and abides may not have made the same match.'

As they scraped the plates and filled the dishwasher, Joe leaned in close to Yasmin, his breath tickling her ear. 'Let's sneak out,' he said. 'Half-time debrief.'

It was a mild September night, thick with the scent of jasmine and rosemary. He wrapped an arm around her and they crossed the patio and lawn, passed beneath an arbour, and entered the rose garden.

'Okay?' he said. 'You doing okay? Hope you appreciated my containment strategies when Harry threatened to get out of hand.'

'Yes,' she said, laughing. 'I'm fine. And your mum's been brilliant, she can handle anyone.'

'She can. I'll give her that. Not that your parents need handling. Let's sit out here for a bit and look at the stars.'

They sat on the bench, holding hands. The cool air in her nostrils was sating, like a glass of water on a hot day.

'Had a bit of a freak-out at work,' said Joe. 'It was scary. I don't remember ever being that scared before. She just bled and bled and – I know this is stupid – I was shocked. You know, just kind of stunned.' He shook his head. 'As though something like that had never happened before.'

'What happened?'

'I froze. It was just me and the newly qualified midwife who'd called me in, and the husband was looking at me, this sort of panicky hopeful look, and I just went into this state of . . . I don't know what else to call it – shock.'

Yasmin squeezed his hand. 'But it was okay, wasn't it?' Joe was three years older than Yasmin, and a registrar in obstetrics and gynaecology.

'The thing is,' he said slowly, 'I had two emergency caesareans and a ruptured ovarian torsion and didn't bat an eyelid and then . . . ' He trailed off.

Joe looks like his mother, Ma had whispered when the biriyani was heating in the oven. He didn't. Harriet had sharp cheekbones, arched eyebrows, her eyes were a stinging shade of blue, like the sky on a scorching day. Joe's eyes were blue as well but they weren't sharp like Harriet's.

'But it was okay,' said Yasmin, needing to hear him confirm it. 'And the baby was okay.'

'Thank God.'

She looked at him carefully. Maybe Ma was right after all. There was a resemblance. His cheeks were softer, fuller, but sat high on his face like Harriet's. His chin was different. His eyes were a paler shade but almond-shaped, like hers. His hair a darker shade of blond. His nose was similar but less imperious.

'I love you,' she said.

'Yeah?' He feigned surprise. 'You sure?'

'Mmm,' she said. 'Well . . . let me think.' She leaned her head on his shoulder and looked up at the stars, mere pinpricks in the velvet sky worn thin by the city lights.

'I'll take that as a yes. Listen, Harry wants to have it here. The reception. What do you think?'

'Oh,' said Yasmin. 'But we'd still keep it small, right?' They'd agreed they didn't want a big production, just the register office followed by a meal. The honeymoon would be at Harriet's villa in Tuscany.

'She'd invite some of her friends I guess but yeah, it's up to us to say what we want.' He paused. 'The benefit would be that when she organises something it's always, you know, totally organised. And work's so busy. For both of us.'

'Guess it makes sense.'

'Okay, then we'll give her the green light.' He sounded relieved, as though he'd expected her to raise more objections.

She thought they would get up now and go back in, but he showed no sign of stirring and she was content to stay where she was, inside the warmth of his arm and shoulder, with the scent of autumn mingling with his good, clean, linen-cupboard scent.

The first time they met was at someone's leaving drinks in The Crosskeys, the pub across the road from work. He stood there, pint in one hand, in the other a stool, dangling by one wooden leg. Mind if I sit here? She looked up from her conversation. Brown leather bomber jacket, battered in a way that said vintage. Linen shirt. Dark blond, in need of a haircut. Dimple in his chin. Full cheeks, full upper lip. There were spaces at the other end of the table. Did he want to sit with her? Had his question been to her? She cast her eyes down. Orange laces in his trainers that looked box fresh.

When she sensed he was about to move away she looked up and he smiled. His eyes were blue and steady and kind. You can sit here, she said, and shuffled her chair to make room.

He'd delivered twins that day, he told her. Six weeks premature but perfect, and the proud father had insisted on buying him a drink. Dad had been wetting the babies' heads all afternoon. That guy there, still at the bar. The birth of his children had resolved the mysteries of the universe into an elaborate and incoherent unified theory of everything.

He made her laugh. They talked until closing time.

Over the next few weeks they talked. On the phone, on Messenger, on email, which she found endearingly quaint, and in person. Or went for walks in the scrubby park that lay just south of the hospital. He asked her so many questions about her life, was so intensely interested in everything she said, she felt sorry she wasn't more interesting. Nevertheless, she liked it. No one else had ever paid her such close attention, including Kashif, and he had been her boyfriend for two years.

You know what's happened, don't you? Rania told her. You've entered the friend zone. If he's not even tried to kiss you by now then I'm afraid you're too far into the friend zone for him to risk anything. Sometimes Rania was too much. She'd never even had a boyfriend but Rania always had to be the expert. I'll do it then, said Yasmin, I'll kiss him, it's not like the man always has to make the first move.

But she didn't, of course. How could she? She couldn't make a fool of herself like that. If he wanted to kiss her he would.

And he did. They were in the park, idling by the pond watching a cormorant spread its ink-black wings. He turned and kissed her on the lips, and the kiss was long and sweet. Compared to how Kashif used to mash his lips on hers and chomp his jaw up and down, it was delicate, it was searching. She could almost say it was chaste.

'When I was fifteen ...' They were walking back towards the house. The lights went on behind the folding glass doors that opened to the patio. Harriet would emerge any moment in search of them.

'When you were fifteen,' Joe prompted.

'When I was fifteen ...' The story felt stuck inside her but she was going to get it out. It pushed at her diaphragm like a hiatus hernia. It was a blockage that had to be cleared. 'When my dad finally became a partner at his practice, we went out for dinner with the senior partner and his wife. And ... my mum was sick on the table. God, it was awful. I was mortified. The senior partner's wife only had one arm, the other was just a stump poking out of her dress. Her blouse, actually.'

'What? No, really?' Joe was laughing and also groaning because he could tell it still made her squirm. 'Wait. You're telling me the stump made her puke?'

'Oh, no! No! It was the bacon. She'd just found out that the little pink bits in the coq au vin were tiny pieces of pig. She'd thought she was being so adventurous eating chicken cooked in wine, even though my dad had told her the alcohol would be burned off. And she was getting up, sort of leaping up, and out it all came. It splashed off the plates, the sound was horrendous and it really *sprayed*. It wasn't a neat little heap, it went all over the place, including this poor woman. She sat there with vomit dripping off her stump.'

'Christ,' said Joe. 'If I'd known what I was getting mixed up with here.'

'Then my mother tried to wipe the stump with a napkin, and the woman didn't want her to, and there was a sort of tussle and her husband got involved and my father too. All the waiters came over, the manager, a few of the other diners. I literally thought I was going to die.' By the time she finished the story she was laughing too, and they stood on the lawn laughing together as Harriet appeared behind the plate glass and waved at them, and Joe put a hand on Yasmin's shoulder and said, 'That's brilliant, I can't believe you haven't told me that story before.'

THE SHAHADA

Harriet, at the head of the table, sat on her chair in half-lotus position, feet tucked one under, one over her slender thighs. 'I have a proposal. The wedding reception should be here, the garden is practically begging for a marquee, there's space for a band, more than one probably, and God knows this kitchen is big enough for caterers and . . . whatever.' She gestured vaguely towards the glass-walled extension with its sectional sofas and freshly lit lamps and mid-century modern chairs. She inclined her sleek blonde head conspiratorially close to Ma.

Ma trembled with pleasure. 'Very kind, but the children must . . . and my husband . . .' She looked meaningfully at Yasmin and then Shaokat.

'Joe mentioned it,' said Yasmin, 'and we're really grateful.'

'I am the father of the bride,' said Shaokat solemnly. 'I must be allowed to bear the cost.'

'I won't spend a penny,' said Harriet.

'Spend a penny,' said Ma quietly to herself.

'Though, isn't it the custom in India,' Harriet continued, 'for the groom's family to pay for the reception?'

'But the wedding itself will be at the register office,' said

Shaokat. 'This is a matter of a few pounds only. No, it is for me to pay for the celebration.'

'We're going to keep it small, though,' said Yasmin. 'We don't want a lot of expense.' If Harriet took over, the cost would be more than Baba could possibly imagine. But if Baba took over there'd be disposable plates, plastic chairs and paper chains for decorations. It would be like the annual 'community day' he used to organise at the surgery.

'We don't want a lot of fuss,' said Joe.

Yes, Ma was right, thought Yasmin. Somehow, she hadn't noticed the resemblance before. Joe was a gentler version of his mother. His eyes less piercing, more candid and searching. He was attentive where she was sharply observant. Avid where she was acute. Harriet shone her light from above. It could be blinding. But Joe lit you up because he shone from below.

'Cooking will be mine,' said Ma, 'I will cook everything.'

'Of course,' said Harriet. She turned to her son and gave him a long, appraising look. 'Joseph, darling, you are aware, aren't you, that a small Indian wedding means two to three hundred guests. At least.'

'But we're not having a—' Yasmin began to protest.

Harriet talked over her. 'Sister, how many hundreds did you have at your wedding?'

Ma, in a fit of excitement, had greeted Harriet not as Mrs Sangster, as she'd planned, but as 'My sister, isn't it'. Throughout the meal Harriet had proved keen to return the compliment.

Anisah dabbed her napkin over her mouth and nose, almost up to her eyes. Whatever she was saying behind it was inaudible.

'What are we thinking,' said Joe to Yasmin, 'forty guests? Fifty tops?'

Harriet placed a jewelled hand on the top of Joe's arm and massaged his biceps. 'Stop trying to steamroller your bride! Fifty tops! You're a vile, unfeeling brute and you don't deserve her.'

'He is a very good boy,' said Ma, emerging from the napkin, 'and deserving also. My daughter and your son are equal.'

Yasmin's spine prickled with embarrassment. Ma, who took everything literally, had spoken in valiant tones. As though Joe needed her to stand up for him.

Harriet looked amused. 'You're too kind. But yes, he's not really so bad.'

'Our daughter is precious to us,' said Shaokat, who had been ruminating hard. Yasmin dreaded what was coming next. He didn't understand, any better than Ma, that affection could be expressed in insults. This was a level of Englishness to which he could never aspire. Shaokat wetted his lips. 'She has chosen such an excellent young man, such an excellent family, that is the most important thing.'

Harriet still looked amused but when she thanked Baba she sounded not only pleased but also touched. She began to talk about her love of India. In Delhi she had spent a month working with a women's group that campaigned on reproductive rights; on another visit the intention was to set up an experimental theatre project working with slum kids, but the funding never materialised ... In Kerala she'd spent a week at an Ayurvedic retreat that cleansed every part of her body and mind. On every trip she'd eaten her meals with the five digits of her right hand and it was certainly an enhancement of the senses ...'

Ma listened and moved her head in a manner that indicated supreme satisfaction with Harriet's every word. Baba had relaxed sufficiently to undo the top button of his shirt. Joe leaned back with his hands laced behind his head. He closed his eyes. His shirt rode up as he stretched and the top of his appendix scar was just visible above the waistband of his jeans.

Ma leaned closer to Yasmin while Harriet talked on. She pointed at a framed print of emerald-green and custard-yellow splodges on the wall opposite. She smelled of cumin seeds and the Yardley Lily of the Valley eau de toilette that she purchased in discount bulk at Superdrug.

'Joe has painted?' Ma whispered it, cupping a hand around her mouth, and Yasmin had difficulty not rolling her eyes. 'I should have done this for you and Arif. All those paintings you did at primary school and I have not kept even one of them.'

'It's a Howard Hodgkin,' whispered Yasmin. 'The painting – it's by a famous artist.' She only knew this because Joe had told her. Nevertheless, she was mildly pained by her mother's ignorance.

'The first time I went was with Neil – that's Joe's father – he was on an assignment for *National Geographic*. We'd met only four days previously but he absolutely insisted I go with him. He was a very persuasive man when he wanted to be.' She smiled brightly at Joe, who had opened his eyes at the mention of his father.

'May I offer my condolences,' said Shaokat. 'I did not realise your husband had passed away. Yasmin did not mention this, only that Joe grew up with you alone.'

Harriet's blue eyes danced. She clapped her hands. 'Oh, I did rather eulogise him, didn't I? No, he's far from dead. Joe, do you want to invite him to the wedding? It's up to you. It's entirely up to you if you want your father to be there.'

'Haven't thought about it,' said Joe. He yawned. 'Probably wouldn't turn up anyway.'

Yasmin had never met Joe's father. She knew he was a photographer who lived close to the Scottish border. He'd moved out soon after Joe was born and lived in Hampstead until Joe was a teenager. Sometimes Joe stayed with him or was taken out for the day but Neil was an unreliable care-giver so Harriet rarely entrusted her son to him. On one occasion Harriet had called social services after she found Neil passed out drunk on the sofa and Joe at the bottom of the stairs with a mild concussion and a deep cut on his lip. Joe hardly talked about his dad. When he did, he seemed at worst indifferent and at best mildly amused.

He said all Neil had ever given him was a cleft chin, although really it was just a dimple not a deformity like he made it sound.

'He lives far away?' said Anisah.

'Now he does,' said Harriet. 'He didn't turn out to be the paternal type.'

'We must not impose on you longer,' said Shaokat. 'And you must visit us in our home.'

'It's only half past nine,' said Harriet. 'You can't possibly abscond. We hardly got started on the wedding plans.'

'Actually,' said Yasmin, 'I'm on an early shift tomorrow, so . . . ' It was probably best to withdraw now while the Ghoramis could get out of Primrose Hill relatively unscathed.

Harriet ignored her. 'I want to get your opinion on something,' she said to Shaokat. Clearly she'd worked out which buttons to press. Shaokat, duly gratified, removed his bifocals in order to concentrate. 'Muslim marriages aren't legally recognised in this country. Why shouldn't they be?' She paused. 'Or Hindu or Sikh or any other religion for that matter. What's your opinion?'

'An interesting question,' said Shaokat. 'There are many angles to consider.' He furrowed his brow. Normal conversation was quite beyond him. He had to deliver his judgements from above.

Ma seemed to want to say something, but when she opened her mouth only a series of clucking sounds came out.

Harriet turned towards her. 'Yes,' she said, as though Ma had managed an intelligible sentence. 'It's a *feminist issue* because women in this country, Muslim women in particular, are discovering when their marriages break down that they were not, in fact, legally married in the first instance and that they have no rights at all. Why don't we accord the same rights to all communities?'

Where was this going? Yasmin tapped a little rhythm on her placemat to attract Joe's attention. After the exchange about his dad he appeared to have tuned out.

He noticed but misread the message and reached across the

table to refill Yasmin's wine glass. 'I agree,' he said. 'Why should you have different rights if you get married in a church?'

Harriet held out her own glass for a top-up. 'People get married in church, and even though they believe in God as much as they believe in Santa Claus, it's legally valid and their rights are protected. But for people who *actually believe*, who take their vows before Allah, the marriage is worthless in the eyes of society, in the letter of the law. They should be given the same status, that's only fair, there should be equality.'

Harriet, an atheist, was championing the rights of true believers. She could argue anything, any position. Yasmin – despite her sinking feeling – admired the way Harriet's mind darted, her panoramic intellect, her insatiable curiosity. Ma and Baba had a new thought only once a decade. That was probably an overestimate. Their views never changed. Baba had no time for religion and now was the time for him to say so out loud. Come on, Baba! Speak!

'Right, there should be,' said Joe, as though the conversation was entirely theoretical. Perhaps it was. 'But,' he smiled at Yasmin, 'since we're going to a registry office it doesn't affect us, fortunately.'

'But what will your relatives feel,' Harriet lowered her voice conspiratorially, addressing herself to Anisah, 'about having only a registry office marriage? What do *you* feel about it?'

'One sister is coming from Mumbai,' said Ma. 'Rashida is a lecturer, and she never married. Another sister, Amina, will come from Harrisonburg, Virginia. Amina is devout. Yes, very devout. She married a dentist and they have three children, all grown now but –' with a touch of pride, '– my daughter is the first to make the marriage.'

'How difficult would it be,' said Harriet, 'to secure the services of an imam? If one were required or desired?'

'Baba,' said Yasmin. But Shaokat was staring at the white

leather stools lined up beneath the breakfast bar. He was mid-cogitation and would not speak until he was ready.

'No difficulty,' said Anisah.

'Well, I think that's settled then.' Harriet practically sang the words.

'Hang on,' said Joe. 'What did I miss?' Harriet again put her hand on his biceps and he frowned but didn't shrug her off.

'If there are no objections the proposal is to arrange an Islamic ceremony . . . there will have to be a civil ceremony too, of course. Shaokat, what's your opinion?'

'My opinion . . .' began Shaokat, and Yasmin noticed just then how unnaturally tight against the table he sat, his chair tucked in so close that his torso seemed almost to sit on top of the oak slab. 'My opinion is that my wife is the one you should ask, since she shoulders the burden of faith for the two of us.'

'If Joe is not objecting . . . ' said Anisah eagerly. Her round cheeks shone with hope.

'Hang on,' said Yasmin. 'What about me?'

'He will decide, isn't it?' said Ma, not looking at Yasmin.

Harriet directed her gaze at her son. 'I'm looking forward to seeing how many *impeccable liberals* of our acquaintance turn out to be Islamophobes.'

Yasmin slid low in her chair so she could kick Joe's leg under the table. It wasn't easy because he wasn't directly opposite, but she managed to make contact. He squinted at her earnestly, trying to read her mind.

'There are more Islamophobes in India than in the whole of Europe,' said Baba. 'That is why Modi came to power. His greatest achievement in the eyes of many was the pogrom in Gujarat when he was Chief Minister.'

'Don't get me started on Modi,' cried Harriet. 'Yes, Islamophobia is everywhere, but not in this house! Joseph, isn't that right?'

Joe tilted his head, still observing Yasmin. She widened her eyes in desperation.

'It's fine with me,' he said.

'Bravo!' said Harriet. 'Will you, sister, select the imam? Will he be from your local mosque?'

'I pray at home,' said Ma, 'but also I attend sisters' majlis in Croydon every week. It is a sort of bookclub, but for studying the Qu'ran and the Hadith. I will ask Imam Siddiq. Inshallah, he will be most happy.'

'But it's up to Yasmin,' said Joe, finally catching on as Yasmin shook her head. 'Can't have a wedding without a bride.'

They all looked at Yasmin. And now she hesitated.

Joe looked confused. He shrugged an apology. Baba prepared responses to whatever her response might be. Harriet fizzed with determination, as though she might levitate off her chair. Ma pleaded with her eyes.

She would say no, she decided that was best even though it would cause some awkwardness. Better a little awkwardness now than a lot later on.

'When you were a little girl,' said Ma, 'you always said your prayers. Arif was more difficult. But you always said your prayers with me. Every day.' She sniffed and rubbed her nose.

'Yes, Ma,' said Yasmin. There was a risk Ma would begin to sob if she said no.

'Every day,' Ma repeated.

'I said yes, Ma. Yes. It's fine.'

'Yes?'

There was, Yasmin realised, still a chance Ma would succumb to a weeping jag. 'Yes!' she repeated, rather aggressively. 'If Joe doesn't mind.' But it was hopeless now. Joe wouldn't sit there and overrule her. He'd handed her the opportunity to put an end to this and she'd blown it. Now they'd have Imam Siddiq at their wedding, with his big yellow teeth and oiled hair. They'd have to endure him croaking on and on in Arabic and when he'd maxed out on recitations he'd switch to English for the sermon, and that would be worse.

Joe blew her a kiss across the table. Yasmin forced a smile. Ma kissed her on the cheek. Even Shaokat looked pleased, although he had never said a good word about imams in his life. Perhaps he was pleased for Anisah. Or for Harriet, whose plan it had been, after all. Perhaps he was simply glad his daughter had shown herself to be a good daughter, and a compliant daughter-in-law.

'Joe will convert,' Anisah said directly to Harriet, as if the youngsters could now be safely left out of the arrangements. 'But don't worry, it is simple only. Even on the wedding day itself, he can do it. Only he has to say the Shahada, and it is done. La ilaha illa Allah, Muhammad rasoolu Allah.'

'Is it really? It's done with a sentence? Well, Joseph, consider yourself lucky. If you were marrying a Roman Catholic, think what a palaver *that* would be! A simple sentence, how beautiful, what does it say?'

'There is no true god but God,' said Anisah, 'and Muhammad is his Prophet.'

'You and I,' said Harriet, 'are going to be such good friends.'

Harriet had siphoned Ma off to a window seat, instructing the others to *talk doctor stuff*. Harriet sat again in half lotus on the green damask cushions, facing Anisah who had her legs tucked awkwardly up to one side. Harriet's hair was smooth as a sheet, her limbs precisely angled. Anisah's hair – ever wayward – frizzed out of her bun. She was loose everywhere, her body slack and untidy like a skein of unravelled wool that had been hastily balled up again. The pair spoke in low and urgent tones, and only an occasional word drifted as far as the table – family, flights, invitation, and also – unfathomably – asparagus.

41

Yasmin was hot with regret. She should, at the very least, have said she needed time to think. It had all happened too fast. But she'd tell Baba she'd changed her mind and he would agree with her; he'd want minimum fuss. There were no relatives on his side to please. He hadn't set foot in a mosque since he left India. And he was a secular Muslim, he was fond of saying, as many Jewish people were secular Jews.

Shaokat needed no encouragement when it came to talking doctor stuff. 'When I first became a GP, I used to run antenatal clinics. This is a thing of the past. A patient came to see me – she had tonsillitis and also a baby in a sling. I had not even known about her pregnancy.'

'I've got the best job,' said Joe apologetically. 'Despite the Health Secretary's determination to make every single junior doctor's life a misery. Look at this.' He whipped his phone from his pocket and showed Yasmin and Shaokat a text: *We named him Joseph! Thank you!! Xxx* There was a photo attachment of a translucent face tight-shut against the world.

'Sweet,' said Yasmin. 'But ... you give your number out to patients? We're not supposed to. The Trust has a blanket rule.'

'True,' said Joe. 'But sometimes the rules are a bit ridiculous. There's a notice up in the department – any staff member who gets caught taking tea or a biscuit from the ward trolley will be subject to disciplinary action. For taking a custard cream. Seriously? They're not even branded! Cut-price supermarket own label, basics range cardboard creams. We should never have abandoned the industrial action.'

Shaokat ran his tongue around his lips. Earlier in the month, when the first of five planned strike days by junior doctors had been called off, he had expressed his hope that the matter had effectively drawn to a close. Medicine was a calling, a vocation, not an assembly line. It was beneath the dignity of junior doctors to behave like factory workers. Yasmin, despite voting in favour of industrial action last November, carried on working as normal during the subsequent January and February strike days for fear of Baba's disapproval. But when the all-out strike happened in April, she had been out on the picket line with Joe. It was part of their budding romance. One she preferred to conceal.

'Do you miss doing the antenatal clinics?' she asked, hoping to deflect him from preaching against the strikes.

'I have been reading,' he said, 'about amniotic band syndrome.' He asked Joe how often he'd encountered this rare condition, the success rate of detecting it with ultrasound, the complexities of corrective foetal surgery.

He said nothing objectionable. But his suit was too big across the shoulders. Had he shrunk after all, perhaps in width rather than height? And it was his best suit but it looked shabby here in Primrose Hill. It would have been better if he'd dressed casually, thought Yasmin, forgetting for a moment that other than a tracksuit her father possessed no casual clothes.

'Well,' said Shaokat, his enquiries satisfied, 'an obstetrician, a GP, and an elderly care doctor – within one family we deliver the National Health Service, from the cradle to the grave.'

'I've not totally decided yet,' said Yasmin. She would rotate out of elderly care in a few months. The plan had always been to return to geriatrics as her specialty but how this plan had taken shape was somewhat mysterious. Shaokat bestowed a smile on her, as if amused by this sudden flight of fancy.

'I will be proud,' said Shaokat, 'to call you my son.' He made a kind of stiff, seated bow to Joe and turned to Yasmin. She braced for a lengthy speech about the nature of fatherhood, or advice for their joint future. But he only said, 'If your mother can be prevailed upon, I believe we should begin the journey home.'

THE COMEDOWN

The leave-taking was riddled with enthusiasm and promises. Ma hugged Harriet long and tight, and Harriet, although she was more air-kisser than hugger, wrapped her arms nearly right the way around Anisah. Now, you won't forget, and you will come, and of course I won't and of course I will, and how wonderful, and very-very this and that – until they at last broke apart.

In the car they quickly fell silent. A mist had settled over the city, and the headlights cut a narrow lane of black road, orange halos of streetlights above, silver bands of lights rising and falling as the oncoming traffic streamed by.

They were coming down off their highs. Harriet was a drug and her parents were first-time users. They'd be irritable now; it was inevitable.

'I hope,' said Baba, 'you will not ask that Siddiq fellow to perform the nikah. That man is not holy. He is nothing but a hypocrite.'

'Hypocrite?' said Ma. 'What are you talking, hypocrite? Do you know him? You don't know. How can you call him names like this?'

'I know of him,' said Baba, 'and that is enough.'

Ma grumbled beneath her breath in Bengali. Yasmin could

not make out the words, but knew it meant Ma was making up her mind that this imam would be the one to marry her daughter unless her husband prevented it by killing her, her daughter or the imam himself.

'Also, is it not forbidden to recite the Shahada unless one is sincere? Joe is not a Muslim, he does not wish to become a Muslim; for myself I have no objection, I am secular. But I thought that you would dislike it very much. Is it not a mockery of the faith? Of the Siddiq fellow I make no such enquiry, as long as it lines his pocket he will not care.'

Ma gave no reply.

'It was dreamed up in a moment,' said Baba, 'it can just as easily be undone. What do you say, Mini? How do you feel about it now?'

'Easily?' said Ma quickly, sensing danger. 'Easily for you to say when you have no relatives, born under a bush and not one invitation will you send back home!'

'Better be quiet now,' said Baba. He issued it like a careful instruction, a doctor's suggestion to take bed rest.

'Let's talk about it tomorrow,' said Yasmin. 'We're all too tired tonight.'

'If Joe recites Shahada,' said Ma, 'he can become Muslim in his heart. It puts the seed inside, and maybe it takes some time but the seed will grow. Let him only recite and open his heart.'

Ma thought she'd notched him up as a convert! Yasmin had to stop this now. 'But, Ma—' she began.

'Tomorrow,' said Baba. 'Tonight we have all said more than enough.'

ST BARNABAS

St Barnabas Hospital was an agglomeration of defiantly mismatched buildings that straddled the land between two major road junctions, a municipal park and a low-rise block of housing association flats to the west that had been earmarked for demolition and gradually cleared of residents. Another outpatients' department would be built, and then most likely another, as the hospital sprawled ever outwards. The neoclassical façade of the original nineteenth-century building faced the main road. Next to it a red-brick mausoleum of towers and turrets housed the day surgery unit. Behind and to each side St Barnabas mutated into a mixture of concrete bunkers, brutalist multi-storey blocks, curved buildings clad in orange and lime-green plastics, Portakabins, ambulance parks, car parks, service roads, shops, lecture theatre, research centre, dental institute and other more mysterious entities with names such as Max Huber Unit or Leonard Ross House.

Yasmin hurried across the 'village green', a stretch of grey paving that lay in the geographic centre of the hospital. She was late.

'Oh, thank fucking *fuck* you're here,' said Dr Arnott. 'Sometimes, I think I should have stuck to pole dancing. The pay is better, the hours are more civilised. The clients sometimes try to feel you up but at least they don't shit on the floor.'

'One of those nights?' said Yasmin. 'Sorry. Train.'

'Mr Ahmed set fire to a wastepaper basket in the nurses' station, trying to have a sly smoke. It's a miracle we weren't forced to evacuate, health and safety having, you know, gone mad as they say. What's-her-name, the large lady with the bedsores, has been touch-and-go all night. The gentleman in bay D, the one with pneumonia, passed away and I'm sorry I can't even remember his name right now. And this morning, for your special delight, Mrs Antonova has barricaded herself in the TV room. Rest is in the notes. I'm off. Good luck!'

'Thanks,' said Yasmin. 'Umm, Catherine . . .'

'What?'

'Were you really a pole dancer?'

Dr Arnott, who was younger than Yasmin, still in her Foundation training, regarded her sympathetically. 'Only all through college. I've got a practice pole at home, if you want me to teach you sometime?'

'Cool,' said Yasmin, feeling vaguely undermined. Should she already know how to pole dance? 'Maybe. I mean, thanks.'

'No problem,' said Dr Arnott, walking away. She turned and called back, 'Forgot to say, Pepperdine's doing his round super early so you may want to get your arse in gear.'

'Amoxicillin, 500 milligrams, three times per day. Bed rest. Nurse will see to you.' Dr Griffiths prescribed the same treatment for every patient.

Yasmin was checking up on an eighty-seven-year-old man admitted via A&E during the night, complaining of abdominal pain.

'So it's nothing serious?' said the man, addressing Dr Griffiths.

Yasmin looked down at the paperwork to check the patient's

name. 'Mr Renfrew,' she said, 'I need to examine you, if that's okay. Shouldn't take long. If you just pull your top up so I can have a quick feel of your stomach.'

'Listen, Nurse,' said Mr Renfrew, 'I'm not being funny, but best just do what you're told. Okay?'

She'd introduced herself, of course (I'm Yasmin, I'm one of the doctors), but that clearly hadn't sunk in. Not surprising. When you were old and ill you didn't necessarily get everything first time.

Slightly more surprising was Mr Renfrew's willingness to put his faith in Dr Griffiths. Yasmin looked over her shoulder. Dr Griffiths was busy with his stethoscope, which he held inside his pyjama top. He listened carefully to his own heartbeat, cocking his head thoughtfully to one side.

'Amoxicillin, 500 milligrams. Mmm. Mmm. Three times per day, with food.'

He did have a good bedside manner. He spoke with gentle but absolute authority, undermined only by his slippers, pyjamas and the long string of drool hanging from the left side of his withered lips.

'I'm Dr Ghorami,' said Yasmin. 'This gentleman was a GP, but he retired about thirty years ago. He should be in bed in the ward next door.' From the corner of her eye she spotted Anna, one of the health care assistants, hurrying over to capture the fugitive.

Mr Renfrew said, 'I'm not being funny, but at my age I don't think it's right. This is what I get. Messed about. No offence.'

'Dr Griffiths,' said Anna, taking his arm, 'time to get back to the surgery. You've got a full waiting room!'

'None taken,' said Yasmin to Mr Renfrew. He looked like a sweetheart. He had a cloud of white hair, a face as round as a baby's bottom, and his chin quivered when he spoke, as though he was about to burst into tears. It had probably been a long night.

'I'll come back later,' said Yasmin. 'Try to get some rest.'

Mrs Adeyemi sat on the edge of her bed, in her coat and shoes, packed bag at her side. Yasmin needed to do the paperwork so she could be discharged with all the medicines she had to take home. It was the kind of thing that upset Pepperdine, seeing patients hanging around for discharge, preventing a bed from being released. Yasmin didn't want to be subjected to one of his baleful looks. But she had spent nearly half an hour dealing with the siege situation in the television room. This happened from time to time, but usually it was one of the dementia patients. Mrs Antonova was sharp as a tack. Yasmin managed to lure her out with a banana and a tangerine (from her own lunchbox) and the promise that she personally would sort out the radiator behind Mrs Antonova's bed that was stuck on the hotter-than-hell setting.

Yasmin logged on to a computer terminal at the nurses' station. If she could just get a clear ten minutes, she could let poor Mrs Adeyemi go home.

'You know what, Yasmin?' said Niamh. 'I walked over twelve kilometres at work yesterday.'

Niamh was one of the nurses, one of the dwindling band of actual staff nurses. There seemed to be more and more agency staff every day. You hardly learned someone's name before they disappeared again.

'Never need to go to the gym,' said Yasmin. She could feel Niamh hovering, wanting to talk. Right now, though, she had to concentrate. Pepperdine would be here for his rounds any moment. After Mrs Antonova she'd been up to the ICU to check on the lady with bedsores and a chest infection who'd deteriorated overnight and been transferred. Then there was Mr Renfrew, although she hadn't got very far with him.

'You say that, Yasmin, but actually . . . ' Niamh insinuated herself into a chair, flicked off her shoes and put her feet up on the desk. She was around Yasmin's age, maybe a couple of years older. Niamh would have been one of the popular girls at school because she was beautiful, because she was confident. She had copper-coloured hair and alabaster skin. She always made a beeline for Yasmin, determined to make conversation as if they were friends. It was because Niamh was what Baba would call workshy, finding excuses not to attend to her tasks. But there was a bit of Yasmin that was nonetheless flattered: the part of her that was sure Niamh wouldn't have been seen dead with her at school.

'Actually, the kind of walking nurses do at work doesn't relieve stress or have cardiac benefits. That's been proved. And the pain in my feet! Plantar fasciitis, I reckon.' She began to massage her foot.

'Where exactly are you experiencing pain?'

'Centre of the heel, both feet. Oh, look – here comes Nancy. And how are we today?'

'No, no, no.' Nancy was tiny. A sheet of grey hair hung from her skull. A desperate look animated her eyes.

'Not supposed to be over here, are you, Nancy?' said Niamh. 'Honestly, Yasmin, it's getting beyond a joke. They don't control them properly, and if the dementia patients are always over here it's scary for others. Know what I mean?'

'No!' shrieked Nancy. 'Shit, balls, shit.' She crammed her bony fingers in her mouth.

'All right,' said Niamh, her voice dropping an octave. 'All right, then,' she repeated as she rounded the desk. 'Let's get you back to bed.'

Anna, the health care assistant who had wrangled Dr Griffiths, came running.

'She's quick, very quick,' said Anna, out of breath. 'Mrs

Pattinson, we got to get you ready for the hairdresser, don't we? Come – let's go. Come.' With a little more coaxing, Anna finally led her away.

'You know what, Yasmin?' said Niamh, returning to her chair. 'I'm not gonna lie. When the HCAs are that large – I won't say fat because, bless her, it's probably genetic – but when the HCAs are that large it's hardly surprising they can't even keep up with the ninety year olds. Sad, but true.'

'Anna can run,' said Yasmin. 'She's been running all over the place this morning already.' She really had to focus on the forms for Mrs Adeyemi.

'Well, if you can call that running! I do feel sorry for them, though, these West African ladies. You know what I mean? They obviously can't help being that size.'

'That's a bit ...' Yasmin hesitated. 'Bit of a generalisation,' she concluded lamely.

'Well, excuse me for sympathising.' Niamh sat forward. 'Would you say plantar fasciitis counts as an industrial injury?'

'I think you should go to your GP, that would be the best thing. Get it checked out properly.'

'Oh, I will, don't you worry. Shit, he's here.' Niamh sprang up. If her feet hurt as she did so, it wasn't discernible in any way.

Pepperdine stood just inside the door. For a moment the ward grew almost silent, then the bustle and hum of activity intensified.

'Miserable bugger,' said Niamh under her breath, neatening her hair, straightening her uniform. 'I'd fuck him, I would,' she said, as if they had been discussing it. 'I'd do it for all of us, because he obviously needs it. Uptight, or what? And you know what, Yasmin, he's not bad looking. For his age. You know he's never been married. Honestly, I'd do it. I'd fuck him. I'd take one for the team.'

OCCAM'S RAZOR

The general elderly care ward was really two wards knocked together, eight female bays of three beds and, beyond the central nurses' station, eight male bays. A metal rail with a flimsy bluish curtain ringed each bed. The curtains were flags of privacy. They tended towards the symbolic rather than the functional. Next to each bed stood a bedside table, a cupboard for personal belongings and a hard slippery armchair for visitors. More than once Yasmin had witnessed an exhausted wife or husband or daughter slide into sleep and then on to the floor. The walls had the colour and texture of dried sage leaves, as if they might crumble at any moment. The warm yeasty smell of urine was cut with a sharper note of disinfectant. Despite the tall windows the ceiling lights blazed all day, which for some reason always made Yasmin feel tired. She stifled a yawn.

The round was taking for ever. In the acute care unit a patient had had a grand-mal seizure, which had provided Pepperdine with an unmissable teaching opportunity. The 'dementia-friendly' ward was inevitably slow.

Yasmin's concentration was flagging. She was terrorised by an image that came to her suddenly of Harriet on her door-step waving goodbye to the Fiat Multipla, and then collapsing with laughter when the carful of Ghoramis had turned out of the drive.

'Are you, ah, with us, Yasmin? Um ... yes, good ...' said Pepperdine, when she fell too far behind. The medical students flocked immediately around him like goslings and he flapped a hand to shoo them on.

'Sorry. Of course,' said Yasmin. He wasn't scary like some of the consultants and he wasn't over-friendly like some of the others. He was also her supervisor and he liked her, at least she thought he did. It was hard to tell.

'Hello, Elsie,' said Julie, the ward sister, when the retinue had relocated to the next bay. 'We're a little bit worried about Elsie. She's not moved her bowels in four days.'

'Mrs Munro,' said Pepperdine, 'how are you feeling?' He disapproved of calling patients by their first names, even if they had said that you could or even that you should.

'Not bad,' said Mrs Munro, 'little tired today, Doctor.' She sat on top of the bedcovers, propped against a thin pillow, and a tremor ran down her right arm and leg.

Pepperdine, with Mrs Munro's permission, invited one of the students to examine her.

Julie slid off and quickly returned with another pillow that by a sleight of hand she conjured behind Mrs Munro without disturbing her in the least.

'And so?' said Pepperdine.

The student looked preposterously young, even to Yasmin. The colour rose in his cheeks. 'The constipation could be due to the Parkinson's? Or even the antidepressants? She's on, like, citalopram?'

'Thank you, Max. Would anyone else like to make an observation? Anyone?' Pepperdine gazed sadly at the gaggle of students. One young woman bobbed her head as if trying to duck out of the way. Answers were slowly volunteered. Irritable bowel syndrome, hypothyroidism, inactivity, nerve damage, stress, or – this one whispered – colon cancer. Pepperdine nodded slowly to all.

'Dr Ghorami, perhaps you have, ah, something to contribute?'

Yasmin moved in closer to the bedside. She bent down to the patient. Mrs Munro's head quivered from side to side. 'We won't disturb you much longer,' said Yasmin, 'I'd just like to ask – how's your appetite?'

'Hollow legs,' said Mrs Munro. 'That's what my mother used to say about me. Long time ago now, of course. I don't get hungry these days.'

'Got to eat, though, haven't we, Elsie,' said Julie. 'Have you not finished your breakfast this morning?' She looked strained. Yasmin smiled at her, and Julie stretched her lips briefly in return.

Julie didn't waste smiles easily. Her mouth was thin and organised in a straight line. If you stood close enough you could see she had multiple piercings in the lobes and cartilage of both ears, her right eyebrow and her left nostril. They spoke of a past life, though Julie certainly did not. She wore no jewellery, not even studs in her earlobes, as if like a reformed addict she had renounced all of her piercings. Niamh had told Yasmin there was a piercing in Julie's tongue, and another in an intimate part of her anatomy. But Niamh said many things.

'I think that might account for it,' said Yasmin.

The breakfast tray of porridge, toast and a yogurt pot lay clearly untouched on the bedside table. This was not unusual. Old and sick people often didn't feel like eating. But right now it offered evidence of an awful possibility. Yasmin knew Julie had thought of it too.

Four days without food, maybe longer.

Pepperdine let the silence grow. Yasmin looked at his long, serious face. He was tall, leanly built and carried with him an air of remote benevolence. Miserable bugger, Niamh called him, but he wasn't like that at all.

'I'm sorry,' said Mrs Munro. 'I don't mean to be a bother.'

At the far end of the ward, lunch trays were already being distributed.

They all watched Mrs Munro's shaking arm and head. Nurses or HCAs were supposed to feed patients who couldn't feed themselves, and mostly they did. But the ones who didn't want to be a bother were easily overlooked.

'Never a bother,' said Pepperdine. 'You'll keep an eye out?' he said to Julie, mildly.

'Won't happen again.' Her face and her voice were tight. Pepperdine was always courteous and meticulous and everyone wanted his respect. No one was sure they had earned it, including Julie, who was otherwise unflappable.

'Occam's razor,' said Pepperdine. 'Never be blind to the obvious answer. No food in equals no waste out.' He nodded to Yasmin and she felt happy and slightly bashful, as though he'd praised her to the skies.

They had reached Mrs Adeyemi, who sat neat as a pin, feet pressed together in bright blue canvas post-op shoes. It dawned on Yasmin that in addition to her medications, Mrs Adeyemi was going to need a walking frame. And she'd need help at home, though it wasn't clear from her records if that was available. Yasmin needed to speak to Leslie, the social worker, and Leslie was so busy . . .

'Oh dear,' said Pepperdine to Mrs Adeyemi, 'what's this? Are we, um, keeping you waiting?'

'Just need to finish the paperwork,' said Yasmin.

'I see,' he said. 'I see.'

He turned his attention to the next bed, which was vacant. 'We have an escapee.' The students tittered.

The empty bed was Mrs Antonova's. Someone had managed to force open the window.

'The radiators aren't working properly,' said Julie. 'We can't turn them down. Some of the patients complain about being too hot so we open a window, then of course there's a draught and we get other complaints.'

'Ah,' said Pepperdine gravely, 'here we have a perfect example of the Trust's efficiency drive. Maintenance has been contracted out — out of existence, some might say — and patients are thus incentivised to compete amongst each other in a free market for climate control.'

'I promised her I'd fix it,' said Yasmin. Pepperdine looked at her. She wished she'd kept her mouth shut, but now she had to go on. 'Mrs Antonova. She wouldn't come out of the television room.'

'Are you a doctor or a miracle worker?'

The students tittered again.

'I bribed her with a tangerine and a banana,' said Yasmin, 'but she's a tough negotiator.'

Pepperdine nodded, but she braced herself for mockery. It didn't come. 'Good,' he said. 'Very good.'

NO SUCH THING AS SEX

'I messed up, didn't I?' Joe sat on the examination couch and she stood between his legs. He wore a pair of navy moleskin trousers and a white linen shirt. The other male medics wore office shirts with stiff collars, without ties. She ran her fingers through his fringe.

'It's okay.' They'd talked after Yasmin got home. Then he'd sent half a dozen messages saying sorry for not cottoning on.

'Harry will forget about it probably. If we just don't mention it again.'

'*She* might. Ma won't.'

'So you'll tell her that's not what you want?'

'I think so. I was going to this morning but she was so happy she made parathas for breakfast, and I didn't have the heart.' Maybe it would have been kinder if she had. The longer Ma nursed fantasies about having a nikah, the more upset she'd be when Yasmin killed them off.

He squeezed her legs between his knees. 'Parathas for breakfast? Okay, so this *might* be another example of me being slow on the uptake, but what's the significance?'

'She only makes them for breakfast on birthdays. Obviously!' She rapped her knuckles on his forehead. 'Everyone knows that!'

'Of course. Well, if she's *that* excited about it . . . should we just . . . ?'

'You've never met Imam Siddiq.'

'Fair enough.' His steady blue eyes held her gaze. 'But would it have to be him? Couldn't you get someone else as . . . as a compromise?'

'But it's not what we want,' she said. It came out as a bleat. It wasn't even what Ma had wanted. Or if it was she would never have mentioned it until Harriet interfered. Yasmin sat down on the swivel chair. She swung it round. The room where he'd just finished a gynae clinic was cramped. The desk was cluttered with boxes of condoms, morning-after pills and disposable gloves, tubes of KY, blood pressure cuffs and a life-size pelvic skeleton – hip bones, sacrum with coccyx and two lumbar vertebrae.

'Hey, listen,' said Joe, 'I'm just feeling my way, okay? You've talked about how you were brought up Muslim and I know you're not observant, but you told me you still pray some-times and—'

'Not very often,' said Yasmin, interrupting. 'Hardly at all.'

'Okay. I get it.'

'And my father has no idea how much a marquee and everything would cost. Hiring the chairs and tables and cen-trepieces and dance floor and everything else. He's probably thinking he could buy a big tent from Argos.'

'But Harry can pay. It's not an issue.'

'Baba doesn't want her to.'

'Tell him I'll pay. Does that work?'

'No, he'd be insulted.'

'Then . . . Harry can tell him to pay her back for everything she arranges and you can come up with a figure that's suitable. She won't mind whatever it is.'

'I mind,' said Yasmin. 'It's getting too complicated. Why don't we just book the registry office and get married now? We don't want all the fuss, do we?' It suddenly seemed ludicrous they were waiting another six months.

Joe looked baffled. 'Well, we could do. But what about your relatives from abroad? Doesn't your mum really want them to come?'

Yasmin shrugged. 'It's not a big deal.'

'Not for you. But for—'

'Fine,' she said, cutting him off. 'Forget it. We'll wait six bloody months.'

He laughed. 'It was you who didn't want to rush anything. Remember?'

'Yes, but that was before . . .' What was it before? Before Harriet interfered. But she couldn't say that. Harriet had welcomed Yasmin with open arms and she'd made every effort with Ma and Baba, and Yasmin had no right to feel angry with her about anything. 'Let's just rent a place together,' she said. 'We can get married later, but let's move in together now.'

'Yasmin,' he said, 'what is it? There's something you're not telling me.'

'Nothing,' she said, feeling foolish. She looked down at his shoes. Pale grey trainers and purple laces today. He had laces in every colour of the rainbow and a few more besides. Said it was a 'style cheat' he'd read in a waiting-room magazine when he was sixteen. It was something that had just stuck. 'I want us to live together, that's all. Soon.'

'Me too.' He sighed. 'But your parents would be upset, right?' He came over to crouch beside her and looked at her earnestly. She was being a selfish bitch. She was being unreasonable. She wound her fingers around the back of his neck.

'Sorry,' she said. 'Sorry. I don't know what's got into me.'

'Have you got time for lunch? We'll have a picnic. Wait here. I'll go and get it.'

*

She didn't wait there, she went to the toilet. When she'd washed her hands she appraised herself in the mirror. She wished her lips were fuller and her nose less round. That's what she used to wish, anyway, and the thought arose still, automatically, without the feeling of longing that used to accompany it. Her face was all right as it was. Her eyes counted for a lot. The lashes, too. They didn't need mascara. All she used on them was Vaseline. Under this awful light her hair looked thick and shiny but uniform in length and colour, a shoulder-length fall of black. But outside, when they went for this mysterious twenty-minute picnic, the way it was cut in layers would show. The colours would show: chestnut, auburn, mahogany.

It was you who didn't want to rush anything.

She slipped a finger down her sweater and touched the engagement ring, a sapphire clustered with diamonds, strung on the silver chain around her neck. Rings weren't allowed. The Trust permitted only wedding bands.

When he proposed they'd only known each other five months. It was a month before he even kissed her, then four months later he took her to Paris for the weekend and proposed by the Medici Fountain. She said yes immediately.

That night, lying in bed in the hotel behind the Luxembourg Gardens, she asked what she'd wanted to ask for the previous four months: Why didn't you kiss me the first time? Or the second or third or sixth?

In the past, he said, he'd jumped into bed with a lot of girls. You know what Tinder dates are like.

Not really, she said.

Have you really only had one boyfriend?

Yes, she said. She'd told him about Kashif, but she'd made him sound nicer than he really was. Didn't mention the two boys at school, but she hadn't slept with them so they didn't count. And after Kashif she'd slept with another student, but

only once, and the things he wanted – expected – her to do . . .
Well, she'd almost blotted them out.

I just wanted to do it right, he said, answering her question.
I wanted to do it properly. I've tried the other way and believe
me it wasn't working. It wasn't working for me.

They sat on a bench on the 'village green', in a patch of sun.
The picnic was packets of crisps and chocolate bars from the
vending machine.

He'd told her about the fourteen-year-old girl he'd seen in
the clinic that morning. The girl was worried that her *privates
looked funny* and her mother agreed she *didn't look right*. Women
worried about their labia because they compared themselves
to what they saw in porn. But this girl was fourteen! The GP
hadn't convinced the mother there was nothing wrong with her
daughter. When Joe reassured them that the girl was perfectly
normal, she definitely didn't need an operation to reduce the size
of her labia, the girl burst into tears and the mother said, *You're
telling us we have to go private, that's what you mean.*

'I should have shown them the photo of Harry,' he said. 'You
know *that* one. There you go – look, here's a natural woman.
Just be proud of your body exactly as it is.'

Joe had never referred to the infamous photo before. He'd
talked a bit about her book that described her polyamorous
pursuits, and it was clear he admired her courage and openness
as well as her prose style. The only criticism he made was that
the memoir occasionally lapsed into boastfulness.

'Definitely,' she said. There was nothing to be embarrassed
about. Joe wasn't embarrassed. But he hadn't grown up in the
Ghorami household where there was no such thing as sex.

'Oh, I signed up with another two estate agents. Three or four
flats that look interesting. But not amazing. We're going to find
somewhere that is. Trust me, it will be incredible.' He smiled at

his own over-enthusiasm. She loved that about him – the way he managed to combine fervour with humour, to be intense and simultaneously chilled. She loved his earnestness, and his readiness to laugh at it.

She looked at the dimple in his chin. 'Will you invite your father to the wedding? Did you give it any more thought?'

His face darkened as a cloud drifted across the sun. 'My father? I don't know. I've only seen him maybe four or five times since I was fifteen. He's a drunk and a liar and a cheat. And those are his *best* qualities. Wait, hang on, so there's going to be a wedding, is there? Because not so long ago you wanted to call it off.'

'No, I didn't.' She laughed. 'You idiot.'

'I love you too,' he said.

SANDOR

The patient was an engaging young man: intelligent, articulate, in possession of an abundance of self-deprecating charm. Acutely aware of his privilege. Acutely in denial of his pain. Sandor wondered if he should jump in now. He'd heard enough about all that the patient had not suffered, all the disadvantages with which he had not been burdened, the blessings bestowed and the endless reasons why he should not be as he was.

Wait, he decided. One thing Sandor had learned this past year was that Brits were more entrenched in the hierarchy of pain than Americans. On the whole, Americans were less inclined to dismiss their own suffering because someone, somewhere, had it way worse.

Sandor leaned back and crossed his legs. The thrill of occupying Robert's armchair had waned surprisingly little. If his father-in-law was up there looking down he'd be white-lipped with cold, cold rage to see Sandor in his study, in baggy corduroys and moth-eaten sweater, practising voodoo on aberrant drinkers, gamblers, drug-users, all manner of addicts: the weak-willed, the feckless, or those unfortunates inflicted with 'chemical imbalances' or maladapted brains. Dr Robert Elliot Heathcote-Drummond FRCPsych, FRS, recipient of the

Gaskell Medal and Officer of the Order of the British Empire, dealt only in sickness and cures. Pills, incarceration, electroconvulsive therapy. Everything else was for the birds.

'In some ways,' said Sandor, because the patient had come to the end of his litany of fortunate events, 'you've already taken the most difficult step in your recovery simply by being here. I'd like to take a moment to acknowledge that and for us both to acknowledge your courage in seeking help. You feel uncomfortable with praise?'

'Urf,' said the patient, his articulacy deserting him. 'Umm.' He shook his head and his hair fell into his eyes. 'Recovery? I don't know. I mean . . . when you put it like that I feel like a bit of a fraud because . . . '

'Because? You're not sick?' Sandor smiled. 'You're not an addict?'

'I don't know if I even qualify. As an addict. I guess what I'm saying is *recovery* feels like letting myself off the hook. As though I'm not responsible for anything.' The boy – his rosy cheeks and full upper lip made him look young – was addicted to self-criticism.

'If we consider the Latin root – *recuperare*, to get again – perhaps that might be helpful. What have you lost, that you want to find again?' Sandor paused. The English tended to be uneasy with this type of question. They laughed, or looked embarrassed, or answered a different question that had not been asked.

The silence stretched and Sandor kept his gaze on the coffee table, a round of smoked glass on interlocking carved teak legs. It was mid-century modern, a piece of vintage Danish design known as the Spider table, and it really was a beauty, although Melissa said you didn't have to be a shrink to figure out why Sandor preserved Robert's study intact. His wife wasn't wrong, of course. But Sandor liked the table. And this armchair. The wide armrests topped with beech were useful for resting his notes. He loved the rosewood mini-bar and the two-tier cocktail table with stern metal legs and jaunty mosaic inlay. The desk with walnut drawers and silver-plate handles, and the grey lacquered frame in an art deco design. The only thing he'd changed was the couch because black leather and chrome was too inhospitable.

'Perhaps it's a question for another day,' said Sandor. 'Let's keep going with the family history. You've told me what your parents *didn't* do. They didn't beat you, et cetera.' He raised his eyebrows in what he hoped was a jocular manner. 'I'm curious to know what you *did* experience during your childhood. Locating the source of the trauma isn't always easy, but it's always worthwhile.'

'But I haven't experienced any trauma.'

'Okay. I understand. Your father left when you were very young. Why don't you tell me more about that?'

The patient talked and Sandor prompted him now and again with a question and took an occasional note. The boy was eager to please. His manner was open and sincere. He was educated, his clothes expensive and understated, his gaze direct. His words were thoughtful. And clueless. He didn't know if he *qualified* as an addict. Of course, at some level, he knew. Why else seek out therapy from the author of books such as *Fix: Drug Addiction and the Quest for Life* and *Thirst: Finding Freedom from Alcohol*?

He was a family therapist too, that was always part of his billing. An essential part, because addictions were almost invariably rooted within the family history.

'Say more. About being an only child. You said you felt special. Your mother made you feel special. In what ways did she do that?'

The boy pressed a thumb knuckle deep into his chin. 'Well, by always putting me first? Talking to me like an equal?

Confiding in me?' He slid into the millennials' habit of turning statements into questions.

Sandor nodded and looked down at his papers. The boy had a name and it was there, somewhere on the intake form.

'So it wasn't exactly a *normal* sort of childhood.' The boy – but he wasn't a boy, he was close to thirty – gave a laugh, to underline how well he knew the meaninglessness of such a statement. 'I guess nobody's is.'

'How do you feel when you say that? That it wasn't a normal childhood.'

'I feel that I'm being a bit self-indulgent?'

'Okay. I understand. But let's try again. When I say *feel* I mean an emotion you experience somewhere in your body. Maybe in your chest, your throat, your gut – doesn't matter where. Take your time. Take a breath or two. It wasn't a normal childhood. How does it feel to share this information with me?'

'Umm, I think that it's probably more of a question I'm asking you indirectly. Is that what you're getting at? If I think more deeply about it, yes, I'm asking for your opinion about whether you think there's something abnormal about it, but I was hedging around instead of being direct.'

Sandor remembered the patient's name. He knew it would come back to him. The poor boy: for his entire life his every need had been met except for the essential ones, and those were so far from being met that he wasn't even aware of them. 'Yes, this is a smart analysis, I've no doubt.' Sandor nodded to show he appreciated his patient's acuity. 'But I'll share a little trick I've learned about the naming – the identification – of feelings. If you use the word "that", it prevents you from naming a feeling. I feel that ... or I think that ... It doesn't work. Sad is a feeling. Angry is a feeling. I feel sad. I feel angry. I feel scared. I feel hurt. You see? A "that" will always trip you up.'

'I feel ... '

'Yes.'

'I feel . . . like a bad person.'

'*Like* is another disabling word.'

'I feel . . . bad, weak, wrong.'

They were coming towards the end of their first session together – ninety minutes for the first, the subsequent sessions would be fifty – and already Sandor had an inkling of how this might play out. A picture had begun to form. But it was important not to rush ahead of the patient. And not to turn first impressions into firm judgements. He felt sad for this boy, who was unable to feel sad for himself.

'That sounds really tough,' said Sandor.

'Why am I like this? What's wrong with me?' The pink cheeks turned red.

'Why are you an addict?'

The boy struggled with the word. Joe was not a boy. He was a young man. And Sandor was old. Every time he passed a mirror these days, Sandor noted how age was hollowing out his face, so that his big nose grew bigger while his cheeks sank inwards and his eyes sank backwards in his skull. Sixty-four years old but these days he felt more like a centenarian. Particularly on the days he had to catch his breath halfway up the stairs. The dark rings around his eyes reminded him of his first patients, back in Brooklyn, the meth-heads and heroin addicts and the other unloved people who had taught him so much and to whom he owed everything.

Sandor watched the struggle play out in Joe's pale blue eyes. He was bad, weak, wrong. Was he an *addict*? Did he *qualify*?

Finally, he said, 'Yes.'

It was a breakthrough. The first step, at least. 'Think of it this way,' said Sandor. 'Addiction is not the primary problem. The addiction is always an attempt to *solve* a problem. It is the person's unconscious attempt to escape from pain. So the question,

Joe, is not: why the addiction? It is: why the pain? That is what we will attempt to solve together in these sessions.'

When he'd seen Joe out, Sandor had an hour to himself. After that his day was filled with appointments. Although he'd promised Melissa he would see only a handful of patients, cut down on his work hours, he found it hard to turn people away. Sandor pulled off his loafers and lay down on the sofa. A wave of nostalgia rolled over him. The first time Melissa had brought Sandor home to this house he was a grad student but Robert made him feel like a kid, the way he had repeated back his name, Sandor Bartok, as though it was some kind of prank. Yes, sir! said Sandor, standing to attention in flared jeans and spiral tie-dye T-shirt, silently cursing Melissa, who stood behind her father shaking with mirth.

International relations, said Robert, is that what you're studying, or is that what you're doing with my daughter? Back then Sandor was studying at the London School of Economics and Melissa was an undergraduate, two years into her BSc in Economics. Anthropology, said Robert, when he discovered it had been Sandor's major as an undergrad, is about studying chaps in loincloths. So what on earth are you doing in London? Melissa said, He's studying you, Daddy. You and your tribe.

Walking him to the bus stop after dinner she giggled all the way. Daddy, she said, had never met a real live hippy before. Mummy, she said, had chosen her life as a martyr to Daddy and deserved nobody's pity in return.

When Melissa's mother died, Melissa began wondering out loud about returning to London now that Adam was grown. A week with Robert after the funeral (her mother no longer ignored but beatified) nipped that in the bud. But after Robert passed, Melissa once again raised the possibility of return. With Adam living in Berlin, it made just as much sense to be in London as New York. Sandor agreed. The plan had been to live in the house until it was sold, but a year had passed and now it was home.

Yes, sir!

Bell-bottom jeans and tie-dye T-shirt.

Yes, sir!

Sandor smiled and closed his eyes.

CHAI WALLAH

Arif lay on the sofa eating a bag of Chilli Heatwave Doritos and scrolling through his phone. His big toes poked through the holes in his socks. He'd left the sitting-room door wide open and when Yasmin walked past, trying to hurry straight up to her room, he called out.

'So I heard about it. Ma is well excited.'

Yasmin leaned against the doorframe. 'Arif,' she said, 'I'm knackered. I'm not in the mood. And I've got studying to do.'

He tossed the Doritos on to the table and swung his legs down. 'I'm not in the mood either.' He gave her a helpless kind of look. 'It's okay. Go.'

She let her bag slide to the floor, and sat down next to him.

'What?' she said. 'What's wrong?'

He looked around at the cornicing, as if the answer might be secreted in the layer of dust up there.

'Joe's converting then,' he said. 'Good man.'

He had Shaokat's slender nose. Yasmin had often envied it, because she had inherited Anisah's round one, but she noticed now the way it made Arif look pinched and rather peevish. It didn't work the same way on Shaokat's stern face.

'We'll see,' said Yasmin. She didn't feel like discussing it, certainly not with Arif. 'I'm going to my room.'

'You remember that girl,' said Arif, sitting up. 'I was with her in the shop that time.'

Lucy-as-you'd-guess. 'She seemed nice,' said Yasmin. She waited, but Arif had expended his entire energy on getting this far. 'Lucy? I take it she's your girlfriend.'

They heard the front door open, the familiar slap of Shaokat's brogues along the tiled hall. He always returned promptly after the surgery closed now his seniority had relieved him of all those home visits that used to swallow up his evenings.

It only then occurred to Yasmin that Ma hadn't popped her head out of the kitchen, and that she couldn't smell anything cooking.

'Where's Ma?' she said to Arif.

'Out for tea with your mother-in-law.'

Arif tried to slink off but Baba told him to stay. If he wanted to treat the place as a boarding house and act like a lodger, like a stranger, then he was welcome to pay rent and take no further part in family life. Shaokat turned his wooden chair away from the table and sat straight as a judge, facing his children. Arif put his feet on the onyx-top coffee table. His big toes, naked and protuberant, suddenly looked obscene. He waggled them suggestively.

Yasmin perched on the arm of the sofa. She hoped Shaokat would leave Arif alone. But she knew Arif's ingratitude pained her father, after decades of struggle to attain a four-bedroom home in a cul-de-sac, with a porch for umbrellas and shoes, and a garden over a hundred feet long, and two children put through university, all their fees paid by him (*that's* what Baba did with his money); it pained him to enter that dream home and ignore the dust and the clutter, the piles of charity-shop bargains; it pained him that the garden was scarred by flapping polytunnels and mud trenches from Anisah's sporadic bursts of agricultural activity. It pained him but he never complained. In fact, he took care to encourage and praise Ma's many and varied half-baked projects. And though he often tried to avert his eyes from Arif sometimes he could not help but see. Arif was not helping matters by munching aggravatingly on the Doritos and picking insolently at his teeth.

'I had a patient today, Baba, I was hoping to discuss with you.'

Mr Renfrew, who had been so reluctant to be examined earlier, was happy to be centre of attention on the consultant's round. He bestowed on Pepperdine his detailed medical history, including an appendectomy over sixty years ago, a bout of dengue fever contracted in the Philippines, and a disquisition on the NHS's failure to effectively treat his carpal tunnel syndrome. Yasmin outlined the more relevant parts of his medical history and her observations, and Baba took off his glasses the better to ruminate on the details. He asked some questions and then steered her towards a differential diagnosis by reminding her of a case challenge they'd studied together, and suggesting that IgG4 pancreatitis should certainly be tested for.

Yasmin hoped Ma would come home now so Arif could make his escape. What was Harriet doing with her anyway? And wasn't it too late to be having tea? But Ma did not come, and Baba turned his attention to his son.

'Now, tell us what you have been doing with your day.'

Arif threw a Dorito in the air and failed to catch it in his mouth. He left it lying on his crotch.

Baba let the silence expand and fill the room.

When she could bear it no longer Yasmin stirred herself to speak, but Baba held up his hand to signal her to be quiet.

'Some job applications, perhaps?'

'Yeah,' said Arif. 'Job applications. All day.'

'I see. Would you care to show them to me?'

'Can't. Posted them. They're in the post.'

'No emails? No online applications? Nothing you can show at all?'

'Nothing,' said Arif. He straightened the Dorito packet and funnelled the crumbs into his mouth.

Shaokat's suit today was double-breasted and he'd kept it fastened. His tie, striped in shades of brown, was a little askew and one tip of his shirt collar was very slightly frayed, but everything about his clothes, the way he sat, his neatly combed hair said that he worked hard, he made an effort, and above all that he *cared*. Arif's jeans were dirty. His hair, which he kept long, looked greasy. The way he lay, limbs splayed on the sofa and across the coffee table, said the opposite: that he didn't give a fuck.

It was still an effort, though. Caring less about not caring, thought Yasmin, would be a whole lot easier.

Shaokat peered at Arif as if from a great distance, though he could easily have reached out and touched him without leaving his seat.

'Indeed,' he said, 'this is apposite. Nothing. Apposite to your situation, which is that you have nothing to show for anything.'

Arif got slowly to his feet. 'Yeah, thanks. Thanks for that. That really helps. Thanks for your support. You think I haven't applied for jobs? Is that what you think?' He was moving towards the door, but then he turned and came back again. His voice rose in volume and also in pitch. 'I've applied for . . . I don't know . . . lost count. Hundreds of jobs, and what have I had? Five interviews and six months in a call centre, one month in telesales. You say there's no discrimination, you think I'm lazy, you think it's all my fault, but let me tell you something, yeah, you're 74 per cent more likely to make a successful application if you have a white-sounding name. So thanks very much, I'm so grateful to you for pointing out to me that I have nothing to show for anything!'

'Sit down,' said Shaokat. 'Calm yourself.' He waited but

Arif remained standing. 'Very well, you choose for yourself how best to behave. And now, with your permission, I will tell something to you.'

'Sit down,' Yasmin whispered. 'Please.'

Arif ignored her. He was so evidently riven with indecision about whether to storm out of the room that he seemed almost to vibrate on the spot. 'Here it comes,' he said, 'here it comes! Your glorious rise from the dunghills of the poorest village in West Bengal.'

Shaokat undid his jacket and smoothed his tie. 'I apologise that I have, on previous occasions, bored you with the story of my life. Your satirical representation correctly identifies that the tale is far from heroic, and I am aware that in your eyes I am nothing more than a mediocrity.'

Yasmin wanted to protest but knew her father would not wish to be interrupted. He was cogitating, or perhaps just pausing to let his words sink in. She glanced at Arif, and thought she detected a little softening. He had spoken so wildly, and the way his voice had lifted almost to a squeak betrayed how much his emotions had run out of control.

The truth was that Shaokat rarely talked about his childhood. He'd told them a few things. The school he attended from the age of five to eleven had only three brick walls. The fourth was a sheet of corrugated iron that was pushed aside to serve as both window and door. He first learned to write his letters on the dirt floor with a stick before graduating to a slate board, thence to paper when supplies allowed. He had no brothers or sisters, because his mother died soon after he was born and his father remained a widower until his own death, from cholera, when Shaokat had barely turned twelve.

For two years he lived with an uncle and continued attending the secondary school in the next village, three miles away, a journey he made on foot carrying his shoes strung together over his shoulder so as not to wear out the leather. But his uncle could not continue feeding him indefinitely, not with nine children of his own, and at fourteen years old Shaokat was sent to Calcutta to work for a chai wallah, a distant relative of somebody or other. The chai wallah, blessed with a prime spot on Park Street, had expanded his operation to a second urn.

Whenever Yasmin thought about how her father's life had begun she experienced a swell in her ribcage, pride of course, but also fear, as if there was still a chance that he would never escape the jaws of poverty, as if he might never embark on the long and difficult journey, or might travel but never arrive.

Arif, she knew, felt differently. When he had complained, a few weeks ago, that his laptop was old and slow, Baba had reminded him how he had first learned to write letters in the dirt. You win again, said Arif.

'This is what I want to say to you,' said Shaokat.

Arif rolled his eyes at this preamble. He stood so hunched he turned his entire body into a question mark. Well?

'You may wish to consider the possibility that the so-called prejudice you have thus far encountered has something more to do with your third-class degree in sociology and something less to do with your name. A name which, I should say, has been serviceable to me and also your sister.'

'Chood,' said Arif, shaking his head in disbelief. 'Chood.' Somehow he could swear in Bengali in front of his father. In English he could not.

'Go back to college,' Shaokat said, a flicker of urgency quickening his words. 'Maybe you will have to retake one or two A-levels, and then you can go to a decent university this time. What about accountancy? When you were a boy you loved maths, you were so quick with numbers —' this was said with tenderness, but then, '– and it is so puzzling, that you have abilities you decide not to use.'

'Accountant,' said Arif. His face contorted. 'Accountant or doctor, that's it, isn't it? That's the choice.'

'You prefer technology?' said Shaokat, reasonably. 'You are making apps, that is your assertion. Why not do it properly? Take a degree in computer science. You will find no persecution, I assure you, on account of your name.'

Arif exploded. 'ACCOUNTANT! DOCTOR! INDIAN I.T. NERD! I DON'T WANT ANY OF THAT!'

'What *do* you want then?' Yasmin jumped up. She was almost shouting herself. 'What is wrong with you? Can't you see Baba is trying to help?'

'Help? He's trying to help? He knows why I got a bad degree. He *knows* the reason. And he brings it up to insult me.'

'It's not like that, Arif,' said Yasmin. 'You're twisting everything.'

'Enough, Mini,' said Shaokat. 'No need to get excited.'

Yasmin sat down and looked at her hands.

'I was twenty-three when I married your mother,' said Shaokat. 'One year younger than you are now, Arif. Only after that I attended university. Seven years in Calcutta to qualify as a doctor, and when I came to London I studied for more exams. I was thirty-eight when I had my first proper job, not as a locum, a permanent job. What I'm saying to you, my son, is there are many years ahead. You are angry because you feel your life is wasted. I am telling you that has not happened yet. You choose the course and the university, and I will find money for the fees.' He rubbed his temples and closed his eyes.

'No chance,' said Arif. 'Already I have to hear about how you spent all that money on my education. You think I'd let you pay for another degree? So I can spend the rest of my life being grateful for something I never even wanted. And you! What about you? You claim you're like this self-made whatever, this

rose that grew out of the cow pat, all under your own steam . . . '
He waved his arms to compensate for his inarticulacy. 'But Ma's
family paid for all that. Without them you'd still be pouring tea
and sweeping up bits of clay.'

On the first of their two family trips to Calcutta, Baba had
taken them to Park Street to show them the exact spot where
he used to work. The pitch was occupied by a jelabee stand,
but there were plenty of chai wallahs elsewhere and Yasmin
and Arif had been thrilled by the bhars, the little clay cups
that they drank from before smashing them on the street. Baba
was humble. He shared his history openly. And now Arif was
throwing it back in his face.

Yasmin glared at her brother. She gave him the finger, and
mouthed *shut up*. When she glanced back at Shaokat he had
opened his eyes.

'Yes and no,' said Shaokat. 'You have perhaps forgotten the
fact that I had left the tea business by the age of sixteen. I had
bettered myself. Medical college was paid for by my father-in-
law, this is true. But I paid back every penny to that family.
With interest. Which their faith didn't prevent them from
charging. Their investment was secure and sound.'

'Investment?' said Yasmin. It was news to her that he'd paid
them back. But he was nothing if not proud. 'Because they saw
your potential? Just like Ma did when you met.'

'Yes, Mini, of course. You are correct. It happened like that, as
you know.' He stood up and moved his chair towards the table.
He adjusted it until he had the placement exactly right. 'Now,
I have some reading to do. Arif, you may consider my offer or
reject it out of hand as you please. But within one month you
must either commence steps towards your further education or
find employment. If you do neither you will be on your own.'
He turned his back before continuing. 'Sweep the streets if you
have to. We all have to start somewhere.'

ZAMZAM

'So where did you go? What did you talk about?' Two days ago she'd spent the evening agonising about the prospect of Harriet meeting Ma. Now she was quizzing her mother as if she'd been on a date!

'Look,' said Anisah, unzipping the red and blue check nylon laundry bag she favoured for transporting shopping. 'Pizza!' She pulled out four boxes with the finagled surprise of a magician plucking a rabbit from a hat. 'This one has many sorts of cheese.'

The only time Yasmin could recall pizza in the house was when white school friends had come and she'd demanded English food for dinner. Somehow she'd failed to realise curry was as English as pizza and most likely more of a treat.

'Ma, I really want you to be involved with everything, you know, with the wedding, but me and Joe aren't sure—'

'Wedding, we did not discuss,' said Anisah, cutting her off. She and Harriet obviously had more important things to talk about. She switched on the radio and kept it turned down low. If Ma was in the kitchen the radio had to be on, voices running like water in the background.

'We're not sure about having the imam. I know it would mean a lot to you. And Amina-auntie and Rashida-auntie, but—'

'When you were small I told you so many stories from the Qu'ran. Remember how much you loved to listen?' Anisah unfastened her heavy gold earrings and pulled on her earlobes, as if they hadn't been stretched enough over the years. 'You remember the story of Ibrahim? When he destroys the idols in the temple of Akkadian? This one was your favourite. Is he not frightened when they throw him on the burning pyre? Always you were asking like this.'

'And you said, no, he knows Allah will save him.'

'The flames turn into—'

'Flowers.'

'Flowers,' repeated Anisah, beaming. She buzzed around the kitchen narrating the tale of the slave girl, Hajira, who had been given to Sarah, Ibrahim's wife. Yasmin filled the water jug, took glasses down from the cupboards, chopped a chilli and a quarter of an onion and mixed them with a little water, salt and a pinch of sugar to serve on the side. Hajira bore a son, Ismail, for Ibrahim, and Sarah grew jealous of mother and child. It was confusing the way Ma emphasised how much Ibrahim and Sarah loved each other. Sarah was barren and offered Hajira to Ibrahim. If Ibrahim loved Sarah, who was so beautiful she had to fend off pharaohs, then why wasn't she enough? And if Sarah, out of love, offered Hajira to her husband, surely she expected he would refuse? It sounded like the exact opposite of a love marriage, yet Ma told it as a romantic tale.

Ma kept talking and moving and tidying. She wore her best salwar, jade green and pinched tight at the ankles, with a black button-up shirt and a salmon-pink cardigan. It was as if she had again had difficulty deciding between outfits and had simply decided to mix the two.

'Hajira is alone in the desert, baby Ismail cries and cries.' Anisah's voice was bright with wonder. She had fallen into a past time, when she would sit Yasmin and Arif together on her soft lap and wrap them to her tightly, cocooning them with stories from the Qu'ran and the Hadith.

They used to pray together, Yasmin and Arif with Ma, and Yasmin had somehow thought – was encouraged to think? – Baba prayed separately, in his room or at work. When she discovered the truth it disturbed her deeply. She included him especially hard in her dua and hoped devoutly it would count for something. She would have performed his namaz for him if she could.

By the time she reached secondary school, Yasmin had begun to drift from Anisah's orbit into Shaokat's. He extolled the virtues of science. He taught her the importance of a testable hypothesis. The crowning glory of evidence. He too told her stories, and they too were often of worlds invisible to the eye. He spoke about Galen, van Leeuwenhoek, Mendel, Pasteur, Watson and Crick. Yasmin had never seen Shaitaan, houris, the Angel Jibreel, or a fire-bleeding ifrit. But when Shaokat bought her a Bausch & Lomb microscope she could see bacteria, cytoplasm, vacuoles and chloroplasts.

As a boy, Arif moaned or bristled when it was time to unroll the prayer mats. Anisah was keen for her son to lead the namaz, which he knew well enough from about eight years old. He messed around so much she would give up on it for weeks at a time before starting her campaign again. She reminded him of the Hadith that said: order your children to pray from the age of seven, and beat them if they neglect it when they are ten. Arif took it as licence. He had two more years. Anyway, there was no chance of Anisah hitting him; her chastisements were gentle as warm summer rain. They all knew, the three of them, that once Arif reached puberty his mother could no longer lead her son in prayer. But it was Yasmin who broke away. Studies, Shaokat said, came first and foremost.

'When Hajira runs back to Ismail,' said Ma, 'the angel guards him but the spring water flows so fast she is afraid her baby will drown.'

'Zamzam, zamzam!' said Yasmin.

'Zamzam,' said Ma. 'Stop!' She pulled the oven door open. 'And this is how the holy water of Mecca gets its name. Always I finish the story this way.' She put down her oven gloves and enveloped Yasmin in her pink-cardiganed arms and Lily of the Valley eau de toilette. 'Oh, Mrs Sangster is wonderful woman. Very-very kind and wonderful woman.'

'What did you talk about?' Impossible to imagine Ma and Harriet having a heart-to-heart!

'All sorts of things.'

'Like what?'

'Feminism,' said Ma. 'Pizza will be ready now.'

Yasmin smiled. 'So Harriet's turning you into a feminist, is she?'

'Oh, no,' said Ma, beaming. 'Already I am feminist.'

BLACKLIST

'He's a hypocrite.' Arif lay flat on his back on his bed. Yasmin sat on his desk, having cleared a space just large enough. 'Hypocrite. Idiot. Arsehole.'

'Okay,' said Yasmin, 'even if he is—' She broke off. Trying to reason with her brother was always a hopeless task.

'So you're agreeing?'

'That's not what I meant.'

'He knows why I got a shit degree. He *knows*. But he's never acknowledged *his* part in it.'

'Wouldn't it be better,' said Yasmin, 'to focus on yourself, decide what *you* want? It's not about anyone else.'

'And also, right, I'm definitely on some kind of list. Home Office list, like . . . a blacklist. I sent in a request. FOI request, that's Freedom of Information, but what have I had back?' He sat up. 'Jack shit.'

'Might be better to think about the future rather than going over the past,' said Yasmin. They'd eaten the pizzas in near silence, Arif sullen, Shaokat forbearing, Ma in a reverie.

'Mind you,' he said, 'mind you, that kind of list, no way they're giving out the information. That kind of information isn't fucking free.'

'They said there'd be no record,' said Yasmin.

'No, they didn't,' said Arif, 'they said I wouldn't *have* a record. A criminal record. On account of me not committing any crime. Doesn't mean there's no record at all.'

'Oh, Arif,' said Yasmin. She sighed and leaned over to touch his guitar, propped up against the wall. 'Haven't heard you play that in a while.'

'You know what he said about them doing a dawn raid on his only beloved son?'

'I was there,' Yasmin murmured.

'He said it was a courtesy because the neighbours wouldn't see. Such a lot to be grateful for! And then he goes to see Fintan Faherty and he says, thank you Professor Faherty for bringing to my attention that my only beloved son is a Muslim, I will put a stop to it at once.'

'That's what you think, is it?' said Yasmin. 'That's what you really and truly think?'

'I don't *think*, I know. *Professor* Faherty! He wasn't a professor. Just some junior lecturer who couldn't tell the difference between a research project and a terrorist. I'm sick of pretending like it never happened. I'm sick of being the leper in my own home.'

Arif had it all so muddled. They hardly talked about it, but it had happened four years ago, when Arif had just started his second year of university.

A librarian had alerted Mr Faherty, who had reported the concern to the police. It seemed to Yasmin that Mr Faherty should have talked to Arif first. If he had he would have understood that Arif was simply (and for once) a keen student, intent on researching his thesis about Islamism in the UK. Baba, however, saw it differently. Arif's stupidity was colossal, his breaches flagrant, his attitude cavalier. Let him stay at the police station, he yelled at Ma, when she begged him to go and get her son.

Baba always indulged her but not this time. He can rot there! If I bring him here I will kill him with my two hands. This nonsense stops now. He will not bring more shame on this house!

Baba meant the disgrace of the police entering and searching his home. But Yasmin suspected the shame went deeper – it was the shame of failing to raise a good son. The shame of having a son who disrespected him.

Once he'd finished venting, Baba went straight to the station and brought Arif home. But Arif just turned around and left. For a couple of months, he stayed away. When his friends grew tired of him sleeping on their sofas he returned, without announcement or discussion, with his guitar and dumbbells and duffel bag. Before the disgrace, Baba had agreed Arif could rent a room somewhere closer to campus, but the offer had evidently been withdrawn. Yasmin knew Arif was bitter about this punishment that was in his eyes everlasting, but she had never been given the same offer that Arif had fucked up for himself. It was always assumed she would remain at home throughout the entire five years of her medical degree. *The best medical schools in the world are in London. There is no reason for you to go to Leeds.*

For a while, Arif continued to wear the topi that Baba slapped off his head on the first day of his return. He went to mosque, a manoeuvre he committed with a mix of ostentation and subterfuge. He flaunted his tasbih. Yasmin worried. Arif had been studying how young Muslim men became radicalised. What if his experience turned him into one of his own subjects? When he came home he hated everyone. The police who – he was convinced – had bugged his laptop. His father. The lecturer. The librarian. The students who didn't protest on his behalf.

Perhaps this was how it happened. It scared her. She was scared for him. Arif had put on a mask, but what if he started to believe it was his true face? Her brother would become an

84

Islamist. She knew the chance of it happening was remote, but that didn't stop her worrying.

Ma didn't help. To the obligatory five daily fard prayers she added rakats of sunnah and nafl, setting her prayer mat in the sitting room so that there was hardly a time between sunrise and sunset when it could be used for anything else. Arif was often out of the house or sleeping the day away, but he joined her when afflicted by a bout of holiness, especially if Baba was at home. He worked harder on his beard than on prayer.

Ma couldn't see that she was making it worse for Arif. She thought the pressure was all from Baba, but she was pressing in too so that Arif had little room to breathe.

'Can't you say something to Ma?' said Yasmin.

'What should I say?' asked Baba. 'How should I complain to your mother about her faith?'

'You told Arif to stop going to mosque.'

'I was angry. And if he stops going it will be because he is too lazy, not because of anything I said to him. Arif smokes. He drinks. Probably he does other things as well. I do not pry. You think there is a religious bone in his body? Everything – mosque, skull cap, beard – everything is all for show.'

Arif stopped going to mosque. He turned in his research paper only half-written and showed Yasmin how he had printed CENSORED BY THE SECURITY SERVICES over the heading, although this was very far from the truth. He had simply given up. He persevered, however, in blaming Mr Faherty for every single low grade he got, including his final exams. Much preferable to facing up to the fact that nobody outside this house cared or even knew about his atrocious results.

Gradually, Yasmin relaxed. Becoming an Islamist entailed too much dedication for Arif. It was just another passing phase, and Arif had had plenty of them.

*

Yasmin said, 'You know you're being ridiculous. Nobody's treating you like a leper. You just sat down to dinner with your family.' She wondered if her brother would ever find his niche. He was, in equal measure, listless and restless. He had searched but had not found his tribe.

'Yeah. Joyous occasion,' said Arif. 'Lovely family meal.'

Arif expended so much energy defining himself in opposition to other people, other musical tastes, other fashions, other views, other politics, other members of his own family that he was too exhausted to know who he really was. He thought she was weak and he was strong because he rebelled and she did not. But it took strength to work hard and do your duty, and it was she who had what she wanted in this world. He didn't even know what he wanted. She felt sorry for him.

'Do you want to tell me something or not?'

'Not,' said Arif, as if she'd asked if he would like her to pull out a tooth.

'Okay,' said Yasmin. 'I'm going.'

'Fine. Go.'

'I am!'

'Get out then.'

'Make me!'

That got a smile.

'What does Baba say about Siddiq doing the nikah? He tried to stop his own son being a Muslim, but it's okay for his son-in-law.'

'Jaa taa!' said Yasmin. Too much bullshit to untangle so she wouldn't even try.

'Bhallage na!' Arif lay back down, flattened by his burdens, real or imagined.

They always spoke English together. Yasmin's Bengali was getting rusty, she hardly used it and putting sentences together was hard. Arif spoke Bengali with Ma when it was just the two of them. Sometimes Yasmin would walk in and hear them and feel she was intruding somehow.

But she'd spoken to her brother in Bengali and he had responded in kind. And although all they had exchanged were expressions of exasperation, her instinct had been right. It had created an intimacy between them, not friendship, not understanding, but something deeper that she could not explain.

She picked up a grimy baseball cap from the desk and threw it, trying to spin it like a Frisbee. It landed on his chest.

'Good shot.'

'I was aiming for your face.'

'I am totally fucked.'

'No,' she said firmly. 'You are not. Your life's hardly started. Forget about everyone else. This is only about you, just think about yourself.'

Arif rolled on to his side towards her and his face was half in the pillow, one eye staring up at her, wild and scared. 'I can't, Apa. Not any more. I've got to think about Lucy and the baby. That's two other people and what am I going to do now?'

'Kyabla,' said Yasmin. You dummy. She said it gently and Arif picked up the cap and hid the rest of his face.

THE THINGS THAT COULD
NOT BE MENTIONED

Arif swore her to secrecy. She was the only person he'd told. Lucy was five months pregnant, and Arif had known for two months he was going to be a dad. Lucy had bought a Moses basket and was picking out baby names. She's so happy, said Arif, twisting his body. That's good, Yasmin told him. I know, said Arif, clearly in agony, I know.

Yasmin lay in bed going over it all again.

She'd got him talking about Lucy and her family. There was no point making things worse by asking him anything practical like what he was actually going to do, how he planned on raising a child when he had singularly failed to grow up himself. It turned out Arif had been seeing Lucy for nearly a year. Longer than Yasmin had been with Joe, he pointed out, as if that meant anything.

Lucy was a receptionist at an orthodontist practice in Eltham and lived with her mum and grandmother in a maisonette in Mottingham. The grandmother's name was Sheila but everyone called her La-La, which was her stage name from when she was a dancer with a troupe called Legs & Co that appeared on *Top of the Pops* when it was one of the most popular shows on TV. La-La wasn't a regular member, she only filled in now and then, but she could have married a record producer or even a pop star (apparently her conquests changed all the time) but she fell in love with a local boy, a milkman, and married him, even though she'd had proposals from members of The Specials, Mott the Hoople and Ultravox. Arif sat up as he chewed this over. It seemed unlikely, he said, because those bands were all really different, synth rock, glam rock and ska, so you'd think they'd all have different tastes, but you never knew and La-La was still amazing even at her age and that's where Lucy got her looks.

He lit up as he said it. Yasmin kept him talking, and it was as if they had agreed between themselves all the things that could not be mentioned, not yet, and all the paths they should avoid that would lead them to Ma and Baba and whatever abyss might lie beyond.

What happened to the milkman?

The milkman ran off with some tart from the Coldharbour Estate who'd had a win on the Pools.

Poor La-La.

Not really. They hated each other after a couple of years. But Lucy's mum – Janine – she's had it tough.

Time to sleep. Yasmin stared at the curtains. Ma made them when Yasmin was about ten years old. Blue with sprigs of jasmine, the state flower of West Bengal. The curtains were too short when she first hung them so she'd let down the hem like a pair of outgrown trousers, and every moonlit night the light shone through the pinpricks left behind in the fabric where it had been unstitched.

Lucy's father was a window cleaner working on high-rise buildings in the City, and Lucy was only six months old when Tony's harness broke. She never knew him, but even so she carried a photo of him around in her purse. The way Arif told the story made it sound like Tony was the ideal sort of father, an icon to watch over you, a pocket-sized talisman.

Janine got a settlement from Tony's employer, bought the council maisonette and added a red front door to make it stand out from the dark brown all the council tenants had. She painted it every couple of years but most of the maisonettes had been sold off by now and all the front doors were different and Janine was sick of it, all the garish colours, and was thinking of going back to brown.

The baby was due in four months.

Two months before the wedding.

She had to work out what Arif needed to do. God knows he wasn't capable of working it out for himself. Would it be better to tell Ma first and let her tell Baba? Or tell them both together?

If Arif got a job, just any job, would that ameliorate the situation or make it worse? On the one hand it would demonstrate responsibility. On the other, it would show he had narrowed his choices into a dead end. If he applied for another degree course before he broke the news would that soften the blow?

Arif would keep putting off any decisions. He'd carry on skulking in his room and not facing up to reality and then he'd drop this bomb that would overshadow everything.

Between Harriet and Ma and Imam Siddiq and Arif and the baby, the wedding would be ruined.

She closed her eyes, turned on her side and hugged a pillow to her chest. The wedding was only a day. A single day in an entire life. It didn't matter. Let it be a disaster. She was lucky. She loved Joe and he loved her, and there was nothing to fret about.

HARRIET

She has spent a fruitless hour in the study. This room is not a good place to write, and never has been despite the book-lined walls, the softness of the sunlight filtered through the acacia outside the floor-to-ceiling window, and the beauty of the Regency desk – faded rosewood strung in boxwood, satinwood and ebony. Those cracked-leather spines lined up against her. It is hubris, she decides, that's the problem. Sitting at such a desk, in such company, to begin scratching on a pad the life and times of Harriet Sangster.

Rosalita has chosen pink gladioli again for the tall blue vase and this should not matter but it does. It would be easy to tell her: No more gladioli! But Rosalita takes pride in her floral arrangements and it would be a slap in the face, akin to saying her casseroles are too salty or her tartes Tatin too sweet. Which they are, but never mind, never mind.

No, she cannot write in here.

Where, then?

The kitchen is out of bounds because Rosalita is steaming – steaming! – the floor. Totally unnecessary and quite possibly damaging to the limestone, but never mind, never mind. The dining room? A mausoleum. Not right at all. The drawing room? Too big.

She drifts upstairs and finally settles. She has tossed the Smythson notebook. Its gilt-edged pale blue featherweight pages are incompatible with the memoir as she wishes to write it – raw, unvarnished, real. An A4 refill pad lies on her dressing table.

The first 'memoir' wasn't really a memoir, it was a thesis dressed up as one. And it was widely – most often deliberately – misunderstood. Nevertheless, it had value. It was an intervention. It bore weight. In the field of sexual politics, female sexuality, gender and identity it began to change the conversation. And long before polyamory or *fluidity* was being written about by every Tom, Dick and Harriet. That was a book worth writing. She knew why she had written it.

These days everyone writes memoirs. But what are they for? Reading them is like eavesdropping outside the confession box. Nothing is risked. One knows the sinner will say the Hail Marys and be absolved of their sins. And yet.

Here she is, Montblanc in hand, ready to begin.

The blank page is maddening. She raises her head and looks once more in the mirror. She has chosen to sit at her dressing table because when she writes a false word she will know it from the look on her face.

Why now?

Why look back now? Is there no more living to be done? Is the road all behind you now that . . .

Now that he's leaving.

He's left before, hasn't he? And come back. This time he won't come back and that's how it should be, children are meant to leave their parents. He's not moving to Timbuktu, he'll be in Hampstead or Highgate. Or at worst Kentish Town. Must make an appointment with Lily soon, that right cheek needs topping up. God knows what's in those little needles of hers, but it's worth every penny. What would Daddy say? What do you think, Daddy, about me writing about you and Mother?

Harry, my girl, grab the bull by the horn and give it a good kick in the testicles.

Oh, I miss you, Daddy. Even now. I wish you'd lived to see my baby. My boy. You'd love him, Daddy, as much as you loved me.

She smiles at herself in the mirror. Her fine nostrils flare and the neat brown arches above her eyes flex. If Daddy had been a coalminer rather than an eminent surgeon. If he was an alcoholic who died when she was a child, rather than in her twenties. If Mother had been some kind of victim, an abused woman, rather than a beauty and socialite. If she'd been cruel, rather than merely distant. Then one could carve a satisfying narrative.

Anisah Ghorami – there's a story! Not one to envy, of course … No, of course not. It is Harriet's life, Harriet's upbringing, Harriet's career, Harriet's house that is enviable.

She draws the pen slowly down the paper, crossing out the whole blank page.

PIETY LEVEL

'I'm never getting married.' Rania waved at the waiter. She used both arms at full stretch as if flagging a plane along a runway.

'What happened this time?'

'Fucking nightmare!' She sat with one black platform boot resting on the low drinks table. Rania was only five foot two but took up the space of a larger person. Her voice was big too and the bar was small. Several people turned round to check if it really was the girl in the jeans and headscarf who had sworn so loudly and with such authority.

'Come on, tell!' At Rania's request they'd met in the bar of a hotel in Victoria. Usually they ate at cheap restaurants, or had dinner at Rania's flat.

'Seriously,' said Rania, 'I'm giving up. Over and out. Done.' Rania had met a number of matrimonial prospects from Muslim dating websites, and apps including Minder (*Swipe. Match. Marry.*) and Muzmatch. Over the last few months she had labelled these encounters in a variety of ways, from dull to *catastrophically fucking dull*.

'Since when did you give up on anything?'

'Alhamdulillah,' said Rania, 'I never have to go on another date. Or view another profile. I don't have to get messages

94

saying I have a "match" when some guy has ticked the same box for piety level, never mind that he's a welder in Huddersfield.'

'A glass of house white wine, please,' said Yasmin to the waiter. He had taken his time coming over, possibly due to Rania's belligerent signalling.

'Same,' said Rania.

Yasmin laughed. Rania didn't drink.

The waiter didn't find it funny. 'We don't serve no-alcohol wine here.' He had ice-pick scars on his cheeks and nose, presumably the result of acne in his younger years.

'I want wine with alcohol. What's the point of wine without alcohol?'

The waiter shrugged.

'And bring us some olives, please.'

Yasmin and Rania had been friends since the third week of secondary school. One lunchtime, Yasmin found herself cornered by three older boys. Where are you from and why don't you go back there and you smell bad and why don't you wash properly and all the usual things. They didn't even seem to believe what they were saying. They seemed bored but it was raining too hard to go out and play football.

Rania appeared out of nowhere and said, Hey, pick on someone your own size, you fucking idiots, which was funny because she was an eleven-year-old girl in a hijab and short for her age. The boys were too surprised to laugh straightaway. Rania kicked the biggest lad between the legs and hit another on the back with a chair. Two boys rolled on the floor and the other quickly backed away. Don't let me catch you again, she said. She jerked her head at Yasmin and Yasmin followed her out of the room and down the corridor. I hope you don't get in trouble. Rania giggled. That surprised Yasmin almost as much as the ninja attack. What are they going to do? Admit they got beaten up by a little Muslim girl? No way.

'You know Omar Khayyam wrote a lot about wine,' said Rania, sniffing her glass. 'Rumi, too.'

'But you don't drink.' Yasmin wanted to take the glass from Rania's hand. The waiter watched Rania drink, arms folded across his chest, as if he too disliked what he saw.

'So what? I decided I want to try it once in my life. And plenty of Muslims drink.' Rania pointed at Yasmin. 'Exhibit A.' Rania was a solicitor with a small firm that worked on immigration cases, industrial disputes and human rights. Exhibit A was one of her favourite phrases, although she admitted she'd never been able to use it in a professional capacity.

'My father likes a whisky now and then,' said Yasmin. 'So it never seemed like a big deal to me. On the other hand, he's not religious.'

'My father drinks,' said Rania. 'He thinks I don't know. It's a big secret. My mother pretends she doesn't know. I pretend I don't know that she pretends she doesn't know. And my father pretends there's nothing to know.'

'Why now? Why tonight?'

'Why not tonight?' Rania took another sip. At each sip she pulled a face. 'Okay, if you really must know, I read about the Iranian Ministry of Culture banning all mention of the word "wine" from books. Because they want to stop the Western cultural onslaught, so they say. But they don't know their own history. You know there are Islamic wine jugs from fifteenth-century Persia?'

Yasmin waited.

'Life isn't black and white,' said Rania. 'That's all.'

'Fair enough. What do you think so far? Of the wine?'

'Too early to reach a verdict, I'll try a glass of red as well. But tell me about the wedding plans! And how did it go with your parents and his mother? You said you were dreading it.'

'It was fine,' said Yasmin, 'until Harriet decided we should have the whole thing at her house and have a nikah for good measure.'

'What! That's brilliant. Tell!'

Yasmin told her more. Rania glossed over any possible difficulties. She made it sound as though Imam Siddiq would be barely noticeable and as though the whole ceremony wouldn't be a spectacle to be gawked at by Harriet's friends. She approved vehemently of Harriet's dissection of the unequal marriage laws. And she even approved of Anisah's decision to attend Harriet's next salon, as if nothing could be more natural. Yasmin picked at the fake leather on the overstuffed banquette seat. She tried to convey to Rania some of her unease about Harriet commandeering the wedding, but only succeeded in sounding petty.

She couldn't wait, though, until she didn't have to stay at Harriet's house. Harriet was such a big presence it felt like Yasmin and Joe were never truly alone. One morning when Joe was in the en-suite shower room Harriet swept into the bedroom. She had to talk to him immediately because she was leaving to give a lecture somewhere. She walked straight in on him. Yasmin was shocked. Imagine if Baba walked in on her when she was naked in the shower cubicle! But Joe didn't even mention it. Yasmin's prudish upbringing was the problem. Joe didn't have hang-ups about his body because Harriet hadn't brought him up to be ashamed of his own nakedness.

She thought about his body. The mole on the underside of his right arm, the freckles across his shoulders, his appendectomy scar. His body wasn't hard like Kashif's, which was all knotted muscle and tendon from hours of lifting weights at the gym.

Kashif was on the short side and put on weight easily. He over-compensated by pumping iron, but Joe didn't have anything to compensate for.

'Hello? Can you hear me?'

'Oh, sorry,' said Yasmin. 'What did you say?'

Rania giggled. 'Can't remember now.'

Rania had drunk a large glass of white wine and the same quantity of red. She'd ordered a rosé as well and appeared to have overcome her initial distaste. She buried her nose in the glass and inhaled. How drunk was she? For the first time since they had known each other, Yasmin felt a sense of responsibility for Rania. Rania could usually take care of herself.

'Hey!' said Rania. She leaned in close, a curl of auburn hair springing loose from her hijab. 'My parents' marriage is shit. You know that, right?'

'They argue. You always said they have rows.'

'You see, maybe that's the reason ...'

Rania's chin was practically on Yasmin's shoulder. Her eyeliner was drawn with precision, two neat black lines framing upper and lower lids and sweeping out towards the temple without intersecting. It was a style Rania called 'the fishtail'.

'Reason?' said Yasmin.

'Why I won't marry. But you!' Rania pulled back and hiccuped. 'Your parents ... you see! True love. I remember that story you wrote about it at school. I was jealous, you know.'

'Well, I'm sure I wrote it with rose-tinted spectacles,' said Yasmin. The story had got her in trouble at home but she'd never told Rania that.

'I know what I'm going to do,' said Rania. 'I'm going to try spirits. Gin. Or whisky. No! A vodka shot. We'll have some vodka please!' She waved at the waiter. He grimaced and shook his head.

'Are you sure?' said Yasmin. Rania was too drunk already. 'Why don't we go and get something to eat.'

'Service, please,' said Rania loudly, thumping the table. 'Why's everyone staring?'

'Because you're shouting!' Yasmin looked on in dismay as the waiter brought two shot glasses and a tiny bowl of crisps.

'Keep it down, ladies. People want to enjoy their drinks in peace.'

'Sorry,' said Yasmin.

Rania disposed of one shot in one swallow. 'It burns!' She clutched her throat and grinned. 'You know how much whisky gets drunk in Pakistan? You know how many Saudi men come here and go to pubs and clubs? That's nothing to anyone. One woman in a headscarf drinks one shmall sot of vodka and everyone looks.' She giggled. 'Small shot!' She picked up the other glass.

'You're still yelling. If you don't want people to look, you've got to be a bit quieter.'

'I *am* speaking quietly,' said Rania. 'Shall we order another drink?'

'No! And maybe you better put that glass down before it spills.'

'I'm having another drink,' said Rania. Her announcement seemed to silence the entire bar. She got to her feet somewhat unsteadily. 'You can all watch if you want,' she declared, holding the glass aloft.

'Rania,' said Yasmin, tugging at her sleeve. 'You need to sober up.' The waiter was filming them on his phone!

'One more drink!' chanted Rania. She downed the vodka, then continued her chant. 'One more drink! Come on, I'm never, ever, ever, ever, never, never . . . ' She looked faintly surprised at this new disability, this loss of control of her tongue.

The waiter tucked away his phone. He came over with the bill and a scowl. 'No more drinks,' he said. 'You need to pay and go.'

LOVE MARRIAGE

Yasmin could not remember being told the story. She did not recall, for instance, being lifted on to her mother's lap and imbibing it like the tale of Khadija and Muhammad, or Yusuf and Zulaikha. She had no recollection of Shaokat pressing his hands together and parsing the essential elements, carefully ordering and structuring the information as he did when he talked about Lister or Fleming.

It was as if she had always known. As though she had been born with the knowledge. Still, she thirsted for more.

'What was the first thing you said to each other?' she asked, while Anisah pulled up onions in the back garden, a smear of mud across her face.

'I don't know.'

'You do.'

'Only ten years old and so cheeky!'

'You have to know.'

'Hello. Okay? We said hello.' Ma, squatting on her haunches, stabbed the earth with a trowel. Usually, she liked to chat while she gardened. But not this time.

'Who said it first?'

'You don't see how busy I am?'

'What did Naana and Naani say when you said you wanted to marry?'

'Abba and Amma said okay.'

Yasmin squatted down next to Anisah. 'Is that *all*? Is that all they said? And why do you call them Abba and Amma, but we say Baba and Ma? Why? Ma?' She tugged at a browning onion top. 'Ma! You're not listening!'

'I don't know,' said Ma. She sighed. 'Always asking for reasons! I am your ma. Okay? I did not want to be Amma. Here – take. Take the onions and wash for me.'

Yasmin dumped the onions in the kitchen sink, took a pad and pen from the drawer and found Shaokat in the garage, performing his weekly exercise routine with a pair of Indian clubs.

From her perch on top of the freezer she initiated the interview.

'So, you and Ma met in the library. What was the first thing you said to each other?'

Shaokat windmilled his arms so fast the clubs became blurry. 'Did you know that the national library of India is in Calcutta? It has over two million books. But it was the state library where I met your mother. Have you finished your homework?'

'Yes. Did you speak to her first? What did you say?'

'It was a long time ago, Mini. I must concentrate on the routine or it will not have the desired effect. Indian clubs are not only for strength, core stability, flexibility, they work also at the neural level – you know this word? – they build the connection between the body and the mind.'

'But Baba, what happened? Did you ask her her name?'

'The first time I saw her I knew I would marry her.'

'You always say that. But what did you do? What did you say?'

'Go and help your mother, Mini. I will finish my exercise.'

One of Shaokat's regulars at the chai stall needed a boy to sweep the courtyard, carry parcels, wash the car and see what else needed doing and do it without being asked. Shaokat was delighted with his new lodgings at the back of a storeroom, with a window and a strip of flypaper, and a shelf to call his own. His new employer was a kind man, a professor at the university in the department of physiology, who saw that the boy was quick and capable. When the professor found Shaokat trying to read one of his discarded scientific journals, he enrolled him in night school.

Six and a half years later, when Shaokat had graduated from houseboy to driver and finished his secondary education, the professor accepted a job in Bombay. He moved there with his family, leaving Shaokat to pack up the house and send on the furniture. The house was to be sold and Shaokat was welcome to stay in the storeroom until the new owners took the keys.

Shaokat dreamed of becoming a doctor. His grades were good enough to get into medical school but there was no way. He had to find another job, and soon. His wages were meagre, and as the professor had, with untold kindness, paid for night school, Shaokat had never had a pay rise. After paying for books and the other essentials, he was never able to save. When he met Anisah, he was penniless and about to be homeless as well. Anisah's father, Hashim Hussein, was the proprietor of Hussein Industries, manufacturers of bed sheets, mosquito nets, blankets, towels and uniforms. Shaokat's father was a landless labourer who died in a cholera outbreak.

But they fell in love anyway. That much she knew.

When she was fourteen she had to write a story for English homework. Choose one of the following:

Write a story entitled 'Lost'

Write a story about a chance meeting that changes someone's life

Yasmin knew straightaway what she'd write about. She still

didn't know all the details (though she had asked again in many more subtle and sophisticated ways), but somehow she knew everything she needed to know.

It was a picture she had when she closed her eyes. It was a feeling in her stomach. An atmospheric disturbance. A glimpse in the dark.

She wrote it and when the teacher said it was good, that she should enter it for a competition, she tingled to the root of every single hair on her body and scalp.

Baba, will you read my story? I got full marks and the teacher said there's this competition. I should enter it. That's what he said, anyway.

After he had finished he folded up his glasses. It was a long time before he spoke. Yasmin's hands had grown hot and sweaty, and then gone very cold.

Does it entertain you? Does it amuse you to make up these things?

Yes, Baba. I mean, no, Baba.

You have written things that you do not know. That you cannot know.

It's creative writing, Baba. Mr Curtis really liked it. You can read what he's written at the end.

You do not know what I said to your mother in the library in Calcutta. You were not there. You were not born. You do not know what she said to me. And yet you have written as if you were at the next table. Tell me – how are you different from a liar? How is this creative writing different from lies?

Mr Curtis was disappointed Yasmin would not be entering the competition. He asked for an explanation and Yasmin said that her father would not like it. I can speak to him for you, said Mr Curtis. Please don't, said Yasmin, and he had to reassure her three times that he would not.

SANDOR

'I want you to stay with that for a moment. The feeling of disgust you experience after one of these sexual encounters. Close your eyes.' Sandor paused. The boy looked terrified. 'Okay. Let's try this – are there other words that come to mind to describe the way you feel at those times?'

'Revulsion.' Joe's eyes remained wide open. His hands clenched. 'Distaste, abhorrence, repugnance, aversion, loathing . . . How am I doing?'

'You're doing great.' The listing of synonyms was a defensive move, though of course the boy was unaware of that. He was afraid to close his eyes and connect with his body, and this disconnection from the body was another sign. With this type of trauma (if indeed Sandor's instincts proved correct) the survivor, almost without exception, had a difficult time being comfortable with his body. The addiction – *ostensibly* – was an escape *to* the body, whereas in fact it represented obliteration, an attempt at flight *from* the body as the locus of so many forbidden feelings.

'What does your fiancée know about your sexual history? Is it something you've shared with her?'

'She knows I've dated around a lot. That I was sick of the whole casual sex thing. I always intended to come clean when the time was right. I thought it would be a reset. I kept thinking: When she knows me better. You know? Like – surprise! Guess what? Did I do a good job fooling you?' He laughed and rubbed his hands over his thighs. 'I'm a fuck-up. I fucked up again.'

'Joe,' said Sandor, 'every addict I've ever worked with considers themselves a fuck-up. Until they come to understand the root cause of their addiction and how they've used it as a way to medicate their feelings.'

'It's a vicious circle. I feel bad so I do it and it makes me feel better for about one second and then I feel worse so I do it again.'

'A succinct and accurate definition of addiction. I'd like to explore a bit more about how this addiction shows up for you. You haven't mentioned pornography. How would you characterise your relationship with porn?'

'I don't ... I'm not into porn. I've seen some. Boys at school – you know how boys are. Things get passed around.' He shrugged. 'I'm against it. It's degrading to women.'

'The photograph of your mother you mentioned last week. Was it one of the things that got passed around?'

'It didn't bother me that much. Believe me, I've thought about it – can I pin the blame on Harry? But honestly, I was proud of her. I was glad she wasn't like the other mums. And all the boys wanted to meet her. I was more embarrassed when she'd start talking to my friends about Derrida or Baudrillard.' Joe rolled his eyes. '*That* was excruciating.'

'Ha! Yes, I understand.' The boy was so engagingly frank. And so utterly in denial. It wasn't going to be easy to help him access his pain. His rage. 'What about masturbation? Excessive masturbation?'

'What's excessive?'

'If it impedes your life in any way, or if it triggers feelings of disgust or remorse.'

'No.'

'Prostitutes?'

'No! Never. I wouldn't degrade a woman like that.'

'So, hook-ups and sex parties. Would you like to tell me more about these parties?'

'I stopped going to them before I even met Yasmin.'

'They're organised events?'

'I never went dogging in a car park.' A slow, sheepish smile spread across his face. 'God, I really am a prick. And a terrible snob.'

'And the hook-ups? They're from dating sites? How many in a week?'

'My last binge, pre-Yasmin . . . was pretty out of hand. Every day. Sometimes two in one night.'

'It affected your work? You'd be overtired?'

'Usually it's just turn up, have sex, go. Half an hour. Sometimes less. It's more the distraction that's a problem. On a day off from work it could be one hook-up or as many as five. Scrolling, swiping, obsessing . . . I'd binge for a couple of weeks, stop for a month or two and think: I'm never doing that again.'

'How did you feel about these women?'

'They always knew the score. I never pretended – I was straight up about what it was and they were on for it. And if any woman ever changed her mind that was totally cool, I never pressured anyone into anything. I checked. Every step of the way. I never touched without consent.' Joe put his hands on top of his head and squeezed his skull. 'Why do I feel like some sort of rapist now?'

Sandor let the question hang. It was a question the boy needed to answer for himself. Of course the act of denying inappropriate or non-consensual contact was necessarily discomforting. But the underlying discomfort stemmed from the contradiction between the transactional nature of the encounters and the values the patient aspired to uphold.

Joe closed his eyes and screwed up his face. He appeared to be holding his breath.

'Let it out,' said Sandor. 'Take a sip of water. Breathe.'

'I'm okay. I'm okay. But I fucked up again.'

'Yes. This is something you told me towards the beginning of our session.'

'I slept with someone. This week.'

'Yes, I assumed so.'

'Oh. Right.' Joe looked away. Scratched his eye. 'Well, should I talk about it?' He picked up the glass of water. Sandor poured a fresh glass for every patient. In over thirty years of practice, he had initiated each session with the exact same ritual.

'Do you want to talk about it?'

'I don't *want* to. But should I?'

The boy was a people pleaser. As a physician he was a member of a caring profession. It fitted the profile. It fitted Sandor's hunch about him. 'Is it of particular significance, this encounter?'

Joe put down the glass without drinking. 'Not the actual encounter . . . no, it wasn't *special*. But I'm coming to therapy, I'm getting married, I'm nearly thirty years old and I can't control myself? Why did I do it? And it was someone connected to work. I've always been so careful to keep things separate and now—' He broke off. 'What's *wrong* with me?'

'I understand the frustration. Would it be too strong to say despair?' Joe shook his head and Sandor continued. 'Possibly these feelings are exacerbated by your uncertainty about whether you qualify as an addict. For example, when I've worked with a heroin addict and he or she tells me at the start of treatment that they've used, are using regularly, this is not a shock or a cause of puzzlement. If you do not understand your addiction as an addiction but instead try to figure out each act individually it will only hinder the healing process.

First, we need to figure out the causes. Down the road we can look at triggers, situations to avoid and so on. Does this make sense to you?'

'Yes and no. Heroin, any kind of substance abuse, they're physical addictions. And, you know ...' Joe smiled weakly. 'Look, I'm aware of the science – some of it – and I'm here, so ...'

'So you might already know that brain scans of people having orgasms resemble scans of heroin rushes. And that the brain response of sex addicts exposed to sexual stimuli mirrors the brain response of drug addicts exposed to drug-related stimuli. The dorsal orbital prefrontal cortex lights up the exact same way as it does for substance addicts.'

'You don't get DTs when you stop screwing around.'

Sandor laughed. He liked this kid. 'Okay, Doc. I can point you in the direction of the relevant literature on the mesolimbic dopamine pathway. As I'm sure you already know, it connects the ventral tegmental area to the nucleus accumbens – the areas tied to impulsivity, pleasure reinforcement learning and reward. The cycle of sensitisation and desensitisation involved in the addiction has an impact on the brain's reward centre, which can no longer return to its homeostatic set point. With sex addiction, obviously we're not talking about the physiological effects of a specific substance. It's about the negative affect of the altered set point of the reward system. Which helps explain, perhaps, why you took a bigger risk this week. It's akin to a drug addict needing an increasingly higher dose to get high.' It was a common pattern: At least I've never let it affect my work, says the patient, shortly before derailing his career with a workplace sex scandal. At least I've never hurt anyone close to me, says the patient, only weeks before waking up in bed with the husband of her best friend.

'Jesus,' said Joe.

'Maybe it's difficult to accept, because, of course, we want to be in charge of our desire, of our self.'

'But do I tell her? Should I tell Yasmin I slept with someone?'

'How do you feel about that?'

'I feel that—'

'No *that*, remember.'

'I feel . . .' He paused and smiled apologetically. 'Scared. I feel scared.'

'Okay. How do you feel about telling her about your addiction?'

'Fuck,' said Joe. 'No! No way.'

'It makes you feel . . . ?'

'Fucking terrified.

'I get it.' It would be part of the recovery process but everything in good time. 'I can't tell you what to do about telling Yasmin you slept with someone this week. It's a decision only you can make. What I can tell you is that part of the journey – the healing journey – is about honesty. Being honest with yourself and those around you. That doesn't mean you have to rush into anything. In fact, there's quite a good argument for first understanding your own behaviour before attempting to explain it to others.'

'Right. So I shouldn't tell her anything?'

Sandor observed the boy. His shoulders had slumped. 'I'm wondering if sleeping with someone this week was perhaps a subconscious attempt to put your relationship at risk. Perhaps to end it altogether?'

Joe shook his head. 'No, I love her. I love Yasmin.'

'Of course. And you believe that if you reveal yourself she will not love you.' He paused for a couple of moments. 'Better, then, to break up the engagement for the sake of a single misdemeanour. Hearts might break, yours included, but you remain hidden. That way she'll never know how you – how did you put it? – *fooled* her into caring for you.'

'No! I didn't plan anything like that.'

'No, you didn't. I didn't mean to suggest that you did. I merely offer an interpretation of this acting out. Sometimes our actions spring from motives we obscure from ourselves.'

'I'm not going to tell her. Because that's not what I want at all. I don't want it to break us up.'

Sandor nodded. 'Good. That's settled then. We haven't talked much about your relationship yet. Perhaps we should use the remaining time to explore it?'

'Yes, okay.'

'Let's start with sex. How would you describe your sexual relations with your fiancée?'

Joe shrugged. 'Normal. Fine. There's not a lot to tell.'

Sandor waited. He crossed his legs.

'What do you want to know exactly?'

'Only whatever you want me to know.'

'It's normal. Once or twice a week.'

'You are not highly sexed with her? Or she with you?'

'She's attractive. There's no problem or anything. She's only had one boyfriend before me so she's not, you know, very experienced. We make love. That's the difference. With Yasmin it's not about sex.'

'She doesn't enjoy sex?'

'I didn't say that.'

'She wouldn't have sex only for pleasure, for physical enjoyment, for fun? With a stranger or near-stranger? She never hooked up with anyone?'

'Not that I know of. It wouldn't matter to me if she had, if that's what you're getting at.'

'Okay. I understand. Tell me more about her. You said she's a doctor also?'

Joe talked about Yasmin and Sandor scribbled an occasional note. Her age, her ethnicity, the fact that Joe fell 'instantly in love' but waited weeks before the first kiss. Everything so far was adding up. The beginning of the relationship was rapid and fervent. Sudden and sweeping (and imagined) commitment from the boy's side, which he was careful to conceal. The bond, of course, was to the fantasy of the ideal or perfect person who represented liberation from his psychic prison. The headlong commitment was fuelled not only by this fantasy, but also by the patient's emotional indigence.

'I know I could make her happy,' said Joe. 'I *do* make her happy. If we find a way through somehow . . . this sounds crazy but I know I'll be a good husband.'

'One day, I'm sure you will be.'

'All this stuff we're talking about . . . my childhood, all that . . . how will it actually help? We get to the root of the addiction – but what then? Does that mean I'll be able to control it? I'll be cured?' He smiled to undercut the desperation in his question, in his voice.

'It's not *quite* so simple, I'm afraid.'

'Then why is it so important to know? Why is it like this holy grail?'

'Because it shortens the odds against us,' said Sandor. 'It affords us the *opportunity* to take control. Because what we do not know controls us.'

HARRIET

She puts down the pen and reads through the last few pages. Dear God, she thinks, how self-indulgent! There is nothing of consequence in what she has written. She looks in the dressing-table mirror and dislikes what she sees. Crow's feet and self-pity. Tomorrow there is the gala dinner at the Savoy where she will receive an award for Lifetime Services to the Arts. She tries out a gracious smile.

She's being put out to grass. Naturally, the *enfant terrible* stage can't last for ever. But the *grande dame* stage is not only dull, it's oppressive. It's *ageing*.

At least this month's salon was revivified by Anisah's presence. She did wonderfully well. Everyone adored her and the salon had been going stale for so long, it needed something new. Yes, Anisah was a resounding success. She has a talent for being herself and she touched everyone. They all remarked on it.

The girl is not the equal of the mother, but Joseph has nevertheless chosen wisely. Yasmin is clever but not too clever, pretty but not too pretty. She will be steadfast and loyal and family values are in her Indian DNA. The extended family is not an alien concept to her, and mother-in-law means something different in her culture, something beyond the punchline of a crass joke.

Family values! 'Good grief,' says Harriet aloud. 'When did you become such a traditionalist? A reactionary!'

She puts the A4 pad in the dressing-table drawer and hunts in the jewellery box for the earrings she has in mind for tomorrow evening.

What will Yasmin be wearing? she wonders. With a little coaching the girl could look quite striking. No, perhaps not striking, but more attractive. She doesn't make the most of herself. The dreary pastel palette! Those prim and shapeless shift dresses!

Harriet drifts to her dressing room and passes a hand along the rack of evening gowns. What to wear? What impression does she want to give when she gets up on stage to receive her Lifetime Achievement Award? Now *this* dress would be fantastic on Yasmin. This colour. But it wouldn't fit, and even if it would it would be entirely wrong to suggest it. That kind of mother-in-law would *deserve* to be the butt of the joke.

She pulls out dresses and rehearses an acceptance speech in her head and for the first time since Joe announced his engagement the anxiety leaves her. She has been, she realises with a sudden flash of insight while trying on a midnight-blue silk column dress, a little selfish in her fears. She feels generous and bountiful and truly happy that Yasmin will become part of her family.

CATERPILLAR

They were late because of the argument and had missed the drinks reception. A waiter led them along a plush carpeted hallway to the banqueting suite of the Savoy Hotel. A young woman in a black bandage dress checked their names on a clipboard and ushered them across the floor around the flamboyantly dressed tables with their bird of paradise centrepieces and napkins folded into crowns.

The argument was stupid. It wasn't about anything. Yasmin had asked Joe to do up her dress and when the zip caught he made a joke about it being too tight. She refused to accept his apology and then she ended up in tears.

It was because of Niamh, of course. What Niamh had said about Joe.

'Here they are,' Harriet cried as they reached the table. Gold bangles cascaded down her forearms. 'Now, Joe, you're over there, and Yasmin you are here, just one seat away from me so we will talk to each other across Malcolm because Malcolm has turned into Cassandra this evening and I'm not listening to another word.'

Joe kissed Harriet and took his seat on the other side of the table. She should have asked him on the way to Park Lane. There was nothing in it. Niamh was a liar. But she didn't want to risk a scene in the taxi, or arrive at the awards dinner in the middle of an awkward conversation.

'Yasmin, meet Belinda,' said Harriet, waving a breadstick at the silver-haired woman sitting on Yasmin's right. 'Belinda, this is Yasmin, my son's fiancée.'

Belinda evaluated Yasmin. She did this openly, as if looking from behind a one-way mirror.

'Good,' said Belinda. 'Good. And where are you from, Yasmin?' Belinda had a large mole under her right nostril, black in the middle and brown around the edges. That was not good.

'I'm from . . .'

London? Sometimes London was enough. More often than not, it was insufficient. Yasmin sighed to herself. If you didn't elaborate further then the follow-up questions made it seem like you'd been evasive. She could say, My parents are from India but I'm from London. But that felt like a denial, a renunciation of some kind.

There was a third way. 'I'm Indian,' she said.

'India, I adore India. You know, I've made three documentaries in India, one in Mumbai and two in Jaipur; have you been to the festival?'

'Which festival?' The mole was slightly asymmetrical and the borders were indistinct. It could well be cancerous.

Belinda laughed. 'Touché! The literary festival. I was talking about the literary festival and of course as a Hindu you have so many festivals. Foolish of me to make assumptions . . .'

She couldn't be bothered to correct Belinda. It was easier to nod her head every now and then to indicate she was listening, which she was not.

There was no way Joe had slept with Niamh's friend. No way. As if he'd pick up a nurse!

As if he'd be unfaithful at all.

I'm doing you a favour, actually, telling you. Because she's married, as it happens, and she swore me to absolute secrecy but I thought it's not fair if I don't warn you. I guess a lot of people wouldn't, they'd leave you in the dark, but that's just not who I am.

It wasn't true. She'd ask him this evening. She had to ask, even though he'd be insulted by the question. And maybe Niamh *had* done her a favour because now Yasmin didn't give a damn about Imam Siddiq and his clownish kurta pyjama and his big yellow teeth. She could hardly believe she'd worried about something so trivial. Even Arif becoming a father was nothing to worry about. Well, it was. But not in terms of the wedding. Nothing short of death could spoil the wedding. Death or infidelity.

' . . . local fixer,' Belinda was saying, 'who was only four foot eight, and he had vitiligo, poor chap, looked like a little Friesian calf, but by God could he get things done . . . '

Yasmin stuffed a breadstick into her mouth and nodded at Belinda. She hoped the food would come soon. This evening Harriet would be receiving an award. There would be awards for many varieties of arts. Theatre, film, books, television, radio, perhaps other things as well. Yasmin had never seen the TV show, an arts programme that sponsored the awards. Nobody watched it, Joe had assured her. Why, then, were all these people – some of whom she recognised from television – why were they here?

Thankfully, waiters began to stream out of the kitchen and swoop around tables. Yasmin was hungry.

'Yasmin? Remind me – how many days does Durga Puja last?'

'Umm,' said Yasmin. 'I think . . . ' She was saved by a voice ringing out from the stage that was suddenly lit up at the front of the room.

'Don't worry,' said the man at the podium, 'we'll let you have your dinner in peace. The crew is just running some last-minute checks. Well, the mic seems to be working.' He was old but youthful, with a quiff of dark hair and rosy cheeks. His voice was slightly nasal, a little bit Yorkshire, a little bit posh. He smiled, displaying veneered teeth and a sense of ownership. This room belonged to him. There were two television cameras on the stage, and two roving cameramen already filming the audience.

'We love you, Marvin,' someone shouted out from the floor.

'I'm afraid the winners have already been decided,' said Marvin. 'But please – feel free to continue sucking up.'

The appetiser was some kind of foamy tower, clad in smoked salmon and standing on a bed of frizzy lettuce leaves. Belinda had turned her attentions to the guest on her other side. Yasmin was glad of the respite. She ate a dab of the seafood mousse and a lot of the smoked salmon. Joe looked so handsome in black tie. He'd put wax in his hair and it was swept back off his forehead. He looked like the hero of an old black-and-white movie. The elderly woman on his left was clearly thrilled to have his undivided attention.

Yasmin speared a piece of lettuce. It was so springy it nearly bounced off her fork. She would buy new underwear, she decided. Get rid of all those knickers that were well past their sell-by date. No more sleeping in old T-shirts either when she stayed the night. She had to make more effort. She needed to be sexier.

Was she good enough in bed? What if she wasn't? She wasn't passionate enough. She couldn't let herself go. Kashif didn't expect that from her. But for Joe it would be different and she had to give that some thought.

She stabbed her fork into a curly leaf. As she raised it up to her mouth, something moved against the tines: a small green caterpillar, rolling into a tight protective ball. She studied it closely as it began to unfurl again. It was brighter than the leaf and covered in tiny white bristles. Each flank was studded with yellow circles stamped with black dots, like two rows of beady eyes. Its body was scalloped along each edge as though it had been cut out of cloth with a pair of pinking shears.

'Yasmin?'

She put the fork down. Caterpillar to butterfly. It didn't seem possible.

'Yasmin,' repeated Harriet. 'Come and sit next to me. We have some catching up to do.'

ANTHROPOLOGY

Harriet's dress was so tailored and sequinned it could have a life of its own, in a penthouse, with a limousine and chauffeur. On a lesser mortal there would be a danger of the dress wearing the owner, but Harriet looked like she owned it and maybe the atelier as well. When Yasmin looked at Harriet's meticulous eyebrows, her own itched. She had forgotten, again, to pluck.

'So what do you make of it?' said Harriet, sweeping a hand regally about the place. 'All these bright young things and old farts, adoring ourselves.'

'I'm enjoying it,' said Yasmin. 'A lot,' she added unconvincingly.

'Really? Well, it's sweet of you to say so anyway. These rubber-chicken bashes require feats of endurance! I must tell you your mother is a remarkable woman. Quite remarkable.'

'Thank you.'

'Oh, don't thank me. Getting to know her is . . . let me say, I consider it a privilege. She's so strong and refreshing.'

'Like a cup of tea,' said Yasmin. She laughed and hoped her irritation didn't show. Harriet had taken ownership of Anisah, added her to one of her many collections.

'Everyone loved her at the salon,' said Harriet. A few days ago, Ma attended Harriet's salon to talk about Islam, especially the nikah ceremony, as a primer of what to expect on the wedding day. She travelled to Primrose Hill on several buses wearing her green and gold silk sari with a grey duffel coat on top and socks and sliders on her feet. For an overnight bag she took a Louis Vuitton tote she had bought in an Oxfam shop and which was glaringly fake.

'And when she told me,' Harriet went on, 'the story of how she came to be married to your father! Oh, I was in tears!'

'Yes, it's quite a story. But I grew up with it, so . . .' So it was ordinary. Dal bhat. Lentils and rice. Meat and potatoes. Yasmin implied this with a smile. But she always knew it was special.

Harriet gave her a piercing look. 'You should ask her to tell it to you again. Ah, here's the rubber chicken. Let's eat and be grateful for all our many blessings.'

Dessert was passion fruit pavlova and Yasmin was beginning to despair of the evening ever coming to an end. The awards ceremony had not even begun. How much longer before she could talk to Joe? He would be shocked. He would laugh. Or he'd be angry. Maybe both. Then they'd laugh together and get into bed.

'Nathan!' Harriet rose to greet a willowy young man, both hands outstretched. He took hold of them and stood there uncertainly, not knowing what to do with these dazzling gifts.

'Nathan is an up-and-coming novelist,' said Harriet, directing him to Malcolm's vacated seat. Malcolm had gone to interview some fucking starlet, as he put it. 'Nathan Clarke: a name to watch out for!'

Nathan reached to shake Yasmin's hand. He had a darting manner, thirsty and watchful. His hair stuck out from his temples as if he had been mildly electrocuted. 'If I ever get published. Another rejection yesterday.'

'And has Angela introduced you to anyone useful this evening?' Harriet turned to Yasmin. 'Angela is his agent.' And back to Nathan. 'Don't worry about rejections. They will make you a better writer.'

Nathan looked as if he would like to disagree. But he was wary. He coughed into a closed fist.

'What's your book about?' said Yasmin.

Nathan brightened. 'It's an eco thriller set in the near future, about guerrilla activists who break into a billionaire's compound in New Zealand that he's built in case of some worldwide apocalypse.'

'Sounds gripping,' said Yasmin.

'What have you read recently? Anything good?'

'Yes,' said Harriet archly. 'I'm curious too.'

Magazines. A snatched few minutes at work here and there. Half an hour on the train. Twenty minutes in the bath. Textbooks. Journals.

'I've got exams coming up,' she said. 'So not much.' At school she read all sorts of novels, serious ones from the school library, fat paperbacks with gold block lettering on the covers that got passed around the playground. The vast stack of mildewed hardbacks that Anisah brought home from the British Heart Foundation shop to furnish the front-room shelves, which turned out to be full of silverfish and larder beetles. Shaokat made a bonfire of them while Yasmin was halfway through *Bleak House*. Even when she was at medical school she read fiction, always with a guilty conscience about wasting her time.

'Nathan,' said Harriet, 'would you allow me to give you a little career advice?'

'Of course. Please do.'

'You have talent. Angela says so and she is never mistaken about these things. But your talent is being misplaced. What I mean to say is you're writing in the wrong genre. That's why Angela's having difficulty placing you.'

Nathan pressed his long fingers together on the table.

'Thrillers sell, don't they?' His eyes darted at Harriet, at Yasmin, the bird of paradise flowers, his fingertips.

'You must write about whatever you want,' said Harriet. 'Creative freedom is paramount. But if you want to get published – and that is an entirely honourable goal – then perhaps a way forward would be to occupy a different space. If I were you, I would choose another story, something a little closer to home.'

'Closer to home,' repeated Nathan, and fell silent.

Because he's black, thought Yasmin. But he was too polite to challenge Harriet, and Yasmin was insufficiently brave.

The table was almost empty. Nathan had been whisked away by Angela. Harriet had gone to do the rounds. Then Yasmin went to the bathroom and when she got back, Joe had left. Guests weaved between tables and waiters on their way to the bathrooms or to greet each other, or simply to stretch their legs while the tables were cleared before the ceremony finally began. It had been a long evening and it was far from over. She hoped Harriet received her award soon and then maybe they wouldn't have to stay to the bitter end.

You should ask her to tell it to you again.

Why? Was Harriet suggesting she knew something about Ma that Yasmin didn't? When Ma returned to Tatton Hill the day after the salon she declared the evening 'very successful'. But she was restless, out of sorts. At the weekend she set up a trestle table on the pavement and stacked it with items she declared were 'depriving her of oxygen'. A phrase she'd clearly got second hand with cloudy purpose, like one of her charity-shop purchases. On the table she placed an ice-cream maker, a bread machine, three half-empty embroidery kits, several balls of purple mohair wool, a box of tiles that had been destined for the downstairs cloak-room, a rail of spotlights, and forty-three items of blue Denby crockery from a range that had been discontinued.

She quarrelled with Baba when he removed the items to the garage and forbade her to turn the cul-de-sac into a bazaar. She quarrelled with Mr Hartley, the next-door neighbour. And she quarrelled with Arif for getting under her feet, a crime he'd never been accused of previously.

Ma probably felt uncomfortable at Harriet's house, though she enjoyed being centre of attention at the salon. Deep down, perhaps she knew she was being studied like an exhibit in a human zoo, like some anthropological specimen.

'This Harriet Sangster's table?'

Yasmin confirmed it. The man was dressed in jeans and a short-sleeved khaki shirt. The top four buttons opened to reveal a milky-white patch of chest beneath his weathered neck. In a roomful of people in evening clothes it was an outfit that announced itself. It was the very opposite of casual dress.

'Tell her David Cavendish came by,' he said. But instead of leaving he picked up a spoon and, still standing, tucked into Harriet's untouched pavlova.

'I will,' said Yasmin.

'Don't know why I come to these fucking horrific things.' There was cream on his bottom lip. 'Always the bridesmaid, never the cunt who wins.'

'What are you nominated for?'

'Novel.' He sat down in Harriet's chair. '*The Symphony of Birds*,' he added, looking at her slyly for any possible glimpse of recognition. He wiped a finger round the plate, gathering cream and drips of passion fruit. 'Nobody buys my books, anyway.'

'I'm sorry,' said Yasmin. 'But you're shortlisted for a prize, so that's good. And maybe you'll win.'

He rubbed his fingers on the tablecloth. 'No chance. Look at me. White. Male. Heterosexual. Absolutely no chance.'

'But that's awful! Surely that's not how it works?'

'Not officially, no.' He could say more, his tone suggested, but would keep his counsel. 'What do you do, anyway?'

'I'm a doctor.'

'A real job! What kind of doctor are you?'

'Still training. Geriatrics at the moment.'

David Cavendish wrinkled his nose as if he could smell the ward, the scent of urine and death and disinfectant. 'Rather you than me.' He looked mildly disgusted but also a little more cheerful. At least he'd had the good fortune this evening of finding the one person in the room whose lot in life he could not possibly envy. He stood. 'Tell Harriet . . .' He paused. 'No, on second thoughts, don't tell her anything.'

In the black cab on the way home Yasmin said, 'Someone came looking for you. David Cavendish?'

'Dear David! And how was he this evening? Miserable?' Harriet sat next to Joe on the back seat, and Yasmin, sitting across from them, felt a little jealous, as though Harriet had stolen her place.

'He seemed a bit . . . He said he wouldn't win the book prize because he's—'

'White, middle-class and has a penis?'

'That sort of thing, yes.'

Harriet laughed. 'Oh, yes, they're the new persecuted minority. These men weighed down by their centuries of privilege. David's real problem is – I've said it before and I'll say it again – the novel is over as an art form. He's working in a moribund medium. The novel is dead.'

'Is it?' This was news to Yasmin.

But Harriet's attention was on Joe. She put a hand on his knee. 'Darling, have you been feeling *oppressed* recently?'

'Inevitably so, being, um, white and all that.'

Harriet patted his leg. 'Listen, darlings, you need to decide an actual date. And I'm thinking May would be so much better than March. Or June? June's even better. Now that we'll be using the garden it would make such a difference. The weather in March can be dreadful.'

Joe looked at Yasmin. 'What do you reckon?'

'Let's think about it.'

'Your mother is in favour,' said Harriet.

'She's not the one getting married,' said Yasmin, more sharply than she'd intended.

Harriet yawned and looked out of the window. 'I do *try* to be helpful.'

'We know,' said Joe, 'and we appreciate it.'

'I hope I've been welcoming. I hope I've been hospitable.'

'Oh, you have,' said Yasmin. It was true. Harriet had been nothing but kind to Yasmin and her family. 'May or June would be better. Definitely.'

She waited until they were in bed. 'Niamh said this strange thing today.' It was midnight, almost exactly. Almost a new day beginning.

'Mmm,' he said, sliding an arm across her. 'What did she say?'

'She said you slept with one of her friends. Recently.'

'Oh,' he said. 'Niamh? That's the red-haired nurse? The one you don't like much? The one who's always bugging you.'

'Yes,' she said, 'that one.'

MRS ANTONOVA

A deep stillness had settled over the ward. The high winds of washing, dressing, toileting, consultant rounds, medicine rounds, food trolleys, physiotherapy, occupational therapy, bingo, Scrabble and hairdressing had subsided, leaving the place eerily becalmed. Yasmin looked around. The linen cage was almost bare, only a few white sheets and pillowcases hanging limply over the wire racks. The door of the equipment room stood open to reveal a leaning tower of commodes, loosely piled hoists and a jumble of drip stands. Yellow holdalls of dirty linens lay like sandbags in front of the pharmacy cupboard. Nothing moved.

Visiting hours were often like this. Yasmin tiptoed past the bodies, the closed eyes and open mouths, the rows of arms pinning the bedclothes as if rigor mortis had set in already. She hovered at a bedside, fighting the urge to poke and prod. There was no need to go round checking everyone was still breathing, disturbing everyone's rest. It was only exhaustion. Old age and sickness and sheer exhaustion because washing and dressing started during the night shift at 5.30 a.m. If there were no visitors during visiting hours it was perhaps a blessing because the patients could get some sleep.

Something stirred. Yasmin turned to see Mrs Antonova struggling to sit up in bed.

'Let me help you.' She rushed across. When Yasmin put her hands on her back, Mrs Antonova's ribcage felt so fragile beneath the brushed-cotton nightdress.

'Thank you, pumpkin.' Mrs Antonova called everyone pumpkin, from the cleaners to the consultants. She was ninety-six years old and this was her third stay in hospital in as many months, this time following a fall at home. 'Now if you'd care to do me another favour, just get one of those pillows and hold it over my face. Don't let go until you're absolutely sure.'

'I'm sorry you're feeling that way,' said Yasmin. 'I can prescribe you an antidepressant if you're feeling so low.'

'I'm sure you can, pumpkin. But I'm not depressed.'

Yasmin sat down on the bed and took Mrs Antonova's wrist. Her pulse was a little thready but nothing out of the ordinary for a patient with chronic atrial fibrillation and arrhythmia.

'I'm not depressed, I'm bored,' said Mrs Antonova. 'I'm surrounded by ... ' She peered around and Yasmin was struck by her regal bearing, even in her rucked-up nightgown, with her wig askew. 'By *that!*'

'Mrs Antonova,' said Yasmin, 'do you mind if I sit here with you for a while?'

'Call me Zlata.' Mrs Antonova, since her readmission, seemed devastatingly frail. Impossible now to imagine her being strong enough to push a trolley, which was how she'd wedged the door handle of the television room for the protest she'd staged during a previous stay. But her voice was still full of mischief, and she winked at Yasmin as she said, 'Man trouble, is it?'

'Oh, no,' said Yasmin, wondering how Mrs Antonova knew. Was it that obvious? 'Just thought we could keep each other company.' The gala dinner last night was gruesome. She'd been so tense she'd hated every minute. Afterwards she talked to

Joe about what Niamh had told her, and ... Well, they'd put it behind them. It was done. An unpleasant conversation but she'd never have to have it again.

Mrs Antonova tugged at her wig, making it even more lop-sided. The aubergine-coloured curls, thick and shiny, contrasted impressively with her paper-thin-paper-dry skin. 'Man trouble! I know it when I see it. Married five times, and so it goes.'

'Five times!' said Yasmin. Mrs Antonova, on a previous stay, had told her about three husbands: a Uruguayan dentist who turned out to be homosexual; an Israeli violinist who had spent two years in Treblinka and who, three days after a honeymoon at the Sea of Galilee, committed suicide by jumping in front of a train at Tel Aviv Savidor Central (it was the 9.45 p.m. to Hod HaSharon); and a civil servant from Bexleyheath who, Mrs Antonova indicated by a vague wave of the hand, was not worth talking about.

'Yes, five. Do you know how old I was when I was first married? Sixteen. That's eighty years ago.'

'Goodness! I'd love to hear all about it one day.' She should be catching up on paperwork while the ward was quiet. She should be snatching an opportunity to study for the MRCP exam or update her reflective practice on her e-portfolio. She was behind with everything.

Mrs Antonova leaned towards Yasmin. It was a risky manoeuvre and for a moment Yasmin feared she would topple sideways out of bed. 'You are very busy, pumpkin. Thank you for the visit. It was lovely.' She sounded like she meant it. Her voice had not aged with her; it was playful and strong.

'I'm not busy,' said Yasmin. 'Tell me about your first husband.'

'Dimitri Ivanovich Shestov was fifty-three years old when I married him, and I had just turned sixteen. Of course it wasn't my idea to marry Dimitri, I had no say in the matter. I believe my father owed him money or something silly like that.'

'How awful.' Yasmin felt sorry Mrs Antonova's only 'visitor' was a doctor. She felt sorry for the entire somnolent ward. The cancer wards, at visiting time, turned into a scrum. Cancer made you popular.

'He was the love of my life,' sang Mrs Antonova. Somewhere in the rubble and ruin of her body, Zlata, the sixteen-year-old bride, still lived. 'He was a white Russian, an émigré, like me – do you know about the white émigrés, pumpkin?'

Mrs Antonova explained that she was a baby when her parents fled Moscow in 1921. Her father, Vladimir Antonov, was an academic. Her mother, Nataliya, was only twenty years old when they fled to Istanbul, and eventually Prague, Paris, London. She took with her baby Zlata, a Kornilov tea set and a determination to live in exile the life of a Russian noblewoman. The Kornilov teacups had little gold griffins for handles. The insides were fully gilded, and the outsides were painted with seashells and flowers. 'You know what we were, pumpkin? We were gypsies. Noble gypsies roaming Europe with our teacups and rye bread and Russian pride. Sometimes we had no bread. But Vladimir had his writing and Talia had her cups and they both had their pride. Pride, you know, is a very expensive commodity.'

Mrs Antonova fell silent.

'So what happened with Dimitri?'

'Who?' said Mrs Antonova, closing her eyes.

'The love of your life,' whispered Yasmin.

A RANDOM STAB OF HAPPINESS

'The thing is, Yasmin,' said Niamh, 'I'm not one to be sitting down but my back's gone – with all the lifting – and it's Mr Soames, he needs cleaning and that means lifting, doesn't it?'

Yasmin glanced at the call light flashing on the wall above Niamh's head. 'Where's everyone else? Jacinda? The other HCAs?'

'I know!' said Niamh, as if Yasmin had blamed them for something. Her hair, the colour of a bright new penny, shimmered righteously. 'But I'd be the last person to complain about any colleagues. Not gonna lie, though, Jacinda is downright lazy.'

'Do you want to find her or should I?'

'I was just about to.' Niamh stood up and adjusted her uniform. Nurses could choose between a blue trousers-and-tunic combination or a dress. Niamh always wore a dress, cinched tightly at the waist with a wide black belt and a décolletage that suggested she'd made a few alterations. 'Oh, Yasmin, if you want to talk about it, you know I'm here for you, right?' Niamh inched closer. 'I don't want to pry,' she added, tilting her head innocently.

Yasmin pursed her lips and tried to look quizzical. 'Huh? Oh! *Your friend.* I did ask Joe. Bit embarrassing, but we ended up laughing.'

'I'm sorry, Yasmin, but whatever he's told you, he's lying.'

'It didn't happen – as he pointed out, he has a watertight alibi for that night.'

'Did he tell you he was at a conference or something?'

Yasmin shook her head. Joe didn't lie. He told her the truth. *I'm sorry,* he said, *it just happened. It didn't mean anything.* 'No. Nothing like that. He just reminded me we spent that whole evening and night together.'

She turned and walked out of the ward, and kept walking. Past the burns centre, the pharmacy, plastic surgery, around A&E, through the patient transport area, where those too frail or too poor to make it home alone sat waiting for an ambulance.

She walked along corridors, climbed stairs, wound through unfamiliar passages. From somewhere the smell of fried food. The hushed din of the place, a machine-hum that built and fell remorselessly. Up another flight of steps and out through a fire exit on to a rusting platform where she stood and shouted into the wind.

The ward, which had been so disturbingly calm earlier, had livened up by the time Yasmin returned.

'Mr Sarpong,' said Julie, 'I promise I'll look for your watch, but let's get you back to bed. You mustn't keep wandering about like this.'

Her ward sister's uniform, dark blue with red piping, carried no authority with Mr Sarpong. 'No,' he said. 'I want my watch. Forty years. I worked for them forty years. They gave me a watch. A bloody watch!'

'All right,' said Julie, patting his arm. She'd intercepted his mission from the dementia-friendly ward. Mr Sarpong wore a long-sleeved camouflage-pattern T-shirt, an indignant expression and no clothing on his lower half. Perhaps due to the presence of a very large hydrocele in his scrotum, which was the size of a helium balloon.

'She's got it!' said Mr Sarpong, pointing at Yasmin. 'I want it back!'

'Dr Ghorami doesn't have your watch. Jacinda!' Julie called out to the health care assistant scurrying along with a hoist, a sheet and two packs of wet wipes.

'Mr Macrae exploded,' said Jacinda, still moving rapidly towards one of the male bays. 'All the way up his back. It's got in his hair!'

That explained the smell. Call bells flashed. Nurses hurried by. The locum doctor sat at a bedside taking a pulse. A patient shouted from her bed. The clank and slop of cleaning in progress, and a series of chirps and whistles from Harrison, who self-soothed that way while he worked. All was chaos and Yasmin kicked herself for going walkabout.

From one end of the ward Dr Arnott approached with her hair in a perfect chignon. Her heels machine-gunned down the tiled floor. Pepperdine approached from the other end of the ward, carrying a large stack of files.

'She stole it,' said Mr Sarpong. 'She steals everything.' He shuffled closer to Yasmin. 'Get me a biscuit, then?'

Yasmin glanced sideways towards Pepperdine, hoping he wasn't getting a bad impression of her. Maybe she should have called in sick. She wasn't coping well today. 'It'll be dinner time soon,' she said. It was 4.30 p.m., which meant the dinner trays would be handed out in about half an hour.

'Hi, Yasmin.' Dr Arnott had travelled at warp speed despite her high heels. 'Are we struggling? How can I help?' Catherine had that healthy-and-wealthy look about her. She probably ran marathons. She had definitely been Head Girl.

I'm in the wrong job, thought Yasmin. I'm not cut out for this.

'Yasmin?' said Dr Arnott.

'Biscuit?' said Mr Sarpong, adopting the same inquisitive tone. He'd abandoned, it seemed, all hope of recovering his watch.

Pepperdine arrived and looked sadly at Julie. 'I do see how difficult . . . ah, well, I must get on.' He went on his way.

'Where is Niamh?' said Julie.

'Hungry,' said Mr Sarpong. He tugged at Yasmin's sleeve with one hand. With the other he waved at the pantry. Packets of chocolate bourbons and custard creams were clearly visible through the glass doors.

'I'm sorry,' said Yasmin. 'I can't get them.' The pantry door was locked and only employees of Cotillion, the private company to which all hospital catering was contracted, held the keys.

Mr Sarpong dodged past Yasmin, apparently intent on a smash-and-grab raid. His scrotum bounced alarmingly on his thigh as he lunged forward but Catherine, calm and collected, blocked him. 'I'm Catherine, I'm one of the doctors,' she said. 'Why don't you come with me and we'll see what we can do.'

'She stole it,' he explained amiably, as he allowed Dr Arnott to lead him away.

'We need twice as many nurses on the dementia ward,' said Julie. She looked exhausted. 'Are you okay?'

'Me?' said Yasmin. 'I'm fine.' She turned her head and blinked back a tear.

'Dr Ghorami,' said Pepperdine. 'Ah, have a seat.' He continued writing something in a file.

Yasmin sat down and waited. Pepperdine's office was small and stuffy. He was the Senior Consultant in the Care of the Elderly Department, and in reality he ran it, but Professor Shah was Clinical Director and his office was much bigger. Or so Yasmin had been told. She'd never had cause to go in there.

Pepperdine turned a page and wrote some more. Niamh was right. He wasn't bad looking. For his age. Some lines around his eyes, some grey hair at the temples, but he wasn't *old*. His brow was big but not too big, and balanced out by his jaw. His mouth was nice, not too thin, and not at all miserable. It was only his eyes that looked sad. Maybe they weren't sad, exactly. Preoccupied? He looked like someone. Some Antarctic explorer she'd learned about on a school museum trip. He looked like one of those men in the photos, all lean and stoic, with icicles on their eyebrows.

He put down his pen and looked up. 'Clinics, I presume.'

'Excuse me?'

'What do you have to clock up for CMT? Is it twenty these days? I always forget.'

'Twenty-four in total,' said Yasmin. 'I have ten or eleven so far.' She'd come to his office because she wanted to tell him, as her supervisor, that she'd been having second thoughts about a career in medicine. No, that wasn't accurate. She hadn't been thinking about it. But today, all of a sudden, she'd had enough. She wanted out.

'Getting there,' he said. 'Making progress.' He picked up his pen obviously hoping this wouldn't take much longer. 'Well, the falls clinic, the stroke follow-up clinic and the movement disorders clinic are all badly in need of more manpower. You'll have to remind me which ones you've already covered. On the other hand, it's difficult at the moment to spare anyone from the wards. In the weeds today, weren't we?'

'I think I'm going to quit,' said Yasmin.

'Yes, it's been one of those days.' He leaned back in his chair. His shirt had fold marks across the chest as though he'd put it on straight out of the packet without ironing it first. He'd never been married. If he lived with someone, she decided, the shirt would be ironed. 'Have you tried running? I always find it helps.'

'With what?'

'With stress. Today, for example, I'm battling bureaucracy

trying to figure out why the two Trust doctors I tried to hire had their visa applications turned down. When I go for a run . . . the problem remains but I shall find some, ah, equanimity.'

'I'm not stressed. I'm . . .' What? Sick of it? Not having endless fun every day? What had she thought it would be like, being a doctor? She was supposed to be serving the needs of others, not just serving her own. Niamh had upset her. That was the real reason she was sitting here. It was none of Niamh's business what Joe had or hadn't done. It was between Joe and Yasmin and nobody else.

'Look, 2016 is a miserable year for junior doctors. These new contracts — if you want my opinion they're pretty awful, but I think it's almost certain now they will go ahead. Nobody could blame you for quitting. Are you thinking about Australia? New Zealand? A lot of medics are heading that way.'

'I'm just not sure I should be a doctor,' said Yasmin. 'I think I should be doing something else with my life.'

'Ah,' he said, 'in that case . . .' He nodded vaguely. 'That's for you to decide.'

'Yes,' said Yasmin. She bit the inside of her lip. What did she expect? He'd tell her that the NHS would collapse without her? He'd tell her she was special? 'Thanks,' she said, getting up. 'That's *very* helpful. Thanks for your input.'

She was almost at the door when he called out. 'Wait a minute.'

She turned around, ready to argue, ready to pack it all in right now if he tried to reprimand her for being rude.

'For the record,' he said, 'I don't think you should leave the medical profession. That would be a great pity because from what I've seen you're a very good doctor.' He smiled.

So, he *could* smile! She smiled back at him, a mysterious twinge in her chest. On her way home she diagnosed it as a random stab of happiness.

LOVE CONQUERS ALL

The back gardens of Beechwood Drive sat below a grassy slope of parkland ringed by diseased elms and straggly pines. Beech trees, ancient and majestic, tracked the broad path up to Tatton Hall, which stood at the top of the hill. The house, the twisted baroque parapets just visible from Yasmin's window, had belonged to a great English family of slave traders and was now a community centre and a café.

Yasmin leaned her forehead against the glass and watched Ma harvest vegetables into a rusty wheelbarrow. Anisah cut a butternut squash and held it aloft like a severed head. She inspected the underside carefully for mildew or rot or insects. She wore a yellow cotton sari, the pallu tied around one shoulder to keep it from falling. The sari's rose-pink border was fringed with a layer of mud. Patches of sweat darkened the underarms of her choli. Trust Ma to dress inappropriately for every occasion or activity.

She forced herself back to her desk. It was Saturday and – for once – Yasmin had two clear days in which to study. This morning she had paid the £419 exam fee in order to focus her mind. So far she'd attempted two practice questions. Then she'd started flicking through magazines left behind by a patient or relative in the television room. She read a story about a young woman who married her stepdad, and another about a Canadian lady who had dated a serial killer (she wondered why he had no inside handle on the passenger door of his car). The magazines were out of date and trashy and badly written but she could still bury herself in them, though she seemed incapable of burying herself in her work.

My Fiancé Cheated On Me! She could be in one of those magazines now. Joe had sex with someone else. Though she had – formally, supposedly – forgiven him, her mind returned incessantly to this fact, and every time this 'fact' was shaded differently. Slip-up. Betrayal. Insignificant. Monumental. Deceitful. Honest (he gave a full confession). Enraging. And for some reason she cannot fathom, shaming. The shame was idiopathic. It had no discernible cause. Nonetheless, there it was, the flush of emotion, the warm wet feeling like some kind of chronic internal incontinence.

I'm sorry, it didn't mean anything. She'd cried. Of course she'd cried. He held her and she thought she would quite literally disintegrate, just deliquesce in his arms right there and then. But soon she stiffened. Her ear pressed against his bare chest and the steady beat of his heart filled her with rage. Hours of *whys* and *how could yous* and she was exhausted and he bowed his head in defeat. Suddenly she was afraid. If she lost him ... but she would not. She would not lose him, and she would not throw him away.

She returned to the sample exam paper. *A 79-year-old woman was admitted for elective hip replacement surgery. On examination, she was pale. There was 2-cm splenomegaly and there were small discrete axillary lymph nodes.*

Focus! But even as she began reading the investigations she knew she would not complete the question. She did not care if

137

this hypothetical seventy-nine-year-old woman had acute mye-
loid leukaemia, chronic lymphocytic leukaemia, myelofibrosis
or bubonic plague. She was a bad doctor. All these years of study
and training. What a waste.

Yasmin picked her way between the tin bath filled with wood
and bags of gravel, the bamboo wigwam that hosted runner
beans through the summer, the strawberry plants turning
brown beneath the ripped netting. She'd given up studying.
Ma was in the dilapidated greenhouse, staring vacantly at a
hat stand. What was she thinking about? What did she have
to think about? Ma always kept herself busy but since she'd
started going over to Harriet's two or three times a week she
was acting differently, like she was carrying round some secret
prized possession. It was ridiculous.

Ma startled as Yasmin pushed the greenhouse door open. 'I
came out for tomatoes only.' She flicked up the skirt of her sari
to display the soiled hem, as if she had been unwittingly caught
up in a maelstrom of gardening.

'Ma,' said Yasmin. She hesitated. 'Will you tell me properly
about . . . how you met Baba? How you knew you wanted to
marry him.'

Anisah turned to a tomato plant and began snipping and
plucking. 'I don't know. What can I tell you? I don't know.'

'Did you ever have any doubts?'

'Things were very difficult,' said Ma, elaborating further with
some intricate head movements.

The greenhouse served as refuge of last resort for Ma's
hoarded bric-a-brac and surplus garments. Yasmin sat down on
a black bin-liner stuffed with old clothes and cushions. It gave
off a puff of musty scent that mingled with the heady aroma
of the tomato plants. 'Did you feel like you were taking a risk?
On Baba, I mean.'

'Is there marriage without risk? No. Marriage without risk is impossible.'

'Because . . . I'm taking a risk on Joe.'

'If you love,' said Ma, 'everything else you will manage. Love is most important and when problems come you can tackle them.'

Ma had tackled a lot. It must have taken great courage to tell the Founder and President of Hussein Industries that she wanted to marry a penniless boy without a college degree.

Hashim Hussein – Naana to Yasmin and Arif – wore white kurta pyjamas, as white as his white beard, which was dazzling against his skin. He sat in a cane chair under a ceiling fan in a reception room stuffed with upholstered furniture that made your bottom and back sweat the instant you sat down. The servants moved around him like whipped dogs, eager and watchful and sidling. On their first visit, aged nine and eleven, Arif and Yasmin were presented to him, scrubbed and tongue-tied, shining slicks of coconut oil on their hair. He beckoned to Arif who took a step backwards and Yasmin had to give him a little shove. Naana took hold of Arif, pinching one skinny arm between thumb and forefinger. He inspected him briefly then let go, and Arif ran and threw himself against Ma's legs. Yasmin steeled herself for her turn, but Naana didn't call her forward and she was disappointed. For the rest of the fortnight she waited for a chance to impress him but it didn't come. It never came on the next visit either, the last before both Ma's parents passed away.

Ma must have told her mother first, about Baba. Yasmin and Arif called her Naani. Naani had eyes like burnt currants and the tiniest feet. It was amazing she could walk on them. Her big toes were the size of cashews. Every time she was in the same room with Baba she covered her hair although, Yasmin noticed, she didn't do that for other male relatives. At the time she thought it was a sign of respect. Now she thought it meant Naani never accepted Baba. Yes, Ma was a remarkable woman, just as Harriet said. She didn't let anything get in the way of her love.

'Thank you, Ma,' said Yasmin, her voice cracking a little. She was greatly moved by her mother's love marriage, more than she had been in years. Love, Ma was telling her, not only in words but by example, conquers all.

Anisah picked up the bucket of tomatoes and squeezed past Yasmin, giving her a vague pat on the head as she went.

They moved the spoils of autumn – squashes, marrows, carrots, beetroots, onions – to the kitchen, the pantry, and mainly to the garage, still packed with the remains of Anisah's abortive front-yard table sale. 'I will make many chutneys,' declared Ma, as if struck by sudden inspiration, as if this outcome hadn't already been decided by the agricultural glut surrounding them.

Just outside the kitchen door was a suntrap, between the pebble-dashed wall and the bin shed. They sat there on stools, resting. Ma untied her pallu and used it to mop her face, and Yasmin picked the dirt from under her fingernails.

After some time Anisah said, 'I am living here so long in this house. So many years and years.' She sighed and the brown band of her stomach quivered between the sari and sari blouse. She twitched her little round nose. 'Why we didn't go to Wembley? Indians should live in Wembley or Southall or, best of all, Tooting. Southall is good but in Tooting there are more Muslims.'

Yasmin laughed. 'Have you been doing a survey of Indians in the UK? And why? You love it here!' Ma grumbled and hinted sometimes about how far she had to travel to buy hilsa fish or how there were no Bengalis at sisters' majlis, but really she loved going around on the buses and she met so many different women at majlis from Turkey, Afghanistan, Syria, Somalia, Iraq . . .

'Many Gujaratis in Tooting,' said Ma, 'but some Bengali speakers also. Tower Hamlets there are many. Why should we live here like mice?'

'Mice?' said Yasmin. 'What are you talking about?'

'Mice,' said Ma, quietly but firmly. Her hair, recently hennaed, glowed like boiled beetroot, and her third and fourth fingers were stained with turmeric. 'In Harrow there are Gujaratis also, and in Ilford many Punjabis, even Watford I prefer and they are Tamils but even this is more acceptable.'

'Acceptable?' said Yasmin. 'You love it here.'

'No,' said Anisah. 'Your father has kept me tied up here like . . . like a goat.'

'Baba doesn't stop you doing anything.'

'I wanted to do something with my life,' said Ma. She paused and twisted her fingers into the folds of her sari. She seemed to make up her mind and spoke in a rush, as if her courage would desert her if she waited a second longer. 'But your father is keeping the . . .' she hesitated again, '. . . seg . . . reg . . . gation and what can I do when this is the condition and this is how we live?'

Ma had started university in Calcutta but dropped out after a few months when she met Baba, and that was her decision, no one forced her to do anything. And she *did* do something with her life. She raised a family.

'Ma,' said Yasmin, 'you've got so much going on, so much to keep you busy – there's my wedding to plan for a start!' *And Arif's girlfriend is having a baby. That'll give you something to do.* It was tempting to say it out loud.

'Mrs Sangster says never too late, and better to talk about everything.'

Of course it was Harriet! It was all very well for Harriet to goad Ma into talking about who knows what because the Sangsters discussed everything, but this family was different. In the Ghorami family you didn't blurt things out inconsiderately. God knows where that would lead.

'Mrs Sangster says we are *not thriving without community*.' Ma widened her eyes and leaned into the words just like Harriet.

'Oh, but you know everyone round here,' said Yasmin. 'You've got loads of friends.' She didn't, not really. She had clients for her free meals-on-wheels service. But she'd been happy enough with that. A chat over the garden gate. Cooking. A trip to Poundland. A rummage through the clothes racks at the British Heart Foundation shop. More cooking. Prayers. Family. Knitting, crotchet, pickling, upholstery, gardening, baking, half-baked home improvement projects. And more prayers. Ma was always busy. And she'd been happy enough until Harriet decided to interfere.

'I have been isolated,' said Ma, pronouncing the word carefully, 'too-too long.'

Yasmin sat down again. Segregation! That was the word Ma had struggled to put together, and it only now landed in Yasmin's brain. Ma's life would have been different if they lived in Tooting. But in Tatton Hill you had open spaces, fresh air, good schools. Someone – was it the council? – planted pansies round the bases of the trees in the street. In the winter they put in cyclamen. It was quiet. Everyone minded their own business. Baba was friendly to all the neighbours but he was a private person and he liked to keep himself to himself. Tatton Hill was perfect.

HARUT AND MARUT

Segregation. Isolation. Did Ma really feel that way? Or was Harriet just stirring things up? But maybe Ma was lonely ... maybe she'd felt that way for a long time. She'd gone to make tea and heat up samosas. They were going to have a snack in the sun.

When Yasmin was around thirteen years old and to her great horror developing tender breasts and a disgusting interest in boys, a new family had moved into the cul-de-sac. The Gazis lived in the detached house nearest the park gate. You could drive a car into their front garden on the left and then out of another opening on the right. You never had to back out, like Baba in that maroon Lancia, checking his mirrors a dozen times, with the handbrake semi-engaged. The day they arrived Ma was so excited. At school she'd been friends with a girl called Malika Gazi. Maybe these new Gazis were Bengali. Ma didn't imagine they were related to Malika, or maybe she did. She tripped over the doorstep on her way out with a welcome tray of mango lassi, lacerating her knee and chin. Hobbled but still wildly enthusiastic, she staggered round the kitchen preparing another batch, adding a dash of lime juice, a pinch of ground cardamom. Then she had to sit down because her ankle had puffed up like a luchi in hot oil. Yasmin was despatched with the tray and urgent invitations. There was a drop of blood in one of the glasses, blooming red on the pale mango-tinged yogurt. Yasmin stirred it in with the tip of her finger and then licked her finger clean.

The Gazis' eldest son was fifteen and she had butterflies in her belly when she looked at him. He said he was called Rupert. Later she found out his name was Raseem, but no one ever called him that. Mrs Gazi wore hoop earrings like Jennifer Lopez and a purple bodycon dress with ruched seams and shoes with kitten heels, all that just for ordering the removal men around. Her mobile phone kept ringing and her hoops swung as she tucked it between her shoulder and her ear. It made Yasmin sad. Mrs Gazi wasn't going to be Anisah's new best friend.

They only stayed two years. Yasmin was glad when they went. She hated Rupert by then.

The Gazis, it turned out, were Bengali but not from Calcutta. They were from Birmingham. To Yasmin's mortification, Mrs Gazi seemed mildly amused by Ma's overtures. *Look,* she'd say, *your amma has left me this note but I can't read it. I have enough trouble speaking the language.*

Of course it would have been nice for Ma if the Gazis had turned out to be what she hoped. Or the Patels. They were only two streets over. But Baba had disliked them instantly. Money grubbers, he'd said.

Ma came out with a tray. They sat quietly for a while.

When they'd eaten, Ma said, 'Something is troubling, no? Something you want to tell Ma?'

'I'm okay,' said Yasmin. 'It's just that . . . I guess I thought Joe was perfect . . . but nobody's perfect, are they?'

'Nobody is perfect, but Joe is good. A good boy. See how he takes care of his mother. Not many English like that. Faults you will always find, in any boy.'

'I suppose so. But he . . .' She was suddenly sick of it, the way they danced around each other in this household. All this delicacy. It was unnecessary. It was oppressive. *He had sex with someone else.* She should just say it straight out. 'He let me down and it . . . it hurts.'

Ma patted Yasmin's hand. 'You know about Harut and Marut? Did I tell this story before?'

'Probably,' said Yasmin. She was glad she hadn't blurted it out. It would be too much for Ma. Ma had led a very sheltered life.

Anisah sighed.

'Actually,' said Yasmin, 'I don't think you did.'

Ma rearranged her sari, wrapping the loose end around her shoulders like a shawl. 'I will tell. Very long time ago, under Prophet Idris – he is fifth prophet after Adam – evil was on the earth. The angels are shocked to see how man behaves, all sorts of wickedness. God knows this. He has given to man free will and desire. Also knowledge of right and wrong. But he has created angels from light and they do not sin because they do not have free will.'

Ma paused to pin up a strand of hair that had worked its way out of her untidy bun. There was always a part of her that seemed to be unravelling. Yasmin wished she'd hurry up.

'The angels think they will never commit any sin. God sends two angels, Harut and Marut, to Babylon as men with every human desire. Now, what will happen?'

Yasmin thought she could probably guess but Ma didn't really want her to. 'I don't know,' she said.

'One day,' said Ma, 'a beautiful woman called Zohra invites them to her house. They both have desire for this woman and she says she will give in to them if they worship her god. Harut and Marut, they agree. They worship an idol. They drink wine with Zohra.'

'Fallen angels,' said Yasmin, trying to speed things along.

145

'A beggar sees what they do and he tells them these are immoral things. They chase him into an alley and kill him there. This is the conscience. This way they silence the conscience.'

'Okay,' said Yasmin.

'Harut and Marut run back to Zohra but she has vanished and they are naked and afraid.' Ma paused to let this racy detail sink in. 'They have failed this test. Somewhere near Babylon, these two fallen angels hang upside down in a well, praying for forgiveness. This is their penance until the Day of Judgement on earth.'

'That's a great story,' said Yasmin. 'I better go up and study now.'

Ma began gathering plates and mugs on to the tray. 'It's time for Asr,' she said. 'Will you join? Do you know where your prayer mat is?'

Yasmin shook her head. 'Sorry, I have so much work.'

'You go and do work,' said Ma. She put the tray down and took hold of Yasmin's hands. 'Everything is okay,' she said, 'you will see. Humans always are sinning. Men are not angels. And the angels no longer wonder how humans can sin. They pray for their forgiveness. I will pray also for this.'

INDIAN CLUBS

At the foot of the stairs Yasmin paused. A faint whirring issued from the sitting room. She went to investigate, wondering if Arif was in there. He'd hardly been home for the past fortnight.

As she opened the door she knew, even before she saw, what the sound was. She hadn't recognised it immediately because it was a noise that belonged elsewhere.

'Ah, good, come in and sit,' said Baba.

He had pushed the sofa beneath the window and placed the coffee table on top of it. Yasmin was unsure where to sit. There was the armchair and also the chair at Baba's worktable but she'd have to dodge the clubs flying round his head. They sliced and swooped and skimmed the ceiling, seemed almost to reach the very corners of the room.

Everything was out of place. Baba usually spent Saturdays in the garage or the front room.

She settled on the arm of the sofa, where the yellow flower pattern had turned brown with wear and slops of tea. Anisah rested her mug there when she watched one of her programmes.

Baba wielded the clubs fearlessly, around the back of his head, alternating directions, one in each hand, crossing his body, out to the sides, in opposing circles, changing the rhythm without breaking the flow, swinging one way with the left, another with the right. They were dangerously heavy. You could knock yourself out with one misjudged movement. When they were kids, Yasmin and Arif had taken the whole set of six into the front yard and tried to use them as skittles but they were too heavy to succumb to a tennis ball. They'd resorted to kicking a football to blast them down. Arif got his legs smacked for that.

'There is no space in the garage,' said Baba. 'Your mother has filled it to her heart's content. I must be grateful for her forbearance in not using this room also as a landfill site.' He wore his exercise outfit, a brown tracksuit with a white zip and white flash down the trouser seams. His bare feet, heels together, toes fanned out, were almost the exact same shade as the cloth.

'I will finish soon,' he said, 'and then there is a case challenge I would like to discuss with you.'

'Okay,' said Yasmin.

'You look pale, Mini,' said Baba, bringing the clubs down and rolling his shoulders. 'You should take regular exercise. I will show you some basic movements. No better exercise in the world than Indian clubs. And naturally you can perform the routines outside. For myself I choose to be indoors, but it is a matter of personal preference. Begin with the feet in the ten-to-two position . . . if you can't manage then hip distance apart is acceptable . . .'

He swung a single club in a slow semicircle. Yasmin traced the movement with her eyes, her gaze narrowed to the painted blue band around the thickest part of the club. Ma had married a poor boy, a servant, an ex-chai wallah, a driver who completed secondary school at the age of twenty-three, a penniless orphan, a boy from a mud-and-thatch village. Marriage was always a risk. How would she call off the wedding anyway? Even if she wanted to. Imagine telling Baba. Imagine telling Arif. How humiliating would that be? Imagine poor Ma having to tell her relatives.

'. . . demonstrate again . . . hammer grip to sabre grip . . . look carefully . . . the club is now an extension of your whole arm . . .' Baba transferred the club to his left hand. All the whirling about had coaxed the dust from the cornicing and it glittered above his white-and-grey hair. 'These are basic moves . . . inside pendulum . . . front circle . . . and inside mill.' He laid down the clubs. 'This is enough for the first lesson.'

He began some vigorous arm-stretching and neck-rolling exercise. Always cool down, he explained. Yasmin was relieved to see that he didn't expect her to try out some clubs swings right now. He unzipped his tracksuit top and took it off. A few curls of hair, still dark, pushed out of the neckline of his white cotton vest. His chest and shoulders were broad and his waist narrow from all the regular core strengthening. He picked up the coffee table from the sofa as though it weighed hardly anything and placed it back on the carpet.

He flexed a bicep, and struck it with his other hand. 'Sixty years old,' he said approvingly. 'Now, shall we solve the case challenge together? Or do you prefer to discuss something from your studies for the MRCP exam?'

'Actually . . .' said Yasmin. She preferred to do neither. The front door opened. Yasmin jumped up. 'Arif,' she cried, 'we're in here. Baba is teaching me clubs. Come and try.'

'Come,' said Baba to Arif, 'kneel here.' He pointed at the coffee table. 'Let's see how strong you are. I challenge you to an arm wrestle.'

'Nah,' said Arif, at the living-room door. 'No thanks.' His hair was just long enough to be scraped back and tied into a ponytail. It made him look thinner somehow.

'Are you afraid to lose to an old man?' said Baba. He knelt down and placed his right elbow on the mottled green stone, clenched and opened his fist.

Arif shook his head. 'Got stuff to do.' He attempted to sidle off, melting backwards into the hallway.

'That is excellent,' said Baba. 'Please come and inform us what pressing activities you are undertaking. You have found gainful employment?'

Arif entered the room with the air of compulsion and the shambolic gait of a prisoner whose legs have been shackled. He buckled on to the sofa.

Baba rose to his feet and picked up the clubs. 'Here,' he said to Arif, and threw one softly towards him, 'want to try?'

The club landed on Arif's lap. Arif flicked his gaze down and up and down again, as if considering its lethal potential. Baba slapped the other club against his palm like a truncheon.

'What does that say on your shirt?' Yasmin, still perched on the arm of the sofa, was regretting calling out to Arif.

'Five pillars,' mumbled Arif. He wore a short white kurta over his saggy jeans. It had a round collar, five buttons to the neck, a breast pocket and Arabic writing embroidered in red down the sleeve. He twisted to show Yasmin the other sleeve, also inscribed. 'Allah is the greatest,' he said.

Baba snorted but he relinquished the club and put his track-suit jacket back on. He sat down on his straight-backed chair. 'Have you tried praying for a job?'

'I'm working on something,' said Arif. His shirt was neat and clean but there was always something messy about him. The way he sat was untidy. He flopped around as though he was all flesh and no bone. He seemed to be growing a beard again, although it was difficult to tell because sometimes he just couldn't be bothered to shave.

'The app?' said Baba gravely. 'It is no more than an excuse.'

'A documentary,' said Arif, 'if you really want to know. I'm making a documentary about Islamophobia.'

Baba digested this news. He flexed his bare feet then screwed his toes tight until the joints cracked and popped. 'You are making this yourself? Nobody is paying you?'

Arif shrugged. 'I've pitched it everywhere. I'm going to put it on YouTube.'

In three months' time he would be a father. Would he try to shrug that off too? Yasmin willed him to grow up, start caring, stop expecting the world to change to suit his every need.

'Tell me about this Islamophobia,' said Baba, 'this hatred of Muslims. You have been subjected to this yourself? You are uncovering it on the streets?'

'Every day,' said Arif. 'Can I go now, please?'

'Explain to me,' said Baba. 'Give me examples.'

Arif's demeanour began to change from sullen to agitated. He shifted his weight and scratched his beard. 'There was a mosque in Leeds that was attacked—'

Baba interrupted him. 'This is not your daily experience.'

'Microaggressions,' said Arif, 'every day you get micro-aggressions. There are three different kinds, yeah, there's micro-assaults, like when someone says something deliberate, like derogatory about your religion, like why do you oppress women or something, or they deliberately serve a white person first, ahead of you. Then there's micro-insults which are unconscious, so the perpetrators aren't even aware, but they micro-insult you by saying you speak really good English or telling you you're not really like a Muslim person at all because you're cool. And there's, like, micro-invalidation when they say we're all just human beings and I don't even see you as Asian and everyone's equal and all that crap.'

He was gabbling by the end and Yasmin wasn't sure it all made sense. It was hard to believe anyone complimented Arif on his command of the English language, for instance. And some of his examples didn't seem to be anything at all to do with Islam. In any case, the best strategy was simply to ignore that stuff. Or it would drain you of energy. The more you looked for it, the more you'd find.

'When will you finish the documentary?' asked Yasmin. 'How much have you filmed?' She kept an eye on Baba, who was cogitating with his arms folded across his chest. He always used to take Arif aside, into the front room to lecture him. Nowadays it happened anywhere and everywhere, the kitchen, the sitting room, the hallway. Nothing was orderly any more.

Arif shrugged.

'Microaggressions,' said Baba. 'Very well. I suppose this is what you learned from your sociology degree. I will not argue with you. But I will tell you something. In India nobody is concerned with your micro-assaults. In India when you are assaulted for being Muslim you do not wonder if it was merely a figment of your imagination. Only last week in Delhi two Muslim men were attacked on the street. And the police stood by, guarding the mob. One man was dragged by the beard and beaten with planks while he begged for mercy. The other was kicked and dragged along as he lay unconscious. Both died later of their injuries. They were accused of eating beef. In fact, these lynchings are happening every day.'

Arif stood up. 'You asked me what I was doing but you don't want to know.'

'You are wrong,' said Baba. 'I am deeply curious. What is the purpose of your documentary?'

'It's obvious,' said Arif. Anger reddened his cheeks. 'Today, right, I interviewed two women who've been spat at in the street for wearing hijab. I know what my purpose is!' He hitched his jeans and moved closer to Baba. 'This violence against women has to be stopped.'

'What do you know?' said Baba, and there was thunder in his voice. 'What do you know about violence against women? Do you know in India how it is? Do you care to know before you criticise this country how it is for these women where they came from? Do you think they would be better off elsewhere?'

Arif grabbed the club off the coffee table and began to swing his arm in a slow windmill. 'Why should they go elsewhere? This is their home, right, don't you get that? Their home.' The tip of the club swung close to Baba's knees. Arif took a half step forward. There was a faint breeze and a whooshing sound as he began to speed up, his arm rotating. Another step forward and the club would crash down on Baba's head. Arif wouldn't dare. But then again, he was reckless, stupid, incapable of considering the consequences of his actions.

Yasmin's voice came out high and strangled. 'Arif, put it down!'

Arif redoubled his efforts. It seemed he would wrench his shoulder or lose his balance or let the club fly out of his hand.

Shaokat watched. He didn't flinch or move. He was making his calculations, judging and watching and waiting.

Arif's kurta worked its way up his back. His mouth hung open as if astounded at what his arm had decided to do.

Yasmin got to her feet just as Baba, his reflexes honed from years of practice, shot out his hand and stopped the club as it arced down in a wild, loose trajectory mere inches from his face. The slap of wood on flesh smarted in her ears. She could almost feel the sting.

Her heart raced. Arif stood panting. But Shaokat was utterly calm. He turned to his worktable and donned his spectacles. 'I wish you every success with the documentary.'

She shook her head at her brother. She was so sick of this tension, these scenes, the ever-present threat of something she couldn't name but that filled her with dread. When she was married she'd be rid of it finally. She didn't want to live here any longer. She couldn't wait to go.

'And I remind you,' continued Baba, 'that one month is almost up. I believe we had an agreement. If you are not in employment, paid employment, neither will you be in this house.'

'Don't worry,' said Arif, 'I'm going. I just came to pack my stuff.'

Baba nodded and opened a journal. 'Your allowance is, of course, terminated.'

'Something else to tell you,' said Arif. He looked at Yasmin, warning her he was about to pull the pin.

'Come upstairs,' said Yasmin. 'I'll help you pack.' She didn't for one moment believe he'd actually move out. He'd simply take a few more clothes and come and go and dodge Baba as he always did when things got rough. Unless he actually told Baba about Lucy. If he did that right now then he was finished. Baba would kick him out for good.

'What is it?' said Baba. 'I'm listening.' He kept reading his journal.

Arif looked determined, as if he knew he had to speak now before his bravado, worked up with every spin of the club, dissipated again. His long nose quivered. He opened his mouth. A change came over him. It descended quickly, and Yasmin could see it in the way his shoulders fell.

'No,' said Arif quietly. 'You're not listening. You never do.' He straightened his kurta and walked out.

A MUDDLE AND A MESS

'Tell her goodbye, yeah, tell her I'll come round when he's at work.' Arif stood before the alcove cupboard and pulled a couple of jackets off their hangers. He tossed them into a suitcase and a spider ran out of the striped lining of the lid. Most of Arif's clothes were either crammed into drawers or lay strewn around the floor. A selection was, presumably, already draped around Lucy's bedroom. The wardrobe was almost bare.

It was a symbolic act, this cupboard clearance. A ritual disembowelling of his room. The jackets he'd just tossed in the suitcase he hadn't worn since school. 'She's only out shopping with Mr Hartley,' said Yasmin. 'You can tell her yourself when she's home.'

Arif sniffed loudly. He made a kind of choking sound. He kept his back towards her. 'He's got no self-respect, you know, he's got no identity ... self-hating ... coconut ... he's got no pride ...'

'No pride?' If you had to describe Baba in three words two of them would be proud. The other would be dignified.

'He's not proud of *me*, is he?' He turned around and slid down the wall until he sat on the floor. 'Lucy's proud of me.' He sounded like a seven year old.

'She's proud of you becoming a . . .' Yasmin searched for the word. 'A campaigner? An activist?' The words rang hollow. Arif as a campaigner for what? Muslims? He was so muddled. A muddle and a mess. Where in the five pillars of Islam did it say you should disrespect your parents and have a child out of wedlock? Did Arif realise you had to do more than wear your religion like a badge, wear it – literally in his case – on your sleeve?

Arif shrugged. 'Getting into telly,' he said. He adopted a modest tone. 'Writing and producing. Making a doc.'

'Arif,' said Yasmin gently, 'does making a YouTube video count as getting into telly? Doesn't she . . . don't you . . . ? I mean, you've got a baby coming.'

'You think I don't know?' He sucked his teeth.

'Listen, you can't just drift along. Let me help. I've got money. Enough for a deposit and a few months' rent. Enough to get you on your feet and when you've got a job, we'll tell Ma and Baba about you and Lucy and the baby.' It wouldn't look half as bad, when he wasn't living this man-child life. It would neuter Baba's rage.

'What did *you* want to do?' said Arif. 'What did you want to be?'

'I'm offering you my savings,' said Yasmin. 'Do you want the money or not?'

'No thanks. What did you want to be?'

Yasmin sat stiffly on the end of the bed. 'A doctor, Arif. I wanted to be a doctor.'

When he snorted he sounded like Baba. 'No, you didn't, Apa. *He* wanted you to be a doctor. You went along with it.'

'So what if he did want it? He didn't force me. He . . . he inspired me!'

'You're an appeaser, Apa,' said Arif, sprawled on the floor like a road traffic accident, 'you've always been an appeaser. You're the biggest appeaser since Neville Chamberlain.'

156

'And you're the biggest idiot since . . . since . . .' She'd come up to his room to offer him help and support and this was the thanks she got. 'You're a moron, Chhoto Bhai. I feel sorry for Lucy and that poor baby.'

To her horror, tears welled in his eyes and ran in tramlines down his nose.

'Me too,' said Arif, sniffing loudly. 'I feel sorry for them as well.'

'Oh, Arif,' she said.

He couldn't speak for a couple of minutes, then he wiped his face on his sleeve. 'Wanna see my footage, then?'

'Definitely.'

'I don't want your money,' said Arif, getting up, taking his laptop out of his rucksack. 'Thanks, but I just have to do things my way from now on.'

'Okay,' said Yasmin. 'Fair enough.' She wanted to ask him what his way would entail exactly. But Arif's way probably didn't include such a thing as a plan.

He fired up the laptop. 'Canned some banging interviews today. I was thinking, like, your friend Rania. She'd be interesting; can you ask her if she's up for it?'

'Sure,' said Yasmin, deciding she wouldn't. She could do without Rania for a while. She wished she hadn't told her about Joe sleeping with a nurse. *You'll never be able to trust him. You've got to break it off.* Rania had never even been in a relationship but she had to be the expert on everything. 'Let's watch the video now.'

But as the cursor hovered over the play button a FaceTime call began bubbling and pulsing on the screen.

'About time you two met,' said Arif. 'Did I tell you it's a girl? You're going to have a niece.'

BUN BUNS

Lucy sat back from the screen to display her belly. It was perfectly round, as though she'd swallowed a basketball. Her pink jumper stretched neatly over it. 'Twenty-seven weeks,' she said. Her breasts formed two high smaller balls above, and her face was round too, some water retention perhaps around the jaw, and her widely spaced eyes were trustingly large. If you drew her, thought Yasmin, you'd basically draw a series of circles.

Lucy scooted in so her face filled the screen. Her hair was tied back and a broad dark stripe ran down her centre parting. Big gold hoops hung from her ears. More circles, thought Yasmin.

'I was saying, about time you two met,' said Arif. 'Show her the scan.'

'We already met, silly! Londis, wasn't it? No, Seven Eleven. Hello again.' She gave a little wave.

Yasmin waved back. 'Congratulations. A little girl, Arif tells me. So exciting.' It was absurd, but what else could she say?

'We've been thinking about names,' said Lucy. 'It's exhausting. It's literally making my brain ache.' She held her fingers to her temples to demonstrate. 'Every patient that comes into the surgery, I'm thinking about their names. Even surnames, like there's a Mrs Ladonna comes in. I'm thinking that's a pretty name for a girl, Ladonna. You see what I mean?' She blinked her big round eyes.

'No way,' said Arif, 'we're not calling her Ladonna.'

'No, we're not,' said Lucy, 'definitely not, but you can't help thinking about every single name because you've got to do the absolute best for your child. So far in the top ten we've got, let's see,' she began counting off on her fingers, 'Luna, Maddison, Summer – this is no particular order – Hallie, Harper, Darcy, Willow, Aurora, Peaches and Zina. Which do you like best out of those, Yasmin?'

'Well,' said Yasmin, 'I'm not sure. They're all pretty.'

'Aw,' said Lucy, scrunching her face, 'I know. They're all so sweet, aren't they?'

'Scan,' said Arif, 'show her the scan.'

'It's upstairs, I'll go and get it,' said Lucy. 'Do you think it's okay, Yasmin, that my belly button is starting to stick out? It looks so weird, I'll show you.' She pushed away from the screen, pulled up her top, turned a little to the side. 'See. Doesn't look right.'

'If you're worried you should book an appointment with your GP, but it looks fine to me. Perfectly normal, in fact.' What didn't seem normal was conducting an online consultation with her brother's pregnant girlfriend from his bedroom. But Lucy seemed so perfectly at ease, as if this whole situation wasn't a disaster, as if she took it for granted she was part of the family now, Yasmin wondered if she was a bit simple minded. Arif, for all that he was stupid and lazy, was quite clever. Even without all the other pressures, how long would their relationship last?

'Thanks,' said Lucy, 'it's so lucky you're a doctor.' She covered her belly again. She smiled, showing a perfect row of teeth, probably a perk of the job.

'Before I forget,' said Lucy, 'I was calling to say could you pick up a big bottle of Fanta on your way back, and some double-A batteries for the remote.'

'Sure,' said Arif, 'but you know how it hurts now when you burp. Why don't I get you, like, Ribena or something?'

Now they're getting on to the big issues, thought Yasmin, what kind of soft drinks to buy. Did Lucy have no clue? Did she realise the father of her child was jobless and quite possibly homeless as well? Arif had thrown his life away. If he truly loved this girl then it would be worth it. Ma went against her family. But Arif and Lucy was not a love story, it was a cautionary tale.

They had finished the soft drinks discussion and agreed on black-cherry-flavoured Rubicon. 'I'd like to get you a pram,' said Yasmin. 'You choose one and I'll buy it.'

'We're fine,' said Arif. 'We don't need anything.'

'Now, Bun Buns,' said Lucy, wagging a finger at her man-child, 'Auntie Yasmin can buy a present for her niece. A little outfit, maybe, or some booties, or a hat?'

'Is that Arif? And who's that with him?' A woman's voice in the background.

'It's Yasmin,' said Lucy. 'Say hello!'

She angled the screen away to take in the room and a woman in a canary-yellow jumpsuit.

'Hello, Yasmin. I'm La-La.' She waved, a double-handed, full-armed, wave, like a castaway spotting a rescue boat. The famous showbiz dancer. She had the same platinum hair as Lucy, a similar dark stripe down the parting. 'Seen my cigs anywhere, doll?'

'You can't smoke in here,' said Lucy firmly.

'Well, excuse me,' said La-La, 'I didn't know I wasn't allowed to put my Silk Cuts down in my own living room! Oh! You know what?' She patted a pocket, one of many on her jumpsuit that appeared, from this distance at least, to be composed mainly of belts, buckles, pockets and compartments. 'They're right here on my boob.'

'What's going on?' said another voice, off-screen.

'It's Arif,' came Lucy's voice. 'And Yasmin. Say hello, Mum.'

'Hello, love!' said Lucy's mum, walking into view. Yasmin began to get a sense of just how small this room was in this maisonette in Mottingham. Hardly space enough for three people. The walls were papered with a geometric pattern designed for a much larger room. The ceiling was too low to swing a club. A mantelpiece crammed with framed photos topped an old-fashioned gas fire. And Lucy's mum had to squeeze past La-La, who held up her arms to dramatise how little room to manoeuvre there was. With Arif and a baby there they'd literally be falling over each other.

'Nice to meet you, Yasmin. I'm Janine. Arif, love, we're getting Chinese, do you want that duck thing again because if you do you have to make everyone's pancakes up for them, okay?'

Janine wore what appeared to be a man's dressing gown. Was she getting up at this time in the afternoon or going to bed? She plonked herself on the leather corner sofa that took up over half the floor space, tucked up her feet, and picked up a television remote. 'And get batteries, double A, this thing's practically dead.'

'Will do. See you in a bit,' said Arif. 'Lucy? Hey, Lucy?'

Lucy had disappeared.

How casual they all were. As if there were no issues and nothing to worry about. The way they greeted her as if this was all normal. This baby coming into the world without a care or scarcely a thought. Chinese takeaway in front of the telly and Arif a part of the furniture, a part of the family. She could almost feel jealous, although there was nothing to envy, of course.

The screen lurched around and filled with a blur of black and grey tones. 'See her little fingers?' came Lucy's fluttery voice. 'Can you see how perfect they are?'

'Oh yes, perfect,' said Yasmin, but she couldn't see anything at all.

Lucy's face filled the screen again. 'Your mum was so sweet when I showed her. She looked at it like it was, I don't know, a work of art or something. Then she gave me a great big hug. So lovely she is, your mum.'

Yasmin turned to Arif. 'When was this? She knows? Since when?'

'Why shouldn't she know?' said Arif. He touched his fingers to the screen on Lucy's cheek.

'No,' said Yasmin, 'she should, I mean . . .'

'It's all right,' said Lucy, her gaze wide and innocent, 'she won't tell your dad. He's a bit old fashioned but I respect that, I really do. She won't tell him. Not until it's the right time.'

'That's it then,' he said. 'You'll visit, yeah?' Arif surveyed his bedroom, hands on hips, taking it in from top to bottom as if he'd never see it again.

Yasmin nodded. 'You visit too, okay?' He wasn't really going for good, but he seemed to believe it. At least when Arif came back his family would all be here for him. When Baba went back to his village – he was sixteen or seventeen – to look for his uncle and aunt and cousins they had vanished. People said they had gone across the border to East Pakistan and Baba thought that's where they were but there was no way of finding them. They hadn't even left him a message. How hard he'd worked to make his own family and give them a good life, to give them all that he'd never had. Arif never thought about that.

'Gonna fix this,' said Arif, picking up his guitar. 'Band's getting together again. Probably. Lucy sings, you know.'

'Great,' she said. Arif was severely deluded about this new life as documentary filmmaker and pop star, but Yasmin didn't have the stomach right now to tell him any home truths. 'That's great, Bun Buns!'

'I'm gonna let that slide, just this one time. Okay, Peking duck here I come! That's my Saturday night sorted. Joe taking you out somewhere?'

She shook her head. Joe wanted to meet up, had offered to come round, but she'd refused. Said she forgave him but needed some space. What she meant was she needed to punish him. He'd hurt her and he had to understand he could never do it again.

ADVENTURE PLAYGROUND

Rania sat at the kitchen table eating a bowl of semai. 'This is so delicious, Mrs Ghorami, how do you make it?'

'You have to boil milk for long-long time,' said Ma. 'Some people are using condensed milk but then all flavour is gone. You will not taste the ghee or cardamom or even raisins or cashew nuts. I will write this recipe for you.'

It was late Sunday morning and Yasmin had been in bed when she heard the doorbell and, soon after, Anisah calling her downstairs. She stood at the sink and filled the kettle.

Behind her, Ma said, 'Here is pen and a paper. I will tell and you will write.'

Yasmin gazed at the spider plants on the windowsill. They had self-propagated, trailing shiny little baby plants down the tiles.

The radio was on as usual, the volume turned down low. It sat on the windowsill amongst the greenery. *The deeper one goes, as a writer, into oneself, into the quotidian that necessarily constitutes the I . . .* The radio voice sounded familiar. Yasmin turned up the volume. *. . . which is to say that the locus of the self resides as much in the coffee cup with one's name scrawled upon it by the barista as it lives in the psyche . . .*

Harriet's award ceremony. It was that writer, the one with the khaki shirt and white and pink chest.

. . . The deeper one goes into this self, these selves, the more scrupulous the examination, the more rigorous the personal scrutiny of the I, the more one comes to the conclusion, to the full realisation, that the only fit and proper subject for the novelist, any novelist, is himself. Indeed, it is the only thing that can be written about with integrity.

'Bollocks!' Rania was right behind her. 'Sorry, Mrs Ghorami, didn't mean to swear. The only proper subject for a novelist is himself? Right. Definitely don't want novelists taking an interest in the world. Or making anything up! Who is this idiot?'

Yasmin turned the radio off. 'I need some fresh air. Let's go to the park.'

They trudged along the broad central path flanked by beech trees with their huge domed crowns, dark green flecked with orange and gold. Beechnut cups creaked open beneath their feet. Since they'd left the house they'd said little to each other, but Rania had slipped an arm through Yasmin's and Yasmin had allowed it to stay. When they reached Tatton Hall Rania suggested going into the café. Yasmin looked up at the grey stone walls and sandy architraves, sparkling a little against the bright blue sky.

'Too nice a day. Let's stay outside.'

'Adventure playground?' said Rania. 'Look, there's nobody there.'

They veered left and started down the far slope towards the pirate ship and the high walks and the orange climbing nets. A train jogged along the tracks at the bottom, a stubby Sunday train of four carriages, pausing a while, waiting for three fluorescent jackets to cross the tracks and signal the all-clear. Bonfire smoke twisted lazily from a back garden. A crow hopped ahead on the grass.

The gate was padlocked and bore a notice: *Adventure Playground Closed for Essential Repairs.*

'Over here,' called Rania. 'We can get through.'

'We're supposed to keep out.' But she followed Rania and squeezed through the broken fence. The first time she kissed Rupert Gazi was right over there, behind the tyre wall.

Rania put her head inside a huge concrete drainage pipe covered in graffiti. 'Stinks of piss.'

'See-saw,' said Yasmin.

'Race you,' said Rania.

The see-saw was outsized and you whacked into a rubberised pit when you went down and banged your groin against the metal handlebar when you tipped up. If you got the hang of it and balanced each other then you stopped slamming and banging and floated serenely up and down.

'Oh, that *hurts*,' said Rania, landing hard.

She pushed off vehemently and Yasmin screamed as she bounced up and almost off. 'Rania! No!'

'Are you okay?'

'Yes. Just keep it steady.'

'No. I mean are you *okay*?'

Yasmin nodded.

'You can tell me to mind my own business.'

'Actually, I don't really want to talk about it.'

'That's totally fine. We'll talk about something else.'

But they didn't talk about anything, and after a short time Rania closed her eyes, just as she used to when they were kids. When you closed your eyes on the see-saw you soared and swooped and felt like you were flying and your stomach travelled a little way behind but it caught up eventually.

Yasmin let her head hang back. A single white cloud scudded across the blue. It looked so far away yet when she rode skywards she felt she could touch it if she stretched out her hand. She was fifteen when she kissed Rupert Gazi behind the tyre wall. He was seventeen, filled out his Diesel jeans, rode a moped and sometimes drove his mum's car, although he only had a provisional licence, and he tasted like liquorice and fags. Rupert, Rupert, Rupert, she wrote in her biology exercise book and scribbled over it until the nib ripped the page.

They kissed again at his house, so much saliva, so many teeth, and he asked her to go upstairs with him and she was going to even though he'd put his tongue in her ear. But then Arif turned up with Rupert's younger brother and ruined everything. At night, in bed, she rubbed her fingers between her legs and pushed them inside and pretended it was him. She sucked the end of the duvet, turned on her side and then her stomach and pushed and rubbed until she went rigid and then very soft.

At school he mostly ignored her but she never blamed him. She was two years younger after all, and she wasn't cool even in her own year. It was another few weeks before he pulled up on his moped as she was walking home from the bus stop in her uniform. She was nearly on Beechwood Drive already so there was no reason for him to offer her a lift. When she slid her leg across the seat and put her hands on his bomber jacket she knew they were going to his house. She prayed for Arif to stay away this time.

'I'd forgotten,' said Rania, still with her eyes shut, 'how good this feels. It's like being in a trance.'

Yasmin closed her eyes.

He kissed her in the kitchen without taking out his chewing gum. She followed him up the stairs to his bedroom, unmade bed, curtains still closed. At the threshold she hesitated. He held out his hand. Haven't got all day, he said. He took her hand and pulled her in and kissed her and pushed his chewing gum from his mouth into hers. She tried to pull back, felt like she was choking, couldn't breathe properly, nearly swallowed the gum. He groaned without removing his mouth from hers, he was groaning into her mouth and his hand was under her skirt and in her tights. She pushed him, she tried to turn her head but she was against the wall and he was pressed in so close. He grunted and forced his fingers between her legs, rammed a finger up and finally took his mouth off hers. You been dreaming about this, he said. So stop being difficult.

She kicked his shin. Frigid bitch, he yelled after her as she ran down the stairs.

Somewhere overhead a plane tore up the sky. Yasmin kept her eyes closed. Maybe she was. Maybe she was frigid.

Two years until she kissed another boy. Ying was her first boyfriend. Rupert didn't count. A-level year and Ying started sitting with her in class. They never went on any dates but it first became common knowledge and then it became the truth that Yasmin and Ying were girlfriend and boyfriend. They'd been lumped together and accepted their fate as the two foreign (though they were English) science nerds. They kissed at lunchtime on the way to the chip shop because that was where Year 13s went and that was what they did. Ying had bad sinusitis and that was good because it meant he couldn't clamp mouths for too long, he had to come up for air.

After a term of Ying hurrying to sit next to her, Yasmin had to admit to herself what she'd suspected in the first place. He wanted to copy her work. She didn't mind but she pointed out to him, as gently as possible, that he wouldn't be able to do that in the exams. Ying wore his book bag on his front like a marsupial pouch. He clutched it and scowled and told Yasmin that Ying meant clever and she was too stupid to know that. Yasmin started her medical degree and Ying went to some sort of college to do re-sits.

She'd never had any sexual feelings for him as far as she could recall. What about Kashif? Her second boyfriend and first lover. Was she frigid with Kashif?

'Hey,' called Rania, 'are you sleeping? Yasmin! Wake up!'

The tyre wall was in fact brick with pieces of tyre sticking out for foot and hand holds. Despite her wedge heels, Rania reached the top before Yasmin. The platform where they sat was the highest point in the playground. In the distance you could see the city skyline printed crisply against a gradually whitening canvas, the Shard inked in gunmetal grey, the Gherkin, the Walkie Talkie, the Cheesegrater in shades of purple and blue. Down the hill, across the rail tracks, were the red-brick bungalows where a bonfire smouldered, a block of low-rise flats and the row of shops where she'd run into Lucy and Arif one time that seemed very long ago.

'I've just taken on a new case which is interesting,' said Rania. 'This woman, this mother, got kicked out of her son's school because she was wearing niqab. She went to a parents' meeting and a teacher told her she had to leave. She's suing for discrimination and I think we'll win.'

'You think so? There must be a security issue for the school. They've got to know who's on the premises and if her face is covered . . . '

'She lifted it.' Rania shook her head. She wore a leopard-print headscarf wound like a turban over her hair. With her ripped black jeans, silk shirt and leather jacket she looked like a petite Hells Angel Muslimah channelling a little 1950s glamour. Rania always dressed with attitude. 'When she entered the grounds she lifted the veil at the gate for the security guard, and he didn't give her any problem. So it wasn't about security.'

'Well, there's probably a school policy.' Yasmin wore boyfriend jeans and jumpers at the weekends. For work she wore collared button-down dresses or short-sleeved shifts. She had jackets from Jigsaw and Hobbs. She had a preference for pastel shades. Not a preference, exactly. She didn't know which colours suited her so it was safer not to opt for anything too bold. Rania's clothes said, This is me! Yasmin's said, I am a stranger to myself.

'No. There's no policy. She asked to see the policy but there isn't one. In fact, the headmaster wrote to her explicitly stating the policy didn't exist because there'd been no need for one previously, and they'd be introducing one now. If that's not discrimination I don't know what is.'

'Okay,' said Yasmin. There was no point arguing with Rania. She always had to win. 'What else are you working on?'

Rania dived into a complex immigration case about a client whom the Home Office was trying to deport to Baghdad. Yasmin kept nodding but hardly listened.

Kashif had seemed like a possible husband. He assumed she would definitely be his wife. That was sort of the problem. They were medical students together and Yasmin would spend the night at his hall of residence, or later his grimy Acton flat, and he expected her to make the bed, the cups of tea, empty the waste basket, as though the pattern of their lives had long since been determined and all that was left to them was to play out the days. She told him she wasn't allowed a boyfriend. He fully approved of this preservation of her honour and virginity, especially while fucking her. It was neither the truth nor a lie. At home the matter was avoided and when she stayed over with Kashif she said she was staying with a friend, and it went without saying the friend was a girl. Sex with Kashif wasn't enjoyable, and at first she thought it would get better in time, with experience. Then she wondered if she was frigid. Finally she just accepted it because Kashif had no complaints, never enquired if she was satisfied.

It carried on for over two years and one day she heard him belch and knew that was it, she couldn't do it. He wasn't even in the same room. She'd heard him burp before, of course, and fart, and seen him pick his nose, fish the wax out of his ear with a fingertip. She'd smelt his breath, his armpit, his urine and even his faeces when he'd forgotten again to flush. We're all human, she told herself, we are all secretions and gas and flesh and blood.

She heard him belch like a bullfrog and she picked up her coat and let herself out.

Rania touched Yasmin's sleeve. 'Am I talking too much?'

'Sorry,' said Yasmin. 'No. I *am* listening.' Maybe she was frigid. Sex with Joe was nice, nothing like it had been with Kashif. Joe was tender and attentive and loving . . . but she could never let herself go and maybe that's why he had strayed. She was bad in bed. But he could teach her. She could learn.

'I'm worried about you,' said Rania. 'And I get it – you don't want advice, but why don't you just talk to me? Maybe it will help sort things out in your head.'

'Thanks but it's already sorted.' She shouldn't have told Rania. However long they were married, Rania would always be judging him.

'It's not sorted,' said Rania. 'Trust me. You can't get over something like that in a few days.'

'And how would *you* know?'

'Listen, your fiancé has been unfaithful. That's serious. I know you're in pain and I'm your friend, that's why I'm here for you.'

'Well, I didn't ask you to be.'

'It's okay,' said Rania, patting Yasmin's knee. 'Let it out. Take the anger out on me.'

'I'm not angry!'

'You sound pretty furious.' Rania smiled.

'You're always right.'

'Not always,' said Rania, 'just most of the time.'

'Oh, no,' said Yasmin. 'I've never known you be wrong. Not once. Not one single time.'

'Now you're just being rude.'

'Go on then,' said Yasmin. 'Give me an example. Tell me one example of when you've admitted to being wrong.'

Rania shrugged. 'I think the point is – I'm not wrong now.'

'Really? You're judge and jury as always. Seriously! You've never even had a relationship, Rania. I'd have to be out of my mind to listen to you for relationship advice.'

RULES

She had nothing to be sorry for. Rania shouldn't have turned up uninvited. Rushing over here on a mercy mission, expecting Yasmin to be grateful. She wasn't having it, she wasn't going to let Rania pity her like that. The flame of self-righteousness burned brightly until she reached the ruined park gatehouse. By the time she'd walked down Beechwood Drive it had burned itself out.

She closed the front door as quietly as possible, slipped off her shoes and tiptoed upstairs. *If you are troubling, you know the best thing to do.* Ma kept the Qu'ran in the bedroom, wrapped in dark blue silk. It contained an English translation alongside the Arabic, and it had an entire shelf to itself. In this room in which Ma's compulsive hoarding tendencies were given freest expression, the clear inches of space amplified its status. Yasmin stood before the shelf and bowed her head. She felt a little calmer already. How many years had it been?

Yasmin's fingers hovered over the silk. Her period had started today.

If you are troubling . . .

Ma claimed you could find the answer to anything in life just by sitting for a while reading the Holy Qu'ran. It was just one of the things Ma said. Yasmin didn't even know what she was doing here. Should I marry Joe? Can I trust him? If Ma asked bigger questions maybe she wouldn't address them to an ancient script.

She reached out her hand and lifted the corner of the cloth; the silk ran through her fingers and slipped away.

Her period hadn't really got going yet. She'd only changed her tampon once and it didn't need changing. Probably less than a teaspoon of blood.

But. There were rules.

She sat down on the bed. There were still passages she knew by heart and she could recite them in her head if she wanted to meditate that way. It was only about clearing space in your head, that was the benefit. Ma thought it worked like some sort of miracle, not realising the answers came from her not from the book.

Yasmin got up and lifted her hand to the shelf again. What did she think would happen? What consequence would follow from handling some cardboard and paper? Why should those pages be forbidden to her?

She let her arm drop by her side. She wouldn't touch the Qu'ran until her period ended. You didn't break the rules just because they didn't suit you.

Joe broke the rules. Silly, stupid rules. It was only a biscuit from the wrong trolley. It was only a photo of a baby texted by a grateful patient. It was only sex.

When you started breaking rules you didn't know where to stop. When you only suited yourself, when you acted selfishly, when you started believing all that matters is what *you* want and what *you* think and what *you* feel then that's where it all went wrong and people got hurt, they got terribly, terribly hurt because of you.

'Oh, you are here. Rice will be ready, ten minutes more. I am trying out my new machine.' Ma held up a cardboard box that had 'Lloytron Automatic Rice Cooker' printed on it, above a photograph of a cream and black stainless-steel pot.

'You met her. You met Lucy. Why didn't you say?'

Ma balanced the empty box on top of a spare lampshade still in its cellophane wrapping. She moved around the room, shifting items as if she was tidying up. 'You have met also,' she said. 'Arif called me. You had a very nice conversation.'

'Did he tell you Baba kicked him out yesterday? Did he mention that?'

'Don't worry,' said Ma, 'I will deal with this.' She wobbled her head in a way that suggested she already had things under control. 'I will deal with your father, okay?'

'He's really messed up,' said Yasmin. 'Arif's ruined his life.'

Ma made a clucking noise. 'No. Don't worry. Everything is good. Everything is fine.'

'I'll just go downstairs and tell Baba now then, shall I? If everything is so good.'

Ma looked hurt. 'I will deal with your father.' She rummaged in a dresser drawer and pulled out a parcel wrapped in brown paper and tied up with a fraying shoelace. 'Come. Sit,' she said and cleared some space on the blanket box at the end of the bed. 'My wedding jewellery. Did I ever show you?'

'No,' said Yasmin. And there was her answer! She loved Joe and he loved her. That's all that mattered. Ma, above all people, knew that, and she was giving Yasmin her wedding jewellery.

'All gold,' said Ma, 'and very heavy. You will see.' She untied the parcel and began unravelling the brown paper. Inside the paper was a red velvet bag.

'I bet it's beautiful,' said Yasmin.

'Not beautiful,' said Ma, tugging the drawstring, 'ugly but valuable. I want to sell this ugly necklace and things for money for Arif and the baby. Will you help? If I go, they will try to cheat me, but when they see you, a clever doctor, they will not dare cheating you.'

'If that's what you want,' said Yasmin. Why should Arif get the jewellery? Why should he benefit from his irresponsibility? Why did Ma support only him?

'Look,' said Ma, 'feel how heavy.'

Yasmin stood up and went to the bedroom door. 'I'm going to lie down.'

'But lunch is ready,' said Ma, still weighing the necklace. 'I made your favourite. Chingri macher malai.'

'That's *Arif's* favourite,' cried Yasmin. 'Not mine. And I'm not hungry. Leave me alone.' She ran to her room and slammed the door.

PATHOLOGY

Pathology never picked up the phone. It just rang and rang. There was always someone chasing results so Yasmin didn't entirely blame them. Still, it was frustrating. She'd go down there, it would waste less time.

As she went through the door she saw him walk down the corridor towards her.

'Can we talk?'

They met beside the third window, halfway along. The corridor windows were wire mesh, laminated in obscure glass with a yellowish tinge, designed to let in as little light as possible.

'I've got to run down to the basement,' she said.

'Pathology never answer the phone.' He smiled. 'Neither do you these days.'

'I do,' she said. 'I did.' They'd spoken a couple of days ago, but in the week or so since Harriet's awards dinner he had called and left many messages. Sent a million texts of apology. She'd answered a few, deliberating hard over the words, trying to get the right tone: cool but not hostile.

'I'm not complaining,' Joe said, 'I just wanted to see you and talk.'

'Here? We can't talk here.' A patient in pyjamas and dressing gown trundled by, pushing a drip stand. He paused to cough up his guts, then went on his way.

'I know, but could we see each other this evening?' He wore a grey-green button-down linen shirt with one patch pocket. He had a knack for looking good without looking as if he was trying.

Yasmin glanced down at her powder-blue dress. The square-cut neckline suited her, she knew, and it was definitely a good hair day. She had mascara on her lashes instead of the usual quick dab of Vaseline. She'd been taking more care with her appearance.

'Not this evening,' she said, 'I'm meeting some uni friends I haven't seen for ages.' It was the truth, but even if she was free, she'd make him wait a bit longer. She couldn't let him off so easily.

'Okay,' he said, 'I don't want to push it . . . '

'Just tell me why,' she said. 'Why did you do it?'

He looked down at the floor, biting his bottom lip.

'Is she prettier than me?'

He looked straight at her with his clear blue ardent eyes. 'What? Of course not, how could she be?'

'Is it because I'm not good in bed?'

'Yasmin! No! What the . . . no! Is that how I make you feel?'

He was so urgent, so heartfelt, that she almost crumbled. But not yet. She wouldn't let herself be weak. 'Then, why? Tell me!' It was the wrong place to talk, with people walking by, the rumble of trolleys and the clatter of feet on the stairs, the incessant ping of the lift opening and closing. At any moment Niamh could appear.

Joe ran a hand through his hair. He opened his mouth. He looked winded. 'I don't . . . what . . . there's no explanation . . . I can't . . . '

The lift at the end of the corridor opened again and disgorged a man with a television camera. A woman with a boom followed, and then a man with a big microphone. Professor Shah stepped out next with some kind of entourage of hospital administrators with their yellow lanyards around their necks. The party processed slowly down the corridor, with the camera-man walking backwards.

'It just happened,' said Joe. 'I'm so, so, incredibly sorry. It just happened.'

'How? *How* did it happen? How does something like that *just happen*?'

'Well, okay . . . we met at Graham's house, you know Graham who works at The Royal London—'

'So, all your friends know?' She kept an eye on Professor Shah. His rare appearances on the wards resembled visits from dignitaries. He wore a suit and tie and left the tie dangling down his shirt front although it was supposed to be tucked inside. He didn't remove his jacket and of course he didn't roll up the sleeves.

'Christ, no! Nobody knows. I'm not proud of it!'

'Not even Harriet?'

'No. No way.'

'So, you met at Graham's house and *it just happened*?'

'Oh, God, how did it happen? She put her hand on my leg under the table, brushed against me in the kitchen . . . I feel like I'm making excuses . . . when it was time to leave—'

'Joe!' she said. 'I don't want to hear! I don't want the horrible details about you sleeping with this woman.'

'But . . .' he said. He blinked and pressed a thumb into his chin. 'I'm sorry.'

'If I hadn't found out, would you have told me?'

'I don't know. I hope so, I was planning to . . . but honestly, I don't know because part of me was hoping you'd never know and thinking it would only hurt you for no reason. I'm sorry. That's pathetic.'

She looked at him and he was so miserable she took pity. 'Okay,' she said, 'thanks for being honest.' At least he didn't tell her the glib and easy lie that he would definitely have confessed his infidelity. She had to give him some credit at least. 'Look who's coming,' she said.

He turned to look over his shoulder. 'That's Shah, right? He loves himself, doesn't he?'

'Shh,' said Yasmin. 'He'll hear.' The retinue was almost upon them.

'Look at that quiff,' Joe whispered, 'do you think it's dyed? He must dye it.'

'Should we ask him?' She touched Joe's arm, a quick light touch and his eyes lit up. She was sick of punishing him. When he suffered, she suffered too.

The cameraman moonwalked past them and Yasmin and Joe flattened against the dingy window to allow Shah and his courtiers plenty of space.

Professor Shah stopped right next to them and turned to the man with the microphone. 'Allow me to introduce some members of the team. It's all about good teamwork, in any department, but especially in geriatrics, which is necessarily multidisciplinary.'

The cameraman shuffled forward and pointed the camera at Yasmin. The boom swung overhead.

'This is ...' Professor Shah paused. He didn't know who Yasmin was, though he'd recognised her from the wards. 'Better if she introduces herself.' He looked smug. He always looked pleased with himself. Perhaps it was just the way his face was made.

'Yes,' said the man with the microphone, thrusting it in front of Yasmin, 'could you say your name and a sentence or two about what it's like working with Professor Shah?'

'It's for a documentary,' said one of the admin people. 'You'll have to sign a release form. I'll make sure we get one to you. I'm Clare, I'm a press officer for the Trust.'

'I'm Dr Yasmin Ghorami, I'm a junior doctor.' What else should she say? 'The department is very well run. In my opinion,' she added, 'it's an excellent department.'

'Great,' said the mic man. 'Great. And could we get you as well?' He moved the mic over to Joe. 'Same sort of thing.'

'I'm Dr Joe,' said Joe. 'I'm a registrar at Barney's, and Professor Shah is a legend.'

'Terrific,' said the mic man. He looked at the cameraman. 'I think we've got that?' The cameraman gave a thumbs-up.

'I didn't plant them,' said Professor Shah, 'I swear. It looks like a set-up. I'm rather embarrassed by such generous accolades.' He held a hairy hand to his heart. 'Well, shall we proceed to the ward?'

They fell about laughing as soon as the doors had swung closed.

'Professor Shah is a legend! He loved it,' said Yasmin, 'he took it seriously!'

'That's what legends do.'

'Dr Joe!' For some reason it was funny. 'Dr Joe!'

'What? What's so funny about that?' But he was laughing too.

'I don't know,' she said, 'I don't know.' When she'd caught her breath she said, 'I'd better go. Lab results to chase.'

'So, we can't meet up tonight.'

'Not tonight,' she said. 'But soon. And I want us to find a flat south of the river. I don't want to move north.' The way it came out it sounded as though she was setting him a test. Maybe she was. She'd agreed to move north because that's what he wanted and she didn't have strong feelings then. But she'd been thinking about it and it would be better if they didn't live so close to Harriet.

'That's fine. We will. It'll be closer to work anyway.' He

181

looked relieved. He rolled his shoulders. 'When will I see you? When are you free?'

'Tomorrow, straight after work.'

'Tomorrow.' He grinned. 'Great, tomorrow! But straight after work I have an appointment with my therapist. I started seeing a therapist.' He rolled his eyes. 'Sounds so self-indulgent when I say it out loud.'

'Oh, what kind of therapist? Why? No, I mean it's not self-indulgent, I'm sure. I'm sure it's a good thing, but what made you decide?'

'My father. Thinking about my dad, whether to invite him to the wedding or not. Abandonment issues. I've got abandonment issues, apparently.'

'Well, it's good,' said Yasmin. 'It's great you're dealing with them. It's better not to bury these things, I guess.'

'That's the theory. Can I take you out for dinner after that?'

'Sure,' she said, 'somewhere fancy. You can take me somewhere nice.'

'Absolutely! Where would you like to go?'

'No, you think of somewhere. Don't make *me* do the work.' She began to walk away and she felt his eyes on her and she felt good in this dress that skimmed so nicely over her stomach and fitted tightly but not too tightly on her bum. She stopped and turned back and he was looking, just the way she'd imagined. She walked back to him. 'Listen, I think you should also talk to your therapist about how *it just happened*. If you don't understand it, maybe the therapist will.'

'Yes, I'll do that,' said Joe. He put a hand on her cheek.

'Promise?'

'I promise,' he said.

SANDOR

'How does your fiancée feel about you living with your mother? Does it cause tension between you?' Sandor took note of the patient's irritation, a hardening around the eyes.

'They get on really well. And Yasmin lives with her parents so it's just normal. It's fine.'

'That's a word you used before to describe your relationship – normal. This idea of normality occupies a central place or meaning for you?'

'I don't know how to answer that. Is it a bad thing?' Joe smiled his charming smile. It gave him a bashful, slightly vulnerable quality. Was he aware of that? Was it cultivated? Perhaps yes, perhaps no, but either way it no doubt was helpful when it came to sexual pursuits.

'Let's come back to your mother. In our last session you talked about being the man of the house. Was this a responsibility that weighed heavily? Did you resent it at times?'

Joe shook his head. 'There were always guys around. I guess she was being careful to reassure me I was, you know, number one. The others were coming and going and I was there to stay. It was comforting.'

'And you required comforting because?'

'I didn't *require* it. No more than any other kid. It's not a crime to make your child feel secure.'

'And did you?'

'I think so. Yes, as far as I can remember. We've always been close. Look, I'm not trying to be difficult but where is this going? Because, you know, I'm still pretty much in the dark. You're the expert and I'm sorry if this sounds rude but could you just clue me in to how this is supposed to work?'

'My questions disturb you in some way? They feel, perhaps, invasive?' Sandor smiled at the patient, to show he had taken no offence. They're not patients, his father-in-law had said, they're customers. Robert had taken exception to some of the services provided at The Red Maple, the private clinic Sandor had run for a number of years. Acupuncture and reflexology, said Robert, were voodoo by any other name. Many therapists said 'client', but Sandor disliked the term.

'I know psychotherapy is . . . ' Joe looked around as if surprised at his surroundings. 'I know what it is, it's just that . . . '

Sandor waited. Sometimes the most important work was done in the silences.

'It feels like you're judging her. Because she was unconventional she must have been a bad mother. But she wasn't. Isn't. She's not perfect but she was the only person who cared about me when I was growing up. No one else cared, certainly not my dad.'

'Would you say you were a lonely child?'

'No. The opposite, sometimes.'

'In what way?'

'Too many people. Mostly I loved how the house was full of interesting people. Filmmakers, artists, writers, designers, politicians, all sorts. I was a lucky kid. Really. Not many kids get to grow up around all of that.'

'It must have been confusing sometimes, all the coming and going. Destabilising, perhaps?'

Joe shrugged. 'There are worse ways to grow up, I'm sure.'

'Yes? Meaning what?'

'Being neglected. Abused. Beaten. Starved. Take your pick.'

'And this invalidates your own suffering?'

'I wouldn't say I've suffered anything!'

'Okay,' said Sandor. 'And yet. Here we are.' He paused. Allow the patient time and space. In his early days as a therapist, allergic to the Freudian model, he talked too much, said too much too soon.

'I don't know,' said Joe.

'I'm wondering if it was frightening, at times, to be exposed to evidence of your mother's sexuality from a young age. Do you feel that she breached boundaries by disclosing intimate information about her personal life to you?'

Joe laughed. 'To me? She told the world! If anything, I was . . . sometimes I was jealous. Maybe that's the wrong word. I wanted the attention all for myself, or something. So I'd go and hide in the summerhouse at the bottom of the garden and fantasise about how sorry she'd be when she couldn't find me. She'd be sorry for being too distracted to pay proper attention to *the man of the house*.' He leaned into the phrase to mock this childish vision of his own importance. 'Honestly, I was a brat.'

At the very bottom of things, thought Sandor, there is always this: the addict's belief that they are unlovable. 'For a child it can feel threatening – you perceive your mother as the sole source of love and affection, and your position is being challenged. You said you felt jealous of your mother's relationships. Could you say more about that?'

'It wasn't sexual.'

'I didn't suggest that it was.'

'I thought that's what you were getting at.'

'What makes you think so?'

Joe screwed up his face. 'I don't know. Because all of this is

about sex? Sex addiction. Because I feel like you're implying . . .
not really implying . . . but leading me down a road that ends
up . . .'

'Where?'

'With me having an Oedipus complex. And I don't! I definitely don't.'

'I agree.' Of course, the need for denial was interesting.

'Okay,' said Joe. 'And anyway, she stopped having boy-
friends – or at least stopped bringing them home – when I was
about twelve, until I was seventeen or eighteen.'

'Why was that?'

'So I never felt like I had to compete with them. Teenage boys
don't want men coming into their territory, it just ends up with
conflict, so Harry put me first.'

'Did she? Put you first?' Joe would stick to this story for as
long as he could. It had taken Sandor years to truly understand
that in these cases it was vital for the patient to believe that
his only caregiver had done everything within her power to
care for him.

'Yes,' said Joe. 'She did.'

'Does she have a partner now?'

'No. Says she's finished with all that. Says she's done with sex.'

'Since when?'

'Since . . . around the time I moved back home, um, about
three years now.'

'And soon you'll be leaving her all alone. I'm wondering if
that induces any feelings of guilt?' It was no coincidence. Once
she'd got him home again, she'd renounced the possibility of
other partners. She wanted to keep Joe there with her.

'I'm not going far.' He shifted on the soft beige sofa, crossing
his leg so his ankle rested on the opposite knee. His shoe wagged
up and down. 'I'm not moving to Australia. Guilt? A bit, of
course. But that's normal, isn't it?'

'Normality seems to be something you crave. Was it something you were denied? Do you feel angry with your mother for depriving you of it?'

'Look,' said Joe, fiddling with his shoelace, 'if you knew Harry you'd know she can be infuriating. But I'm not angry with her in some fundamental way. She did her best, and that's all anyone can do.'

'And sometimes a parent's best is also damaging for the child. Is it possible you have some unacknowledged anger towards your mother? Anger might be fuelling – may indeed be causing – your addiction? When you have sex with one woman after another, when you make use of the female body in this way, perhaps what you are expressing is a kind of sublimated hostility.'

'Towards my *mother*?' Joe laughed to disguise his anger at Sandor. He was unable to sit with his negative emotions. It was ingrained in him to gloss them over, hide them from himself. 'Are you back on the Oedipus thing again?'

'Actually, no. I've never been there. I don't mean to suggest that you have a desire to sleep with your mother. Merely that you are, deep down, furious with her.'

'Why?' Joe threw back his head, addressing his question to the heavens. 'Why would I be furious with her? I'm not hostile to women. Sometimes Harry's a pain in the arse, but so what? So fucking what?'

Sandor nodded. 'I hear you.' Time was nearly up, and he'd pushed it as far as he could today. Joe wasn't ready to go further yet. But it was all adding up. All the indicators pointed in the same direction – the difficulty identifying personal needs, the caregiving role, the intemperate commitment, the ensuing fear of emotional flooding and subsequent sabotage, the sexual dysfunction and compulsive behaviour, the battle to feel validated because on the surface no violation of rights or personhood had occurred. It was textbook. Aloofness from the opposite sex parent. Another box checked. That one required more exploration. Next time.

'Sorry,' said Joe. 'For swearing.'

'In this room if we are sad we cry, if we are amused we laugh, if we are angry we shout or curse. As long as we don't hit each other, it's all good. Okay?'

'Okay.'

'One last question for today. The shoelaces – what's the story with them? Last week was red, right?'

'Just my little thing.' Joe lifted his foot and inspected it. 'Something I saw in some magazine once, in a dentist's waiting room. Style cheats for men. How to stand out without much effort. Have a fancy tie, or bright socks, or a scarf or pocket square. Stuff like that. It said it was a good way to get into conversation with girls. Women would approach you at the bar to compliment your tie or whatever. I was still at school and I was shy with girls. Didn't have a clue, obviously, how tongue-in-cheek that article was. Anyway, I decided laces would be my thing, and I've done it ever since. It just stuck.'

'And with the girls? Did it work with the girls?'

'Funnily enough,' said Joe, 'it did. It was amazing how easy it was.'

'You think it was the laces that made the difference?'

'Obviously, it wasn't . . . ' He trailed off.

'What changed was your belief. When you let go of the belief that you were shy, it was as if the world itself had changed. Impossibilities became possible. This is how it can be with addictions. Sometimes the most important thing an addict can give up is a belief about himself.'

HARRIET

Harriet lays the twenty tall stems next to the kitchen sink. If Joe wants to waste his time and money on a shrink it's entirely up to him. She will say nothing. If there's one thing she knows as a parent it's to stand back.

Rosalita is clanking about in the pantry, rearranging jars and packets and tins, wiping shelves and moving serving dishes from one cupboard to another. Last week Harriet suggested Rosalita put her feet up and have a cup of tea. Everything that needed doing had been done. Rosalita took offence. This week she has been making as much extra work for herself as possible. As if to prove herself indispensable. The reality is that Rosalita doesn't have enough work to do. The house is so rarely full these days. But Harriet would not dream of cutting her hours or letting her go.

She half fills a vase with water and gauges the length of the stems before beginning to trim and split a little way into the wood. If she hadn't brought up the subject when the Ghoramis came for dinner ... though it would have arisen naturally at some point. Neil is still Joseph's father, worse luck. If he wants to invite him to the wedding that is entirely up to him. If he wants to consult a therapist about it, he can just go ahead.

He's angry with his father. No. He's *carrying a lot of anger*.

Therapy jargon. Darling, of course you're angry! He was a shitty father. He needs a therapist to help him stop being angry. It was hard not to say: Why, darling? Why on earth should you stop?

Thank goodness she held back. The Hungarian would have a field day. She finishes arranging the deeply cupped roses with sprigs of myrtle and stems of fiddlehead fern, and stands back to look. Bartok. Something Bartok. He'd insinuate she was blocking her son's emotional development. Some such rubbish. They always go for the mother. There's a deep-rooted sexism at work in the whole psychoanalytic industry. She makes a few final adjustments to the flowers and carries the vase to the hall.

It is time to sit down and write. She must drag herself upstairs to her makeshift desk in her bedroom. Take out her pad of lined paper. Uncap her pen. Joseph will find his own way with his father. Reach his own conclusions. It's hard to imagine how she could ever have wanted to settle down with Neil. She did want that. For a short time she was set on the idea of marriage and more children, of lifelong incarceration with a man who drank gin gimlets and took second-rate photographs, who betrayed her while she was pregnant, betrayed his brother by fucking his girlfriend, betrayed everyone and everything, including the small amount of talent he possessed.

Anyway, she is grateful that Neil was such a total and utter shit. After Daddy died, she was so lost and sad she grabbed on to the nearest man and it could have turned out so much worse. If Neil had been the kind and steady type, she'd have stayed with him and suffocated. Died of boredom. Learned to make quiche.

Joseph, of course, benefited hugely. She has lived her life for him. No man has ever come between them. Nor woman. The lovers she had were always secondary. She has always put her child first.

*

She has something in mind to write about today but when she sits down at the dressing table she is crippled by doubt. In the mirror she surveys the lushness of the bedroom furnishings, the antique Italian cabinet of blackened wood with ebony and scagliola cartouches, the silk pillows heaped high on the bed, the fauteuil chair lined with Mother's creamy-gold mink coat. The coat is the only thing she has of Mother's, apart from the jewellery, and there is little of that left because Daddy got rid of most of it soon after she died. But it was Daddy who gave her the coat, on her eighteenth birthday. He stored it for her.

Harriet hears the front doorbell and has to resist the urge to rush down to answer it. Rosalita doesn't take kindly to Harriet usurping her. It's quite ridiculous the way she can't do whatever she likes in her own home! But never mind, never mind. The only reason she wants to run downstairs is to avoid getting on with writing. It will only be a parcel of some kind. Nobody drops round these days. It's not done any more. Harriet used to leave the door unlocked in the days when people would come and go without arranging appointments days, weeks, months in advance.

Poor Daddy. She hasn't done him justice. Hasn't written at all well about him. Easier to write about Mother's ice-cold beauty and frozen heart. Even a mink coat couldn't thaw her. She blamed him, of course, for Hector's death. When she'd had too much to drink at parties – she *always* had too much to drink at parties – she'd say, Have you met my husband, the brilliant physician? We had a son, you know, but he had a seizure at sixteenth months and Ludo unfortunately couldn't be disturbed because he was in theatre. He's a very brilliant doctor, my husband. Very important.

She'd always flirted with men in the way that was expected – even demanded – of a hostess and beautiful woman. But after Hector died, when she eventually got out of bed, the way she carried herself changed. Harriet was only seven but she saw it: the way Mother acted, especially when she flirted, made everyone uncomfortable.

Daddy rose above it. Ludo Sangster was the most clubbable surgeon in London, in the whole of the country. He was a big man, almost six foot three and big boned. His thighs filled that fauteuil when he sat in it. He was a big man in his profession. He was a big man in his appetite for life. Ludo Sangster never said no to an experience. He sang baritone, danced the boogaloo and the twist, rode to hounds, drove across Africa, shacked up with that girl in Chiang Mai, bought a bar in Mayfair and sold it for a fortune to an Arab. He was a big-hearted man who set up a free clinic in Thailand and trained local doctors. That was his legacy, he said, on his deathbed. His second-biggest legacy, after his daughter.

Harriet was fifteen when Mother died of ovarian cancer. She couldn't cry, but Daddy wept like a baby. Do you forgive me? he kept saying to Mother, over and over. Mother died in her own bed with her face to the wall and Daddy lay his big warm body next to hers and sobbed. Do you forgive me? Do you forgive me? Harriet held his big, fine hand and said, Don't, Daddy, don't. She knew they'd be better off without Mother. She was right. As soon as the funeral was over Daddy recovered. He took her skiing in Gstaad and that's where he met Aurelia, the first in a long line of women desperate to become Harriet's stepmother. Harriet didn't worry about it. Daddy said he'd never marry again and he always kept his promises to her.

LIKE A PRISONER

'So, I'm guessing you're a bit stressed out.' Catherine Arnott crossed her legs and the outline of her thighs strained against her skirt. They looked easily strong enough to grip a pole and dangle upside down.

'Who isn't?' Yasmin tapped away at the terminal in the departmental office. In fact, she was feeling fine today. At first, she'd expected Niamh to spread gossip and keep attacking her with unwanted condolences, but it had been about a month now and so far, so good. She'd sensed no whispering behind her back. Perhaps she wasn't interesting enough to be gossiped about.

'Yes, I thought so. I thought you must be.' Catherine scooted her chair away from her desk to sit closer. She obviously wanted to chat.

'Same for everyone here,' said Yasmin. 'How are you managing?' They'd fixed a date: Saturday, 17 June 2017. Maybe she should invite Catherine. She and Joe had started lists. School friends, university, work, people they never had time to see except on Facebook.

'*Me?* I'm fine. I was just a bit worried about you. Haven't been hauled up yet?'

'Hauled up? What do you mean?'

'Management. I don't have to tell you what arseholes they are. All they ever think about is PR.'

'What are you talking about?'

'The other day – when you had a row with that woman in the patient lounge.'

'I wouldn't call it a row.' Maybe it was. Since she knew instantly what Dr Arnott meant. 'She got pretty loud . . . but . . . how do you know about it?'

'Overheard her complaining to Julie a bit later. Complete bitch, if you ask me. Not that I know exactly what happened. What actually happened then?'

What happened was that a nurse told Yasmin a relative wanted to speak to a doctor about her uncle's diagnosis and care plan. Mrs Rowland was waiting in the television room. A large-boned woman, freckled face, a wraparound dress that severed her ample chest from her ample stomach. She had a no-nonsense expression and when she spoke her words had a don't-test-my-patience tone. Yasmin introduced herself.

Can I see a doctor qualified in Britain?

No problem. I qualified in London. How can I help?

I mean a British doctor.

I'm British. I was born here. Is that okay?

Mrs Rowland pursed her lips. It was clear she felt she'd been crossed, as if Yasmin's replies were in some way impertinent, as if Yasmin was trying to make her look like a fool. But she didn't know what to say. She looked around the lounge for inspiration but there was none to be had from the solitary patient – not her uncle – snoozing in front of the muted television set.

Would it help if I showed you my passport?

Yasmin should have kept quiet. She shouldn't have said anything more. Baba would have been disappointed in her. *Don't get excited, Mini. Don't get involved in things that are trivial.*

Do you mean you want to see a white doctor? Is that what you mean?

Mrs Rowland was sorely aggrieved.

How dare you? Don't you dare play the race card with me! Are you calling me a racist? Me? There's not a racist bone in my body. Not one! I've paid taxes all my life and so has my uncle, and I'm entitled to ask for a British doctor without getting insulted and abused.

You think you're the one who's been insulted?

Mrs Rowland raised a finger and stabbed the air repeatedly.

Are you calling me a racist? Yes or no.

Draw your own conclusions. Would you like me to discuss your uncle's care with you?

What I'd like . . . what I'd like right now is an apology. You need to say sorry and you need to say it now or else!

'God!' said Catherine when Yasmin had finished. 'Total bitch! And when – *if* – they do haul you up, tell them where to stick it.'

'You don't think Julie will . . . ?'

'Oh, no! Julie just told her to fill in a PALS form if she was unhappy. Got rid of her as quick as she could.'

Yasmin sighed. 'If I'd been a bit more polite . . . ' It was hardly the first time she'd encountered a certain reluctance or disappointment from a patient or relative when they set eyes on her. But it was always something in their expression, or manner, or at most it was a joke or throwaway comment, always followed by the words, *no offence*. Mrs Rowland had given voice to something Yasmin had sensed before, but told herself she was probably imagining. That's why Yasmin had failed to control herself.

'Sorry, but that's rubbish. Even if she does make a complaint against you, it would be worth it. *Per angusta ad augusta*, as my mother always says.'

Yasmin had assumed that Catherine Arnott with her creamy

195

skin with blue undertones, her sturdy legs and even sturdier manner was as English as it was possible to be. But her mother, apparently, was Italian or Spanish or something. Even people from here, it seemed, were also from somewhere else. She waited for Catherine to translate.

'I'd better finish my notes,' said Catherine.

'Me too. What is it your mother says?'

'Oh, I guess you never learned Latin? Through difficulty to greatness. From trial to triumph.' Dr Arnott smiled. 'My mother says a lot of stupid things.'

Yasmin had got into the habit of spending as much time as possible with Mrs Antonova during visiting hours. Usually that wasn't much time at all but this afternoon, despite the chaos this morning, she managed a bit longer.

'I like hearing him sing. That cleaner. Harrison.' Mrs Antonova motioned with her big bony hand, as if conducting one of Harrison's atonal lullabies.

'He certainly practises a lot.' Yasmin wondered if Mrs Antonova's hands really were large, or just looked that way because the rest of her had shrunk. Perhaps, when she was younger, she had been complimented on her slender fingers and small hands.

'Appalling, the way they treat him. I've told him to join a union. Get a pay rise.'

They'd been severely short staffed until more agency nurses and auxiliaries turned up around lunchtime. Pepperdine arrived for his round and surveyed the dirty linens and food trays with an expression of anguish. Julie was driven to such despair she shouted at Harrison for knocking over his bucket in the middle of the ward.

Harrison muttered darkly about transferring to somewhere more civilised. In the management suite you didn't have to mop at all because there was carpet, and there were always leftover sandwiches. Mrs Antonova supported Harrison loudly. Her body seemed to get a little smaller every day but her voice was still at full volume. She was disgusted with the hospital.

'And what did he say?' Harrison was the only regular cleaner in the department, on the hospital staff, while the other cleaners came and went through an agency. According to Julie he was the father of Professor Shah's wife's fitness instructor, and that's why he was still on the payroll after the cleaning was 'contracted out' to a private firm.

'He said he's meeting the Prime Minister next week to discuss it. He's not all there, you know.'

'I know. How are you feeling today, Zlata?'

'Pah! Like a prisoner. I want to go outside, but nobody takes me. I have no freedom, not even the freedom to die.'

'Now ...'

'That lucky, lucky lady who died last week. She was only eighty-nine, and it should have been my turn. I'm ninety-six. I had a stroke a few years back but *my* stroke was only piddling.'

'I'll take you outside,' said Yasmin. 'But I can't take you far.'

'Far? I don't want to go far. I'm not asking to go to the seaside or Disneyland.' She scratched at her wig. 'Dimitri, my first husband, he died at fifty-eight. Only fifty-eight. We'd been married five years. It was my twenty-first birthday party. Not my actual birthday but the day of my party. Oh, it was a grand affair! There was an ice sculpture of a swan. It was filled with vodka and you drank from its beak. Imagine. We were all so drunk, and when he fell down we thought it was the vodka, but he'd had ... ' She was short of breath, ' ... a heart attack.' Inside the dried apple core of her face her eyes began to well.

'And he was the love of your life.' Yasmin suddenly felt like crying too. She dug her fingernails into her palm to stop herself. It wasn't professional.

'And so it goes, pumpkin. This wig is itching like hell!' Mrs Antonova pushed her fingers deeper inside the aubergine curls and scratched extravagantly but in vain.

'Do you want me to take it off for you?' She should check Mrs Antonova's scalp for any rashes or even lesions caused by the wig.

'No, and I don't want to sit here naked either. Tcha! I do have a little pride left, you know.'

'Well, I'll let you get some rest.'

'Don't mind me. Sometimes I speak and it's my mother's voice that comes out. The princess who has lost everything except her way of ordering people around.'

They talked a while longer before Yasmin had to go.

'Thank you for the visit,' said Mrs Antonova, as she always did. 'Will you pass my book and my glasses? I'd like to read a little.'

Yasmin pulled down the bed's metal arm that folded in various directions and formations to be used for holding equipment or a food tray, or in this case as a book stand. She propped *A Tale of Two Cities* open at page one. 'Is that a good height? A bit higher?' Mrs Antonova nodded and Yasmin inched the contraption up but it wouldn't stay in place and sank back down.

'It's fine. I can manage. You know what would be lovely? A biscuit. Missed the tea trolley, I was dozing. But I know a doctor has better things to do than fetching snacks.' She batted her few remaining eyelashes and smiled a gummy smile.

Yasmin looked at the locked pantry. There might be biscuits at the nurses' station. 'I'll go and find you something.'

The rest of the day dragged terribly. What did *you* want to be? Arif's dumb question had been rattling around her head for weeks. She'd wanted to be a doctor but she wasn't turning out to be a very good one. She'd much rather sit with Mrs Antonova and listen to her stories than organise laparoscopies and check blood results.

Finally, it was time to go home.

She reached for the chain around her neck as she left the ward. It had become a habit. The instant she clocked off she slipped the engagement ring on her finger. She walked down the corridor, past a porter pushing an empty wheelchair, nurses in green scrubs, patients in dressing gowns, catering staff in white coats. She was fed up and agitated. And angry. About what? Mrs Rowland? It was so trivial she'd forgotten about it until Catherine brought it up. But she wouldn't get in trouble for it, would she?

She was in such a hurry she almost ran straight into Niamh.

'How's it going, Yasmin? You look upset.'

'Do I? I'm fine.'

Niamh reached out and touched the sapphire on Yasmin's left hand. 'Oh, I didn't realise! So you're still . . . ?'

'Engaged. Yes.'

'If you ever want to talk. He's told you the truth now, hasn't he? About sleeping with my friend.'

Yasmin kept her mouth closed.

'Don't feel embarrassed. I get how embarrassing it would be to call it off. But you've got to be true to yourself. To be very honest with you, Yasmin, that's all that matters. Being true to yourself.'

'Not necessarily. Sometimes it's not,' said Yasmin. She looked at Niamh's flawless skin, her radiant copper hair and scheming green eyes.

'Like when?'

'Like when your true self is a nasty piece of work, for instance.'

'Well, obviously not then. Listen, I know we don't know each other very well . . .' Niamh spoke softly. She had drawn no inference. 'But I know what it's like to have your heart broken, and if you need a friend I'm here.'

'Thanks,' said Yasmin stiffly.

She blundered down the corridor banging into people. She wanted to bang her head against the wall. She could kill Niamh. And her friend. She could kill Joe. *It just happened.* Sex didn't just happen. It didn't happen automatically, like breathing. She wrenched the ring from her finger and dropped it into her bag. Things didn't just happen, they had causes, required actions. Thoughts and desires and actions. It wasn't all preordained. Harut and Marut still hung upside down in a well for exercising their free will so poorly. What had Joe's punishment been? Only one month had passed since he'd committed his sin. She'd let him off so lightly! And she was the one still suffering.

She reached the lobby. As she crossed it she saw Pepperdine, waiting for someone, hands in his overcoat pockets.

'Ah, Yasmin,' he said, 'are you in a rush this evening?'

She shook her head. She read the posters on the wall that she already knew by heart: Don't Bring Norovirus Into Our Hospital. A&E Is For Emergencies Only. Just Ask: Could It Be Sepsis?

'We've not had a chance to catch up for a while. And you look like you could use one. Drink,' he clarified.

'Yes,' said Yasmin. 'I could.'

SAME

The pub was crowded. She thought maybe they'd end up as part of a larger group of Barney's staff, him at the centre, her at the periphery, drifting away unnoticed after one drink. But he steered her to a small table by a window before going off to the bar.

They talked about work, of course: the department, then the hospital as a whole, then the state of the NHS. The rest of the strikes, planned for this month – October – and the months following, had been cancelled the previous day. She told him about standing on the picket line in April. How there'd been so much support from patients, from drivers tooting their horns as they went by, from members of the public who brought sandwiches for the doctors, or stopped by to say they'd written to their MP or rung into a radio station to express their support. They discussed how it had all soured so quickly, how they'd been portrayed in the press as wanting to bring the government down.

Don't get involved, Mini. Baba gave his usual advice, of course. Yasmin didn't mention that to Pepperdine. Didn't mention either that she'd stood on the picket line with Joe. Did Pepperdine even know she was engaged?

'So, did you make up your mind?' He was looking somewhere behind her, over her shoulder as he spoke.

'About what?'

'About quitting medicine.'

So that's why they were here. Of course it was. Why else would he invite her for a drink? 'Yes,' she said. 'I'm not quitting. Unless I actually come up with something else I could do. Which is kind of unlikely.'

'Good. I'm glad.' His hair was a little grey at the temples, but he wasn't really that old. His bottom lip was a little cracked. Probably, he never thought about things like chapstick. She had to say something. It was her turn to speak.

'What do you do when you're not at work?' She felt bold as she said it.

He looked her straight in the eye. They held each other's gaze for a moment longer than normal. It was only a moment longer but she knew it, and she knew he knew it too.

He gestured vaguely and his eyes flitted away. 'I run. I go to the theatre, to dinner. I read. The usual things. I guess I'm quite dull. Predictable.'

Niamh thought he was attractive, was always trying to get his attention, thrusting her chest and fiddling with her bra strap. He took no notice. Niamh said she would fuck him, but Yasmin didn't find him attractive at all.

'What about you?'

'Same. The usual.'

'Have I said something wrong?'

Yasmin looked away from him, out of the window at the slow caravan of traffic grinding uphill from the city towards the suburbs. Across the road in the hospital campus a few patients stood in the smoking shelter, shoulders hunched tight beneath dressing gowns.

'No,' she said.

'I'm a bit of a failure when it comes to small talk, I'm afraid.'

She looked at him then. His lips parted slightly as though he was willing but unable to say more. His hair, short and thick, stood up over his heavy brow. Niamh would love to get her fingers in it. But Niamh would never get the chance.

'Same,' she said. 'Me too.'

He put on his coat. 'Time to go home.'

By unspoken agreement they walked to the corner and across a side road. Nothing more had been said but her heart raced. Was it going to *just happen*? Just sex. What if she just let it happen tonight?

'Where do you have to get to?' he said.

'Primrose Hill. I'll get the tube and change for the Northern Line.'

'I'm Chalk Farm. I'll drop you somewhere easier. Camden. If you want.'

She started to say she didn't want to put him to any trouble but he was already walking towards the staff car park and she followed, as if sutured loosely but securely to his coat-tail.

They drove north. The dashboard glowed like phosphorus. The car smelled of leather and peppermint. Yasmin stole a look at Pepperdine.

He kept his eyes on the road.

She said, 'I think I was a bit rude to you back there, in the pub.'

At a red light he looked at her and shook his head. 'No. You weren't.'

She waited for more but he drove and stayed silent. He seemed far away, forgetting – it seemed to her – that Yasmin was even there.

Eventually, he said, 'I'll take you all the way, no sense in you having to mess about with the tube. What's the address?'

'No,' said Yasmin. 'I don't want you to.'

'I insist.'

'No,' Yasmin repeated. 'I don't want to go there. I don't want to go to Primrose Hill.'

For some time there was only the steady pulse of the traffic and the less steady beat of her heart.

He said, 'Where do you want to go?'

It didn't just happen. You made it happen or you didn't. It didn't *just happen* to anyone. 'Home with you, that's what I want.'

This time he didn't pause. 'Good,' he said. 'Same.'

FOR THE RECORD

She had made a terrible mistake. Yasmin closed the bathroom door and turned the key. As they walked up the short flight of steps to the front door he'd asked if she'd prefer wine or another gin and tonic. But she hadn't wanted a drink, had seized the moment, seized him, in fact, and practically dragged him up to his bedroom. She had pounced, and having pounced, she remembered and now she was looking in the mirror of the bathroom cabinet and wondering how the hell she could back out of this gracefully.

There was no way.

She opened the cabinet, partly curious, mostly to get rid of the sight of her own horrified face. Toothpaste, too many packs of soap, he'd over-bought, a razor, shaving gel for sensitive skin.

How could she forget she had her period?

What was she going to say? She wasn't bleeding lightly, either, like at the beginning or the end. It wasn't something that could go unremarked if they went ahead and did what they clearly had been going to do.

But she couldn't go through with it now; of that she was certain. Perhaps she could sneak down the stairs and let herself out. Her bag was in the hall. Not sure where she left her coat but she could go without.

She did namaz with Ma for the first time in ages and she had been bleeding then. Some scholars said it was forbidden, but many gave other interpretations that allowed it. And Ma always said girls could pray any time, Purity is in the heart. Allah welcomed everyone.

Regarding intercourse there was no room for interpretation. It was off limits. Period. That was Joe's joke when she explained it to him. He didn't mind in the least. He said abstinence made it all the more special the rest of the time. With Kashif it had been different. There was no question of intercourse during that time of the month. But he seemed to resent it, as if she was bleeding out of spite.

Her shoes were in the bedroom. Maybe she could do without those. If she called an Uber and waited in a side street.

The cabinet door swung to, though she had not touched it, closing with a magnetised click.

Oh God, her eyebrows! How long since she'd plucked them? Why had she stopped seeing them? Them? Why use the plural? Only one fat eyebrow crawling across her brow.

'Are you okay in there?'

'Yes,' she said. 'Absolutely fine.'

He sat on the end of the bed. Yasmin stood in front of him and despite everything she pulled in her stomach and regretted never having done the crunches and bicycles she'd so often read about. They only took a few minutes every morning and if she'd done them her stomach would be toned.

There was nothing for it but to tell him straight. 'I've got my period. Sorry. So we can't . . . I don't know why I didn't think of it before.'

Pepperdine sat there in his shirt and underwear. He'd removed his jacket, and Yasmin had more or less ripped the shirt open, undone his belt and pulled his trousers off. Yasmin was still fully clothed. This gave her some measure of confidence, though this evidence of her previously unbridled enthusiasm was somewhat unnerving.

'Okay,' he said. 'I don't understand, but okay.'

'Sorry,' she repeated. With his hair messed up he looked edible. Niamh would be insane with jealousy.

'If you don't want to, it's perfectly fine. You don't have to make up a reason. You're allowed to, ah, change your mind.'

'Really. I have my period.'

'You said that already. But what difference does that make?'

She shrugged. Maybe she *was* frigid. If she could let herself go they'd already be doing it, she wouldn't be worrying about some stupid ancient rule.

He rubbed the back of his neck. 'In some cultures, I know there are taboos around menstruation.'

'Yes. Thank you. I'm aware of that.' She should pick up her shoes and walk away before she did any more damage. First she'd tried to have sex with him and now she was on the attack, for no reason other than she had embarrassed herself.

To her surprise he began to laugh. 'I guess you are.'

'I'd better go,' said Yasmin. She swallowed. Her tongue felt too big for her mouth.

'Sure. If that's what you want.' He lay back on the bed.

Yasmin nodded and picked up her shoes. When she was at the door he said, 'For the record, I'd very much like you to stay.'

She turned back to the room and looked around as if taking an inventory to commit it to memory. She allowed herself to look at him and her shoes fell from her hand. She pulled off her blouse as she went to him. He sat up and kissed her on the stomach and this time she didn't remember to suck in.

207

HARAM

'Ask me anything. What do you want to know?'

They lay on their backs, hands barely touching. A faint glimmer from the street framed the window over which the blind was drawn, a floating rectangle of black. Before she'd let him remove her underwear she had reached over to turn off the lamp. It was easier to lose herself in the dark. Easier, as well, to talk.

'Okay,' she said. 'How old are you?'

'Forty-six.'

He didn't sound apologetic about it. Yasmin was relieved. No jokes about being old enough to be her father. Just the number. Just the fact.

'What's your first name?'

'You're kidding.'

The sweat on her body was cooling, and she was starting to shiver a little but didn't want to move. The duvet, she was fairly sure, was somewhere on the floor. Under the window the outline of the chaise longue looked like a body bag. The slight shimmer to the right was a wall of handleless closets. The room was minimalist, like Pepperdine.

'No, really. I've forgotten. I know the initials. Mr J. A. Pepperdine on your office door. Everyone calls you Pepperdine.'

'I know. It's James.'

'James,' she said. 'What does the A stand for?'

'Archibald.'

'Archibald?'

'That's funny, is it?'

'Archibald! Of course it's funny.'

He moved a hand to her breast, circled the nipple with his thumb.

'It's a family name. I assure you I wouldn't make fun of any names handed down in your family. Do you mind if I do this while you laugh?' He replaced the thumb with his mouth.

They had done everything. There was nothing left to do and she could hardly believe they would do it all over again. It was a one-off, a spectacular, a carnal cabaret in the dark. Every shape that could be made, they had made it. The trigonometry of sex. She touched her own body as much as she touched his. Hands on the floor, feet on the floor, hands on the bed, feet over his shoulders, hands on the wall. At first she had egged herself on. In for a penny, in for a pound. A phrase from a patient on the dementia ward who repeated it endlessly. She banished it. And was free.

The movements gradually became less frantic, distilled to an essential rhythm. He moved deeper inside. She had a sensation of tunnelling, through him into herself.

His mouth was on her nipple. She stopped laughing. 'Oh my God,' she said.

They lay in the dark again afterwards. She was drifting, thoughts rose and fell like ocean waves. An ice swan filled with vodka. Her coat on the banisters. The sapphire, Niamh touched it, and now it's at the bottom of the bag. Don't lose it. Up and down. Up and down. The see-saw, see-saw. So sleepy. Rania, she had to call Rania and apologise. She had to call Joe.

She sat up in a panic. No, it was okay. He was out with friends. Not expecting to see her tonight.

Pepperdine's breath came slow and deep and suddenly she was frightened. She didn't want him sleeping. She'd done something bad, and she didn't want to be alone with it.

'So I can ask you anything?' He didn't stir so she nudged him and repeated it, louder this time. 'So I can ask you anything?'

'Mmm. What?' He yawned. 'Yes. Feel free.'

What did she really want to know? Relationship history? He'd already told her he lived alone.

'I can't think of anything now.'

'I suppose I could be insulted. I'm so dull, am I?' He rolled on his back.

'I have to tell you something.' Did he already know?

'Okay.'

'I'm engaged.'

'Ah. I see.' He was silent for a while. 'Congratulations.'

'I thought you might already know. I mean, people at work, they know.'

'I didn't.'

She waited but he didn't say anything else.

'I guess I should have told you but this isn't ... you know ... ' It wouldn't have made any difference, that's what she meant. They weren't embarking on a relationship. 'This was ... just sex ... so, I guess ... '

'I won't tell anyone. If that's what you're worried about.'

It hadn't crossed her mind. 'No. I'm not worried about that.'

'It never happened, as far as I'm concerned.'

'It was good, though, wasn't it?'

His hand found hers but he didn't take it, just let the knuckles touch. 'I suppose it was okay.'

'Okay?' She punched him softly in the ribs. 'Okay? You're saying it was *okay*!'

210

'Average.'

She thumped him again and he rolled on top of her. 'I'm glad I didn't know.'

'Can I stay the night?'

'Yes. I want you to. I'm going to the bathroom. And then maybe we should get some sleep.'

When he had gone she remained motionless, staring into the dark. It was haram. So what? She tried to shake it off. She did many things that were forbidden. It was haram. It was a sin. Wrong in so many ways. So what? So what? So what? From now on she would do as she pleased, just like everyone else. She felt for the bedside lamp, groping along the cabinet on her side of the bed. It must have fallen off. Nothing there but a book that she knocked off as well. She crawled to the other side. Where the hell was the lamp? She traced her fingers over the headboard and up the wall, found a switch for the ceiling light.

The overhead light came on and she closed her eyes against the sudden brightness. She opened them and let out a yelp. It was horrific. Under cover of darkness a murder had taken place, perhaps a wholesale slaughter, how else could there be so much blood? It was everywhere. Blood on the sheets, on the pillows, smeared on the lamp now visible on the floor. Blood on the carpet. Blood on the bedside cabinet. Bloody handprints on the wall. It was a crime scene. Blood on her body. She held her hands out in front of her, turned the palms slowly up. More blood. More evidence.

She jumped out of bed. She knew the sheets would be stained but *this* she had not expected. This still from a horror film. She had to get out of here fast. Her heart thumped but she was frozen, didn't know which way to move. She spotted her tampon, half hanging off a chair. He must have thrown it. Or maybe she did it. She looked again at the wall, the dazzling whiteness, the red hands fanned out in a semicircle. If she had a lighter she'd burn the place down.

'What's the matter?' said Pepperdine. 'Sorry to take so long, had a shower, and I thought we might need these.' He held up a pile of folded linen.

Yasmin snatched up a pillow and hugged it, covering herself.

'Preserving your modesty? Fair enough.' If the state of the room disturbed him it didn't show in his face. He was naked and unconcerned, as if nothing untoward had happened here.

'Maybe it's best if I go home,' said Yasmin, edging towards the bedroom door. 'Shower first if you don't mind.'

'You'll feel worse if you run off now. That's my opinion, anyway.' He went to the bed and started stripping off the sheet. 'It's only a drop of blood.'

'More than a drop,' said Yasmin. She threw the pillow at him and he caught it.

'Have your shower while I clear up. Don't run away.'

He slept and she lay next to him on the freshly made bed and could not sleep. She felt terrible. She shouldn't have done it. What a horrible thing she'd done. But Joe had fucked someone else. Not like this. Surely, not like this. What difference did it make? Should she ask him: how was it with that woman? Did it blow your mind? Did you see stars? Did you come so hard your legs gave way?

It had never been like that for her. Not with Kashif. Not with Joe either. Only tonight, with Pepperdine. What did that mean? Only that she wasn't frigid. At least that was one thing she'd learned.

How would it be at work? Would it be awkward between them? It would be, at first. How much awkwardness? What level of embarrassment? How much shame if she caught his eye?

Her thoughts drifted. Ma's yellow sari billowed on the

washing line. Baba's clubs whirled round his head. Arif strummed his guitar, Arif had gone . . . Lucy blew bubbles and a baby's face, laughing, their baby . . . can't remember the baby's name, no there's no baby yet.

An arm wrapped around her and Yasmin shifted her body, settled closer in to the warmth. It felt nice. She didn't feel bad any more. The shame had left her. It had bled out of her all over the bedroom, and she gave herself up to sleep.

HERE SHE IS

It was one of the worst shifts ever. Two agency nurses assigned to the dementia-friendly ward walked out after their first hour on the job. Niamh refused to move across to help out because although she was the most flexible person she knew and more than willing to do everything she was asked, she couldn't put her safety in jeopardy in an understaffed ward of aggressive patients. She was sure that the RCN would back her, if necessary. Julie was white with rage, which seemed to make all the empty piercings in her ears turn red.

Yasmin was exhausted. The dementia-friendly ward was always demanding and beside the staff shortage she'd slept poorly for the last fortnight, since that night with Pepperdine. Guilty conscience. *Guilt is the most useless of all the emotions. The most pathetic. The most self-involved.* Harriet Sangster had ordained it, and Yasmin now knew it was true.

A patient with Creutzfeldt-Jakob, an electrician before losing his life to the disease, kept climbing on chairs and trying to rip down wiring or prise light fittings apart. Two orderlies had to be drafted in to help restrain him. CJD had ravaged his brain and he could speak only a few stock phrases. *We'll have to see about that. In for a penny, in for a pound.* In a few months, perhaps sooner, he would deteriorate physically, even to the point where he could no longer swallow. But today it took two large men to stop him breaking into the fuse cupboard. A female patient with Pick's disease and consequently without inhibition, made lusty and increasingly aggressive attempts to lure the orderlies – preferably both at once – into her bed.

Mr Sarpong had greeted Yasmin like a long-lost friend, the stolen watch forgotten. Thankfully, since his hydrocelectomy, he no longer insisted on removing his pyjama bottoms. He lived with irreversible brain damage from Korsakoff's, and was soon immersed in another narrative of loss. This time his daughter was being held hostage in the utility room or the bathroom or elsewhere on the premises. The last time he saw her, according to Anna, the HCA, was two weeks ago, here in the ward, when she had explained she was going on holiday but of course he didn't remember. His confabulation was typical of Korsakoff's, the way he came up with an explanation to fit the facts at hand. Maybe it's typical of everyone, thought Yasmin, as she examined Mrs Garcia, who lay motionless and open-mouthed.

'You can see it in the eyes,' said Anna, hovering over Mrs Garcia like a new parent over the crib. 'See, Doctor, there, she did it again.'

Yasmin peered at Mrs Garcia's eyes. Old scuffed marbles, with about as much sign of life.

'What did she do exactly?' said Yasmin. Mrs Garcia had advanced vascular dementia and, as far as Yasmin could tell, was beyond any sort of communication. The deep grooves that ran down from either side of her nose bracketed off her mouth, as if to put all words, all language, in permanent parentheses.

'When she narrows the eyes like that she's feeling some pain. Her third time in here, you get to know. Believe me.'

Yasmin did. If anyone got to know it would be Anna.

215

'How long since that's been changed?' said Yasmin, looking at the empty urine bag.

'This morning,' said Anna, 'but she's hardly passing water anyway.'

'Maybe a urinary tract infection,' said Yasmin, 'or kidneys, perhaps. I'll take a blood sample. Thank you, Anna.'

Anna nodded, patted Mrs Garcia's clawed hand and hurried off to stop a patient escaping. Although the doors only opened with a card or code, they were often propped open to wheel in equipment or supplies.

Yasmin looked for a vein. Sometimes with elderly patients the veins were raised like fat green worms burrowing along beneath the skin. With others, like Mrs Garcia, drawing blood from a vein was like trying to light a candle without a wick. Yasmin patted the skin, three cautious little taps that did nothing to alter the waxy hollow of Mrs Garcia's elbow. No point asking her to make a fist. It was up to Yasmin to get the blood pumping. She lifted Mrs Garcia's forearm, raised it up to her shoulder and back down. A faint blue-green line appeared and Yasmin swabbed with antiseptic, inserted the needle and slid a tube into the holder. The wine-dark blood ran quick and rich. When she held a cotton pad over the scratch the blood kept coming and she needed a second pad. Mrs Garcia turned her head on the pillow and looked at Yasmin as if to say: See, I am here, still alive.

'Here she is. Here she is,' said Professor Shah, sweeping out an arm, stopping Yasmin in her tracks just outside the ward.

He had never before paid her the slightest attention. 'Were you looking for me?' It seemed highly unlikely. He wasn't in the habit of seeking out junior doctors. Nor did he make many appearances on the ward. It was universally known and accepted that Professor Shah, because of his research and teaching commitments and his other work at very expensive private care homes, could only rarely entangle himself with patients. He had papers to publish and lectures to deliver from podiums in many countries, and awards that had to be accepted no matter the burdens on his time. Besides he was an absolute angel with the staff, unlike some of the consultants (mentioning no names) who were unreasonably demanding. And if, as inevitably happened from time to time, a complaint was lodged by a relative about the care that mum or dad or grandma was receiving it was Professor Shah who was called in to defuse the situation. He knew exactly which buttons to press, which wires to cut to avoid a blow-up.

'I've been hearing things about you.' Professor Shah looked Yasmin up and down, a full and frank scan from head to toe and back again.

'Oh? That sounds ominous.'

'Not at all. I hear you stood up to a certain lady with dubious opinions. Good for you!' Professor Shah was a celebrity in geriatrics. He was the Omar Sharif of elderly care, and that was official because he had been described as such by an interviewer in an article for the *British Medical Journal*. Yasmin didn't know who Omar Sharif was until she googled him, and saw the photos that looked very much like Professor Shah in a Cossack hat. And now Professor Shah was impressed with her, for some reason she had yet to understand.

'A certain lady?'

'A patient's relative, a sister or aunt or niece – you gave her a dressing-down for being racist. I'm impressed! It's too easy to be faint-hearted about these things, to avoid confrontation at all costs, to be too afraid of giving offence.'

'I didn't really . . . I wouldn't say I gave her a dressing-down.'

'I see I've embarrassed you. Not many trainees have your gift of modesty.' He smiled at her with his heavy eyelids half-shuttered. It was the look of a man who finds himself irresistible. 'You have adequate supervision and so forth? If you need anything my door is always open.'

Professor Shah's office door had always been closed any time Yasmin had walked past. 'That's good to know,' she said.

A VIEWING

'It's perfect,' said Harriet. 'Definitely overpriced, but I'm sure they'll be open to offers. That's the upside of the referendum. Before June it might have gone for even more, but it's absurdly overpriced now.' She gazed coolly at the estate agent. He said the seller was 'very motivated', and went to wait outside in the hallway.

'Do you love it, darlings?' Harriet spread her arms. She'd taken off her camel coat and draped it on the sofa. She wore an elegant cream silk blouse tucked into a pair of tailored black trousers.

'The light's amazing,' said Joe. 'And we've seen so many places where they've put a kitchen in the corner of the sitting room to make it a two-bed flat. Or walled the kitchen off so you don't get the double aspect, and it messes up the proportions of the room.'

It was a beautiful room. The flat, on the top two floors of a slender townhouse, overlooked a broad patch of green cut with a footpath and cycleway. It was in Islington, which should have ruled it out because Joe had agreed to move south of the river, but here they were. At a viewing arranged by Harriet.

'I like the fireplace, and the shutters,' said Yasmin. 'It's gorgeous, but I don't think it's quite right for us. And the location . . .' She looked at Joe for back-up.

'You'd have room to grow,' said Harriet. 'You could easily put two children's rooms in the dormer space, keep the second bedroom as a study or a spare.' She wrapped her arms around Joe from behind and leaned her cheek on his shoulder. 'He'll make a fabulous father, won't he?'

'Definitely,' said Yasmin. 'But this is out of our price range anyway, even if they're open to offers. And we've decided on south of the river actually.'

Harriet squeezed her arms around Joe's chest as if she'd never let go. 'You mustn't worry about finances. I see no point waiting until I'm dead before my money is of any use to you. Yasmin, you agree, don't you? Joseph, your bride doesn't want to live in a damp flat in Camberwell when there's no need for it, *absolutely no need.*'

Harriet dropped them off in Primrose Hill. She had a private view at an art gallery to attend. They sat in the kitchen.

'Sorry,' he said. 'I can see you're angry and I'm sorry. I just thought it was worth a look.'

'I'm not angry.' She smiled and shook her head. Pepperdine. She shook her head again to get rid of him.

'You look pissed off. Are you starting to hate her?'

'Who? Your mum?'

'She means well.'

'I know.' She was dizzy. Everything was black at the edges.

'She gets excited. When she's trying to help, she can be overenthusiastic.'

'It's fine. Really. It doesn't matter.' Another attack. It would pass.

'What is it then?'

A desire to hide in a small dark place. A rising sense of panic.

'Are you okay?'

An impulse to confess.

'Do you have a headache?'

'Yes,' she said. 'A headache. Could you find some paracetamol?'

Why? Why had she done it? To get her own back on Joe? To make things even? She wasn't that low. That petty. For two weeks she'd been trying out different versions of the story. Because if she couldn't explain it to herself, she couldn't explain it to Joe. She couldn't tell him.

At least now she knew how difficult it must have been for him to admit the truth. She understood why he didn't just tell her straight away. It wasn't that easy. She understood him now in a way that wasn't possible before. It would bring them closer. Already had. She knew how it felt when you cheated. She knew it didn't mean you were a bad person. She'd cheated and she wasn't bad.

Although maybe she was. He'd told the truth and she hadn't. Yet. But she would.

She turned on her side and rearranged the cushions under her head. Joe had brought her pills and a blanket and made her lie down on the L-shaped sofa that faced the patio doors. Have a rest, he said, pulling the blanket up under her chin. Sorry, she said, it was supposed to be our fun day off together, and I've got to go home this afternoon. Just rest, he said.

He thought she was angry with Harriet. Maybe she was. In the car on the way back from Islington she said she was writing another memoir. The first had caused outrage because she'd written frankly about open relationships. But these days, she said, the visibility of non-monogamy suggests *a challenge to the dominant assumptions* about the feasibility of lifelong sexual fidelity. It's becoming *virtually the norm* for millennials.

No wonder Joe had slipped. Since infancy he'd had it drummed into him that sex was no big deal. And he'd discovered for himself that it was a self-fulfilling prophecy. He'd had enough of casual encounters, Tinder dates, one-night stands. He *wanted* sex to be meaningful. He *wanted* marriage. He *wanted* lifelong sexual fidelity.

She dozed a little and when she woke they ate the mushroom quiche Rosalita had made for lunch. Then they went upstairs.

He rolled off her and sighed.

'You can just ... go ahead. Really. I don't mind.'

'Not like that,' said Joe.

'Sorry,' said Yasmin.

'You haven't forgiven me.' He propped himself on an elbow and in the low light of the curtained bedroom his eyes looked dark and wet like river stones.

'It's not that. I'm tired. And I'm worried about Arif.'

'The baby? Does your father know yet?'

'No. It's all such a mess. He'll be expecting Arif to slink home with his tail between his legs. It's the middle of November and the baby's due mid-January!'

'Wasn't your mum going to tell him?'

'Exactly!' I will deal with your father, she'd said. But she hadn't done anything, except secretly start knitting baby clothes.

'How's Arif doing? Should I come with you to see him?'

'Thanks, but I think it's better if it's just me and Ma. So we can grill him about how he intends to get his act together.' She'd spoken to Arif a few times on the phone, but only Ma had seen him. Yasmin had been busy with her own problems recently.

'The thing about babies,' said Joe. He interrupted himself to kiss her forehead. 'I see it every day at work. Even when things are difficult, they bring a lot of joy. And it'll be the same in your family. You shouldn't worry. You'll see.'

'I'm sure you're right.' She wasn't sure at all.

'Hey, I called my dad. For the first time since ... I don't know when.'

'How did it go?'

'Okay. Better than okay, actually. Told him I'm engaged and he says to send his love.' He raised an eyebrow. 'Bizarrely, he sounded pretty much like a dad. He's looking forward to meeting you.'

'Joe,' she said, 'that's wonderful! This therapist is really helping then?'

'Yeah. Yes, I guess he is.'

'And did you tell him? You know, about . . .'

He nodded.

'What did he say?'

'That honesty is the most important thing. Being honest with you, and with myself.'

'Of course,' she said, quite shocked at the brazen words that were about to spill from her mouth. 'As long as we're honest with each other we can get through anything.'

VISITORS

Anisah had laid out a tea set on the coffee table: cups and sau-cers, teapot, milk jug, and cake stand, all blue with orange and yellow flowers and pink polka dots thrown in for good measure. The cake stand was filled with glistening sweetmeats, sandesh, ladoo, jelabee.

'Do you like?' She twisted her cup this way and that on its saucer.

'They're gorgeous!' said Lucy. She held her cup aloft and pursed her lips as if she might give it a kiss.

Yasmin was still recovering from the shock of finding Lucy and Arif in the sitting room with Ma. Her first thought had been, What if Baba walks in? But of course he wouldn't finish surgery for another couple of hours. Lucy, in the flesh, was even more round. With her legs tucked sideways under a cushion on the sofa, she looked less like a series of circles and more like one spherical object. There was nothing heavy about her, though; despite her pregnancy she looked to Yasmin more like a pretty balloon that might float up any moment into the air. Arif anchored Lucy by the left hand.

'Yasmin, do you like?' said Ma.

'Yes, Ma. British Heart Foundation?'

'Oh, no,' said Ma, as though the question was ridiculous. 'Oxfam.'

'I was just telling about how we first met,' said Lucy. 'Me and Arif,' she added for the avoidance of doubt.

'*Caravan's* Pool Hall,' said Arif. He and Lucy wrinkled their noses at each other. 'It's Kavanagh's, but— '

'I always called it Caravan's by mistake!'

Ma laughed with her hand over her mouth, surprised and delighted by this romantic titbit.

'What made you fall for Arif?' asked Yasmin.

'Let's see,' said Lucy. She sat forward, and Arif released her hand to show Lucy had a free rein to say what she pleased. 'Okay, well, he's kind. He's a kind person. I saw that straight away. And he's a really good listener. You know, a lot of men can't even pretend they're listening, have you noticed? They just glaze over until they get a chance to talk about themselves. But Arif's not like that.'

'Like what?' said Arif. 'Sorry, what did you say?'

'Like ... oh, ha!' She rolled against him. Her hair, freshly bleached, had lost its broad stripe. 'And he's funny! When we started getting serious, after a couple of months, something like that, you know what else I really liked about him? His ambition. He's so ambitious for his future, our future now, and I've always been, you know, just one little foot in front of the other, and I really respect how he's got big plans and everything.'

Lucy gazed adoringly at Arif; Ma did the same. Arif, sandwiched between them on the sofa, sat up straighter to meet these high expectations. He put his arms round the two women's shoulders and looked at Yasmin as if to say, what do you think of me now?

Yasmin mouthed the words silently, *Bun Buns.*

Behind Ma's head, Arif raised a middle-finger salute at his sister, but he smiled at her as well.

'What about you?' asked Yasmin. 'Do you enjoy your job? Will you go back to work after maternity leave?'

'I'm lucky because I do enjoy it, even though I just fell into it when I left school and I thought it would only be temporary but I'm still there. I was going to study to be a dental hygienist, you have to get a diploma, two-year full-time course, and Norman – my boss – said he'd definitely hire me back as a hygienist when I qualified. But then my mum went on long-term sick and Nana's retired. So! And now the baby's on her way ... but I still want to get qualified when I can.' Lucy brimmed – practically bounced – with enthusiasm.

Yasmin's heart went out to her. Lucy was pretty and warm and vibrant. She clearly worked hard and supported her family. Her career plan was so much more sensible than Arif's vague ambitions that were really no more than longings and dreams.

'I'm sure it'll work out,' said Yasmin.

'I just really like teeth,' said Lucy, showing off her own perfect set.

'Teeth are very important,' said Ma. 'How would we manage without teeth?'

'Exactly,' said Lucy. 'That's exactly how I feel!'

'I will take care of baby when you go for studies,' said Ma. 'And your mother and grandmother will also take care.'

'Thank you,' said Lucy. 'She's a lucky girl already this baby, with so many people to look after her.'

'What about me?' Arif tipped his head to lean against Lucy's, his black hair against her white-blonde. 'Do I get a turn at looking after my own daughter?'

Everyone laughed. Laughter filled the room and Yasmin was suddenly buoyant with love for this baby, her niece, this blameless, hapless creature. Joe was right, a baby, any baby, always brings joy.

'I see we have visitors.'

They hadn't heard the front door opening, or the click of Baba's brogues down the hall. The room fell silent. Yasmin froze. Ma jumped to her feet, cup and saucer clattering. Lucy held her stomach between her palms, and Arif hugged her close to him.

CONSULTATION

'An antacid will not harm the baby,' said Baba. 'Keep a bottle of Gaviscon handy and this will help with heartburn and reflux.'

'I will then,' said Lucy. Her face, which had whitened at the sight of Shaokat, was beginning to pink up again. 'I didn't want to take any medicines, you know, to be on the safe side.'

'A wise approach,' said Baba. 'But it is unnecessary to suffer indigestion. Any morning sickness? Usually it passes by this stage in the pregnancy.' He sat on his straight-backed chair facing directly towards Lucy and continued the consultation he had initiated straight away, as if one of his patients had dropped by unexpectedly at home. His manner was professional and courteous and increasingly put Lucy at ease.

'Only the first couple of months so I was lucky because La-La says – that's my granny – she says she had it bad with Mum. And my mum had it bad with me and when she was eight months gone . . .'

Lucy rattled on, a long tale that began with high blood pressure and a pre-eclampsia scare and segued into a description of her father and his job cleaning the windows of high-rise buildings that made him sound like a trapeze artist, which was possibly an under-dramatisation given how things turned out.

Ma sat with her head bowed. She wanted to make more tea but had been deterred by a look from her husband from providing distractions from the interview now taking place. Even by her own standards Anisah's outfit today was preposterous. She wore mint-green leggings under a candy-pink striped dress. Over the dress she'd layered a white jumper cropped at the point where her waist, if she had one, would have been. To this ensemble she had added a sleeveless cardigan, loosely woven out of some kind of rough khaki-coloured fibre. It looked like it was knitted from garden twine. Yasmin watched Ma tangling her fingers in the long string of amber beads that hung down to her stomach. Why couldn't Ma dress like a normal person? Despite the seriousness of the situation the old question arose automatically.

Arif sat with his fists clenched on his knees. He stared into the middle distance and by the way he stuck out his jaw Yasmin saw that he intended to look tough and determined. His Adam's apple bobbed up and down as he swallowed. It emphasised how scrawny his neck was, how easily it would snap.

Lucy was still talking, lulled by Shaokat's questioning into a sense of security that Yasmin – and surely Ma and Arif – knew to be false. Baba was too dignified, too much a gentleman, to be anything other than polite to a pregnant young woman, a stranger in his house. Besides, he disliked agitation, excitement: he would assess the situation calmly without indecent haste, reach his conclusions and deliver his verdict.

'I've got a photo in my purse,' said Lucy, reaching for her handbag. 'Here he is, that's my dad.' She passed the photograph to Shaokat. Ma's lips moved silently as her fingers worked the amber nuggets of her necklace as if they were prayer beads. Baba inspected the photo then took off his bifocals.

'Such a tragedy,' he said. 'Your father looks like a fine young man. Actually, window cleaning is the most dangerous profession – if I may use that term – in the UK.' He spoke in ruminative tones. The investigations had closed but the deliberations were ongoing. 'I have a patient who fell from his ladder and spent nearly a year in a wheelchair as a result. He was worried about his future insurance premiums after he made a claim – they were already sky high. I did a little research at the time, and according to the insurance industry it is more dangerous to be a window cleaner than anything else, including being a soldier, policeman or fireman.'

Lucy's lower lip wobbled. 'I'm so proud of him. I wish I'd known him. I was only a baby when he died.'

'As I say, a tragedy.' Baba, still seated, gave a stiff-backed bow. He had on his darkest brown suit and in the failing light of the late afternoon it looked almost black.

Yasmin thought she should switch on a lamp or two. If she got up now and circulated around the room, making conversation, drawing the curtains, bustling and prompting Lucy and Arif out of the front door then – what? – what would that achieve? The question was, in any case, pointless. Yasmin was as paralysed as Ma and Arif, waiting for Baba to make his move.

Baba stood and put his glasses on again. The lenses glinted darkly as headlights from a passing car swept across the room. Yasmin tried to read his expression but all she saw was her own reflection, two distorted images with huge heads and tiny bodies, one in each lens. The headlights vanished, the noisy rabble of the engine chasing behind and all was in shadow.

Baba switched on a lamp. 'Lucy, it was a pleasure to meet you. Arif, I will see you in the front room now.'

UNBLEMISHED INNOCENCE

'Do you think he liked me?' Lucy's eyes were huge with antici-
pation. 'Did I do okay?'

'Oh, yes!' said Ma.

'Definitely,' said Yasmin. She had expected Arif to put up
resistance to being summoned by Baba into the front room.
Arif could have refused, could have told him to say whatever he
had to say in front of Lucy, could have walked out of the house.
Instead he followed Baba without a word, hitching his beltless
jeans with sudden vehemence. They slid back to his hipbones
before he reached the door.

Ma's head moved in mysterious ways. Lucy explored the contours of her stomach. The three women sat in silence, straining
to hear what was happening between the men.

After a minute or two Yasmin said, 'Sounds peaceful enough
through there.' You could only hear their voices by concentrating hard, and then only faintly. Perhaps a peace deal had been
struck. Perhaps Baba had decided to accept what could not be
changed. Maybe Arif had given assurances, made promises
about his future, even apologised for things in the past. The
unalterable fact and unblemished innocence of the baby had
performed a miracle and healed the rift!

'She's kicking,' said Lucy. 'Give me your hand, there, just there!'

Ma, with her hand beneath Lucy's jumper, closed her eyes and smiled. 'This little baby girl is strong. Yasmin, come and feel.'

Yasmin knelt by the sofa and Ma made space while Lucy guided Yasmin's hand. 'Oh,' said Yasmin, and again, 'oh!'

Arif's voice grew louder and drifted into the sitting room, no discernible words, but the tone was unmistakable. Lucy pulled her sweater back over the stretch panel of her maternity jeans.

'Have another ladoo,' said Ma to Lucy, putting one on a plate.

Baba's voice came now, a low rumble like a distant earthquake.

Yasmin pushed the tea set aside and sat on the coffee table to stay close to Lucy who, faced with the greasy orange ball of sweetmeat, had begun to look nauseous. Yasmin eased the plate from her fingers.

Arif's voice rose again. The words remained indistinct but the anger was audible in the silences that chopped up every sentence: thud, thud, thud.

'Did I do okay? Honestly?'

'You were brilliant and he definitely liked you. I could tell. Arif hasn't been getting along with our father, that's all. If they're arguing that's nothing new.' It was false reassurance but she didn't know what else to say.

'Thank goodness,' said Lucy. 'Arif thought he might go mad about the baby, but he just sat there and asked me loads of questions about due dates and antenatal classes and everything, didn't he? I kept saying to Arif, you think he'll be all uptight and everything but you never know, he might be thrilled he's got a granddaughter, or will have soon.'

Ma shrugged herself out of her macramé sleeveless cardigan. She showed it off to Lucy. 'See, I knitted. But now I knit for baby, soft-soft wool only.'

BE QUIET! LET ME SPEAK!

Ma jumped up. All was silent.

They obeyed Baba's order as if it had been directed at them. Tears welled in Lucy's eyes.

'It's all right,' said Yasmin. 'It'll be okay.'

'Should we go in there?' Lucy whispered.

'No, there's no need,' Yasmin whispered back. She forced herself to speak in a normal voice. 'They won't be much longer, I'm sure.'

'You are family now,' said Ma, shuffling her bottom along the sofa, tucking in closer to Lucy. 'We are family. The blood is there. He will give his blessing.' Her voice was thick with hope and stubbornness. The emotion of the moment made her break into Bengali. 'Bhalobashar nouka pahar boie jae.'

Lucy gazed into Ma's face as if she knew exactly what she'd said.

An almighty crack rang out from the front room. A fist hammered down on the table? A heavy object dropped from a height? A head slammed against a wall? Ma and Lucy held onto each other. Yasmin hugged herself.

The door opened and Lucy shrieked such a high-pitched shriek it was barely audible. The door stood open but long seconds passed before Arif materialised. He had a gash across his forehead. His right eye was already beginning to swell and close.

LOST

Shaokat had removed his jacket. His shirt, sweat-soaked at the armpits, had ridden out of his trousers at the back. He paced up and down the sitting room with long strides and abrupt turns as if thwarted suddenly by an unexpected wall.

'I will not tolerate it,' he said, not quite shouting. 'I have tolerated too much.'

Ma sat on the sofa next to Yasmin and wept silently, her plump cheeks all shiny and red. She massaged her mint-green knees as if they had begun to ache unbearably.

'You are all making a fool of me in my home! Is that how it is? Laughing behind my back.'

Yasmin opened her mouth to protest but he looked at her with such tightly wound fury that she closed it again. When Arif had come in with the wound on his forehead, his eye beginning to puff and darken, blood trickling down and over the bridge of his nose to one side of his mouth, all he said was let's go, to Lucy. He wouldn't let Yasmin take a proper look at the gash, raising his arm to fend her off. He even pushed Ma away. Lucy trembled visibly but to her great credit hugged both Yasmin and Anisah and thanked them even while Arif pulled her away.

'He came at me, do you understand?' Baba stopped by the

radiator, his soaked shirtsleeves steaming in the updraught of hot air. 'You understand, Mini. You saw how he was with the clubs. It was my head that nearly got cracked. You remember. You saw how close it was.'

Yasmin nodded dumbly. Her heart beat too fast. When Baba became agitated, when he was pushed too far, it was a terrible thing to behold. That ever-present threat, the one she thought she couldn't name – it wasn't so mysterious. It was this: Baba's rage. It had been building for a long time because of Arif's irresponsibility, his laziness, his lack of respect. And getting his girlfriend pregnant would have been bad enough, but this ... the way Baba found out, by accident, the secret they'd all been keeping from him ... was the final straw.

Shaokat resumed his striding. Yasmin snuck a look at Anisah, still weeping, saliva bubbles popping softly on her lips.

'The boy came at me. Like this.' He lunged forward, arms swinging, eyes bulging behind his spectacles. 'I protected myself. Like this.' He felled his assailant with a lightning-quick strike. 'His head struck the corner of the desk.'

It was the second time Shaokat had given this demonstration, but Anisah cried out as if the actual deed had been committed in front of her eyes. 'At least you should take to hospital,' she said, lifting her sweater to rub her nose and hide her face.

'Hospital?' roared Shaokat. 'There are two doctors in this house!' He threw the words down like a winning hand.

Even from her fleeting assessment, Yasmin was confident the cut would heal itself. No need to sit for hours in Accident and Emergency. Head wounds just bled a lot. Baba must have looked and reached the same conclusion. Arif would have a black eye for a couple of weeks and a scar that would take some years to fade.

There are two doctors in this house. No need for hospital.

But he meant so much more than that.

Against the odds – incalculably large – he had become a doctor. His daughter had become one too. What he had started she continued. He held the winning hand. And she was his ace.

'He will never set foot in this house again, do you hear me? I forbid it. Do you understand?'

'No,' said Ma. Her face when she pulled the jumper down was set in its most stubborn cast. 'I do not understand. Your granddaughter also you will forbid?'

Shaokat at last sat on his chair, his posture stiffened, which Yasmin took as a good sign. He was calming down. All that loose-jointed ranting was frightening. He was regaining his bearing and dignity.

He didn't answer the question immediately and Yasmin wanted to say something on the innocent child's behalf. She should say something about Arif too – he was hardly more than a kid, although that was really the problem. That haunted look in his good eye. But if she said anything now perhaps it would only stir things up again.

She held her tongue.

Baba tucked his shirt into his trousers, accomplishing the manoeuvre without altering the straight line of his back.

'Arif is lost,' he said. His voice was contemplative, heavy with regret. 'He is no longer my son. I have no son and no grandchild.'

Ma's amber beads swung as she heaved herself to her feet. 'If he is not your son,' she said quietly, 'then I am not your wife.'

Later, lying on her bed, Yasmin listened to the sounds of cupboard doors opening and closing, the squeak of drawers, the muffled thumps that signalled Anisah pretending to carry out her threat to leave her husband.

Where will you go? Baba, clearly, did not believe she was capable.

I will go.

Yes. But where? Mumbai, to your sister? Or to the one in Virginia?

I will go.

Then better pack your bags.

If I leave I will not come back.

Ma had been staging theatricals in her bedroom since then and Yasmin, on her bed with her textbooks, kept trying to interpret every sound. There was no dinner. No enticing smells drifting up the stairs. The house smelled of air freshener, Yardley's lavender water, a memory of fried chillies, a whisper of cardamom and – beneath all that – something else that smelled like sadness but was probably carpet dust.

Ma stopped banging around. Yasmin crept out of her room and stood on the landing listening to the hum of the house, the water knocking in the pipes, settling down. She tiptoed across the landing to the white wooden banisters that ran along from the stairs to the airing cupboard. Her parents' bedroom was dark.

Back in her room she extricated a book from her black leather saddlebag. She sat cross-legged on the bed with the book resting on her knees. She burrowed into it and it carried her far away.

'I am happy to see you are studying.' Baba stood at the end of her bed.

She had been lost, but she came back quickly. 'Yes, Baba.' Casually, she laid her forearm across the open pages. Medical texts anchored the duvet at all corners. Yasmin sat in the middle, back against the wall, head a few inches under the shelf. All was orderly. All correct.

'Even in these conditions,' said Baba, 'when your brother cannot control himself. When even your mother is unable to think clearly. You are studying because the exam is so important. This is how I was also. This is how we flourish in this world. I am so proud.'

'Thank you, Baba.'

When he had gone she rearranged herself lengthways on the bed to continue reading the large-print edition of *The Voyage Out*. It was a gift from Mrs Antonova. She wished she hadn't agreed to take the MRCP exam in January. It was only to please Baba. She could have waited another year.

She sank back into the book. Occasionally she surfaced and reassured herself there was no way Ma would leave them. Ma would stay. Leaving would be giving in and she wouldn't do that, she would remain and agitate quietly until Arif and Lucy and the baby were, if not exactly welcomed here, at least allowed.

The next morning there was a note on the kitchen table.

Mrs Sangster kindly is giving me refuge in her lovely home. You can call on mobile any time. I am your loving mother, your brother's loving mother also. Inshallah, I will see you soon.

HARRIET

Her proposal for a documentary radio series on women-led cults through history has been declined by the BBC. She doesn't know the right people there. It's all about who you know, and that used to work in her favour. Not any more. The *New Yorker* turned down her article about liberal guilt. Never mind, never mind. Someone will run it, Harriet is sure. Almost sure.

She is busy enough with a lecture to prepare, and Christmas to plan, and the wedding, and the proofs of The Penis Book will soon be back from the publisher. It needs a title. Though the working title seems to have stuck somehow.

It wasn't so long ago when *she* was the one doing the declining: invitations to speak, requests to write, proposals to front documentaries. Well, she is more than busy. Her old friend will be arriving soon and staying a few days. Or many. Then again, she might not show up. You never knew with Flame.

Anyway, Anisah Ghorami is keeping her on her toes. When Anisah attended the salon, Belinda asked if she would teach her to cook Bengali food. Rachel Tyler said she'd love to learn how to wear a sari and Anisah promised to show her. Emma Carmichael expressed interest in the rituals of Islamic prayer. Emma has dabbled in several religions. What she's really looking for is a cult, without the punitive financial implications. Dear Emma, what a lost soul . . .

She is losing her train of thought. What was she thinking about? Oh, Anisah has her on her toes! In the four weeks since she moved in, there have been five gatherings to arrange. Harriet made it clear: Anisah should not feel under *any* obligation. No more than those Salonistas feel when they toss out 'we *must* do lunch' to people they'd cross the road to avoid. But it has been fun. The house has been busier, and all the better for it. Rosalita is appalled. She says some terribly racist things, but Harriet reminds herself to be gentle, it's not her fault she's ignorant. Anisah is welcome to stay as long as she likes. Her husband is an ass.

And it's been a welcome distraction from this onerous task Harriet has set herself of adding to her memoir every day. Even if no more than a single line. There should be no excuse for not managing that.

Here she is, and an hour has passed and what has she put on the page? Nothing. Not a single word. Not a doodle. Not even a dot.

Joseph is still seeing the Hungarian but says nothing about the sessions. He's become very secretive. It has to be something to do with the Hungarian, or maybe . . . maybe Joseph is having second thoughts about Yasmin.

Harriet looks at herself in the dressing-table mirror. Her eyebrows arch. Her cheekbones are delightfully angled, but the skin beneath the chin is beginning to sag. She turns her head for a side view. Taps the offending droop with two fingers. Yes, perhaps Joseph is getting cold feet. Perhaps that's why he's still seeing the Hungarian, to discuss his feelings about getting married to this girl. It would be awkward, to say the least, if he called the whole thing off, especially with Anisah Ghorami residing on the floor above for who knows how long.

But he can't *still* be discussing Neil with the therapist. How much could there be to say about an absent father? And to what conceivable end? For what purpose?

Her mind is wandering all over! She must write something, if for no other reason than to gain her freedom for the rest of the day. Where did she leave off? Oh yes, she was writing about Daddy, how good he was at compensating for his wife's chilliness towards their sole surviving child.

Most nights, Daddy slept in a guestroom and Harriet, when she woke and couldn't get back to sleep, tiptoed down the landing and slipped into bed with him. He never minded. He was always happy to rub her ear. There was no trouble that could not be vanquished by the steady stroke of his thumb on her lobe. Occasionally his bed was empty and then she listened outside Mother's door with a knot in her stomach. Mostly she heard nothing. Once or twice she heard him snore. Once or twice she heard other noises, as if he was in pain.

She misses him. She will miss Joseph.

Harriet slides the A4 pad into the drawer. She does not want to write anything today.

OTHERING

'So, tell me,' said Rania, as the waiter led them to the table. 'I want an update on everything. They'd seen each other a few times since the day in the adventure playground, but with other school friends, at Rania's parents' house when Rania required back-up at a family do, and once with Joe and a work colleague of Rania's when they went ten pin bowling. Of course, Rania beat everyone hands down. Today was the first opportunity for a heart-to-heart. Yasmin had tried to apologise for her behaviour in the playground but Rania insisted there was no need.

'Where do I start?'

The restaurant was 'Balkan fusion' and called Orient. Only in Shoreditch, as Rania said. The kitchen opened to the dining room as if cooking was a kind of spectator sport. Blue flames glowed beneath iron grills and dripping meats spurted showy plumes now and then when the fat caught alight.

'What about your ma? Gone home yet?' Rania had done her make-up differently. Her eyeliner, dark shimmery green, was drawn in two defiantly thick lines above and below the eyes. The lines met at the outer corners and winged up. It was bold and she got away with it.

'Still at Harriet's. It's crazy. Over four weeks! Does she think she can live with Harriet permanently?' A few days ago, Yasmin had arrived at the house to find Anisah giving a cookery lesson to a coterie of Harriet's friends. They gathered round the six-burner stove while Anisah worked skillets and saucepans and vats of boiling oil in which samosas or bhajis sizzled and crisped.

'Harriet doesn't mind?'

'I think she likes it. She likes showing Ma off to her friends.' Yasmin described the cookery class. She told Rania about Ma's demonstration to an eager audience of how to put on a sari. About an excruciating dinner party when Rosalita became increasingly agitated and finally incensed by Anisah's attempts to help. About an impromptu Indian head massage requested by Harriet and performed with alacrity by Ma, who made up the manoeuvres as she went along.

'Alhamdulillah!' said Rania, laughing. 'You've found your sense of humour again. But now my eyeliner is getting smudged, which is a total disaster. Let me get my mirror out and check.'

'Listen to this,' said Yasmin, 'Harriet was in bed with a bad cold, this was maybe five or six days ago. Ma wants to take a bowl of soup up to her and I try to stop her because Harriet has loads of Indian erotica on display around the room. Ma says no. I say I'll take it, and we end up in a wrestling match. The soup ends up all over the floor.'

'No! So Harriet went hungry? What happened then?' Rania's eyeliner pencil hovered beneath her eye.

What happened was Ma was as stubborn as ever. Yasmin stayed in the kitchen worrying about how shocked Ma would be by the illustration based on a temple sculpture of 'a couple at foreplay', the man's erection the size of his arm; by the array of Shiva lingams; the mural fragment depicting a complex love knot; the painting of a jackal-faced homunculus using his phallus to beat a drum. Yasmin remembered more and more items in the collection and began sweating on her mother's behalf, but when Anisah returned she was unperturbed, quite serene as she tidied up.

'That's hilarious! But seriously, it sounds as though Harriet treats your ma like a pet.'

'I keep thinking the same thing! I'm glad it's not just me.'

'Or like a domestic servant,' said Rania. 'You know, the soup and everything.'

'Oh, no! That's not it. Although Rosalita sometimes looks at her very suspiciously, as though Ma's auditioning for her job.'

'Okay, well, it's definitely orientalism. It's patronising and reductive,' said Rania. She paused to complete the restoration of the jade-green lines around her eyes. 'It's exotification, which is inherently devaluing, potentially misogynist and shaves uncomfortably close to racism.'

'She's not that bad!'

'Maybe,' said Rania, without sounding convinced. 'Let's give her the benefit of the doubt. But the least you could say about it is that she is othering your ma.'

'Fine. Agreed. Although I also have to say that at the least my ma *is* very other, from another planet sometimes never mind another culture.'

'Harsh! But let's order. I'm starving.'

'Me too.' She looked around for a waiter. The restaurant, which had been quiet when they'd come in, was full. Several office Christmas parties with Christmas crackers next to each cutlery set. Plates of skewered mixed meats and rice sailed tantalisingly close to their table as a waiter passed by.

'Let's order lots and share everything,' said Rania.

'The kuzu tandir is *so* good!' Rania put her fork down. 'Now, tell me about Arif. How's he doing? Any sign of your father coming round?'

'Coming round? I wish! I've no idea what to do, how to fix it.'

'Is it your responsibility?'

'There's isn't anyone else.'

'And Arif?'

'Baby's due mid-January and he *still* hasn't got a job. He says he wants to work in television now. That's his brilliant plan.'

'He wants to be an actor? I guess there are more parts for Asians and other minorities these days, but—'

'Not acting. Producing and directing.'

'Oh, well, forget it. That's very white.'

'How do you know?'

'I'm not just an immigration lawyer, Yasmin, I specialise in discrimination issues as well.'

'And I'm not just a doctor, I specialise in majorly fucked-up family issues as well.'

'Look on the bright side,' said Rania. 'If everything's fucked there's nothing else that can go wrong. Am I allowed to ask how things are going with Joe?'

'Of course you are,' said Yasmin. 'I'm sorry I bit your head off when . . . '

'Forget it. Honestly. I have. Or I would have done if you stopped reminding me! What's it like having your ma there when you're staying the night?'

'It's okay. I thought it would be awkward . . . I mean, I pretended to go to a spare bedroom the first few nights. Didn't want to be . . . you know.'

'Disrespectful.'

'But she really doesn't seem to care.'

'And you and Joe, how's it going?'

How should she answer? She looked up at the proudly naked light fittings with orange-filament bulbs. What would Rania say if she told her about Pepperdine?

'It's good. I know you think I'm crazy to forgive him, but—'

Rania cut her off. 'I'm going to be completely honest with

you. At first I *did* think you were crazy. But I've thought about it a lot and I realised I was wrong.' Her amber eyes, framed in glittering green, looked especially beautiful. Rania always wore 'modest' clothes, but sometimes Yasmin wondered if she removed her headscarf, uncovered more, she'd actually look less seductive. 'You love him, for one thing. And he loves you. And if you can only judge a person by their worst action, the thing that perhaps they regret more than anything, then everyone gets a life sentence. That goes against everything I believe in and work for – everyone should get a second chance.'

'Thank you.'

'You're welcome.'

'Could you just say that bit again – about being wrong? I liked hearing that.'

'Don't push it,' said Rania.

FREEDOM

It happened again.

When she went to his office she closed the door behind her. This was the moment she knew. She repudiated this knowledge. *I'm here to discuss a patient, that's all.*

He stood up. He knew the thing that she knew.

The office was insanely hot although he had opened the small portion of the window that wasn't permanently sealed. Sweat glossed the skin above his mouth. His mouth that was neither too full nor too thin. I've called maintenance he said, with a gesture of helplessness. The radiator is intransigent. He came out from behind the desk and she told herself there was nothing unusual about this.

She told him about the patient and he listened, arms folded across his chest, a thirsty look in his eyes.

Yes, he said, I agree with your treatment plan.

She said nothing more.

Is there anything else? He came closer.

Since the night they went to bed they have neither avoided each other nor made eye contact. They have conducted themselves with professionalism and inscrutability.

She shook her head.

He walked to the door and turned the lock.

When he tried to kiss her she backed away. Wait. There is actually something I want to ask you.

Okay, he said. Ask.

Again she shook her head.

I have a meeting in half an hour, he said. And it will take me ten minutes to get there.

The back of her neck was ticklish: excitement or sweat or fear. No, not fear. She was fearless in this moment that she held in the palm of her hand. She kicked off her shoes and reached beneath her dress to roll down her tights. He started to reach for her but she stayed him with a look.

In this moment she is powerful. She is controlling everything. Quickly, she strips off her dress. She smells her own body, the sweat that has moistened her armpits, the conditioner she used this morning, the musky scent of her sex, the cocoa butter on her legs that she hasn't shaved. She stands in front of him in her mismatched bra and pants and they are proof. She offers them to judge and jury as evidence of the unpremeditated nature of the crime.

He licks his lips, an unconscious action that almost makes her laugh. His shoulders rise and fall as his breath slows and deepens. They are standing apart from each other, by the length of a human body at least, but she senses her breath falling in line with his. The lighting is hard, unforgiving, and it makes dark craters of his eyes. Her pubic bone aches. He is going to see her naked. Every imperfection. She has many, and she knows without looking, that the waistband of her skirt has left an imprint around her belly where it dug into the soft flesh.

She is not in control of anything, not even herself.

Take them off, he says. His voice is hoarse. He is unbuckling his belt.

She takes off her bra and slides off her pants and repents how damp they are. Never before has she stood completely naked in front of a man in the full harsh glare of an overhead light. How much foresight and cunning this has taken is clear to her only now. It is terrifying and wonderful to stand in this pitiless office at the end of a long hot shift on the ward, with stubble on her legs, naked, undefended, and mysteriously invulnerable, as if by this very act of self-exposure she has secreted out of harm's way the part of her that is most intimate and valuable.

Now come over here, he says, and she obeys.

The next time it happened she swore it would be the last. *Who am I telling? Can I tell myself something I already know? Are there two of me in here, one highly informed, one entirely innocent?*

She saw him as she crossed the car park on her way to the train station. When he got in his car without a glance in her direction she felt the sting of disappointment. The driver's side window slid slowly down. Her legs were unsteady as she came closer, and then the passenger door opened and suddenly – as if she had been magically transported – she was sitting next to him.

Do you want to talk?

No, she said. Do you?

They stared ahead through the windscreen as the first few scribbles of rain dashed across the glass.

He turned the key in the ignition and she reached for the seatbelt.

When they get to his house she doesn't waste time with questions and he asks nothing of her except to move her body this way or that. She knows it is wrong, that what they are doing is bad, and it feels so good to behave badly with no excuses and just take whatever you want. She is free. She is disgraced, corrupted, debauched. Her back arches, shoulders pressed into the sheets. Her hands clench and unclench. She has dishonoured herself and it is this self-abasement that has opened her up to the furious pleasures of intimacy. She is bad and therefore free. Her grasp is failing, the world is spinning and everything is upside down: freedom leads to abasement, that's the truth. He moves on top of her and she dissolves into her body, which seeks its own verities.

Afterwards, sitting in the back of the Prius, on her way home to Tatton Hill and Baba and the improvised meal they will share while pretending everything is normal, she relived the past hour in her head. The memory was so intense it was contained in a single second, and so expansive it filled an eternity. When the Uber driver turned to prompt her to get out she was startled, and when she opened the garden gate she saw her father's face vanish from the window: he was waiting for her, his good and dutiful daughter. She closed the front door behind her and leaned against it for a moment and closed her eyes.

SANDOR

Joe was on his feet. When he stood up he'd banged his shins hard on the bevelled edge of the Spider table. 'Look, I'm sorry,' he said, 'but this is . . . stupid. It's a waste of time.'

'You're angry.'

'Angry? Of course I'm fucking angry.'

'Okay. Can you just be with the anger?'

'What does that even mean?' His gaze slid towards the door.

Sandor sat back and crossed his legs. He didn't rush to answer. Better to slow things down.

'It means that your default setting appears to be opting out. You would like to leave the session. You're saying you'll quit therapy. I'm suggesting an alternative – stay with the anger, sit down. Let it out.' Sandor smiled up at Joe.

'Fine. Whatever.' Joe slammed his body onto the sofa and despite the deep soft cushions the frame clicked and complained. 'But it's bullshit.'

'What is?'

'Look, I didn't want to be rude but you asked for it. Do you know what I did at work today? I delivered a baby with the umbilical cord tied round her neck. I did an emergency section on a woman with placental abruption. I dealt with an ectopic pregnancy. I did things that *matter*. Do you get that? I am not a victim. What I do is *real*. And you – I'm sorry – you just made up a fucking *theory*. And it's bullshit. It doesn't help at all.' The boy trembled with rage.

'I understand.' The anger disguised the shame. The shame that was too overwhelming in this moment for Joe to allow it to surface. 'I understand,' Sandor repeated. 'You do serious work. Today you saved a life, maybe more than one. And perhaps you fear that if you allow yourself to go down this road of self-knowledge – a road that seems dark and dangerous – you will disintegrate.'

Joe chewed on his top lip. He kept his eyes down. Kindness, in Sandor's experience, was often devastating. It was a great provoker of tears.

'I've worked with sexual addiction for many years and I know how deep the suffering can be. Sometimes the addiction is romanticised and the addict is called a lothario. Sometimes it's perceived as disordered. Or condemned as depraved, or weak-willed and immoral. No matter how it's labelled by the world, the confusion, guilt and despair remain the same. I've worked with addicts who are unable to confront the root cause of their addiction. Sometimes it's simply unbearable, and I do not judge them for that.'

'I *am* able,' said Joe. 'I'm able but . . .' He shook his head.

'For those who are able to confront their past, much pain arises, but the results are always positive.' There had been patients whom Sandor had failed to help. Benjamin Taylor, a compulsive masturbator, had died. It was an accident. Autoerotic asphyxiation: the quest for the petit mort, for oblivion, taken to its logical extreme. Avi Rothman, the rabbi who slept with members of his congregation, who saw no way out but to go to his Maker, although his Maker would not be pleased to see him. Those were names Sandor would never forget. This work too was serious.

'It's so ugly,' said Joe. 'It feels ... obscene. You know? I feel ...' He screwed up his face.

'Defiled? Debased?'

'I feel *insulted*. Like you insulted me and my mother in the worst possible way.'

'Okay. Can you say more?'

Sandor let him get it all out. Last week, their seventh session, they'd focused almost exclusively on the relationship with the mother. Joe had returned to the theme of how he'd been made to feel special. From an early age he'd been her confidant. He'd been the only one she could talk to about his father, and the failed reconciliation attempts that occurred sporadically over the early years. The son was praised for being everything that the father had failed to be. Mother and child would stay up late, talking. Sometimes she cried and said she was lonely. It was a 'privilege'. The rest of the world didn't get to see how vulnerable Harriet Sangster was. He held her as she fell asleep on the sofa, after a bottle of wine. He covered her with a blanket and then he put himself to bed.

The mother disliked the handful of previous girlfriends he'd brought home. She pointed out deficiencies and at first Joe disagreed but quickly came to see she was right. Perhaps, suggested Sandor, your mother doesn't feel threatened by Yasmin. Joe laughed. Harry, he said, doesn't feel threatened by anyone.

Sandor's hunch had been confirmed by every session. It was as clear a case of covert incest as he'd encountered. He'd explained to Joe that this was the term used when a parent turns a child into a surrogate partner but doesn't touch them sexually. Most survivors, he continued, as Joe stared at him in horror, are unaware of this dynamic. Their suffering remains invalidated because they have not been violated physically. While victims of overt incest feel abused, victims of covert incest feel favoured. Special. But being trapped in a psychologically

253

invasive relationship with a parent is noxious and pernicious. Joe put his hands over his ears but Sandor knew he could still hear. The seduction involved is insidious. The sense of violation prodigious but severely obscured. And beneath the mask of privilege lie guilt and shame and rage.

'So that's about it,' said Joe. He drank down the glass of water, knocking it back as if it might put out some fire inside him. He wiped his lips. 'It's gross. Sorry, but it's gross.'

The explanations, of course, had not landed. They rarely did the first time around. All that the patient heard was *incest*. The rest was a blur.

'It's important for me to emphasise,' said Sandor, 'that typically – and certainly, as far as I understand, in your case – the parent has only the best intentions for the child.'

'It's a filthy word,' he said, as if Sandor had been calling him names.

'Indeed,' said Sandor, 'it's a very troubling word. And its usage in this context denotes the seriousness, the far-reaching consequences, of the parent–child relationship. What it does not imply is inappropriate sexual behaviour. There's no conscious sexual feeling on the part of either parent or child.' No need at this stage to point out that the relationship could nevertheless be sexually charged and transgressive. 'The decisive criterion is that the parent–child relationship is used – however inadvertently – to serve the needs of the parent rather than the child.'

Joe shook his head. 'She doted on me.'

'From what you've told me, she leaned on you. Relied on you.'

'So? It's not a crime.'

'In a healthy parent–child relationship, the parent's love is liberating, nourishing, nurturing. When a parent – motivated by loneliness or emptiness or a troubled marriage – makes a child a surrogate partner, the love can feel imprisoning and onerous. Suffocating . . .' Sandor paused. He noted the change in the patient's breathing. 'I'm wondering which of those two patterns sound more familiar to you.' The patient was wedded to the story of his privileged life. But the reality was that being fleeced of a childhood was a grave misfortune.

Joe stared at the art deco desk. A fly buzzed at the window and he turned his head to look. Sandor waited. It was a critical moment in the work. The patient was stuck in the quicksand of delusion and self-condemnation, and it was Sandor's job to help him to free himself. But the patient had to be willing.

Joe looked back at Sandor. He shrugged. Sandor resisted the urge to explain further, cajole. Impose. The work had to be done together or else not at all. That was the difference – the most important difference – between his work and Robert's. Between psychotherapy and psychiatry.

'At least she cared,' said Joe at last.

'Yes.'

'My dad didn't. Neil . . .' The fly smacked against the windowpane three times, buzz-buzz-buzz, three little electric shocks. 'He never gave a fuck. He'd have his girlfriends around when he was supposed to be taking care of me. Couldn't spend one lousy weekend without . . . They got younger and younger as I got older. By the time I was fifteen I thought, Bloody hell the next one will be in school uniform. Then he went up north.' He looked away again, chewing on his lip.

'He abandoned you. For a second time.' It was a readily accessible truth. The father had left. The more damaging truth was difficult to access and more difficult yet to accept.

'I always thought: I'll never be like him. I'll fall in love, settle down. Get married. Have kids . . .' There were tears in his eyes. 'Be faithful.' He laughed. 'Be a good dad.'

The tissue box was empty. Sandor went to the desk and pulled open the walnut-wood drawers. No tissues there either.

Joe rubbed his shirtsleeve across his face. He sniffed. 'Oh God,' he said. 'Sorry. Throwing myself a little pity party.'

'I usually have tissues.' How many tissues had Robert dispensed during the course of his career? Quite possibly none.

Sandor came back to his chair. His knee creaked as he sat down.

'Oh God,' said Joe. The fly buzzed and he twitched as though he'd been stung. 'It's driving me insane.'

'It's very difficult. But we do not gain our freedom until we see the past clearly. This process can be very painful.'

'The fly! The *fly* is driving me insane.' Joe jumped up and ran to the window. He battled with the window lock.

'The key is on the little green pot on the sill.'

'It's gone.' Joe closed the window carefully. He put the key back in the pot and returned to the sofa. 'Even if it's true,' he said, 'what does it mean?' His eyes were red-rimmed but dry. His affect was flat. The fight had gone out of him.

'Not all survivors of covert incest become sex addicts and not all sex addicts have experienced dysfunctional relationships with a parent. But sexual addiction is far from unusual for those who have been trapped in this kind of relationship. Sex addiction is an attempt at separation and self-definition. Does that make any kind of sense to you?'

The boy shrugged. Then he nodded.

'Can you tell me what you're experiencing right now?'

'Not really.'

'Okay. Take some time.'

Eventually, this, delivered in a monotone: 'Why does it matter? Is it relevant?'

'Where did you learn this?' Sandor paused. 'Where did you learn that it doesn't matter what you feel?'

'She cares about me. She's overbearing, maybe ... overprotective, but that's not her fault.'

'It's not a question of fault. Parents do the best they know how for their children. Almost all parents do. And sometimes their best efforts are damaging. We don't seek to blame, only understand.' The most damaging thing was this twisted conception: the warped understanding that his mother's excessive ministrations saved him from a fate far worse. Every beating is an adverse childhood event. But to be beaten *for your own good* is to be scarred for life.

'Sometimes . . .' said Joe, 'I feel . . . sometimes I feel . . .'

'You feel . . . ?' But the boy could not answer. Sandor waited a minute. 'I'm wondering if your mother respects your personal boundaries. How would you describe your coexistence in the same house?'

'I don't know. Fine. It's a big house.'

'She respects your privacy?'

'Sure. She doesn't spy on me. She doesn't hack my phone.'

'She doesn't walk into your bedroom without knocking?'

'Yeah, she does that.'

'She wouldn't walk in on you in the bathroom?'

'It's her house.'

'Meaning?'

'She does what she wants.'

'And if you are in the shower . . . ?'

The boy rubbed his hands over his face. His broad shoulders hunched up by his ears. 'Yeah.'

'Do you think she respects your personal boundaries?'

'Harry doesn't respect boundaries. She breaks them. That's what she does. That's who she is.'

'I see. And who are you? Are you what you do?'

'No,' said Joe, his voice cracking. 'I don't know.'

Thank God it was the last appointment of the day. Sandor was tired. What could one tired old man do to shore up the world?

'How have you been managing? Your impulse control. Have you been coping?'

'Yasmin's mum's moved in.'

'Oh? She's living with . . . ?'

'In the house with me and Harry. Yasmin's there most of the time too.'

'And?'

'And a friend of Harry's. She's called Flame. Last time she was staying she got arrested for chaining herself to a statue at the Tate.'

'I meant, how is it affecting your impulse control?'

'I've been on the apps. I've not . . . nothing's happened, I've not followed through, but . . . '

'You have these apps on your phone? How many?'

'Quite a few.'

'I assume you take care to hide them.' Joe nodded. Addicts knew all the tricks – burying apps inside dull-looking folders, eliminating them from search and suggestion options, hiding them from purchase history. 'Why don't you list them for me? Then perhaps we could talk about how you might feel about deleting them. Even one or two.'

Joe hesitated then reeled them off as quickly as possible: Tingle, Casualx, Pure, AdultFriendFinder, Xmatch, Shagbook, iHookup, e-hookups, NoStringsAttached . . . On it went. A few Sandor hadn't heard of before. It was important Joe faced up to the extent of his compulsion. How much it interfered with his life, with the person that he was or could be.

'Shit,' said Joe. 'That's how I feel. Since you asked. I feel shit. What's the point? What's the fucking point? He halted and took a deep breath. 'Sorry. Never mind. Thank you. I think I know what to do.'

'Delete the apps?' Avi Rothman, at his final session, had thanked Sandor formally for all his help, gone home, eaten dinner, read the Torah, and shot himself in the head with his Ruger LC9.

Joe nodded. But he didn't meet Sandor's gaze.

'Joe,' said Sandor, 'you saved a life today.'

'Two,' said Joe.

'What you do is important in this world. You are important.'

'Sure. Thanks.'

'I'll walk you out.'

'See you next week,' said Joe.

Sandor put a hand on Joe's shoulder. He gripped it. 'You bet. Next week. I'll be waiting for you.'

RESTLESS

The snow had stopped falling and the world through the window had that special stillness, like silence made visible. Yasmin looked over the garden at the black trees edged in white, the shrubs in their lacy shrouds, the diamond gleam of the frozen pond. At work people foretold a white Christmas. Or said that snow now meant no snow on the big day itself.

Joe muttered and turned in his sleep. It was scarcely morning yet. They'd sat up so late, and even afterwards Yasmin had hardly slept.

Joe was still experiencing the abandonment he'd felt as a small child. That's what his therapist said. Joe was in contact with his father now, dealing with it. He thought he didn't need the therapist any more. Yasmin had run her fingers over his appendix scar, across his navel and up to his chest. I'm proud of you, she said.

He asked about Baba. Yasmin stayed in Tatton Hill a few nights a week so Baba wasn't completely on his own. Her bedroom, with its single bed, flat-pack furniture and faded wallpaper was still the bedroom of a child, like the room of someone she used to know. The hours she spent with Baba were excruciating. Your mother is making a fool of herself, Mini. Her stubbornness bears only the bitterest of fruits. She will see. Arif has thrown his life away. He has never understood the value of hard work. He thinks things come easy because he has been given so much. Because he has never experienced hardship, never faced struggle, he does not value what he had, neither can he imagine how difficult he will find it to manage without my support. This girl has dragged him down to her level and he will never find his way back up.

Why can't he be more open-minded? Why does he have to be so hard on Arif?

Joe stroked her hair. It's because he cares. It's because he's frightened. It's because he loves his son.

He has a funny way of showing it.

He does, said Joe.

He does love his son? Or he does have a funny way of showing it?

But Joe didn't answer. He was falling asleep.

They'd talked for hours and hours and it was intoxicating. She exposed herself totally, bared her soul, hidden nothing from him. As soon as he fell asleep the truth came rushing back. She hadn't told him about Pepperdine.

Yasmin leaned her forehead against the windowpane. Her breath steamed up the glass. She hadn't told him yet. She hadn't found the right time. And how could she explain it? It couldn't *just happen* three times. What would be the point, anyway, in telling him? To relieve her guilty conscience? Harriet was so right about guilt. It was self-serving. A way of signalling to herself she must be a decent person, because she felt bad about what she'd done.

'Hey, what time is it?' Joe sat up and rubbed his eyes.

'Early. Go back to sleep.'

'Why are you up? Come to bed.'

When she was under the covers, warming her feet on him, she said, 'Joe, if your mum is fed up of Ma staying here, you've got to tell me. If Ma's outstaying her welcome . . .'

'Bloody hell, your feet are freezing! Trust me, Harriet's more than capable of getting rid of people if she wants to. She's had plenty of experience.'

'It's been snowing again.'

'Has it? Have you been outside making snowmen in bare feet? No, Harry likes having your mum here. I do too. Rosalita's maybe not so keen. She might come to blows with your mother. Found them fighting over a mop yesterday.'

'Oh God,' said Yasmin. 'I don't know why she's always cleaning here. She's never been what you'd call house proud.'

'I watched *Cash in the Attic* with her the other day. She's very good at guessing how much bits of old tat will sell for.'

'I bet she is.'

'Maybe we should take her to furniture auctions when we need stuff for the flat. No new ones coming up, by the way, because of Christmas. It's a good job we moved the wedding to June, don't you think? Imagine if we had to be planning everything now. Harry sticking her nose in is quite useful sometimes.'

'Yes,' said Yasmin. But if Harriet hadn't stuck her nose in in the first place the wedding would be small and simple and easy to plan. 'Joe, when we get our place do you want to do the bedroom like this, in this style? I mean, I like it, but I was thinking of something a bit different.'

'This style? French antiques and wardrobes painted with flowers? You don't think I *chose* this, do you? Harry loves to decorate. And when I say decorate I mean she loves to hire interior designers. No, you can have whatever style you want.'

'Good,' she said. 'Thanks.' It felt like a little victory. As though he'd chosen her over Harriet.

'Better get up.' He turned on his side so they faced each other. He blew his fringe out of his eyes. 'So, listen, do you think your parents will get divorced?'

'Divorced!' She laughed. It was impossible. It had never entered her head. Her parents. Getting divorced? No. Ma would go back to Baba, it was simply a question of when. She kissed him. 'No, you're so sweet but don't worry. There's no way. It could never be like that for them.'

PICKLES

It was only ten past seven when Yasmin went down for breakfast but Anisah was already in the kitchen, pickling. Harriet, at the table, examined layouts for her new book. Her friend, who'd come for a weekend a fortnight ago, sat at the breakfast bar stirring sugar into a bowl of porridge. The sun wasn't up yet but the snow had begun to glitter silver and blue in the garden, promising a crisp and glorious day ahead. In the kitchen all the lights blazed, the underfloor heating warmed the limestone flags to blood temperature, and bunches of holly and sprigs of mistletoe sprouted from the walls.

'Will you like porridge?' said Anisah. 'Or will you like toast?' She wiped her forehead with a tea towel. All six burners were on and both ovens, with an assortment of marrows and squashes set to roast. The kitchen smelled of lemons, ginger and cloves, adding to the festive air. Preserve jars that had been sterilised in pans of boiling water stood in puddles on the countertop among the vegetable peel and seeds.

Since migrating to Primrose Hill Ma had been cheerful and busy, as if abandoning home and husband was nothing out of the ordinary.

'I'll get myself some porridge,' said Yasmin. She hesitated

to sit at the breakfast bar next to Harriet's friend. But Harriet had layouts spread over the table. The part she wasn't using was occupied by splendid wreaths of conifer branches, inlaid with rosehips, seedheads, miniature oranges, gigantic olives and regular-size cinnamon sticks.

The friend was probably in her forties, with close-cropped black hair, burnished skin, and vermilion-varnished lips. She was a performance artist whose work, Yasmin had been informed, explored the notions of transgression, transformation and transcendence. And she was called Flame.

'What time will we go shopping?' Ma said, addressing Flame.

'Two o'clock,' said Flame.

'I am taking her to charity shops for clothes shopping,' said Ma, beaming.

Yasmin winced. Under her apron, Ma wore a shiny blue kameez with gold collar and cuffs. Flame was dressed entirely in black: a polo-neck jumper and leggings, at the ready to commit either burglary or a mime. Difficult to envisage the two of them together on a shopping trip.

'Costumes,' said Flame. 'We're costume shopping.'

'I don't know,' said Ma, giggling.

'Yes, you do. Wardrobe mistress.'

Ma scraped out a vat of molten green lava into a bowl. She was laughing, a little wildly, as if Flame had said something both funny and flattering. Over the past fortnight Yasmin had begun to avoid conversations with Flame. Flame was serious and intense, which made casual interaction impossible. When Yasmin said she'd had a hellish day at work, instead of sympathising – as a normal person would – Flame subjected her to an interrogation about the definition of hell. Ma, though, seemed to enjoy Flame's company. They laughed together at things nobody else found amusing. Flame, right now, was chuckling over her porridge bowl.

'Yasmin, come and look at these pages,' called Harriet. 'Do you prefer the ones with the photographs framed, or is it better like this when the photos melt into white space?'

Yasmin stood behind Harriet and ate a spoonful of tepid oats. The photos were of naked men, full frontal, from thigh to lower torso. New batches had been appearing for the last few weeks and even Anisah, who had initially averted her eyes, no longer found them uncomfortable. They were no more erotic than the photographs in medical texts illustrating gonorrhoea discharge, genital herpes or warts. The lighting was better, the resolution sharper, and the accompanying text based on Harriet's interviews with the subjects rather than anything anatomical or medical. But the most remarkable thing about them was that collectively they became altogether unremarkable. A single penis was bothersome. En masse they seemed weaker, almost pitiful.

'Without frames is better.'

'Bravo,' said Harriet. 'More naked that way. I agree.' She shuffled the pages and inserted a correction in a margin. 'There's something so defenceless, don't you think, about them? The penis has been accorded such power but even the erect penis has *something ridiculous about it*.'

Flame banged her spoon on the counter. 'Try telling that to a woman who's been raped.'

It's happened to her, thought Yasmin. It happened to Flame.

'Absolutely. I don't mean to be unsisterly.' Harriet piled her papers in a messy stack. She was flustered. She shook her head at Flame, as if to say *so sorry*. But when she got up and left the table, she hurried straight to Ma who smiled serenely while dicing a green mango.

Harriet kissed Ma's fat, downy cheek. 'You'll have to teach me. I can't do a thing in the kitchen. It's quite shameful. In fact, I can't make anything or do anything. I can't heal the sick. I can't create beautiful art with my body –' here she looked meaningfully at Flame, '– and I can't make anything good to eat. All I do is spout opinions. Shame on me.'

'Yes, shame on you,' said Flame. Her manner was as spiky as her hair. Still, if she was a rape victim – survivor – it wasn't surprising she was offended by Harriet's comment.

'Oh, no,' said Ma, 'you are my sister. From you I learn many-many things. Also you are writing books. Not many people can do this.'

Harriet smiled, her equilibrium already restored. 'Well, I had better get myself ready. I've a train to catch.'

'Giving a lecture today, no?' said Ma. 'What is it about?'

'Medea – poor Medea, she's a complex character, much maligned, much misunderstood. Monstrous Medea. She *is*, but there's more to her than that.'

Ma beamed. 'Yes? You will tell me later?'

'Of course. Now, where's my bag? Oh, there!' She sailed around the room, collecting items. 'Keys, money, laptop, done!' At the kitchen door she called back to Yasmin: 'Almost forgot! What are your thoughts about save the date cards? I've taken the liberty of having some printed but you must feel free to discard them if you're against. Or if you dislike the design. I won't be offended. You must have whatever style you like.'

'Yasmin will like,' said Ma.

The porridge was cold. Congealed. She scraped it into the bin. She'd lost her appetite. The way things were turning out it was like having an Indian mother-in-law! She was beginning to realise how Baba felt when he moved in with his. Although of course that was the wrong way around, the bride was supposed to go to the groom's family. But the bride's mother wasn't supposed to move in as well! No wonder she was losing sleep, feeling so stressed. The English middle classes don't interfere in their children's matrimonial affairs! Never in her life had she been so wrong.

PALS

A week later the snow had turned to slush. Walking from the train station to Barney's she stood too close to the kerb. A van sped away from the traffic lights soaking her trouser leg in blackish water and ice chips. By mid-morning, when she sat down at a desk in the departmental office the cloth still clung damply to her knee.

'Dr Ghorami, do you have a moment? Jen Stevens, I'm one of the PALS managers.' The woman held out her hand.

The handshake was limp and perfunctory. 'I'm busy, but—'

'I'll be super quick. Just need you to read this letter then sign this form here to acknowledge we've had this conversation and you've received and understood the feedback and that you agree to modify, in future, the language you use when talking to patients or relatives to avoid giving unnecessary offence.' The woman rattled off the words as if they were standard small print. She handed over a clipboard.

'Sorry,' said Yasmin. 'What's this all about?' Thus far in her career she hadn't been involved with the Patient Advice and Liaison Service, because nobody had – until now – complained about her.

'Yasmin, do you have a minute?' Catherine Arnott, of course, looked immaculate in her black and shiny high-heeled pumps. She must have done the sensible thing and changed her shoes at work. Yasmin's bore tidemarks of grit and slush.

'Not right now.'

'No problem, I'll wait.' Catherine sat on the edge of the desk to observe.

Dear Mrs Rowland, the letter began, *I'm sorry if you felt you had a poor experience in our care of the elderly ward when visiting your uncle last month.*

Yasmin scanned quickly down to the end to see who'd signed it: Michael Edgar, Director of Patient Experience.

You entrusted your relative to our care and you are right that you should be made to feel welcome during visiting hours. I understand the incident that occurred with Dr Ghorami caused distress to your uncle and that this, in turn, has caused you great anxiety. It is our intention that all patients and family members are treated with respect and courtesy at all times, and it is never acceptable for a member of staff to 'display open hostility'.

Yasmin's feet suddenly felt heavy, as if they'd been strapped into surgical boots.

To accuse someone of racism is, as you say, a serious allegation. I understand your feelings of anger in relation to this matter, and that you were deeply frustrated by Dr Ghorami's unwillingness at the time of the incident to apologise.

'But I didn't call her a racist. I never used that word. She used it, not me.' She sounded petulant, and nit-picking, as if trying to worm her way out of trouble.

'What we find best in these situations,' the PALS manager began soothingly, 'is to nip it in the bud, take the heat out of it. Or else it just escalates and that's not what anybody wants. We're not saying one side is one hundred per cent right, or anything like that. What we're talking about is feelings. And when someone feels they've been . . . let down . . . it doesn't hurt to say we're sorry you feel like that, and we'll do our best not to let it happen again. Okay?'

Yasmin said nothing. She glanced at Catherine Arnott, who rolled her eyes and shook her head.

'Well, I know you're very busy. If you could just sign the form. Look underneath the letter. Yes, there. It says you acknowledge the incident in question, you've read and understood the letter and agree to undertake sensitivity training at the next available opportunity. The Trust runs them regularly.'

'Her uncle wasn't even there,' said Yasmin. 'How could he have been upset?'

Jen Stevens sighed, as though she'd been forced to explain this many times. 'Yes, Mrs Rowland clearly stated in her complaint that he wasn't actually present, but he became very agitated when she told him about it. Unable to sleep for two nights. Should I leave those papers with you or are you happy to just give me a quick scrawl in that box and then it's all over and done?'

'Happy?' said Yasmin. 'No. I'm not going to sign. If anything, she should be the one apologising.' Professor Shah would back her up. He'd praised her for calling the woman out on her prejudice.

'I'd urge you to reconsider.'

'No,' said Yasmin. 'No way.'

'Arseholes,' said Catherine. She perused the letter. 'It's not even a proper apology. I'm sorry if you *felt* . . . They don't have the guts to stand up to this woman. And they don't have the guts to truly apologise for anything in case anyone ever decides to sue about anything.'

'Maybe I should have signed and got it over with. Probably less hassle for me that way.' Already she was having second thoughts. Maybe she'd been more aggressive than necessary with Mrs Rowland. After all, the woman wasn't abusive, just rude and ignorant. In her six months in A&E, Yasmin had witnessed much worse. One time a drunk who had sliced off the tip of his finger called a nurse a black cunt. The nurse simply walked away.

'But it's the principle that matters!' Catherine dangled the letter between her thumb and forefinger. Then tore it carefully in two.

'Is it?' Perhaps she was in the wrong profession. In medicine you couldn't be so oversensitive.

'Honestly, Yasmin, you've got to stand up for yourself. As my mother always says, never be afraid to create trouble because a troublesome woman is the best kind of woman to be.'

'Maybe your mother's right.'

'Yes,' said Catherine. 'For once.'

BED DEPARTMENT

The ward was dismal with tinsel and the chipped purple baubles that hung from the ceiling. It was cheered, however, by the nurses and HCAs, infected with Christmas spirit and leading the inmates in sporadic outbreaks of festive song. Julie eschewed the singing, but marked her approval by wearing a Santa hat.

The thin blue curtain was drawn around Mrs Antonova's bed. Yasmin lurked outside, suddenly gripped by the certainty that Mrs Antonova had died. Yasmin didn't want to be the one to examine her for the death certificate.

'Either come in or go away!'

Mrs Antonova's voice, as vital as ever, made Yasmin jump.

'Take a good look, pumpkin.' She pointed to her head as Yasmin pulled the curtain aside. 'The wig is with the hairdresser. He said it needs a deep clean, so I asked him to pull the curtain round. You're privileged to see me in all my glory. What do you think?' She offered her crown for inspection.

The top of her head was multicoloured, as if a child had scribbled on it with a bunch of crayons. Scratches and two small lesions, and some kind of weeping dermatitis by the right ear.

'Spectacular,' said Yasmin. 'I'll give you some cortisone cream for the rash.'

Mrs Antonova waved a crabbed hand. 'Don't waste your time. A little itch here and there. So what, at my age!' Every word that began with 'w' carried a shadow of an accent, a ghost of a previous life as the daughter of White Russian émigrés. 'The social worker comes, the occupational therapist, the physiotherapist, doctors, nurses, and now someone comes to nurse my wig. Tcha! What a waste!'

'What did the social worker say? Have they found you somewhere?'

'No room at the inn. Not in the homes the council will pay for. I'm a bed blocker, that's what I am.'

'No, you're not.' That horrible phrase. It wasn't Mrs Antonova's fault she'd been stranded in hospital for months. Yasmin stroked Mrs Antonova's hand, the loose skin shifting like sand beneath her fingers.

'But of course I am!' said Mrs Antonova cheerfully. 'Not for much longer, I hope. Let's talk about something more interesting. Tell me, what happened with your young man?'

'Oh, it's all fine now.' In a low moment, she had found herself confiding in Zlata. She hadn't mentioned details, of course, just said that things seemed so complicated.

'The passion has returned to your relationship?'

'Absolutely,' said Yasmin. It hadn't. Had it been there in the first place? What was passion anyway?

'How are things in the bed department?'

'Fine.'

'Fine? This worries me. When the passion isn't there something is wrong. My third husband, in the bed department, was fine. And he turned out to be a homosexual. Maybe your fiancé is hiding his sexuality.'

She said it with such dramatic flourish, Yasmin laughed. 'That must have been a shock. It's not like that these days. People are open about everything now. Even sex,' she added in a whisper.

273

Zlata rolled her eyes. 'There are three things in life people lie about and that will never change. One is money. Another is the despair and emptiness they feel inside. I'm okay, they tell you. I'm fine.'

'And the third?'

'The third is sex, of course.'

'Probably.'

'Probably, she says! Probably! Listen, pumpkin . . . ' She batted her sparse eyelashes the way she did when she was about to make a request. 'A nip of whisky now and again would be nice. Any single malt would do. A little chat and a nip of whisky and a breath of fresh air. What do you say?'

'Against the rules, I'm afraid. Alcohol's banned by the Trust. And we have to remember your heart condition.' Although it was true that a nip would be fine. If Mrs Antonova was in a nursing home – or even a hospice – she'd be free to make that choice for herself.

'Tcha! It would be a blessing. But I expect I'm asking too much. I'd like to go outside and feel the sun on my skin. Nobody has time to take me.'

'I'm sorry,' said Yasmin. 'I'll take you, I promise.' She'd promised weeks ago, but there was a problem: doctors weren't allowed to wheel patients around. They weren't insured to do it. Yasmin would have to organise a porter, she couldn't just bundle Zlata into a wheelchair and whisk her off on the spur of the moment.

'Ah well, a girl can dream. And will I be receiving a wedding invitation?' She said it teasingly.

'Of course. I'd love you to come.'

Mrs Antonova laughed. 'Well, in that case you better hurry up. I might not be available for very long.'

PLAY BALL

'Professor Shah wants to see you, Yasmin. He said he'd be on the dementia ward. If he's not there go straight up to his office.' Yasmin looked up from her paperwork. The way the light fell on Niamh it burnished a bright white halo in the red-gold hair.

'Fine,' said Yasmin. 'Thanks,' she added when Niamh lingered.

'Saw you this morning. You and your fiancé. Kissing each other goodbye in the car park.'

'Okay,' said Yasmin. Pepperdine was walking towards them, which made her jittery for no reason at all. 'Anyway, thanks for the message.'

'Honestly, I wasn't trying to break you two up. Just thought you deserved to know the truth.'

'Right, thank you, Niamh.'

'I'm really pleased for you. Really, I am. If you've got through it then you're obviously meant to be together. Lots of couples wouldn't survive something like that.'

'Ah, just the person I was hoping to find,' said Pepperdine.

Yasmin lowered her eyes.

'Me? I'm all yours.'

Yasmin looked up to see Niamh jutting a hip at him. He had a nick on his jaw from shaving, and a single bright spot of blood on the collar of his shirt. The beat that her heart skipped was only because of that spot. Blood on the carpet. Blood on the walls.

'How are you getting on?'

'Fine,' said Yasmin. 'Fine. On my way to see Professor Shah.' She smiled a foolish smile and got up.

Niamh touched Pepperdine's arm. 'We were just talking about her fiancé. Saw them canoodling in the car park this morning. They're so in love!'

Yasmin kept smiling as she walked.

Why did Niamh have to stick her nose in? Stay out of my business! Don't go around telling people things about me and Joe. Don't tell Pepperdine I'm ... I'm ...

At the door of the dementia-friendly ward she stopped to catch her breath. Don't tell Pepperdine what? That I'm in love with Joe?

'Excellent timing!' Professor Shah came out before she could go in. 'Now, I hear you wouldn't play ball with Jen Stevens yesterday. Could I encourage you to do so?'

'Oh,' said Yasmin. 'Yes, but it's—'

'It's the way we like to do things here. It's the sensible approach.' His heavy-lidded eyes gave him a self-satisfied air. Like a lion presiding over a carcass, having eaten his fill.

'No, I know, but you see in this particular instance it's different because ...' She struggled to get it out. 'I don't believe she's owed an apology. Mrs Rowland, I mean. You said I'd done the right thing.'

Professor Shah massaged his chin. Despite the bare-below-the-elbow policy he wore a fat gold watch with multiple glinting dials. 'The letter of apology has already been sent. I'm asking you now to be a team player and sign the forms acknowledging your mistake and undertaking to attend the appropriate training course.'

'Really? Sensitivity training? I wasn't rude to her, not really. I didn't call her racist. I didn't use that word. She did. You said I'd done well to stand up to her.' *I'm impressed!* That's what he'd told her. *It's too easy to be faint-hearted . . . too afraid of giving offence.*

'Allow me to give you some advice. One has to pick one's battles. That's all I'm going to say. Do we understand each other now?'

Yasmin nodded. From the corner of her eye she saw Anna waiting. Yasmin smiled at her to let her know she was free.

'Excuse me for disturbing.' Anna addressed her apology to Professor Shah then turned to Yasmin. 'Mr Babangida has something wrong. Can you look at him please, Doctor?'

'Yes, I'll come with you.' She was more than happy to get away.

But Professor Shah decided to grace the ward with his presence again. He twinkled at Anna. 'You lead the way.'

'It boosts morale,' he murmured to Yasmin, 'when the Department Head pays attention to the HCAs.'

Anna clutched her bosom and took a couple of steps backwards as if in the presence of royalty. She all but curtseyed as she turned. Professor Shah was considered by all to be charming. He exuded authority. A woman with a belly like his, thought Yasmin as she trailed behind, would be a figure of fun. For a man, of course, it was different and they could gain a belly without losing respect.

Mr Babangida had Alzheimer's and had been admitted with malnutrition and dehydration. His son who lived with him did his best, but had struggled to get him to eat and drink.

'And how are we today?' Professor Shah deployed the loud stoic tone he favoured for speaking to patients. He sat on the edge of the bed. Mr Babangida was startled. He pulled the bedclothes over his face.

277

Yasmin checked the notes. Putting on weight. Good. She checked the drip. No problems there.

'I think he has pain,' said Anna, massaging the top of her left arm. 'Here, that's where he's feeling it.'

With coaxing from Anna, Mr Babangida submitted to Professor Shah's examination. He moaned and rolled his eyes but in this ward groans and strangled cries always played into the hubbub. A patient wrestling to form words could sound anguished. And wails most commonly signalled not physical pain but despair.

Mr Babangida's moans grew louder.

'Agitation and restlessness,' said Professor Shah, the examination over. 'Some visual disturbance, possibly hallucinations, leading to distress. I'll give him something that will help.' He stood up and nodded to Anna. 'Nothing to worry about, nothing physical. But you were right to flag it up. You HCAs are our eyes and ears. Good work!' He began writing out a prescription.

Yasmin looked at Mr Babangida's long bony fingers gripping the sheets. His head was entirely bald and, despite the weight gain, his face sharply contoured. He had stopped making a noise but mouthed his discomfort silently. She looked at Professor Shah, his bouffant dyed hair swept into a quiff. Puffed up and phoney.

Anna thanked Professor Shah. She shifted her weight side to side and looked worried.

'Okay if I leave this with you?' Professor Shah handed the prescription to Yasmin.

The prescription was for olanzapine, an antipsychotic. It would help keep Mr Babangida quiet; that was certain. 'What about his arm?'

'Nothing wrong with it.'

'Should I order an X-ray, just in case?'

'Just in case? In case what?' Professor Shah smiled. 'In case I

am mistaken? In case *you* should be running the department?'
He tittered and twinkled at Anna as though sharing the joke
with her. Anna looked terrified.

'No, sorry,' said Yasmin.

Professor Shah had gone. Anna too. But Yasmin remained. She
looked at Mr Babangida. What psychotic behaviour had he
displayed? She looked again at the prescription. What if there
was something wrong with his arm? Anna was only a health
care assistant. She had no medical training. But she was deeply
skilled. She'd been right about Mrs Garcia, read the pain in
her eyes. She knew her patients and when she was concerned
it deserved closer attention. Maybe Mr Babangida had fallen.
It could have happened at home without his son realising.
Olanzapine would conceal the problem, not fix it.

Mr Babangida groaned again. Saliva bubbled on his lip.
Yasmin took a tissue and wiped his mouth.

THE BIG PICTURE

When she'd ordered the X-ray she went straight upstairs to Pepperdine's office. She handed him the PALS form.

'I'll speak to Darius,' he said, after she'd talked him through everything. 'It does seem like overkill. As I said, he's anxious to secure this new funding.'

'I don't want you to speak to him. I just want some advice. I can handle it myself.' When she knocked on Pepperdine's office door she hoped he would take the matter in hand, and sort it out with Professor Shah. But now he'd offered she didn't want that. She wanted something else.

'By the way, it's under wraps at the moment because they want to unveil it with trumpets and flags, if and when it's all confirmed.'

'Got it,' said Yasmin. 'I'll keep it to myself.'

If all went well, Pepperdine had explained, Barney's would become a 'Centre of Excellence' for elderly care. It would mean more money, more staff, more training, more beds.

'We'll be able to set up an orthogeriatric ward. We'll have our own specialist stroke unit.' A bead of sweat ran down from his hairline and trickled into his eye. He blinked. 'Might even be enough money left over to mend the damn radiator. God, it's boiling. I'll open the door, it tends to help.'

He jumped up and Yasmin turned her head to watch him do it: open the door she'd closed. His office was always stuffy. It was sparse and neat, all standard-issue furniture and files and nothing more. The only thing that was personal was the gym bag in which he kept his running gear, and a solitary Christmas card of a snowy St Paul's Cathedral on his desk.

'But what do you think I should do?'

'Let me speak to Darius.'

'So you agree I shouldn't sign?' What she wanted was a little emotion. That's what she wanted. A little outrage.

'My advice, since you ask, is don't get into an adversarial position with Darius. Especially now. He doesn't take kindly to ... um ... insubordination at the best of times.' He sat down, laced his fingers together and rested his hands on the desk. Why was he being so cold with her? The spot of blood on his collar. She tried not to look. His sleeves were rolled, the roped muscle of his lean forearms on display.

'Insubordination? You're joking, right?'

His green-grey eyes brooded on some distant horizon and she knew what he was thinking: Stop making a fuss. 'I'm afraid not,' he said finally. 'Darius is on tenterhooks with this Centre of Excellence business. It's between us and one other hospital and we're looking like the winners – but it's still in the balance. So this is an i to be dotted, a t to be crossed. The complaint dealt with and filed. I guess if this woman were to ask what kind of disciplinary action had been taken ... It's a storm in a teacup but you'd be surprised how minor things can escalate.'

'Disciplinary action! He was going to give me a medal not so long ago!' Her armpits were sweating. How did he stand it in here?

'Don't take it personally, Yasmin. Could you perhaps think about the bigger picture? You know how dire the situation is in the dementia-friendly ward. If we get this funding we'll double the capacity at least.'

Don't get excited, Mini. If she'd followed Baba's advice she wouldn't be in this situation. 'I'll think about it.'

'What's the other thing? When you came in, you said there were two things you needed to discuss.'

She'd planned to tell him about Mr Babangida and how she'd gone ahead and ordered the X-ray, but now she had second thoughts. If the X-ray turned out to be pointless it would be another black mark against her.

'Can't remember. Nothing.'

'Okay,' he said. 'Well.'

'Thanks for the advice.'

'Have I upset you in some way?'

'I'm not upset.'

'Angry, then.'

'No.' She bit the inside of her lip. It wasn't fair. He shouldn't be asking her personal questions. They had to keep things professional. They'd managed that so far. 'I just don't want you to think I'm a terrible person.'

'I don't.' He frowned. 'Why would I?'

'Because . . .' She sniffed and cleared her throat. 'Because of what Niamh said.'

'Niamh? What did she say?'

'About me and Joe. My boyfriend. You must think I'm a complete bitch.'

He turned up his palms, that helpless gesture of his that said, like the hospital heating system, this was beyond his area of expertise.

'He cheated on me.' She hadn't meant to blurt it out.

'Ah, I see. And I was . . . um, so to speak . . . revenge.'

'I didn't mean it like that.'

'I wasn't complaining.'

No, he wasn't complaining, he was acting like it was none of his business. He seemed barely interested. She had to pull herself together. 'Right. Anyway, thanks, and I'll think about what you said. The big picture.'

'Are you sure there's nothing else?'

'No, nothing,' she said. 'Actually, yes. Why have you never got married?'

He smiled at her then, a sad closed-lip smile. 'Depends who you ask.'

'I'm asking you.'

'Well, I'd say it's because I was waiting for the right person. But I've been told, more than once, it's because I'm ... ah, *emotionally unavailable*.' He said it as though it was a phrase in a foreign language.

She laughed. 'Sounds about right.'

'Does it?' He laughed as well. 'And I thought it was *you*. I thought it was you who was unavailable.'

MEANS OF ESCAPE

Dinner was the same unappetising mess of vegetables Baba always served up. He had developed a routine, brewing up a big vat on Sundays and making it last all week. By Friday the ingredients had melted into a kind of lightly curried baby food. He cooked rice in one big batch too, and microwaved portions for each meal. The rice was hard as gravel, providing an unpleasant contrast to the sloppy vegetables. This evening Baba had pushed the boat out by making a side dish of potato curry. He had, however, tipped in too much turmeric and the potatoes tasted bitter and looked radioactive.

Yasmin poked the food around on her plate. She wondered where the electric rice cooker had gone, and if Baba could be persuaded to use it and have fresh rice every day. From time to time she suggested she would prepare the evening meal when she was home, an offer made without enthusiasm. Luckily Baba always declined. It had become a point of pride that he was managing perfectly on his own.

'Baba, something interesting happened at work.' She hadn't told him about the incident with Mrs Rowland, and she certainly wasn't going to tell him now. He'd only say she'd been foolish and urge her not to continue the foolishness. She thought he'd like to hear about Mr Babangida, though.

'Every day is interesting for us, Mini. How could it be otherwise? We are doctors.' He spoke in his most light-hearted voice but it made Yasmin sad for him. His days were singularly monotonous.

She told him about Mr Babangida. How she'd ordered the X-ray, though Professor Shah wouldn't be pleased. Mr Babangida had a fracture to his right humerus and needed a cast, not the antipsychotic Professor Shah had prescribed. There was no record of any falls or accidents but his son, his sole carer, couldn't watch him every second of the day. Perhaps Mr Babangida had been too weak when he was admitted even to signal his pain. Thank goodness for Anna. Thank goodness for her vigilance.

'You went against the orders of the head of the department?' Baba's bushy white eyebrows lifted clear of his thick black spectacle frames. 'You defied Professor Shah? And you call this *interesting*?'

'But I was right.' Yasmin ate a forkful of mush. Cauliflower, judging from the vaguely nubbly texture. Baba's reaction was predictable yet she had failed to anticipate it. How could she have expected praise?

'In medicine there is a hierarchy,' he said, labouring over each word. 'You do not go against your superiors. There is a good reason for this, Mini.'

'But in this case, I had no choice. I had to put the patient first. You'd never leave a patient with a broken arm, would you? Just because someone told you to.'

Baba put an irradiated potato in his mouth and engaged in serious mastication. It was an article of faith with him that insufficient chewing led to indigestion and bloating. He took his time.

Yasmin, because she couldn't sit still, got up to clear her plate.

The kitchen was clean and tidy. Baba kept the surfaces clear apart from the cereal boxes that he lined up in height order. It was depressing, all this neatness, an ever-present reminder of what – or rather who – was missing.

'Well, Mini,' he said at last, 'your intention was good. The outcome was also good. But does the end always justify the means? There has to be order. There is an implacable order of things.'

Yasmin stood at the sink. 'What if it's the wrong order?'

'You did your best,' said Baba. He spoke gently. 'I am proud of you. All I ask is that you think carefully in future. Maybe you will consider taking up your concerns with your superiors rather than taking actions that may come down later on your head. Now . . . we have discussed this enough.' He paused a moment. 'How is your mother?'

'She's missing you.' Ma hadn't said she was missing anything about Tatton Hill but she had to be missing Baba, though she didn't show it. Yasmin sighed. The kitchen was more and more desolate without Ma. The radio had been stowed in a cupboard. The spider plants – browned and shrivelled – cleared from the windowsill.

'She knows where I am.'

'Why don't you come tomorrow? Harriet would be pleased to see you too. And Joe, of course.' Baba needed to show Ma how much he cared, how much he needed her, by going to Primrose Hill and apologising. Ma would pack up and come home. All he had to do was swallow his pride.

'She knows where I am,' he repeated.

Baba seemed to have forgotten how much he loved Ma, and how much she loved him. He needed a reminder. 'Baba, what was Ma wearing the first time you saw her?'

He worked meticulously on another piece of potato. 'She was wearing a red sari, and when I saw her face for the first time—'

He broke off and took a handkerchief from his trouser pocket. 'Your mother is a beautiful woman.'

Yasmin's heart swelled. 'A love marriage, Baba, it must have been an extraordinary thing in those days, especially with such different backgrounds.'

'Yes, indeed, it was extraordinary.' Yasmin held her breath. Maybe now he would finally tell her all the things she'd wanted to know about the great romance. When he began to speak again his voice was still soft with emotion, with tenderness. 'It was most extraordinary and wonderful to marry this beautiful, clever girl. She was so shy, your mother, and also so sure about everything, but her family – they were very difficult. Every day I had to hear from them how lucky I was, how generous they were, how grateful I should be to enter their house, to marry their daughter whom I have cared for in every possible way. Every way possible. And do you know how many years it took me to get out from under their . . . ? But I have paid them back every penny.'

He closed his eyes. The tap dripped two loud drops into the stainless-steel sink.

Ma's wedding jewellery still languished in the drawer. Yasmin fingered the worn brown wrapper, the frayed string. She picked up the package to test its weight. Was the jewellery gold-plated or solid gold, and how much was it worth? It had to be thousands. Enough to give Lucy and Arif a kick-start.

Yasmin put the jewellery back and closed the drawer. You didn't sell your wedding jewellery unless your marriage was over. That was its purpose: an insurance against death or abandonment. She picked up a bottle of Yardley's from the dressing table and sprayed it around as a little reminder for Baba.

There were hours to get through before bedtime. Every time she stayed the night at home it was the same. This sense of imprisonment. Slow suffocation. Yasmin stood on the landing calculating means of escape. She needed to get out of this house for a while. Just a walk round the block would be better than nothing. But if Baba saw her leaving he would ask where she was going and wouldn't approve of her strolling around aimlessly in the dark. He might insist on accompanying her as a safety precaution. Although Tatton Hill was a good area there were ruffians, as he called them, even in good neighbourhoods.

Arif, as a teenager, used to swing out of his bedroom window and monkey down the drain. Yasmin threatened to tell but never did. Lurking somewhere inside her was the notion she might one day shimmy down the pipe and run towards something for which she yearned without having the faintest idea what it was. She'd only find out if she took a chance and flung herself at it with blind faith and terminal velocity. She wasn't brave enough. What was it she had longed for? Running off to meet a secret boyfriend? No. Meeting Kashif was easily done by using the front door and skipping off, all innocence. Yet when Arif did his escape act she felt like a coward while telling herself hers was the smart way and his way was dumb.

She could go to Primrose Hill, but Baba would be offended. She stayed away too long, he said. There was no pretence she was doing nightshifts. She was staying with Mrs Sangster and Ma and that was suitable in moderation. Joe had been listless since he'd stopped seeing his therapist. At first Yasmin thought he was coming down with something, but now she wondered if he had low-grade depression. He was listless but also anxious. Jumpy. Irritable with Harriet. Maybe he needed to go back to therapy. Finish what he started. She'd talk to him about making another appointment. Talking about his father must have stirred up so many memories and feelings. He told her about it and she was glad to listen, but all she could do was empathise or cheer him on. He quit therapy too soon.

*

Back in her own bedroom she couldn't settle to anything. Instead of studying for the MRCP exam she studied the pink and cream cabbage roses on the wallpaper. They floated in a black border that ran beneath the picture rail. The pieces of wallpaper didn't all line up and the black band jagged up and down. The pink had faded over the years and the cream roses were browning as if they might at any moment start dropping their petals.

How lonely Baba must be when she wasn't here. And even when she *was* here, hiding in her room. She could have submitted to a case challenge after dinner. She could have indulged him instead of pleading she had too much exam preparation to do. Despite what he said at dinner his job wasn't interesting enough for him. He never admitted it but his tasks were repetitive and boring. Endless coughs and colds to diagnose and flu that wasn't flu. Minor infections, antibiotics, sprains, travel injections, the warts and verruca clinic every other Wednesday morning, shingles, bad backs, constipation . . . What he longed for was acanthamoeba keratitis or auto-brewery syndrome, or some rare genetic condition that challenged his intellect, anything difficult to diagnose. He kept honing his skills, completing case challenges, stockpiling his knowledge for a day when he could finally prove himself. It was a day that would never come.

The sitting-room door stood open, the television blathering out one of 'Ma's soaps'. So called, but they watched them together, Baba and Ma. The back of his head stood proud of the sofa, his hair drooping over his collar because Ma wasn't here to trim it for him. He swilled the whisky in his ruby-red crystal tumbler, his wrist on the arm of the sofa exactly where Ma rested her mug of tea.

He looked so lonely. Years ago, he spent many evenings doing home visits. It was a pity he didn't have those to keep him busy now. Or maybe it was good that he was so lonely. It might spur him on to do what was needed to win his wife back. He had to go to her and promise he'd make things right with Arif.

SANDOR

Sometimes he missed the meth heads and dope fiends. He missed them now, sitting in the stillness of the consulting room. He missed the carnival of humanity in the clinic. The noise, the chaos, the unpredictability. They'd touched his soul, those addicts, they'd taught him. They'd tested his patience beyond breaking point. He'd cheered their successes and mourned their failures. Attended their funerals.

Joe had him worried. A cancellation followed by a no-show. Would he keep his appointment this afternoon?

An hour clear now to work on his paper for the Society for Psychotherapy Research annual conference. *On Clinical Wisdom: Guidance for Practice, Training and Research* would be the keynote lecture and it would be a tough audience. The gold standard for therapeutic techniques these days was to model and measure outcomes mimicking the double-blind testing of the pharmaceutical industry. Symptom relief was the thing. Empirical studies. Cost-benefit analyses within the mental health marketplace. How then to talk about wisdom? Then again, what use is a therapist without it?

Sandor opened up the document on his computer and read through the notes he'd so far compiled. He opened the internet browser and typed Harriet Sangster into the search engine. It was an urge he had so far wisely resisted. There she was, staring back at him, smiling as if she knew, as if she'd caught him spying on her.

He shut down the browser.

Perhaps the true measure of wisdom, he decided, was awareness of one's own foolishness.

'Indeed,' said Sandor, 'there are those who question the usefulness or even the validity of the term.' He'd been so happy to see Joe it had been an effort not to hug him. Joe had been doing some research. That was fine. It was more than fine. It meant he was engaging again. 'Others prefer the term emotional incest,' Sandor continued, 'or emotional sexual abuse, or psychic incest wounds. Perhaps there's a disutility to all labels. Because human beings never fit into neat categories.'

'I wasn't going to come again,' said Joe. 'Well, I was going to . . . Sorry about last week.'

Sandor waved it off. He had black laces today. Did that mean anything?

'I've been thinking about it. Non-stop.'

'Say more. How has that been?'

'Hard. It's been hard.'

'Okay.' Sandor caught a glimpse of himself in the smoked glass of the coffee table. He looked unhealthy. Melissa said if he didn't start exercising she was going to tie him to her treadmill and set it at top speed.

'I chase the highs,' said Joe. 'Not now. Right now my libido is . . . it's dead. But there's a cycle. When I'm in it . . . the pressure builds, and I chase the highs . . . it's the intensity, you know, it's like you're free for that moment, those minutes. And then you're not. The bars come crashing down. I'm rambling. I've been doing a lot of thinking. Thinking back. And it makes sense, the stuff you said.'

So the boy had submitted to the logic. He'd worked it out. But with a patient like Joe, it was easy to fall into the trap of remaining in the realm of theory and intellect. As if mere insight solved everything. 'How are you? How have you been these past weeks?'

'All over the place but . . .'

Still alive, he meant. 'I know,' said Sandor. 'I know.'

'What do I *do*?'

'Do?'

'How do I fix it? Fix myself. Can you write me a prescription, please?'

'Ha!' Sandor crossed his legs.

'I guess not,' said Joe. 'So where does that leave me?'

'Where do you feel you are?'

'I'd rather be an alcoholic.' Joe looked earnestly at Sandor, as if this might be something he could arrange. 'I'd rather be a drug addict. Compared to what I am, they're normal. Or at least there's some sympathy. You know?'

'It's not what you *are*, remember. It's something you *do* that you want to change. A drug addict is more than their addiction. And you are more than yours. Much more.' But he was right about the sympathy. In Sandor's experience there was little enough for drug addicts, almost none for sex addicts who at worst were perceived as deviant or immoral and at best were the butt of heartless jokes.

Joe looked unconvinced but managed a valiant smile.

'How are things with your fiancée?'

'She's had a lot going on. Family problems. Her brother's girlfriend is pregnant and her dad doesn't approve. Her mum's still living with us. Yasmin's a bit stressed. We both are – work, family, house-hunting, wedding plans.'

'Sounds stressful.'

'Just a bit.'

'How does the stress show up for you?'

Joe looked away. 'Right now, today, my desire for sex is zero. Below zero.'

'It's your body's way of managing the addiction. Your libido is suppressed, in order to suppress the addiction. But as you overcome the addiction, I would certainly expect that you will be able to develop healthy sexual relationships.'

'Doesn't feel like it,' said Joe. 'After our last session something happened – nearly happened – that scared the crap out of me.'

'The hook-up sites?'

'Worse.'

'Okay.' Sandor waited. 'There's nothing you could say that would shock me. Or make me judge you.' He had an idea what it would be. 'Does it have anything to do with your place of work?'

'I haven't *done* anything.' Joe gave Sandor a pleading look.

'But you were scared you might?' A sexual encounter with a patient would be the ultimate transgression.

'I was tempted. That's all, I swear. I was tempted and I fuck-ing hate myself.'

'You have to break off the engagement. You should do it right away.'

'What?'

'You asked what you should do. You asked for a prescription. I'm writing one.'

Joe pressed a thumb knuckle into his chin. 'I can't. I don't want to. And I couldn't anyway.'

'What matters most is your recovery. How do you plan to be a good husband, a good father in the future, if you don't attend to your own recovery first?' And there it was: his inner Robert. Could he finally admit that he longed to coerce his patients into doing what was best for them? In his opinion. Which was naturally superior to theirs.

'But I can't,' said Joe. 'After she's forgiven me? I can't break it off with no explanation. I haven't got it in me to be cruel.'

'Then explain.'

Joe shook his head.

'Do you understand it would also be cruel to go ahead and marry this girl? Doesn't she at least deserve to know the truth so she can make an informed decision?'

'The truth. Yes. That I'm . . . ' He paused. A look of exquisite anguish contorted his face. 'I don't think I could get the words out.'

'Joe,' said Sandor. 'Joe? You're feeling overwhelmed.'

'Maybe I could write it down for her. For Yasmin. I think I could do that.'

'On reflection,' said Sandor, 'I think that's not the right place to start. I was getting ahead of myself. I apologise.'

Joe looked at him blankly.

Give the boy some hope, thought Sandor. You panicked. You went straight for the nuclear option. 'Don't speak to Yasmin yet.'

'Don't write the letter?'

'No, don't.'

'What else can I do?' Joe spoke softly. As though speaking to himself. As though he'd already decided he'd run out of options.

'There are steps involved in your recovery. It's a cliché, I know, but it really is a journey. I'm wondering how things are progressing with your father.' Survivors frequently found it easier to deal with their emotions about the same-sex parent. It was easier than confronting their sole caregiver. It was a way for the patient to make progress without blowing up his world.

'We've spoken a few times. He's invited me to go and stay.'

'And will you?'

'If you tell me to.'

'Well, it's up to you. I know it might not feel like it right now,' said Sandor, 'but you've made tremendous progress in such a short time. Truly. I'd like to take a moment to acknowledge that.'

'I deleted all the apps. Not for the first time, though.'

'But perhaps for the last,' said Sandor. 'We'll work on triggers, okay?'

'And I have to talk to Harry, right?'

'We can take things slowly.'

'But at some point . . .'

'Further down the road.'

'Sure. Further down the road.'

'And it's not about accusing, not about assigning blame.'

'It's not about blame,' said Joe. There was a vacant look in his eyes.

'Are you okay? Are you feeling overwhelmed again?'

'I'm fine. I'll do it. I'll do whatever you say.'

'As a first step, you might set some boundaries with her.'

'Yes.'

'You could begin with asking her to respect your privacy.'

Joe seemed not to hear. He stared into the middle distance. Eventually he shook himself, like a dog waking up from a nap. 'If I do it . . . If I do everything, take all the steps, can I be normal? Tell me honestly. How likely is it I'll be normal after that?'

'You mean, will you beat the addiction?'

'Percentage chance. Give me a ballpark. But tell me the truth.'

Sandor knew everything there was to know about addiction. He was acknowledged – sometimes acclaimed – as an expert. But whether a particular person, an individual addict, would be able to overcome his addiction or not? That was something nobody could know.

'Hundred per cent,' said Sandor. Joe needed to believe. Belief was the most important thing Sandor could give him. 'That's the ballpark. One hundred per cent.'

INTERSECTIONALITIES

'Darlings, I saw the most delectable little mews house just off Delancey Street. I know you said south of the river, but sweetheart, it's *made for you*.' Harriet planted a kiss on Joe's cheek as he handed her a gin and tonic with ice and a slice of grapefruit.

'Is it all cobbles outside?' Joe was fresh from the shower, his hair still wet, his feet bare. He was in jeans and a grey hoodie that Harriet had declared ghastly. You don't have to wear it, he'd said.

'Cobbles?'

'I hate them.'

'I'll book a viewing. This close to Christmas there'll be nothing else coming on the market.'

'For God's sake,' said Joe. 'Could you stop? Just stop.'

'I don't know. Maybe we should take a look.' Yasmin, slicing cucumber at the counter, nicked her thumb. She'd never seen Joe look so grim-faced. He'd gone back to therapy this week and said he should never have quit. It was something he had to see through. It hadn't made him more relaxed. Maybe it was a bad idea to go back. What was the point of therapy if it didn't make you happier?

'No, no,' said Harriet. 'Joseph has made his feelings clear.'

Joe rolled his eyes. 'You're bleeding,' he said.

'It's nothing.' Yasmin went to the sink and ran water over her thumb.

'Let me see,' he said over her shoulder. His breath tickled her cheek.

'It's stopped.' She held up her thumb to display the flap of sliced skin. His arms wrapped around her waist. Scarlet globules bubbled out of her thumb and ran down her wrist. Blood on the carpet. Blood on the wall. The beat that her heart skipped didn't mean anything.

'I'll get a plaster.' Joe let her go.

She squeezed more blood from her thumb.

'Shall I take over?' said Harriet.

'No, I'm fine. Where's Ma?' Usually Ma presided over the kitchen when Rosalita left for the day. Ma was never out in the evenings. She had nowhere to go.

'With Flame,' said Harriet. 'Flame is in rehearsals, her show opens in January, and Anisah went along. They've become close, as I guess you've noticed.'

'Mm,' said Yasmin. She'd taken as little notice of Flame as possible. The white marble countertops smelled of Dettol. Rosalita disliked the lingering smell of Ma's cooking. Today Rosalita had won the battle for the evening meal (there was a shepherd's pie in the oven) and scent-marked her territory. Anisah, despite all evidence to the contrary, persisted in her belief that Rosalita welcomed her help with chores and meals. Rosalita traditionally took two weeks off at Christmas to visit family but insisted she wanted to work this year, until Harriet promised her that Ma would not be cooking the Christmas dinner for the household and the eight invited guests. She had hired a private chef to take care of everything.

'She's quite remarkable,' said Harriet.

'Flame?'

Harriet shook her glossy blonde head. 'Your mother.'

'I know. My father's missing her a lot.' She hoped Harriet would sympathise. It was too difficult say it outright: you've got to send my mother back to him.

Harriet did not take the bait. 'Of course.'

'I'm worried about him.' She'd laughed when Joe mentioned divorce. But maybe Harriet had told him something.

'Do send him my love,' said Harriet.

Yasmin opened the vast Sub-Zero fridge and pulled open the crisper compartment. Which leaves should she use for the salad? Radicchio, lollo rosso, frisée endive or all three? In the Ghorami household salad meant kachumbar, a mix of onion, cucumber, tomato, green chillies and coriander leaves. In the Sangster house the word could mean almost anything.

They'd started eating dinner by the time Ma flustered in, laden with jumbo PVC laundry bags. She was followed by Flame, whose sleek uncluttered silhouette contrasted with Anisah's riotous assembly of shapes and colours.

'Tube train problems,' said Ma, releasing the bags at her feet. One toppled over and a jumble of clothes tumbled out. 'Due to person on the track.' Her cardigan was buttoned wrongly so it hung low on the left side.

'Selfish bastard,' said Flame, glissading from doorway to dining chair. 'Suicides should stick to off-peak.'

Ma moved her head from side to side in a ritual pattern. It was the way she responded when Arif received a school detention or said something rude.

'What?' Flame shrugged her narrow shoulders at Ma.

Ma giggled, and clapped a hand over her mouth. 'Oh! There is another here! Very beautiful.' The Christmas trees had been delivered today, completing the festive adornments. There were three. One in the kitchen, a second in the sitting room and a third in the entrance hall that was the height of a telegraph pole and the width of a terraced house.

'What's this?' Harriet gestured expansively at the litter of bags. 'No, leave them, no, just sit and eat.'

'Costumes,' said Ma. She sat down next to Flame. 'I will sew.'

'And did you enjoy the rehearsal?'

'Oh, yes,' sighed Ma. 'I have learned so much. I want to learn more about Greek myths and tragedies.'

'Anisah was brilliant,' said Flame.

Yasmin stared at Flame, her spiky black hair, penknife nose and bright red lipstick. 'Brilliant in what way?'

'Gave me a new angle on the chorus. Saw straight away the significance, what the people in the shadows represent. I'd been thinking of them purely as narrators, but there's so much more depth to it now.'

'Oh, great,' said Yasmin. Ma had given her insights about a Greek tragedy? And Flame had taken them seriously?

'Which play?' Joe hadn't taken his usual seat by Harriet, who always sat at the head of the table. He sat in Yasmin's usual place and she sat next to him, to the right of Harriet.

'*Antigone*. But reinterpreted, and not a play ... I don't stage plays.'

'It's a *feminist retelling* in movement, music and dance, with a chorus recounting the story,' said Harriet. 'And it's wonderfully done.'

'I've heard of Antigone ...' Yasmin stopped, suddenly shy of revealing the extent of her ignorance.

'Daughter of Oedipus and his mother Jocasta. Do help yourself to more shepherd's pie.' Harriet pushed the dish towards Yasmin.

'Or his wife Euryganeia,' said Flame. 'Daughter of Jocasta or Euryganeia. Sister of Polynices.'

'Oh, yes,' said Yasmin, as if she'd just needed a reminder. 'And what did Ma say about the chorus that was so useful?'

'Go ahead, tell her!'

'No,' said Ma, laughing, 'you tell.'

'Okay, okay.' She laughed along with Ma, as if they had some private joke.

'What's so funny?' said Yasmin.

Flame ignored her. 'Anisah,' she said, 'enriched the reading by seeing what I had failed to see: that the people in the shadows – the chorus – represent the many people in the world today who exist without full citizenship, either within or between states. Who are not accorded full human status. Who operate in a shadowy realm, and haunt the public sphere like Antigone haunts Creon.'

'Wow,' said Joe. 'That's smart!' He reached across the table for a high five and Anisah, after a moment's confusion, met him halfway.

'Great,' said Yasmin. What the fuck? Ma? Ma thought of all that? Surely Flame was taking the piss. Although, when she wasn't laughing with Ma, she always looked deadly serious.

Ma giggled. 'I didn't say like this.'

'You said it better.' Flame put her elbows on the table and pressed her hands together in prayer position. Her forearms were sinewy from the heavy labour of using her body to interpret the world. 'I'd been so focused on gender and building on the work of my predecessors, in the artistic sense, artists like Carolee Schneemann . . . I hadn't thought through the intersectionalities.'

'Who?' said Yasmin.

Harriet jumped in. 'A performance artist, a visual experimental artist. She was a pioneer of multi-media works on the body, gender and sexuality. Specifically, she is famous for a work called *Interior Scroll*, a performance piece in which she reads from a scroll that she pulls out of her vagina.'

301

'She explores the power of the vagina in the creative process,' Flame added.

'Oh, yes,' said Ma, with a sigh of contentment. As if she had been in search of such a person all her life. As if talk of vaginas at the dinner table didn't bother her in the slightest.

Yasmin was agog. At home, Ma blushed at anything even slightly sexual. The television had to be turned off if couples started snogging or there was any mention of genitals.

'Don't wear yourself out with those alterations,' Flame told Ma. She picked a piece of fluff from Ma's cardigan sleeve, raised it to her lips and blew it off the tip of her finger.

'I will sew,' said Ma, 'because when you make your performance it is beautiful and everything must be perfect also.' Ma, the mistress of the bodged job, the half-baked scheme, the incomplete project, was pledging perfection.

'Well, I'm sure you'll be a wonderful wardrobe mistress.' Harriet poured herself more wine, then got up. 'The save the date cards are back from the printer. I do hope you'll approve. I went for simple and classic, though of course for the invitations you may want a more elaborate Indian style.'

Yasmin looked at Joe. He managed a smile but still looked out of sorts. Perhaps he was coming down with something.

'This style is excellent,' said Ma, caressing the thick cream card Harriet handed to her. She passed it across the table to Yasmin.

Yasmin and Joseph are getting married!

Save the date: Saturday, 17 June 2017

Details to follow

Yasmin stared at the card and words began to blur. She looked up and everything was blurry, Ma's face, the lantern lights strung across the window, the yellow and green splodgy painting. Her chest hurt. *And I thought it was you who was unavailable.*

'Your father should inform Imam Siddiq so he can pray istikhara – we should seek the blessing.'

'No,' said Yasmin. 'We don't want that, Joe and I decided we don't want a nikah after all.'

'Darlings—'

Anisah interrupted Harriet. 'It is okay. Only for you to decide. There is time and if your mind changes it can be arranged even one month or one week before. Inshallah, you will want. If you don't want, it is okay. But we must have gaye holud, no? You will be happy if I arrange?'

'What is it?' said Joe.

'The bride gets rubbed in turmeric paste,' said Yasmin.

'I'm on for that!' He squeezed her hand, and she didn't know how she could sit there and allow herself to be comforted by her fiancé when the cause of her distress was her own cheating and lying, but somehow she could. She did.

'You don't get to come. Ma, I don't know. Can we talk about this some other time?'

Ma smiled bravely. Yasmin hoped she wouldn't cry.

'Why don't you just do what she wants?' said Flame.

'Because,' said Yasmin. She shook her head. Flame seemed to take pride in blurting out her thoughts and opinions. Could she not help herself? Was there something wrong with her? Or did she think it was cool and artistic to be rude to everyone?

'Anisah,' said Harriet, jumping in. Whatever her faults, Harriet was not oblivious to the rules of social interaction. 'Anisah, I don't know how you would even find the time to arrange more ceremonies or celebrations. What with the costumes and also the chutneys! Yasmin, your mother is going into business.'

Ma laughed but didn't deny it.

303

'The chutney business?'

'I'm designing a label,' said Flame.

'A label?' Ma already labelled her jars. She wrote the date of bottling and the main ingredients with marker pen on sticky labels from a roll.

'To start only five or six flavours,' said Ma, as if this made the whole enterprise practicable. 'For selling to *delicatessen*,' she pronounced the word with care and pride, 'and also I will sell at farmers' market, these are very popular.'

'You're joking!' She had to go in hard to save Ma from herself. 'You don't know anything about business. You have to be organised, for a start. What about Arif and Lucy? The baby's due next month and they're going to need all the help they can get. And you don't know anything about money or selling, it'll be a disaster, Ma! What do you—' She broke off because Joe put his hand on her leg, just above the knee, and squeezed.

'I love your chutneys,' he said. 'I predict you'll make a fortune.'

Ma smiled at Joe.

Flame glared at Yasmin.

'Who's for dessert?' said Harriet.

A DOG CRAWLED ROUND A WELL

She would apologise to Ma. She'd been too harsh with her. Ma's bedroom door was ajar. Anisah would be at the dressing table brushing her hair or rubbing Yardley's English Rose Nourishing Hand Cream into her face.

But the room was empty, the bed turned down or perhaps still unmade from last night. The wardrobe doors, tied together by a scarf looped through the handles, didn't quite close. Ma had overstuffed it, but at least she kept her room tidy. She hadn't turned the place into a jumble sale. Yet.

Where was she?

The save the date card was propped against a jar on the dressing table. Yasmin picked it up. *And I thought it was you who was unavailable.* What did he want from her? Damn him. It was only sex. He never said he wanted anything more. He was ruining everything. He wasn't suitable at all. He was too old. Too silent. And if Joe hadn't betrayed her with that nurse ... Why did Joe have to go and do something so stupid?

She heard footsteps and turned to see Anisah slip through the door wearing a wedding dress.

'Ma! Be careful,' she said as Ma tripped on the trailing fabric. 'Oh! What is it?' cried Ma. 'What happened?' She raised her hands in alarm. Her hair, undone and unbrushed, tumbled around her shoulders in great black swathes flecked with grey. On closer inspection the floor-length white frothy garment was a voluminous nightgown. It gathered beneath her chest and puddled over her feet. It made her look chaste and rather beautiful, if slightly deranged – like a Bengali Miss Havisham.

'Nothing's happened,' said Yasmin. 'Where were you? I was looking for you.'

'Eesh! I was with Flame, we were talking . . . ' Ma seized her hairbrush and began her strenuous brushing routine.

'About the chutney business? The labels? Ma, I'm sorry for what I said. You should try selling some of your pickles. Everybody loves them. Just don't . . . you know . . . get carried away.'

'Everything slow-slow,' said Ma, decelerating the stroke of her brush.

'So, you had a nice day with her? With Flame.'

'Yes, she is very nice.'

'She can be a bit . . . insensitive, can't she?'

'Always we are laughing and joking,' said Ma. 'I enjoy very much. And I am learning so much from Flame. From Mrs Sangster too, but with Flame it is different.'

'In what way?'

Ma's nose twitched with some emotion that Yasmin could not identify. 'Mrs Sangster tells me so much. Sometimes she reads to me from her lectures. She learns from me also, about Islam, for example. But from Flame I learn about . . . ' She tugged at a knot in her hair. 'Me. I learn about myself.'

'Like what, for instance?' Yasmin smiled at the thought of Ma being on some journey of self-discovery.

'Many things,' said Ma.

'Such as?'

'I can give a good *interpretation*,' she said the word carefully, 'of the chorus in a Greek tragedy. I will never think so, without Flame telling me. Also, I have skills. Sewing and cooking. Because of Flame I am learning to use these skills professionally. They are worth something.'

'They are,' said Yasmin. 'Definitely. We *all* value you, you know?'

'Okay,' said Ma.

'I'm going to bed.' Yasmin hugged her mother tight, reassuring herself she was still Ma, that she wasn't about to undergo some indelible transformation facilitated by Flame. She inhaled deeply. Ma didn't smell of cumin today, there was the usual light high note of Yardley's and something deeper and richer Yasmin couldn't identify.

'You will marry in way you want. I will do only what you ask. Nothing else.'

'Thanks, Ma. Could you tell Harriet to butt out as well? I'm sure she'd be delighted if we just went back to our original plan and she didn't have to do anything.'

'Oh, no,' said Ma, scandalised. Despite her newly discovered talent for critical analysis of classic texts, irony remained beyond her comprehension. 'She *wants* to give a big party and proper celebration. This is important for her.'

'I don't know, Ma. I don't know if I'm doing the right thing.' One floor below, Joe was in bed waiting for her and she was up here betraying him.

Ma put down the brush. 'Tell me. What is it?'

'Nothing. I'm just tired.'

'You are very troubling. I see it in your eyes and I feel it. Because your flesh is my flesh, your blood is my blood.'

'I don't *know*,' said Yasmin, crumpling, resting her forehead on Ma's lacy shoulder. 'He cheated on me . . . he slept with another woman. He's . . . he's *ruined everything*.' It came out as a wail.

Ma put her arms around her and patted her back.

'What do I *do*?' Yasmin said.

'You are angry. He has given pain and you are angry. He behaved in a bad way. This is very wrong.'

'Yes, I'm angry. I'm *so* angry with him.' She wasn't. She couldn't be. Not since she slept with Pepperdine. What a fraud she was, heaping all the blame on Joe.

'But you love,' said Ma. 'However much you love, this much you feel anger. They are same. When love is small, anger is small also.'

'Maybe,' said Yasmin. 'But should I marry him? After what he's done?'

Ma said nothing. What did she *want* her to say? How could Ma, who'd led such a sheltered life, understand any of the complexities of modern love and relationships?

Ma let her go and Yasmin lifted her face from the lacy nightgown.

'I don't know,' said Ma. 'You have told him how you feel?'

'Sort of. Yes. No, not really.' She hadn't told him about Pepperdine. It would be easier to call off the wedding. Kinder to Joe as well. And if she told him, he'd tell Harriet who would tell Ma, and there was no need to involve everyone. She still loved him, though. He was so good to her. They were so suited to each other and she'd never find another man as suitable as him.

'Sit down here with me,' said Ma, sinking onto the bed. She patted the rumpled duvet. 'I will tell a story. Will you like?'

'Yes, Ma.' Yasmin curled up on the duvet with her head on Ma's lap. She closed her eyes and waited for a comfortingly familiar tale to begin. Ma stroked her hair. She took her time. And when she began it was a story Yasmin had never heard before.

'A dog crawled round a well, dying of thirst. It was a hot day. Burning hot. And the people stood or sat in shade of date palms,

308

or they drew water from this well. A woman came near. She was prostitute from the prostitutes of Bani Israel. Some men called out crude comments but these she ignored. She was used to such things and she kept her confidence.

'The dog's tongue hung out from the mouth and it panted and cried. So terribly it was suffering. Not one single person spared one drop of water for this poor dog. Perhaps they did not even notice how it suffered because it was only a low animal. It was beneath them to notice its pain.

'The prostitute had no bucket. She had not come for using the well. But she took off her shoe and tied it to her veil. Like this she drew up water and offered to the dog. And because of her compassion she was forgiven. All sins cleaned from her. It was so reported by Abu Huraira, may God have mercy on him, and on all of us.'

GORY DETAILS

He was sitting up in bed when she finally kissed Ma goodnight and stole into his bedroom. 'Talk to me,' he said. 'What's going on?'

'Nothing's going on. You weren't waiting up for me, were you?'

'Couldn't sleep.'

'What's wrong?' She slid under the covers and he dropped his arm around her shoulders.

'Nothing much. Just feels like the world's about to end. 2016: the year when things got so badly fucked that the world could never recover.'

'Brexit? He Who Shall Not Be Named?' Harriet had met Hillary Clinton at a Democrats Abroad fundraiser decades ago. When she lost to a man who did unspeakable things to women a period of mourning had been declared. Harriet vowed never to utter the name of the man who would next year be sworn in as Moron-in-Chief of the Free World.

'He's the icing on the cake. Brexit, sixty million refugees, environmental disaster . . . save the date cards printed in a really ugly font. Thought you were going to throw up when you saw it.'

She laughed uneasily. 'Oh, yeah, right. I'm sorry. It was just

Ma with all the nikah and istikhara stuff. Stressed me out.'
What was wrong with her? How did she get to be so shameless?
One minute she was with Ma blaming Joe, the next with Joe
blaming Ma.

'So, we're still sending them out? You haven't gone off me?'

She looked at his sweet, boyish face. The dimple on his chin.
'No, of course not.'

'Of course we're not sending them out? Or the other one?'

'Don't be silly. But we should wait until after Christmas.
Things get lost in the post, or overlooked – too many envelopes.'

'But we're not having the nikah?'

'None of that stuff.'

'Your mum doesn't mind?'

'No, I talked to her. Anyway, it was *your* mum who suggested it.'

'Sorry.'

'You seemed pissed off with her this evening.'

'Did I?'

'You were quite rude to her.'

'So were you, to your mother.'

'I know. I apologised. Joe, listen, I've got to tell you something.' It couldn't go on like this. Evasions and delays and
half-truths. And lies. 'I'm ... I ...' She couldn't form another
word, a curious, groaning gurgle spilled from her mouth. It
was the kind of sound she heard so often on the dementia-
friendly ward.

'Are you choking? Are you okay? Do you need water?'

'No, I'm fine. I have to get this off my chest. I want you to
know ...'

He smiled at her. 'Have you murdered someone?'

She shook her head.

'Look,' he said, 'whatever it is, I'm sure you'll feel better as
soon as you say it.'

'No, I won't. I've done something bad. Something terrible.'

'Right, let's hear it.' He sounded amused. 'Somehow I doubt it's going to be so terrible. You haven't got a single bad bone in your body. You're the sanest, the nicest, the best person I've ever met.'

'I haven't studied for the MRCP exam. My father's going to be so upset with me.'

'Haven't studied? You've sat up late so many nights. You shouldn't be anxious. You'll ace it, I bet.'

'All I've done is lie down on that velvet sofa in your mum's library and read novels. I've only been pretending to work! I've been lying. To you, to him, to myself. I'm not even going to take the exam.' She burst into tears of frustration. The nicest person he'd ever met! How could she tell him!

'Yasmin,' he said, and held her close. He kissed the top of her head. 'You are amazing, you know that, right? Fuck the exam. What does it matter? Do it in another year. Who cares!'

She allowed herself to be comforted. She dried her eyes. 'I'm not even sure if I still want to be a doctor. Or if I ever wanted it. My father wanted me to do medicine, so I did.'

'So, quit and do something else.'

'Like what, though? What else could I do?'

'Anything you like. I'll support you while you retrain or whatever.'

'You really think I could?'

'Anything. I do.'

'Thank you.' She rearranged herself so she could look in his eyes. Those eyes that looked into her and saw things that no one else saw. Wasn't that what people meant when they said they'd met their soulmate?

'I want to talk to you about something as well.' He smiled but he was grim-faced again. 'Look, maybe this isn't the best time, but there's never a good time. There's never going to be a good time so it may as well be now.' He put his hands to his head and massaged his temples.

'Headache?'

'Yes. No, not really.'

'I think you're coming down with something. Let me feel your glands.'

'I want us to always be honest with each other,' he said. His voice was raspy. 'And I think . . . my therapist says . . . '

'What does your therapist say?'

'Forget the therapist. He says I should tell you later, but I have to do this now.'

'Okay,' she said. 'Go on, then.' But he closed his eyes and didn't speak. The lamplight was low and his bare chest looked golden against the white pillowcases. She moved around to sit cross-legged on top of the covers, facing him. He kept working his mouth and swallowing. It looked like he was trying to stop himself throwing up.

'Sorry,' he said, and opened his eyes. 'I haven't told you everything about my relationship history before we met. And it's important for you to know everything before we get married. I've slept with a lot of women.'

'Oh, God! Stop! I know that already.' She didn't want to hear it. Not now, not later.

'You don't . . . you don't know everything. My sexual history, I'm not proud of it, and there's stuff I haven't told you. When I said I—'

She put a hand over his mouth. 'Please! Spare me the gory details.'

When she took her hand away, he said, 'I want to start with a clean slate because—'

She clamped his mouth again. 'I don't want to know. Okay?' This therapist was an idiot. Why would she want to hear more than Joe had already told her? Maybe the therapist got off on all the intimate details. Maybe he was some kind of pervert.

Joe nodded.

'Don't tell me. Promise?'

He nodded again.

'I don't feel very well,' he said, when she released his mouth once again.

'You poor thing. Let me feel.' She felt his forehead. 'God, Joe, you're boiling. You're burning up!'

HARRIET

From the car she has watched one delivery man and then another at the front door, and a woman — the wife, she presumes — sign for the parcels. The woman left the house around twenty minutes ago, laughing and talking, phone pressed to her ear. Harriet resents this woman, the way she goes about her day without a care in the world.

The side door is where the clients emerge at ten to the hour, and where they shuffle their feet and check the time before pressing the bell exactly on the o'clock. She hopes to God that Joseph does not have an appointment today. If he spotted her car outside . . .

What is she doing here?

She has looked him up, the Hungarian who is in fact American, and besides being a family therapist, which is how Joseph billed him, he is an addiction specialist. Of course, she asked if that bore any relevance in his choice of therapist, but Joseph is non-communicative these days. She wishes he would talk to her properly, as he used to, instead of mumbling and skulking away. Whatever is going on in that room there behind that peeling side door, it is driving a wedge between them. No surprise — they always have it in for the mother, these therapists.

Ten minutes would be enough. Between clients. Ten seconds. That's all she needs.

Her son is not an addict, she knows that. He barely drinks. He doesn't binge eat or take drugs. That's not why she's here. Nevertheless, she will ask the question of this Bartok, and he will say nothing, but if there is something to know she will see it in his eyes.

Thirty seconds, face to face with the American, and the primary purpose of this is not, in fact, to glean information. She is not that stupid. What she wants is for him to see her. For him to see her and know that she is human, flesh and blood.

The side door opens and a young man emerges, looking left and right before hurrying up the garden path.

Harriet's hand is on the car-door handle, beginning to pull. It's now or never. She takes a breath, looks in the rear-view mirror. You foolish woman, she says. How foolish! She turns the key in the ignition and drives away.

DEEN

'A good sister who doesn't talk to other men. A sister who doesn't show the skin of her arms and legs, only shows her face and hands.' Rania sat cross-legged on the daybed in her living room, scrolling through a dating website. 'What else? Oh, yes, this one I particularly loved: I hate make-up on the face. Your make-up is not beauty. Lot of charming guys out there in the halal dating world.' She laughed but looked nonetheless despondent.

'Irresistible,' said Yasmin. 'When are you meeting him?'

'Never. Inshallah.' Rania groaned. Her wavy auburn hair fell around her shoulders. She looked defiant and utterly gorgeous.

'Let me try,' said Yasmin. 'I'll find someone.'

Rania handed over her laptop and picked up her phone. 'I've started tweeting about it. Not that *those* guys are going to get the benefit of my very great wisdom. But you've got to start somewhere.'

'What are you saying in your tweet?'

'I'm saying it's not exactly appealing when men only list what they *don't* want women to do. Don't talk to other men. Don't wear make-up. Don't do this, don't do that! Guys! We're looking for husbands, not prison guards. If confining me is going to make you happier then you really need to sort your head out.'

'Looking for a Muslimah who cares about her deen,' Yasmin read aloud from a profile. 'That's a bit more positive.'

'Correct,' said Rania. 'With emphasis on *bit*. That's about as positive as it gets. Nothing about personal qualities, interests, education, certainly not sense of humour – and if you don't care about your deen then you're not a Muslim; it's like saying, looking for a Muslim who is a Muslim.' She rolled her eyes. 'I envy you. Honestly, I know you had a bit of a bump in the road but at least you've found him. You know, *the one*. Halal dating is so difficult. Honestly, I could scream. Maybe I should do it your way. Every time I try this shit I swear I'll never do it again! How's Joe, by the way?'

'Still sick. Swollen glands, sore throat. Sends his love.'

Yasmin browsed more profiles. 'Well, from my extensive online survey, I reckon reverts are the worst in terms of focusing on negatives. Don't do this and don't do that.'

'Maybe. What I want to know is: why are there so many more educated women than men on all these sites? Look at the drop-down menu – so many men tick *prefer not to say*. If you prefer not to say what your level of education is it's pretty obvious what that means.'

'That the blokes are more modest? They don't want to boast about their doctorates?'

'Ha! That must be it!' She was dressed like a workman in a blue denim boiler suit. She looked tiny in it, and tough, and somehow also feminine. 'Anyway, enough of that.' She took the laptop from Yasmin and closed the lid. 'So everyone's being kicked out of here. Got to start looking for a new place to live.'

'Oh, no! Why? Wait – *everyone*?' Rania's flat was a one-bed sublet in a tower block in Elephant and Castle. The view from the seventeenth floor compensated for the stink in the lift, the dodgy plumbing, the frequently jammed rubbish chutes, the inadequate heating.

'Knocking it down. Developers. Council's sold it off, desperate for the cash, I guess. My landlord's taking a payoff, not getting rehoused and that's that.'

'I like this place, I'll miss it.' The flat was small, the ceiling was scarred by damp, and one wall had an ugly electric fire inflicted on it, but Rania had made it nice. She'd painted everywhere in shades of terracotta that made it feel tranquil. There was a long-armed planter chair with deep cream cushions, the daybed they were lounging on, and an assortment of drum stools in various sizes, some leather, others upholstered in bright fabrics. Most of Rania's furniture was second hand, bought at junk shops. The exception was a pair of hand-carved chairs with camel bone and mother-of-pearl inlays that came from her dead grandparents' home in Morocco. They were too precious and uncomfortable to actually be used.

'Me too,' said Rania. 'I'll miss the cheap rent. But I was starting to feel bad about subletting a council flat anyway. One-bed flats are definitely out of my budget . . . *so* . . . I'll just have to deal with having housemates and sharing a bathroom with strangers.'

'On, no. Don't you know anyone who's looking too?'

'I'll survive. Has the heating gone off?' She jumped up and felt the radiator. 'Bloody hell! I'll try to get the fire on. Sometimes it works and sometimes it doesn't.' She squatted down by the three-bar grill attached to the far wall. 'Anyway, too many people in the block have found out I do immigration cases and if I live here much longer they'll be queuing on the fucking landing.' A faint glow appeared on the lowest bar and then disappeared. She wiggled some wires beneath the fire. 'And I'm sick of freezing. Look how sunny it is out there and it's like a fridge in here. So, tell me what happened with that guy at work.'

'What guy?' Yasmin shifted uncomfortably. Pepperdine? But she hadn't told Rania anything. She couldn't mean Pepperdine.

'The one trying to bully you into admitting you abused a patient. No, a patient's relative. This fire's coming on now.'

'Oh, Shah! Darius Shah. I did what he wanted just to get him off my back. It wasn't worth all the fuss.' The truth was, Shah had it in for her now anyway. He mocked her in front of the medical students on a ward round when she'd answered a question about spinal osteomyelitis and made a mistake. He'd told her to perform an enema on a patient, a task that by unspoken rule was meted out only to doctors like Catherine who were still in their Foundation training years. He cracked 'jokes' about ordering X-rays for sore throats or diarrhoea. It was his firmly professed opinion that the fracture in Mr Babangida's humerus would have healed just as quickly without a cast. That, in fact, the cast caused more distress to the patient than the injury.

'Really? You're going on a diversity training course as punishment for calling someone racist when that's what they are?'

'I didn't call her—' She broke off and giggled. 'I *know*! It's ridiculous. But what can you do?'

Rania gave Yasmin a look that said there was a lot you could do. 'What did Joe say about it?'

'Haven't told him.'

'Because he'd point out you're crazy for going along with it.'

'Because Harriet would end up hearing about it and . . . she'd just bang on, and I'd find it annoying.' Harriet would relish the opportunity to rehearse once again her free-flowing opinions about *the capacity of bourgeois structures to resist and neutralise change*. Diversity training, according to Harriet, was a means of preserving the existing order without changing it significantly. The old order had to be torn down.

Rania gave her a look. 'Fine. I won't bang on!' She pulled her phone from her boiler-suit pocket. 'Twenty re-tweets for the first tweet,' she said. 'And twenty-nine re-tweets for the second. And a hundred and something likes!'

'The tweets you sent just now?'

'Yep. Shamefully, I get more pleasure out of tweeting about modest fashion and halal dating than I do out of drafting appeals against deportation orders.'

'Does that make you a terrible person? Oh, I have to ask you something. I keep forgetting.' On the way to Rania's, she'd got off the tube at Oxford Circus to buy baby clothes, because tomorrow she was going to Mottingham to see Arif and Lucy. It was the Saturday before Christmas and sunny so of course it was the worst place in the world to be. She'd grabbed a few dresses and bonnets and bootees from Baby Gap and escaped as fast as possible. 'Arif wants to interview you for a documentary he's making on Islamophobia. Are you up for it? It's not proper – he'll probably just put it on YouTube. If he ever finishes it.'

'Sure. No problem.' Rania went to the window and rested her backside on the narrow sill. She looked out. 'I'll miss this view.' She tossed her hair. The sun, melting into a bed of cloud, lit her up from behind. 'I've been asked to take part in a TV show, actually. Next month. They want me to talk about hijab. I know they'll want me to talk about oppression rather than fashion. But I think I'll do it anyway.'

'At this rate,' said Yasmin, 'you're going to need an agent.'

'Forget telly. Who's watching? But social media ... you know something, I think I *could* make a difference. If I get my numbers up, more followers, I could become an influencer. I could use it to talk about some important stuff as well.' She checked her phone again and smiled at however many re-tweets she had now.

'Like a Muslimah Kim Kardashian?'

'Right. But with less product placement. Listen ... ' She put a hand on Yasmin's arm. 'You could complain about that bullshit at work. If you need some legal advice, I happen to know a good lawyer.'

'Me too,' said Yasmin. 'A brilliant one.' She *had* complained to Pepperdine about the way Professor Shah picked on her. *Why is he always on the wards now? Is it just so he can harass me?* Pepperdine said, *Ah, I see.* Which was infuriating. And: *Darius is anxious to be seen because he knows there are unannounced inspections regarding the awarding of Centre of Excellence status.* Which made her seem paranoid. And this: *Yasmin, why don't we talk after work so we can talk properly. Only talk.* Which scared her in case he wanted to do more than talk. And scared her in case he did not.

Rania grinned. 'I'm just saying – I'm here for you.'

'I know,' said Yasmin, putting her arms around her brilliant friend.

KEEP IT HUNDRED

Arif, as agreed, met Yasmin at the bus stop. He stooped to give her a hug and although of course she knew he was taller it was still surprising because he was her little brother and here he was, bending down to give her a reassuring squeeze.

'You look well,' she said, stepping back to take him in. He was clean-shaven, and his hair had been layered and styled. It still covered his ears but it had shape and life instead of hanging limply around his face.

'Likewise, Apa. We're going this way.' He pointed down the treeless road towards the low-rise blocks shouldered by a terraced parade of local businesses. Christmas lights flashed urgently in the convenience-shop windows. An inflatable Santa tethered to a shop front leaned at a desperate angle, his belly inches from the cracked flagstones.

'Your turn to meet the in-laws,' said Arif. 'Listen, I feel bad about the things I said about Harriet. She's all right. When Ma turned up with her it was like—'

'She was here? Harriet?'

'Yeah, with Ma last week. Brought all these cognitive development baby toys.'

'Oh, God! What did they make of her?'

'Harriet's trill. So, no problem, yeah.'

'Trill?'

'Seriously,' said Arif, grinning. 'You've been living in an old folks' home too long.'

'Sorry for not being a teenager. Oh, hang on, neither are you. '

'Trill means true and real, Apa. She keeps it hundred, know what I mean.'

'I really don't.'

'See the houses over there with the wheelie-bin sheds in front, that's where we are, fifth along, red door.'

He held her arm as they crossed the road, as though she was the child and he the adult.

'And here we are,' he said, affecting what he'd call a posh voice, though it was just normal for the middle-class person he was trying not to be. 'Keeping it hundred is a slang term for acting in a way that's true to oneself and aligned with one's values, as well as being honest with and respectful towards others.' He slotted the key in the front door. 'Just raise your hand if you need anything else translating, yeah?'

The maisonette, reached through a claustrophobic hallway and up a skin-tight staircase clogged with purple and silver tinsel, occupied the first and second floors. Lucy waddled out to greet them on the landing, wearing tracksuit bottoms and a stretchy top that had ridden up, revealing the dark vertical line running up to her protruding belly button.

'Yasmin! Look at you! Love your coat, where did you get your shoes, I'm enormous aren't I, come in, let me give you a kiss, we're having pizza, hope you like pizza, or we can order something else, we've got loads of menus.'

'Hiya, Yasmin!' La-La called over Lucy's shoulder. 'Is it Yaz or Yasmin? Remember me? La-La. Lucy, get out the way a minute, stop hogging her!'

'Hawaiian or pepperoni, or a bit of both? Give the poor girl some air!' Janine, holding two large Domino's boxes, led the way to the sitting room.

'Now, where did we put Yasmin's presents?' said Lucy. 'Mum, did you put them under the tree or keep them separate?'

Arif put his hand on Yasmin's back and steered her gently forward. 'See,' he said in her ear, 'now you're part of the family.'

Two hours later he walked her to the bus stop because Lucy insisted. He'd never walked her anywhere before, and now he'd done it twice in one evening.

They sat in the shelter and three double-deckers went by, none going her way.

'Must have just missed one,' said Yasmin. She rubbed her hands together. It was a cold night but not the crisp and frosty kind. It was the cold of a dark, dank cellar.

'Yeah.' Arif sat on the seat with his legs stuck out straight, head against the back wall of the bus shelter, almost sliding off the narrow plank of plastic.

'You don't have to wait.'

'Yeah.'

'I should have thought to bring Christmas presents.' They'd given her a jar of pink bath salts, bubble bath and a set of thank-you cards and envelopes. You always need them after Christmas, said Lucy. Don't waste one on us, though, said Janine. She doesn't need instructions about how to use them, said La-La.

'Nah,' said Arif. 'You bought the baby clothes.'

'But I should have.' She and Arif never exchanged Christmas gifts.

Arif shook his head. 'Never mind about that. Did you like *them*? Do you like Lucy?'

'Yes,' she said, and meant it. 'They're so nice. All of them. Lucy's lovely, and you'd better be good to her.' They'd eaten slices of pizza with the television on and the conversation threading around the game show.

Now he's got to get the next three questions right or he loses everything. Has Arif not told you about his job? Mystery shopper, phone shops this month, and don't forget to ask him when you need a new one, he knows all the deals. Look, Yasmin, listen, medical questions. Go on, go on, oh, that's so easy, gastro refers to the stomach, even I know that.

'Told you,' said Arif, grinning. He seemed to have filled out in the past couple of months, even his arms had flesh on them.

'You did. Hey, how did you get the tree in there?' In proportion to the room the Christmas tree was huge. It blocked out the entire window and partially obscured the television, which didn't seem to bother anyone. Vast quantities of tinsel, fairy lights, and glittery baubles obliterated almost all traces of greenery. On two walls Christmas cards hung on lengths of string that sagged in the middle like washing lines.

'In pieces,' said Arif. 'It's fake. You didn't think it was real?'

'Actually, I did.' At home, though they didn't officially celebrate, Ma who was mad for fairy lights lit up the garden as well as the house. She sprayed the windows with cans of fake snow.

'How's Joe? Shame he couldn't come.'

He's really sorry too. In bed with a throat infection. But the antibiotics will sort it out in another day or so.'

'Next time, yeah.'

'Arif, if you just go to Baba and talk to him—'

'Are you for real? You're fucking kidding! Look! Look at this – in case you've forgotten.' He pointed at the silvery scar above his right eye.

'Listen, he was mortified. You should have seen him. It was an accident.'

'I don't wanna argue so just leave it, okay?'

'But Arif ...' He'd always fallen in line previously, loping home when he'd finished sulking, when he needed money. 'For the baby's sake. For Ma's sake – she can't live with Harriet for the rest of her life! And she won't go back until you make it up with Baba.'

'Do you remember how much we hated him?'

'Who?' She wished Arif would stop being so selfish.

'Baba. You especially loathed him.'

'Me? I did?'

'I'm the one who got his head banged up, Apa. And you're the one with amnesia?' His laugh rang hollow.

'Let's just leave it, like you said.' She spoke sharply. 'Let's not have a pointless argument.'

'You hated his guts. Until you were, what, ten? Eleven? Then you flipped. You took his side against me and Ma.'

'What are you talking about? Seriously, Chhoto Bhai, you've got to stop messing around. How are you going to support a family with part-time casual work? You've got to sort yourself out. Get a career, for fuck's sake!'

Arif wasn't listening. 'He made you comb his hair after dinner ... don't pretend you don't remember. He made you pull out the white ones and you had to pick over his scalp like a little monkey, a little seething monkey on a chain. No wonder you hated him!'

'I did not!' she shouted. 'Grow up!' It was Arif who hated Baba. Arif used to be so scared of him. When Yasmin calmed Baba down it was mainly for Arif's sake. And he *blamed* her for it now! She'd shouted at him so loudly passers-by on the other side of the road had turned around to look at her.

Arif slid lower on the bench, his old sullen self again. 'He only smacked me, or threw shoes or whatever, and yelled. But you're the one he tortured psychologically.'

'Thanks for your concern,' she said. 'But it appears I managed to survive. Quite well, in fact. If you hadn't noticed.'

327

'He flipped you. You got Stockholm syndrome and guess what: you're still his prisoner. Time to face facts, Apa.'

He spoke softly, almost pleadingly, but it was infuriating. She jumped up. It was time for him to face facts, to hear a few hard home truths.

Don't get excited, Mini.

It was pointless to get worked up. She had to be the reasonable one. Arif wasn't capable. 'Okay,' she said, keeping her voice soft. 'So he's evil and I'm weak. What about Ma?'

'What about her?'

'Why didn't she protect us?'

'Protect us? What the fuck are you talking about?'

'I don't know,' said Yasmin. *The greatest appeaser since Neville Chamberlain.* Maybe Arif was right and she was wrong. Maybe she'd built her entire life on lies, on stupid stories she'd concocted.

He was laughing and shaking his head. 'What are you laughing at?'

'Your bus just went past.'

She turned and watched the back of the bus shrink fitfully down the road.

'Fuck. Why didn't you tell me?'

'We were having too much fun.'

She sat down.

He punched her arm. 'Didn't see. I mean it was too late when I saw.'

'Whatever.'

They waited in silence for a while.

'Did you ask Rania about being in my documentary?'

'Oh, yes. She's on for it. How's it going?'

'Low key, working on it. Gonna be my calling card when I go knocking on doors at every television production company.'

'Good for you.' She elbowed him affectionately. 'Plenty of

Islamophobes for you to interview round here, I guess.' She pointed at the swastika graffitied on the bus shelter.

'I like it round here. Least you know what you're dealing with. Not like Tatton Hill where people hide their prejudice.'

'You do know not all white people are racist, don't you?' She laughed, but not mockingly. 'At least Joe and Lucy, and La-La and Janine.'

'I was talking about our father.'

'He's racist as well now, is he?'

'He's prejudiced. Baba's prejudiced against Lucy. You saw the way he treated her.'

'He was polite.'

'Yeah, polite. He thought she was trash.'

'Oh, Arif,' she said. But she couldn't deny it. 'He'll come around. It was just unfortunate how it happened. Must have been a bit of a shock, finding out like that.'

'You don't have to make excuses for him.'

'Sorry. I'll stop. Listen, are you going to raise your daughter as a Muslim or a Christian? Have you and Lucy talked about it?'

'It's not that deep,' said Arif. 'We believe in Jesus, he's a prophet, we respect him, so Christmas is okay and what else is there? That's all they believe in.'

'You may have a point.' She was glad she'd missed the first bus.

He stood up. 'I see your bus coming now.'

A minute later it lumbered to a halt and the doors hissed open. 'I'll see you . . . ' said Yasmin. 'I don't know when but soon.' She boarded and as the doors closed, she turned. 'And Arif, I like your hair like that.'

She tapped her bankcard and sat downstairs and waved to him as the bus pulled away.

He cupped his hands round his mouth and shouted: 'Keep it hundred, Apa!'

CHRISTMAS DAY

She hadn't planned to come and now she wished she hadn't. It was nearly ten o'clock at night and she'd been on shift until five and then waited another hour for Joe to finish his shift before going to Primrose Hill for Christmas dinner with Harriet, Ma and Flame and eight more of Harriet's friends. Harriet had hired (at God knows what cost) a French private chef and two Polish (Yasmin guessed) women to serve and clear. Dinner was nevertheless exhausting.

And then she'd got an Uber all the way south to see Baba and spend the night and now she knew she'd made a mistake. They sat across the table in the kitchen because he insisted on serving food although she told him she wasn't hungry. He claimed to have eaten already but he was thinner than ever and stank of whisky. The way he ladled the sloppy curry onto her plate told her he was both drunk and angry.

Yesterday, when she called to wish him a happy Christmas he pretended to be surprised. It's just another day, he said. Another day all alone was what he meant. If you want to be charitable, he said, call Mr Hartley, he's sitting all day alone with his cat. He is missing your mother. Probably he's eating cat food.

Charitable. That's why he looked so furious. He thought she was here out of pity.

'You come here at midnight,' said Baba, getting up. 'Like this is a boarding house! I serve you and you don't even touch your plate! This is how you show your gratitude.' He loomed over Yasmin, and again she smelled the whisky on his breath. He wore his brown tracksuit zipped up to his chin and white hairs spurted from his ears.

'It's only ten o'clock,' she said, stupidly.

'I know what time it is,' he said. He picked up the pan from which he'd served her.

'Sorry. I thought you'd be pleased that . . . pleased to see me. I'm sorry it's late. I was working today. Shall I tell you about it? The consultant on call came in dressed as Santa Claus and gave out presents to the patients. It's a tradition for the consultant to—' She broke off because he was glowering.

'I am acquainted with the traditions of English hospitals. *You* cannot teach *me* to suck eggs!'

'No, I know, but this consultant is the last person you'd think would put on a fake beard and pad his stomach. And remember the patient I told you about, who's been stuck on the ward for so long . . . ' Pepperdine had pulled aside his long white beard to receive a Christmas kiss from Mrs Antonova. There was a pain in Yasmin's stomach. 'I'm here because I worry about you,' she said. 'We all worry about you. We don't want you to be lonely.'

Baba stared down at the pan he was still holding, the big iron long-handled pan.

'We don't want you to—' she repeated, and Baba hurled the pan across the kitchen. It crashed against a cupboard, hit the counter with an almighty clang and another as it landed on the floor. The reverberations slowly gave way to a dreadful silence.

'You can go to hell, all of you.'

Yasmin's ears rang and her cheeks stung as if he'd slapped both sides of her face.

'I'll clean up,' she said in a whisper. Then, making an effort to speak normally, 'Baba, you look tired. Maybe you should go to bed.'

'Don't tell me what to do. This is my house.' He stepped around the mess, took down a bottle of Johnnie Walker from the cupboard and sloshed a hasty amount into a glass. 'You don't want to live here so get out. Live there with your boyfriend and your mother. I say nothing. But you come *here* and insult me? Go on, get out.' He knocked the whisky down his throat.

'I'm sorry.' She'd been spending fewer and fewer nights at home. And he was right: she *was* here out of pity. 'You must have been lonely.'

'What do you know about it? You think *I* have some problem being alone? You don't know what you're talking about.'

Yasmin swallowed. She was desperate to get out of there and equally desperate not to let him see it.

'I will tell you what it means to be alone since you don't know.' Baba poured himself another dose. 'It means never having a mother, your father dying when you're a child and being sent away. It means working on the pavement and sleeping on the street. Do you understand? You will *never* understand. You and your brother – you are the same!'

'I'm here, Baba.' But she said it so quietly he didn't hear.

'What is *lonely* to you? Is it – spending an hour or two in your bedroom? Do you pity yourself then? Do you feel burdened by your studies? Do you think it was easier for me? If you ever feel the loneliness I felt it will . . . it will . . . ' He made claws of his hands and pressed them strenuously towards each other, fighting an invisible force field. 'It will *crush* you! You will die from it.' He breathed heavily from the exertion.

'I'm sorry, Baba.'

He stared at her, and the back of her neck prickled. She should have changed out of this dress with its sheer puffy sleeves and short skirt that showed her black nyloned thighs when she sat down.

'You are sorry,' he said. He moved towards her and she flinched.

He stood still. Surprised. Shocked. Insulted.

Eventually he spoke. 'Am I a monster?'

'No, Baba,' she croaked.

He moved slowly and sat down – carefully, slowly – opposite her at the table. 'Mini,' he said, 'come near me. Come. Stand next to me.'

'I don't want to.'

'My Mini,' he said. Beneath the white thicket of his brows his eyes were ashy black, the fire in them all burned out. 'Why, what is wrong?'

'I just don't want to.'

'Okay.' He fiddled with his spectacles then put them aside.

For a long few seconds there was only the sound of his breath, which was laboured, the faint tick-tick of the walls, and the soft billowing of the old boiler as it served and warmed the house. This little piece of paradise on earth. It was far from heavenly now.

'Okay. It is okay,' Baba repeated. 'From now on, I will not ask anything of you. Only this one thing: always remember – everything I have done, I have done to the best of my ability.' He bowed his head and mumbled something she didn't catch. He looked at her again. 'I have done everything I could for you, my family. You, your brother and your mother. If I have fallen below the standard, if I have failed in some ways . . . But I have tried to do my duties, and I have the greatest regard for your mother.' He put on his thick-rimmed glasses and got to his feet. 'Remember this, Mini. Please.'

'I will, Baba.'

'That is all I ask.' He patted the table vaguely, as though grateful for its steadfastness. All the fight had gone out of him. 'I am falling behind with my journals. I must study now.' He said it with a smile, poking fun at his endless and pointless self-improvement. 'I hope your studies are going well. The exam is soon, isn't it?'

'Yes, and it's going fine, I think.'

'That is good. Well. Goodnight.' He turned to go.

'Baba – I think I'll go back to Primrose Hill.' She didn't want to stay in her bedroom. On every visit it felt more and more like the room of a child who'd died. Tonight, she couldn't face it.

Baba nodded. 'Happy Christmas,' he said and clasped his hands behind his back as he walked out.

RUNAWAY

She ran up the stone steps and rang the doorbell. I'll be in my office, he'd said, from beneath the cotton-wool beard, if there's anything you want to talk about, I'll be there all day. Tomorrow, he told her, I'm going to Suffolk to stay with my sister, the entire family descends on her every year. He was spending tonight alone. It was practically an invitation. Joe thought she was staying with Baba. Baba thought she'd gone back to Joe. Nobody knew where she was. She was bold and wild and free to do whatever she wanted. He would be shocked and then delighted. Wordlessly, he would reach for her . . .

But when she heard his footsteps in the hallway she panicked and ran back down. Too late! He'd see her running away down the street. If she crouched behind the bins, though . . . squeezed between them and the railings . . . She must have been out of her mind to even think of it! Turning up unannounced. This late. Christmas Day!

She heard the door open. 'Hello?'

She held her breath. She wanted very sincerely to die.

'Hello? Who's there?'

Silently, she prayed: *Cover my shame, pacify my fears, guard me from what is in front of me and behind me, from what is on my right and my left, over my head and under my feet.*

Footsteps descending. Wind whipping through the black iron railings. A stray plastic carton spinning across the flagstones, lodging against her foot. One day she would laugh about this.

She squatted lower and covered her face with her hands like a toddler playing hide-and-seek.

'Yasmin?'

'No,' she said, meaning, *This is not happening.*

'Yasmin. Would you like to come in?'

She sat on the sofa, and despite everything – the lacerating mortification, the despair that led her to it, the fear she was losing her mind – she was hungry to take it all in. It was the first time she'd seen his sitting room. There was little to glean from the white wooden shutters, the straight lines of the chestnut leather sofa and matching armchairs, the cowskin rug, the subdued tones of the striped painting that hung on the wall. But a log fire burned in the fireplace, a war film – Second World War – played on the television with the sound turned down low, and a bottle of red wine – fancy label, half-full – stood on a side-table. So that's how he spent his evening: a fire, a film, a glass of red. She stared at the blue penumbra between the charred black wood and orange flames. She still had her coat on.

What the hell was she going to say to him? He'd gone to fetch another wine glass. Back in a moment, he'd said. And, make yourself at home. No wordless embrace. No, *What the hell are you doing here?*

Perhaps he was calling a psychiatrist right now to have her sectioned.

'Here we are,' he said, returning with the glass. 'Aren't you hot in that coat?' He wore jeans and a faded blue T-shirt with a frayed neckline.

As he sat down, she stood up. He got up again.

'I shouldn't be here,' she said. 'I'd better go.'

He picked up the wine bottle and poured a glass as though he hadn't heard her. Then he was behind her and his hands were on her shoulders, lifting her coat, peeling the sleeves from her arms. She shuddered.

'If you're not in the mood to talk we could watch the film. I only started it a few minutes before you ... arrived. And I could rewind.'

'Okay,' she said. If he was going to pretend this was normal then she would too. What did it matter? Whatever she did now couldn't make things worse. She'd sit and drink wine as if she'd popped round for a movie and a nightcap. 'I don't like war films, though,' she said, succumbing to the urge to be disagreeable. She'd seen so few she had no real opinion. She took her glass and sat down on the sofa. The leather felt buttery, as though the fire had begun to soften it.

'Neither do I, as a rule. But I like this one. *The Thin Red Line.*'

'What's good about it?'

'Um,' he said. 'Well. The cinematography.' He picked up the remote, sat down in an armchair and pressed pause. 'The fever-dream quality. The story – which is really about ... '

He talked and she looked at him, stretching out his long legs to rest his feet on the coffee table, the sinew and muscle of his bare forearms, the stoic set of his mouth. It was suddenly unbearable. How could he sit there playing film critic without showing the slightest interest in why he'd found her out there between the garden waste and the recycling?

'I don't know what to do!' she burst out. 'I'm so unhappy!'

'What happened?' He looked at her gravely. 'My little runaway. What happened?'

'Everything's gone horribly wrong! Everything's terrible!'

'Tell me,' he said. 'Let it out.'

'I can't! I can't make you listen to . . . me talking about my dysfunctional family. About Joe.'

'Yasmin,' he said, 'I want you to. You can tell me anything.'

Later, after they'd caught their breath and lain beneath the bedclothes a while, he got up and returned with a parcel. Holly and silver bells wrapping paper done up with a curly red bow.

'Got you something. Here.'

'Really? Oh no! I didn't get anything for you.' Midnight-blue leather gloves with grey silk lining. 'Thank you. They're beautiful.'

'How's the fit?'

'Perfect.' She wiggled her fingers, to demonstrate how snug they were. 'Are you sure, though? I don't want someone else to go without their present from you tomorrow.'

'They're for you. Look at the tag if you don't believe me.'

'I believe you.' He must have quickly repurposed them, written a new gift tag when he went downstairs. 'How did you know I'd turn up tonight?' She said it teasingly but he looked at her with reproach.

'I thought you might come to my office. I waited there all day.'

'Oh! You should have said.' She laid a gloved hand on his chest, laid her head next to it and counted his heartbeat. Slow. A runner's heart rate.

'What did you think when you found me hiding in your front garden like a total fool?'

'I thought . . . I don't know. I thought you'd better come in.'

'But were you shocked? Were you glad? Or horrified?'

'Not horrified.'

'Thanks a *lot*.'

'What do you want me to say?'

She sat up and took off the gloves.

'Yasmin. I'm glad. I'm glad you're here.'

338

'Fine.' She had told him everything, poured her heart out about Baba. How guilty she felt about him. How confused she felt about Joe. Guilty too, though Harriet said guilt was the most useless of all the emotions. Harriet was part of the problem, always interfering although she didn't mean to, she meant well. But it bothered her in a way she couldn't even define. Arif had caused a rift in the family. Ma had made things ten times more difficult by moving in with Harriet. Yasmin wanted to be honest with Joe, she'd nearly told him already, it was on the tip of her tongue, but if it broke them up then she would be stuck living with Baba, because Arif was banished and Ma had exiled herself and why did it have to be Yasmin who couldn't escape and Arif said she had Stockholm syndrome but she didn't, she just tried to do the right thing. Then she cried, and Pepperdine held her.

And then they went to bed.

'I'm making you angry,' he said. 'No? Disappointing you, then.'

She looked around the bedroom. A cream-coloured chaise longue, a padded bench seat at the bottom of the bed, built-in storage with invisible handles, a ladder-back chair where they'd thrown their clothes. It was all pretty neutral. Like Pepperdine.

'Of course not. You didn't have to let me in. I wasn't *expecting* anything. Well, apart from the obvious.'

'Sex?'

'What else?' she said airily. How strange that he was the one. She looked in his green-grey eyes. He had an air of renunciation about him, an ascetic look, as though he abstained from all earthly pleasures.

'I think there is something else,' he said.

'Oh? Tell me.' How strange that he was the one who'd uncovered her most primal desires.

'I think that's not all you want.'

'What else do I want?'

He drew her down to lie next to him, their heads sharing a pillow. For a long moment all was stillness, all was peace, all was calm. He ran a finger down her cheek, along her jaw, and traced her lips. Cupped her chin in his hand and kissed her mouth.

'What else do I want?' She whispered it this time.

'Friendship.'

He kissed her again but she pulled away and sat up.

'Yes,' she said. 'Of course.'

'Are you going to tell Joe about us?'

'About us? Being friends?'

He lay there on his back and turned up his palms, that infuriating gesture of his. He'd set a trap and she'd walked straight into it. Friendship!

'Yasmin, you're going to have to tell me what you want.'

Friendship. Okay, friendship. What *did* she want? Romance?

'You don't want to live at home with your dad because you'll feel stuck. But you could rent somewhere or . . .' He reached for her but she scrambled away. 'Or you could stay here.'

'No, I couldn't. He'd be so hurt if I left him alone to move in somewhere random, with some random person.'

'Ah, I see,' he said. 'Random.' He brooded a while. 'Life is almost entirely random, as far as I've been able to make out. And I've been very grateful for the random people it's thrown me, especially the ones I've found behind wheelie bins.'

She smiled. She sat on top of the bedclothes with her bum on her heels, naked and on display. With Joe she was still shy of her nakedness. Or maybe she wasn't shy any longer but it had always charmed him, her reluctance, and it was a habit she'd maintained.

'How many people have you found there?'

'Oh, not many. One or two. I guess your parents had an arranged marriage – all planned by their own parents so it was the opposite of random for them. I mean, no chance encounters, no thunderbolts.'

'They had a love marriage, actually.'

'Tell me,' he said.

It was nearly four o'clock in the morning before they fell asleep. 'Do you like the gloves?' he asked her sometime in the hour between three and four when they kept drifting and waking. 'Your hands are always cold.' She kept her eyes closed. 'I love them. I thought you bought them for someone else.' She felt his lips on her forehead. 'There's nobody else,' he said.

BOXING DAY

When she woke, he wasn't there. She closed her eyes again and burrowed under the covers, hoping he'd come back to bed in a minute. Eventually she conceded he wouldn't. She had to get up and face the day. The day after yesterday. And yesterday was one hot mess.

Her dress was folded on an armchair. He must have tidied up. She found her underwear and then slipped the dress on. Black velvet with sheer bell sleeves. Yesterday she'd been so pleased with it, and today it made her feel terrible. At university girls talked about 'the walk of shame'. Yasmin knew what it was – when you walked home after an unplanned sexual encounter in the same clothes you'd worn the previous night – but she'd never walked it before.

She found him downstairs in the kitchen eating a slice of brown toast with marmalade.

'There's coffee in the pot,' he said. 'What else would you like? I've got to leave soon.'

'I'll just get my stuff and go.' It felt like he was throwing her out.

He got up and poured a mug of coffee. 'Milk? Sugar?'
'Just milk.'

He put the mug on the table and pulled out another chair and she sat on it. Sunlight poured through the kitchen window. It was bright in here, too bright, and she shielded her eyes with one hand.

'Still tired?' he said. 'Hungover? I think I have Alka-Seltzer. Should I look for it?' He put a hand on the top of her scalp as though he was some kind of priest and she a supplicant.

She lowered her own hand and looked up at his big, serious face. But she had the feeling he wasn't taking her seriously. Why was he being so casual?

'I don't know what to do,' she said. 'My entire life is entirely messed up.'

'Start with toast,' he said. 'Toast will help.' She watched as he sliced two pieces off the wholemeal loaf.

'I'm serious,' she said. 'I mean it.'

'Same,' he said. 'So do I.'

She drank coffee and contemplated lines of attack. She itched to launch an assault on him and she didn't understand why. But the urge was strong.

'So, you're just going then. You don't want to talk to me. You're going to get in your car and drive off and you wanted me in your bed last night but you can't be bothered to talk to me today and that's just it as far as you're concerned, you've washed your hands, but it's my life that's a mess.'

He had his back to her. He put the bread in the toaster, turned the knob and pushed the lever down. 'I have to leave for Suffolk, yes. I told you that. If I'd known you were going to show up last night—'

'It doesn't matter. Forget it. Forget I said anything.' She wished she had something else to wear, anything but this ridiculous dress. How could he take her seriously sitting here in this dress!

He didn't answer. The toaster pinged.

He gave her the toast on a white plate. He gave her a clean

knife. 'Butter and marmalade there, but if you prefer jam? Or honey?'

She shook her head and sipped coffee and regretted lashing out.

'I know things are complicated at the moment.' He sat down, and she felt small and soft and unhealthy next to him, his long, athletic frame. 'But you'll work them out.'

'I don't want to be a doctor.' She said it with a vehemence that took her by surprise. As if she'd decided that.

'Ah, I thought you'd got over the hump. As it were. We talked about it, and I think you said you'd decided to carry on.'

'My father decided I had to be a doctor. I didn't decide anything.'

'Well, luckily, you turned out to be very good at being one.'

'There are probably other things I could be good at.'

'Yes,' he said. 'Possibly.'

'Joe said he'd support me while I retrain, or if I take time off to think about what I want to be.'

'Ah, good. That's good.'

His face was like granite. It was impossible to hurt him, although why she wanted to hurt him, she didn't know. Did she want him to fall to his knees and sob at the mention of her fiancé? Did she want him to beg her to be with him instead of Joe?

'He's a very kind person. Very supportive.'

'Well, I'm glad. Feel free to take your time over breakfast and I'll leave a key so you can lock the front door behind you and put it through the letterbox.'

'Don't you care *at all*?'

'Yasmin,' he said, 'stop it. I'm not going to play games.'

'What games?' She forced a smile. She felt sick. Sick of herself and her behaviour and being unable to get a grip.

'Goading me. Trying to taunt me. It's beneath you. You're better than that.' He stood up and looked down at her gravely.

'Who are you? My teacher? My headmaster?'

'Yasmin, I like you, I think you're great. But you have a mean streak in you.'

A mean streak! She did not have a mean streak! Joe said she was the nicest person he'd ever met! He said she was too good for him. Who did Pepperdine think he was? She did not have a mean streak! Why did he have to be so nasty to her?

'I don't,' she said, and burst into tears. 'I do not.'

'We all have faults,' said Pepperdine, which was no comfort at all. 'I'm sorry but I have to go,' he said, more gently. 'There's the key. Will you be all right? You should try to eat something; it *will* make you feel better, you know.'

She wiped her cheeks with the backs of her hands. 'I'm all right, stop fussing. Stop treating me like a child.'

'I will if you stop acting like one.' He smiled. 'Do we have ourselves a deal?' He held out his hand as though they would shake on it but she folded her arms and turned her head.

She decided to walk to Primrose Hill, it wasn't far but it would give her enough time to think. She was still wearing the Christmas Day dress and if she'd stayed the night at Beechwood Drive, she would have changed into something else. There were still some clothes in her drawers. She thought and thought until her head ached, until she realised that she didn't need a story after all. She could just as well have chosen to come home in the same clothes, nobody else would remark on it: her worry was a by-product, an excrescence of her guilt. When she reached the driveway she halted and gave herself the once-over. What could give her away? She held out her hands, like a murderer checking for traces of blood under the nails. Her hands were bare, the midnight-blue gloves stuffed in her bag. Her hands were bare. She'd taken off the ring somewhere and forgotten it.

HARRIET

She sneaks into the kitchen and sneaks out with a mug of coffee. The house is being prepared for the party and this never improves Rosalita's mood when she returns from her annual leave after the New Year. Not Another New Year Party. It used to be fun. People loved it, the mid-January one-finger salute to the post-festive backlash. But every year the party feels a little drearier than the last.

Rosalita is banging around in the kitchen, and not only because the house is in disarray. She has not taken well to Anisah Ghorami, and is particularly sour at the moment, but Harriet refuses to be bullied by her housekeeper. She has to draw the line somewhere. Rosalita does not decide who is or isn't welcome in this house. Anisah is most certainly welcome.

Anisah and Flame are becoming close and this too arouses Harriet's protective instincts. But which of the two is most in need of protection? Flame might be intimidating to some, but not to Anisah. That woman has been underestimated all her life. When she told all about how she came to be married . . . even now it brings a tear to Harriet's eye. Anisah is courageous, and quietly formidable.

This will be the last time, Harriet decides, as she steers around the pile of folding-leg tables in the reception hall, the stack of chairs to be put outside for the smokers, the linens and non-slip trays and bottle skips and chillers and ice buckets and the boxes of lighting rig for the garden. She pauses and sips her coffee. No, she won't be hosting this party again. One of the events team – she has her hair in pigtails though she cannot be a day under forty – is opening the door for yet another delivery. Sorry, she says, turning to Harriet. Sorry about this pile-up, we'll get it moved out of the way in a jiffy.

Harriet smiles and waves and says, Oh, don't worry. The hall always looks too bare after the tree comes down, and . . . She trails off because nobody is listening. The woman is busy instructing the delivery men and writing things on her clipboard.

The sitting room too has been denuded of Christmas decorations, and much of the furniture. Harriet stands at the centre and turns slowly, a full circle. This room is too big, she thinks. This house is too big. Joseph will go and she will be all alone. She looks around at the big empty room, the swagged velvet curtains, the logs in the fireplace, the gilt-framed painting over the mantelpiece. Cold white winter sun streams in from the six-pane Georgian sash windows. It settles like frost on the rugs that have not yet been rolled. She stands with her hand on the mantelpiece and wonders if she should go and lie down for a while. Now that she has given up on the memoir, she finds herself distinctly underemployed.

What would Daddy think if he saw her now? He'd make her snap out of it. When he came to visit her at Oxford, he brought his latest girlfriend, who was a dreadful bore. Harriet and Daddy gave her the slip. They left her in the front bar of the King's Arms and left via the back. Daddy took her to dinner then she took him out dancing to show him off to her friends. What about Davina? Harriet kept asking. Don't worry about her, said Daddy, she'll go back to the Randolph and I'll make it up to her tomorrow. *You're* my best girl, he said. He whipped her around the dance floor. Harriet's friends nudged each other. They thought he was her boyfriend. It was hilarious. A glorious night.

Harriet finishes her coffee and puts down her mug.

Those Delft jugs must be put away and the Tiffany lamps. Rosalita will want to take care of those. It would be as well to have a few high round tables in here for people to rest their drinks. No stools, though, or people just sit and sit as if the party should revolve around them. She still knows how to throw a party. That's one thing she's still good for. There should be candle lanterns all around the front garden this year, not just at the entrance. Make it special. Make it fabulous. White dahlias everywhere. White dahlias in tall vases for the house, and white lotuses floating in big steel bowls for the patio, and along the drive.

There's no time to lie down, she realises as she hurries to find Rosalita. There is work to do. There is much work to be done.

HARRIET'S PARTY

In a way, she envied the waiters, busy with their trays of canapés and bowl food – tuna poke, pea and mint risotto and shepherd's pies. There was a knack to circulating at parties and it was one she didn't possess. Yasmin stood with Ma and Flame. Ma wore her most dazzling sari, cream silk with a gold border and a gold choli that was perhaps a little tight under the arms. Her hair was coiled and piled high on her head, studded with diamanté grips.

'Namaste,' said a guest, pressing her hands together and bowing slightly as she passed by. Ma beamed at the woman, an alumnus from her cookery class. Flame whispered something in Ma's ear and they both started laughing.

'She was trying to be friendly,' said Yasmin. She accepted another glass of champagne.

'Not trying hard enough,' said Flame. 'That's the point.'

'Bit harsh,' mumbled Yasmin, although she remembered how irritated she'd been at Harriet's gala dinner when the woman sat next to her just assumed she was a Hindu.

Flame wore sharp black trousers and a heavily beaded mermaid-green blouse, which she had bought on a charity-shop trip with Ma. It was the kind of thing Anisah, with her magpie instincts, might pick for herself and look terrible in, but it looked good on Flame. Ma had started using bright red lipstick, like Flame's, not every day, but often enough, surely, for Flame to notice she'd started copying her.

'Suits her, doesn't it?' said Flame, touching, just barely, a slender white finger to Ma's mouth.

'Mm,' said Yasmin. Was Flame a mind-reader?

'Strong red, strong lips, strong woman,' Flame declared.

'I will cut my hair,' said Ma, touching, just barely, a soft brown finger to Flame's head. 'I will cut it short like yours.' She laughed.

'Come upstairs with me,' said Flame. 'I'll do it. I'll do it right now.' She sounded impatient and terse, as if irritated by Ma's teasing.

Ma just laughed. 'Okay, you go and I will follow.'

Flame slunk off immediately, with Ma rolling behind her. Yasmin decided to sit down somewhere. The sitting room had been mostly cleared of furniture so she retreated with a bowl of risotto and more champagne to the lavishly cushioned window seat to observe the party. She considered, briefly, the possibility that Flame would hack off Ma's hair, but Ma would never go that far for the sake of whatever joke it was they had running between them.

Harriet, who had broken her habitual monochrome with a pleated silver skirt and oxblood blouse, steered Joe from one clot of guests to another, a hand pressed to the small of his back, ever vigilant. Like his bodyguard, thought Yasmin.

It would be different when they were married. She'd stop being so stupid, so stupidly insecure. Pepperdine said she acted like a child. How dare he? He was forty-six and he'd never been married. She'd gone to his office, the first day he returned to work after Christmas. I've lost my ring, have you found it? Blue sapphire with diamonds on a platinum band. *I'm afraid not. How unfortunate.* Nothing else to say. Nothing.

She'd given him the cold shoulder since then and he pretended not to notice. He treated her as normal. She didn't care. She'd be moving on soon anyway, to a cardiac unit in another hospital.

The save the date cards were in a drawer in Joe's bedroom. She made sure she took all of them. We can't send them out, she said, until things are back to normal. Joe agreed. There's too much uncertainty, we can't plan a wedding while my parents are separated. Joe understood. While my dad is estranged from my brother. Joe totally got it. And we have to tell my mother and yours what we've decided and make them accept that it's up to us. We will, said Joe. He was so good. So understanding. He'd even consoled her about losing the ring. It took all her powers of persuasion to stop him buying a replacement. I'll find it, she said, it'll turn up. But it wouldn't. She just knew it would not.

Yasmin drained her glass.

Harriet materialised out of the crowd, holding out her hands. '*There* you are, Yasmin! You mustn't be a wallflower.'

Harriet deposited her with Joe, who looked relieved to see her. 'Here she is, as promised darling,' said Harriet. 'I must fly.'

'Alan's extolling the virtues of Brexit.' Joe wrapped his arm around Yasmin and whispered in her ear.

'The problem with the academic left . . . ' Alan wagged a finger.

'I thought we were the metropolitan elite.' The woman on the receiving end of his finger was short and stout with an unkempt mane and inquisitive face. Like a Shetland pony, thought Yasmin.

'Whatever.' Alan wore a collarless shirt and a moss-green baker-boy cap. He liked to wag his finger as he made his points. 'You shout racism and play identity politics and ordinary people are sick and tired of being accused of being bigots. Also—'

'Why don't we listen to some *other* voices.' The pony-woman gave Yasmin a meaningful look.

Joe's fingers tightened on her waist. 'You're supposed to be the other voice,' he said quietly, just to her.

'I'm a bit drunk,' she whispered back.

'Voting Leave doesn't make you a racist,' said Alan. 'If you feel uncomfortable because English is becoming a foreign language in your own town, your kids' school, doesn't mean you're prejudiced. It's not about race, it's about culture and belonging. If you feel you don't belong in your own country that's a problem. Right?'

'So you voted Leave, did you, Alan?'

'No, Sophie, I didn't.'

'Why don't we ask Yasmin how her community voted?' said Sophie.

Yasmin gave her a little smile. Baba voted for Brexit, she and Arif voted against. Did Ma even vote? What was her community? Would Mr Hartley count? What should she say?

'As a white man,' said Sophie, giving up on Yasmin, 'do you think you have the authority to speak about racism?'

'As a rich woman,' said Alan, 'do you think you have the authority to speak about the working class?'

'How much do you think academics get paid?'

'Middle class, then,' said Alan. 'Class trumps race. Doesn't matter what colour you are, it's how much money you have, the job you do, the circles you move in . . . Yasmin, you're a doctor. Let's hear what you think.'

She tried to look thoughtful. But he wasn't asking her as a doctor. He was asking her as a brown person. An expert. An undeniable authority on issues of race. Alan and Sophie were looking at her, wanting their views legitimated: by the representative of brown-skinned people, of immigrants, of outsiders, or perhaps of insiders but newly minted and therefore doubly

352

loyal, if not loyal then ungrateful or seeking advantage from mere skin colour . . . It was making her head ache . . . it was so much easier dealing with people like Mrs Rowland and telling them to get stuffed . . . although *that* hadn't worked out so well in the end.

'Depends on the situation,' she managed. 'But when my parents first came, there was a lot more racism. They've talked about it. I'm not saying there's no racism now.'

'But you personally,' said Alan joyfully, his finger back in action, 'you personally haven't experienced racism.'

'She just said,' snarled Sophie, 'that racism remains.'

'Actually, Sophie—' Alan began.

'It's not Sophie! My name's not Sophie!' She jabbed a retaliatory finger at him. 'Do you do that to all women? Pretend you can't remember our names to put us in our place?'

'For fuck's sake,' said Alan. 'Calm down.'

'Don't tell me to calm down!' People turned to see what the yelling was about. 'Don't you ever, *ever* tell any woman to calm down!' She turned her back and barged her way to a place of greater safety across the room.

Alan shifted uncomfortably. 'Can't have a decent conversation with anyone these days.' He put his hands in his trouser pockets and jiggled them vigorously to check he still had his balls.

'We'd better mingle too,' said Joe. He took Yasmin's hand and led her through the brilliant and glittering crowd.

They stood on the patio outside the plate-glass doors for a breath of fresh air. Joe said he needed it. Tables and chairs set out for the smokers were mostly empty. A few diehards clumped together round the tables closest to the lawn. Yasmin was freezing. Also, she kept glancing at her reflection in the doors and her outfit was awful: a baby-blue kurta with turquoise embroidery over skinny jeans with high-heel shoes. It was supposed to look like an effortless fusion. It looked a mess. Schizophrenic. She should have known it was a disaster when Ma gave it her seal of approval.

Joe saw her shivering and guided her towards an outdoor heater.

'Sorry you got landed with that lot.'

'They were okay. They meant well.'

'Look me in the eye and tell me you weren't dreading being called on to give a rousing defence of multiculturalism. Or to explain why it's definitely failed.'

'I could have handled it. And it's not as though they even realise they're being a bit . . . '

'Racist,' he finished for her. 'Just say it! Why didn't you tell them?'

'Because . . . ' She paused. Because she'd learned her lesson with Mrs Rowland. Because she had to go on a diversity awareness and sensitivity course. 'It's really bad to call someone racist. It's the worst insult. People get really upset.'

'*Calling* someone racist is worse than *being* racist?'

'I'll put it like this: one is easier to get away with than the other.'

He kissed her. Full on the lips and it felt natural and wholesome. Where was the passion? He was decent, kind and thoughtful, but she wanted more. She needed passion. He looked at her eagerly, the way he did when he tried to anticipate what she wanted. With his new haircut he looked so different that sometimes it startled her. His hair was so short all over it was practically shaved, and the hair that remained was darker, no trace of blond. It made his face more angular. Harder. But when he looked at her like that all she saw was the same old Joe. He kissed her again, gently, and it disturbed her how platonic it felt. How innocent.

'Do you want to go back in?'

'Not yet,' she said. 'Look how clear the sky is tonight. Look at the stars.'

They'd stopped having sex. It had been weeks. They started once and she tried something. You don't have to do that, he said. She was embarrassed. They cuddled every night but he never took it further. When she put her hand there, he said, I'm sorry, I'm just tired. It's okay, she told him. No big deal. But she wanted it. She wanted to feel with him how she'd felt with Pepperdine. How ironic. It had taken her all these years to open herself up to pleasure. But for Joe it wasn't new, it wasn't exciting. He'd slept with so many women. How many? He'd wanted to tell her one night and she'd stopped him. She didn't want to hear about it. No more than he'd want to know about Pepperdine. It would be unkind to tell him in order to relieve her own conscience. Guilt was the most selfish of all the emotions. Harriet said so.

'Joseph! Yasmin! *There* you are.' Harriet spread her batwing sleeves as she swished across the patio. 'Have you been enjoying yourselves?'

'Yes, thanks,' said Yasmin.

Harriet inserted herself between them, taking both their arms. Her earrings, long vines of diamonds, glittered tremendously beneath the string lights festooned above. 'Tell me about all the fascinating conversations you've been having.'

'Interesting one with Alan,' said Yasmin. 'About identity politics. Things have gone too far, apparently.'

'Oh, isn't he preposterous?' Harriet laughed. 'Alan's fighting the liberal establishment with his *trusty sword of truth*. He's quite delusional. Identity politics! I must have it out with him – they've had hundreds and hundreds of years of identity politics these Anglo-Saxon Protestant heterosexual men, and it was all fine and dandy as long as their identity was the only one that counted. Now! We are going inside. Come along!'

*

There had to be a hundred people. A hundred and fifty? Many had arrived fashionably late. Harriet had whisked Joe away to meet someone and Yasmin had gone looking for Ma, who was nowhere to be found. She stood by the library door, observing. A few guests sat on the grand oak staircase as though they too were only here to watch. A small queue had formed at the downstairs cloakroom. And twenty or so people stood around drinking and talking in the hall.

A man by the gilt-framed mirror waved at her. Tall, corkscrew hair, paisley-print shirt, skinny wrists poking from the sleeves. Nathan, that was it. From Harriet's gala dinner. She waved back and he beckoned her over.

'What I'm trying to get across . . .' said the man who was with Nathan. He had a sweaty chest and a hip flask in his hand. 'The self is the only proper subject for fiction. All other claims are preposterous.'

'I disagree,' said Nathan. He turned to Yasmin. 'Been having fun?'

'Sort of. Oh, I think we've met before as well,' she added, recognising David Cavendish.

'I'm David Cavendish,' he said, as if he doubted it. 'Anyway, we live in an age which demands reality, authenticity, immediacy, transparency. Making up characters called Fred and Flora won't do. It won't do at all. The need for fiction is waning because the facts are so pressing. The facts!' He took a swig from the flask.

Baba would agree with him, thought Yasmin. *Tell me – how are you different from a liar? How is this creative writing different from lies?*

Nathan winked at her. 'People want stories. Simple as that.'

'Genre fiction,' said David.

'What genre is *The Bird Orchestra*?'

'*Symphony of Birds*,' snarled David.

'I heard you on the radio,' said Yasmin. 'Saying it's a novel about your life?'

David Cavendish snorted.

'People want shtories,' Nathan said, and hiccuped. He'd seemed quite sober until that point. 'The *environment* is the only proper subject for fiction. How about that!'

'Eco disaster, war, floods, famine, plague – but what do *you* know? You've never experienced any of them.'

You do not know what I said to your mother in the library in Calcutta. You were not there. David Cavendish was certainly on the same page as Baba. No wonder Harriet said the novel was dead.

'Have you read it? *Sympathy of Birds*, I mean.' Nathan swayed towards Yasmin, tall and slender as a birch tree.

'No,' said Yasmin, 'but I think it's brave to write an autobiographical novel, to lay yourself bare . . .'

'It's *autofiction*,' said David, turning to face Yasmin. His eyes were red rimmed. Beads of sweat clung in the crevices of his neck. 'It's not *David fucking Copperfield*.'

'I've read it,' said Nathan. 'Lot of shopping. He prefers Crosse & Blackwell to Heinz baked beans.'

'What about love?' said Yasmin. Perhaps she ought to look for Ma again, make sure she was okay. 'Isn't that a good subject? People always want to read about love.'

'Women's fiction,' said David. 'Only the frivolous and the foolish waste their time with synthetic stories – plots, characters, motives, denouements!'

'Plumbing,' said Nathan. The more David snarled, the more jovial Nathan became. He bent down to whisper in Yasmin's ear. 'Constipation. Barcelona. Arsenal. Fried eggs. Twitter. Diarrhoea. Goethe. Mummy's cameo brooch. Bodmin Moor. Isis. Dog shit.' He straightened up and smiled his gap-toothed smile.

'Let's hear it,' said David Cavendish, suddenly affecting good humour. His eyes betrayed him, twitching with belligerence. 'Share with the rest of the class!'

'People want stories, that's all I'm saying. Or they can just watch reality telly. Or look at the Facebook pages of random strangers.'

'Everybody needs stories,' said Yasmin. She hoped to God that Ma had not permitted Flame to attack her hair with a pair of scissors. What would Baba say if Ma went home with a hedgehog head like Flame's? 'I had this patient once with Korsakoff syndrome, which affects memory, and because he often didn't understand what was going on, he made up stories to try to explain it. But that's what we all do, really, in a way.'

'Thank God we've got a *medical* opinion,' said David.

Nathan reached for David's hipflask. 'May I?'

'Yes, boy,' said David. 'You may indeed.'

Nathan froze. 'What did you say?'

'Yes, boyo – my Welsh roots coming through. Go ahead.' David pressed the leather-clad flask into Nathan's hand.

Nathan drank, licked his lips, and drank again. 'All gone.' He tossed the flask back to David, but it bounced off his chest and landed on the floor. 'Whoops,' said Nathan.

David Cavendish looked at the flask. He looked at Nathan then back at the flask, his little red eyes bulging from his head. He jacked up his shirt sleeves and for a moment Yasmin feared he was going to launch a physical attack. But David just laughed. 'Fuck it,' he said. 'Empty anyway. So, your book's being published when?'

'Oh, great!' said Yasmin, breathing again. 'Congratulations!'

'September,' said Nathan. It came out a little blurry, the s thickening.

'Exciting,' said David.

'Yeah,' said Nathan, 'thanks. That's me done. I'll be off home now.'

'Home! We haven't got started yet. No, fuck the flask, leave it, I know where Harriet keeps the good stuff. Come with me.'

'No, you're all right. I need my bed. Good to meet you,' said Nathan, extending his hand.

David shook hands with him. 'Likewise. Listen, I think it's great that publishers are doing this sort of thing at last. Some people are . . . a bit funny about it, but *I* think it's long overdue.'

'What sort of thing?'

'Giving a leg-up to minorities.'

'So, you're saying that's the reason.' Nathan was still relaxed, his voice quiet and calm.

'Pretty face doesn't hurt. Pretty hair. Don't get upset, mate. It's all good stuff. Interesting backstory I'll bet, polish that up for the interviews.'

'Upset? I'm not upset. Why should I be?'

'Some people would say . . .' said David Cavendish, and paused. He rubbed his jaw. He looked up at Nathan. 'Some people would say a book should be judged purely on the quality of the writing. But I'm not one of them. Minorities should be pro – not protected – what's the word I'm looking for? Promoted? Personally, I'm all for it.'

'That's kind of you,' said Nathan.

'Although it's sad, in a way, that we're not further forward, that we're dividing people up into groups and calling it progress when race is a social construct anyway. I mean, judging people on the colour of their skin used to be a bad thing, right? And I just don't see people in those terms. I don't even *see* colour, personally.'

'Don't you?' said Nathan, very quietly.

'No. I don't.'

'See this?' Nathan held up his fist.

'Now— ' said David, smiling. But that was all he said before Nathan's fist connected with his chin.

'I'm sorry I missed it,' said Flame.

'I did *try* to calm them down,' said Yasmin. The party was over, and they'd gathered in the kitchen.

'Darling, it was quite a show. Vaudeville!' Harriet took off her earrings and massaged her earlobes. 'The hall was *packed*. Anisah, stop tidying!' Harriet swooned onto the sectional sofa. 'The caterers will come back in the morning to finish off. Come and sit down.'

'I will do a few things,' said Ma, scraping food from a platter into the bin. Her hair, thank goodness, was still intact.

'You,' said Flame, 'wardrobe mistress! You're working tomorrow. Bed!'

'No,' said Ma.

'Yes!'

'No,' said Ma, laughing.

'Grr,' said Flame.

Ma chortled manically. What's *wrong* with her, thought Yasmin. Flame's jokes weren't funny at all.

'Now I am tired,' said Ma. 'I will go to bed.'

'Goodnight,' said Flame. As soon as Anisah had gone, Flame yawned and announced her departure as well.

'Brandy,' said Harriet. 'We'll have brandy and then bed. Joe, would you please furnish us with a Remy Martin and do find the balloon glasses? I cannot drink brandy from a tumbler.'

Harriet sat up to sip her brandy. Joe downed his rapidly. Yasmin swirled hers around the glass and just the fumes made her head start to spin.

'Marvin didn't turn up tonight,' said Harriet, her voice

unusually flat. 'Clare pleaded a cold! People who've been attending for decades didn't bother to show up.'

'They'll regret it,' said Joe. 'Everyone will be talking about it now, because of the fight.'

'Of course, if people only realised,' said Harriet, 'how awful writing is, what absolute torture, they'd be surprised how *infrequently* writers descend into public displays of lunacy.'

'Torture?' said Yasmin.

'Agony, darling! Total agony. I'm giving up on the memoir.' She put down her glass and reclined again, gifting her blue-white feet to Joe's lap. 'Would you mind, darling? Those shoes pinched like hell.'

'Gross, Harry,' said Joe. He pushed her feet roughly aside.

'In India, children bow down and kiss their parents' feet,' said Harriet, folding her legs, an unfamiliar, uncertain tone in her voice.

'We're not Indian, mother.'

'Don't be silly, darling.' She had a frog in her throat. She cleared it. 'Well,' she said, getting up slowly, 'you two must hurry up and find somewhere to live. It's clear Joseph has had quite enough of living with me.'

'Joe,' said Yasmin. But he wouldn't look at her. 'Joe, aren't you going to say something?'

'I don't think so.'

Yasmin stared at him. His top lip still curled in distaste as it had when he'd shoved Harriet's feet off his lap. It was true Harriet was overbearing sometimes but this was an overreaction.

'He's just tired,' she said to Harriet, as though Joe was a truculent toddler.

Harriet's nostrils flared. 'I know that,' she said.

BOUNDARIES

On the first Thursday after the party Yasmin had a day off. She was supposed to go and see Baba but couldn't face it. The nights she'd spent at Beechwood Drive since Christmas were awful. Baba sucked all the oxygen out of the house. It was suffocating. Arif had called again. Lucy was due yesterday. They had a bag packed for hospital. Why wasn't the baby coming? The average pregnancy, said Yasmin, is actually closer to ten months than nine. I'm not telling Lucy that, said Arif.

For a long while she stood at the window watching the raindrops, transparent tesserae forming and breaking. And there was the slow steady hiss of the gutters and the lemon scent of the Windolene and the cold glass against her nose. She had to *do something*. Her life was on hold because of Ma.

Ma was still here though she knew it meant the save the date cards stayed in the drawer, the marquee could not be booked, nothing could be planned.

You could stay here, Pepperdine had said. She couldn't. Even if he meant it, which obviously he didn't.

Thinking about him gave her a funny feeling. And it made her angry. Every time she'd seen him at work since Christmas she'd felt so angry it gave her a pain in the chest. I'm afraid not, he said, when she asked if he'd found her engagement ring. Just that and nothing else. Why was she even thinking about him? He had nothing to do with anything. The ring was still lost. It wasn't here or at work or in Tatton Hill or at Pepperdine's. Joe said not to worry, it'll turn up, but it didn't and it wouldn't now.

Harriet had to *make* Ma leave. Only Harriet had the power. It was pointless to try to *influence* Ma. Stubborn as a mule, as always. Ma was behaving irresponsibly, but it was Harriet who was enabling her. And Flame wasn't helping. She was creepy. And she was downstairs with Ma right now making chutneys, encouraging Ma to do who knows what.

She knocked on Harriet's door. Harriet had been out for 'a ghastly lunch' and on returning declared she would be reading in her bedroom if anyone needed her.

'Enter,' said Harriet. 'Ah, Yasmin, yes, yes, come.'

'Thanks. I need to talk . . . ' She didn't know how to start.

Harriet was reclining on the couch, her head against a fluffy sheepskin. Every object and surface in this room invited touch, from the richly embroidered wall hangings to the carved ebony panels of the antique furniture. Even in the gloom of a January afternoon it was sensuous. It was a boudoir. A bedroom for an orgy, though Harriet was avowedly celibate.

'Well?' prompted Harriet.

'There's something I need to ask. A favour. It's a bit awkward, actually.'

'I see. Then allow me to say something before you proceed.' Harriet slid her feet to the floor and stood up. 'It's not a crime to love your own child,' she declared grandly and mysteriously. 'To a fault,' she added. 'I make no apology.'

'Right,' said Yasmin. 'Sure.' Harriet had thrown her off balance.

'Message received,' said Harriet. 'Loud and clear.'

363

'Sorry? What message?'

'Get out and stay out.' Harriet smiled a terrifyingly icy smile. 'Stay out of the wedding arrangements. Don't go into his room without a formal appointment. Do I surmise correctly?'

'No, I didn't—'

Harriet spoke over her. 'Have I not made you welcome in my home, Yasmin? Have I not shown hospitality? To you and also your family. I opened my house. I opened my arms, did I not?'

Yasmin stood dumbfounded. She hadn't said *anything* to Harriet about staying out of the wedding arrangements. When Harriet started up about flower arrangements a couple of days ago Joe said, For fuck's sake, Harry, there's not going to *be* a wedding if you don't keep out of it. It's on hold as it is.

Joe was the one who said it and clearly Harriet had decided Yasmin must have put him up to it. But it was Joe who'd become so irritable with Harriet lately.

'You've been so generous,' Yasmin managed. Her neck, her hands, tingled with embarrassment because that was the truth, and Yasmin had never said thank you. In fact she'd come here to complain about Harriet's generosity and demand that she cut it short.

'I love my son!' Harriet said fiercely. Fervently. No trace of her habitual laconic drawl. She held her chin high. Her long neck was white as a lily; red blooms on her imperial cheeks. 'And I will not ... I *will not* ...' she repeated passionately, 'be humiliated like that again. I do not need permission to enter *any* room in my own home.'

Early yesterday morning Harriet had knocked on Joe's bedroom and, in her usual manner, marched in without waiting for a reply. *Boundaries, Mother!* he yelled at her and Harriet flinched. Harriet Sangster was never afraid but at that moment she looked scared of her son. She went out without saying a word.

'Sorry,' said Yasmin, although again it was Joe who had committed the offence.

Harriet turned away and pressed her hands against the window. Her ringed fingers glistened in the milky rain-sky light. She sniffed two quick tight sniffs. 'Never mind, never mind.' She muttered it into the pane. 'He's been talking to his father, you know. I think that has *something* to do with it.'

'Oh,' said Yasmin. 'I thought that was going well.'

'Therapy,' said Harriet bitterly. 'You realise, of course, the mother *always* gets the blame.'

'He goes to talk about his father.'

Harriet whipped round to face Yasmin. 'Yes, but that's not how therapy works. It's ... oh, never mind!' She cleared her throat. 'Now, what can I do for you?'

'Well ... so ... could you please send Anisah back to my father? I'm very grateful to you for putting her up. You've been enormously kind. But she needs to go back now. My father needs her. And I'm sure you never meant for her to stay here so long.'

'*Send her back?*' Harriet frowned. 'No, I don't think I can. She's free to come or go as she prefers.'

'But the thing about Ma is she needs to be told. She won't pick up on the subtleties.'

'What subtleties? She's more than welcome to stay. I like having her around.'

'Please,' said Yasmin pathetically. If she had to, she'd get down on her knees and beg.

Harriet carried on frowning. She looked Yasmin up and down, weighing something up. 'You know what I think would suit you? Jewel colours – sapphire blue, emerald green, amethyst, citrine. Pastels do nothing for you, and khaki is so drab. You're a pretty girl, Yasmin. Make the most of it.'

Yasmin glanced down at her pink sweatshirt and combat trousers. 'Seriously, Harriet, you don't want Rosalita to quit, do you?' Rosalita had again threatened to leave. Her lips had grown thinner every day until they'd finally disappeared, her mouth a mere crease across her face.

'So Rosalita put you up to this? I'll have a word with her.'

'No! It's what *I* want. Me! Ma has to go.'

'Then tell her yourself.' Harriet shrugged as she crossed the room and sat down at the dressing table. As far as she was concerned the interview was at an end.

'It's not my house. If you tell her it's time to go then she'll go. My father needs her back.'

'Does he? What about what she needs?' Harriet's face, in the three-sided mirror, reflected endlessly. 'Perhaps she needs more time to figure out how to live the rest of her life.'

The rest of her life! Ma already knew what that would be. It didn't need figuring out. 'My parents had a disagreement about Arif, that's all. When she's back home – that's when they can work it out.'

'You do realise that your mother has begun ... a relationship – with Flame?'

'Relationship?' Oh my God! What the fuck! 'They're friends, that's all.'

In the mirror, Harriet smiled.

'Shit,' said Yasmin. 'She hasn't. She can't.'

'That's not all,' said Harriet. 'There are other issues. Anisah needs space, which I am happy to provide.'

'What issues?'

'My dear child,' said Harriet. She opened a jar and rubbed cream into her hands, slowly, sensuously. 'I shouldn't be the one to tell you so go and speak to your mother. I'm not keeping her prisoner.'

'But whatever it is you're making it *worse* by letting her stay. Baba's too proud to come and fetch her and she's too stubborn to go back.'

'Listen to me,' said Harriet sharply. 'It's not that simple. There are things you don't know.'

'Like what? Go on!' She marched closer to Harriet as if she'd beat it out of her if she had to.

Harriet kept her cool. 'Ask her. Or ask him. It shouldn't come from me.'

'You don't know anything.' Her voice was a little shaky.

'Okay.' Harriet sighed. 'I don't want to upset you. We won't fight each other.' She paused. For an eternity she sat there massaging her hands. 'It's complicated. But I'll tell you the straightforward part – your father, over the years, has conducted a number of affairs with other women and your mother has known this and accepted it. Now she's decided she needs a little time and space to herself to think about the future. I'm happy to provide them both. She's a remarkable woman, and I won't turn her out, Yasmin. She has my support. I'm sure she would welcome yours.'

HOME VISITING

'Let's go upstairs, Ma. I need to see you,' said Yasmin. 'On your own,' she added, glancing at Flame.

'I am coming,' said Ma, rinsing her hands at the kitchen sink. 'Do you like? The labels – do you like? Flame has designed for me!'

Flame poured chutney into a square glass jar. The label, which read 'Anisah's Achaars: Authentic Bengal Pickles', was already sticky.

'Nice,' said Yasmin.

'Very beautiful,' said Ma, drying her hands. 'But I could not get any kalo jira for the panchforon so it is not authentic. I will not be able to sell.'

'Yes, it is,' said Flame. 'Yes, you can.'

'Ma,' said Yasmin. 'Let's go.'

'Go,' said Flame to Ma, granting permission where none was needed. Her boot-polish-black hair was gelled into annoying little spikes. How could Ma bear to spend so much time with her?

Yasmin closed Ma's bedroom door and leaned against it as if Ma might try to escape. 'Has Baba ever had an affair?'

'Oh,' said Anisah. She turned away and stood with her back to Yasmin.

'Has he? Has Baba ever had an affair?'

Silence.

'Look at me, Ma. Ma?'

Anisah turned slowly to face Yasmin. A fennel seed clung to one butterball cheek.

'Harriet says he has. More than one. Is she lying?' It was a stupid question. But Baba having an affair was unthinkable: all he did was work and read journals and take care of his family. How could he have affairs when he never went out? Maybe Ma had made it up to justify whatever it was she was doing with Flame. 'Honestly, Ma, he's desperate for you to go home. He loves you. You should hear him, you should see how he's falling apart . . . he can't manage without you. You've got to go back to him.'

Anisah waggled her head defiantly. 'He can manage.'

'He can't! He's miserable!' Yasmin shouted. 'Sorry. It's just . . . this entire family is falling apart. Ma, he'll see sense about Arif and Lucy and the baby. You *know* he will. But if you leave him . . . Ma, haven't you punished him enough?'

'It is not for punishing.'

'What, then?' Flame. But Ma, surely, wouldn't admit it.

'I need time.' There was a pile of clean laundry on the end of the bed. Ma unfolded and refolded a blouse, a skirt, trousers. She shook out a T-shirt then crumpled it into a tight ball.

'Time? You can have as much time as you want at home.'

'He had women,' said Ma. 'Not many. Not recently.' She sat down amid the laundry and kicked off her sandals.

Yasmin slid down the bedroom door until she came to squat on her haunches.

'But how? He never goes out, Ma. He never did.'

'You remember,' said Ma, 'he used to go for home visiting?'

369

'Yes,' said Yasmin. 'Seeing patients at home. Yes.'

'This was how,' said Ma. 'This was when.'

'And you caught him out?'

'Oh, no!' Anisah objected vigorously to this slander. 'Always he was honest. A man has needs.'

So that's why she wasn't shocked about Joe. Ma said she was a feminist. She had no idea what the word meant. 'No, Ma. That's no excuse.' Arif was right. Baba was a hypocrite.

'There are things you don't know,' said Anisah. 'Without knowing you cannot understand.'

'Then tell me.'

Ma bowed her head. She pulled at a loose thread on the sleeve of her cardigan.

'Make me understand, Ma. Tell me. I'm not a child.'

'You are my child,' said Ma.

'But why don't you want me to understand?' moaned Yasmin. 'It's not fair,' she couldn't help adding, though she knew it was the eternal complaint of children.

'I do want. But be patient. These are not easy things for me, and you are pushing. Pushing too much!' She brushed the seed from her cheek.

'I *am* patient. I'm *so* patient, Ma! Look, I'll sit here as long as it takes.' Yasmin shifted from a squat to a cross-legged position. 'Take as much time as you need. Start right at the beginning because I have all the patience in the world and I want to know everything.'

Ma looked at her wistfully. Her eyes misted. 'My angel,' she said, 'I cannot explain it now. One day I will explain to you.'

'Fine,' said Yasmin. She wasn't going to get straight answers out of Ma. She was trying not to be angry with her but it was hard. 'What about Flame? Can you at the very least be honest about what's going on with her? Harriet says you're . . . in a relationship.' It couldn't be true. And if it was Ma would deny it.

'She is my friend.'

'Just a friend? Nothing more?'

'No. She is my special friend.'

'Ma, are you . . . ?' Yasmin stalled. Was she going to say it out loud to her own mother? It was sacrilege. But she had no choice. She couldn't leave room for confusion, and special friend could mean anything. 'Are you a lesbian?'

'Lesbian?' Ma waggled her head as if Yasmin had said something foolish. 'No, I am not lesbian.' Yasmin heaved a sigh of relief before Ma added: 'Only I like Flame.'

'In . . . *that* way?'

'Yes,' said Ma, with no sign of embarrassment.

'What about Baba?' How had it come to this? How had this happened? If only things could go back to the way they were before. When arriving in Primrose Hill in a Fiat Multipla with stacks of curry in Tupperware marked the pinnacle of shame, the very worst of her problems.

Anisah unhooked her earrings. She pulled on her elongated earlobes and gave them a rub. 'It will be okay. You will see.'

'How?' wailed Yasmin. 'How?'

'You will see,' said Ma in her most obdurate voice.

Yasmin got to her feet. Her knees ached. She took a deep breath and inhaled the scent of lightly toasted spices and Yardley's Lily of the Valley. Ma's scent. There was something else in the air as well. The same smell she'd noticed before in here. Honey and musk. It was the perfume that Flame wore.

'Well, I guess he deserves it,' said Yasmin. She'd had enough. She'd tried and there was nothing more she could do. 'Home visiting,' she muttered. 'What a hypocrite.'

'He is not a hypocrite,' said Ma.

'Whatever.' She opened the door. 'I'll find out how he explains it.' How did Ma explain it to herself? Did she think of Baba as Ibrahim and herself as Sarah? And the other women as

Hajira, the slave girl? Ma loved that story. The way she told it was as if Ibrahim and Sarah's marriage was ideal, Sarah's love for her husband so strong but she was barren so she gave him Hajira and let him make love to her. But Ma had given Baba two children, so what was the justification? How could Ma accept it? Why didn't she stand up for herself?

'No! Do not speak to Baba about this. He does not want his children to know these things.'

'I'll bet he doesn't.'

'I am your mother and you will respect my wishes.'

The doorknob was loose. Yasmin rattled it. 'Okay, Ma! Whatever you say.'

Ma looked at her, shiny-eyed. 'It is time for my prayer now. Will you like to pray with me?'

'No,' said Yasmin. 'I will not like.' She started to go out, then turned back. 'Pray hard, Ma. Pray for all of us. Pray for your family.'

SANDOR

'I went up to the neonatal ward today,' said Joe. 'Ages since I went in there.'

'Was it nice to see the results of your handiwork?' The boy had made so much progress it was hard to believe he was the same person who'd turned up at their first session, in denial and terrified. And he looked different too. Since the New Year he'd had his hair cut. Shorn. It made him look older. He'd lost the softness around the cheeks.

'The neonate ward is . . . it's so intense. These incredibly tiny humans wired to all this amazing technology, and rationally you know whether they live or die depends on how premature they are, and the expertise of the doctors and nurses, stuff like that. But what you feel is . . . awed.'

'How do you experience it in the body?'

The last eight sessions they'd worked hard on this: reconnecting to the body in new and healthy ways. Sexual addiction was an attempt to escape from the body, which was the site of so many unwanted and repressed emotions.

'It's kind of enveloping? As though all your nerve endings get supersensitive. A sort of heightened awareness, I guess.'

'Okay. Awareness of what?'

'Awareness of . . .' Joe shrugged. 'The universe? How small we are. How fragile. How everything's connected. It's hard not to feel like the fate of those babies is in the hands of . . .' He trailed off.

'Destiny? A higher power?'

Joe smiled his slow, bashful smile.

'And this embarrasses you?' It took several sessions for Joe to connect with those unwanted feelings, to go deep enough to access his rage.

'The baby boy I delivered a couple of days ago – mum's an addict. Methadone. You get to know them, the addicts, because they get a lot more support. And she's had a really difficult life, Chloe. I like her . . . she's a tough nut but she's funny, you know. You think, How do you do it? How do you survive all that and still find it in you to be cracking jokes?' He paused and ran his hand across his forehead, though he no longer had a fringe to push back. 'Anyway, the birth was straightforward, and the baby was just fine. I was happy for her. She talked about rehab all the time. I don't know if she'll manage it but you can see how much she wants to take care of that baby. She kept saying she wished she could come off the methadone while she was pregnant, but you can't do that because of the neurological damage it might inflict on the foetus. Of course, it's an easy thing to say when there's no chance she has to actually follow through. But I felt for her, really, I did.'

'You saw the baby a couple of days after the birth,' prompted Sandor. By that time withdrawal symptoms would have set in. Babies born addicted to opiates only became sick when with-drawal began.

'He was screaming this high-pitched scream and the nurse told me he had a seizure last night. He has trouble feeding, he's sweating, fever . . . the usual things that happen with neonatal abstinence syndrome. I've seen babies in that kind of state, but it really got to me in a way that it hasn't before.'

'Yes? Say more.' Joe had made so much progress. Sandor felt proud of him. Somewhat paternalistic, but so what? That's how he felt, as if Joe had grown up here in the consulting room.

'He was screaming and trembling, lying there in his cot screaming this unearthly scream. And I was furious all of a sudden ... swallowed up by this almighty rage, with Chloe. This is what she's done to him, this innocent, defenceless baby boy! She should go to jail for this.' He said it all calmly. 'She doesn't deserve to be punished ... but for a few minutes I was completely overcome by rage. So what I'm wondering is ... now that I've *accessed my rage* as you put it, is it going to keep spilling out into other parts of my life?'

'Why do you think the baby triggered that in you?'

Joe shrugged. 'Babies bring out protective instincts in everyone. Except, maybe, sociopaths.'

'Yes. And?'

'He was in pain.'

'Yes. And?'

'It made me angry.'

'It made you angry because?'

'I couldn't help him. I'm a doctor but there's nothing I could do.'

'You said that prior to this you'd felt a connection with this baby boy?'

'I don't know.'

'You were furious with the mother. The mother whom you regard with affection, with compassion for her difficulties. The mother who did the best she could.'

Sandor stopped there. He let Joe sit with it.

'Perhaps,' Sandor resumed, 'you felt a level of compassion for this baby that you still find difficult to feel for yourself.'

'The baby hasn't done anything wrong. He's done nothing to deserve it.'

375

'And did you choose to grow up inside a dysfunctional family? Do you deserve to suffer as a result?' Sandor smiled at Joe.

'I'm assuming those are rhetorical questions,' said Joe.

'For most people, yes. For you, I'm not so sure.'

'Fair enough.' Joe drummed his fingers on his thighs, as he tended to when he was about to take a conversational swerve. 'I've applied for a job up in Edinburgh. And I've got an interview.'

'This has been prompted by ... what?'

'I think what I need is some real distance between us, me and Harry.'

'Sounds good,' said Sandor. It sounded like an evasion strategy, an excuse to delay what had to be done. 'We Yanks love Edinburgh.'

'I might not get it.'

'Other jobs are available. In other distant cities.' Today he'd taken a proper break for lunch and they'd ended up in a slow waltz around the kitchen, Melissa humming in his ear. He was a lucky man. And he was going to start taking better care of himself. Melissa said he should go for a full medical and that it was ridiculous, at his age, he'd never had one. As usual, she was right.

'I thought maybe we could have online sessions.'

'Last week, Joe, we talked about how you might initiate a conversation with your mother. Have you managed to speak to her?'

'Not yet. Had a couple more calls with Neil. That's going okay, I think.'

'In fact, we've spoken about it for a few weeks now ...'

'I was thinking maybe it would be better to leave it for a while. I've been setting boundaries so I'm wondering if there's really a need—'

'Allow me to interrupt you there. There *is* a need. This is not about blaming your mother. It's about assigning responsibility where it belongs. A child does not choose this kind of relation-ship with a parent. You did not choose it, any more than that baby boy you saw chose to have toxins in his bloodstream. And until the truth of it is faced and resolved with your mother you will not be free from the toxicity.'

Joe fiddled with his shoelace. Brown laces today. A green sweater.

Joe sighed. 'I just thought that if I moved away, if I physically removed myself . . .'

'This thought arises, naturally,' said Sandor. 'But here's some-thing I've learned from my patients over the years, especially the drug addicts who often drifted from place to place, town to town, looking for somewhere their lives would be different. What they taught me is that wherever you go, there *you* are. What you seek to leave behind is something inside you.'

Joe sat quietly.

'What about Yasmin? Where are you at with her?'

'Well, I was thinking,' Joe began slowly and shyly, 'and I know this is going to sound crazy but it might not be as crazy as it sounds at first. If I get the job, she could come with me. I haven't talked to her about any of it yet, but we're getting on so well. So it's possible, I think, that she'd come with me and we could just, you know – whoosh!' He dashed a finger through the air like a magic wand.

'Elope? Disappear without trace? Would you tell her about your addiction before the elopement?'

'I don't know. I tried once but she stopped me.'

'So you tried once and that's good enough?'

Joe didn't reply and Sandor let the silence speak for him. No need to spell out just yet what Joe already knew to be true: there was no magic wand, no happily ever after.

'A new job,' said Sandor eventually, 'new colleagues, strange city, far from home. It's the dream of escape. Of reinvention.

You begin again, and the past belongs only to history. But the dream becomes a nightmare, because the job is demanding, you know nobody except your wife who may or may not be aware of your addiction – either way that brings great pressure to bear on the relationship – and hanging over you is the prospect of your mother's arrival for a visit. Would it be surprising in these circumstances to find yourself struggling again with your addiction? It would be a great shame to undo all the good work you've done these last few months.'

Joe hung his head. 'Uff,' he said. 'Urgh.'

'Let it out,' said Sandor. 'And breathe.'

'Aaaargh!'

'Deep breath in. Can you tell me what's going through your mind?'

Joe raised his head but kept his hands clasped over the top as though to keep it from exploding. 'I know you're right. I'm a self-deluding moron! That's what's going through my mind. Dumb as fuck!'

'Would it help if I told you it's common for people in recovery to indulge in this kind of magical thinking? Usually it comes at a point just before a significant breakthrough. Think of it as a last-ditch attempt to find a bridge over the swamp before recognising that you have to plunge in and swim across.'

'Okay,' said Joe, grimly. 'Okay. I'm going to do it. I'm going to cross the swamp.'

'You'll have the conversation with Harriet?'

'What do I say? How do I start?'

'We can role-play if you like. Would you find that helpful?'

Joe smiled. 'Very,' he said. 'You start. You be me and I'll be Harriet.'

TEA AND BISCUITS

It was visiting time and most of the patients were sleeping.

'I have had enough,' announced Mrs Antonova. 'Enough is enough. Wake up. Washing. Dressing. Medications. Breakfast. Nap. Reading. Nap. Lunch. Nap. Blah, blah, blah.' Her voice was thin and wavering. Her vocal cords had suddenly caught up with the rest of her body.

This morning Yasmin had tried once more to get her into a hospice, but Zlata didn't fit any of the criteria. Except that she would die soon. It was disgraceful the way she'd fallen through the cracks in the systems that were supposed to take care of her. The social worker was tearing her hair out because Social Care wouldn't pay for a nursing home place and the Health Trust didn't want to pay for 'continuing care'. So Zlata was stuck in hospital and she'd die before all the forms were redone and the reviews and the meetings happened.

'You'll feel differently when you're in the right place.'

'The right place, pumpkin, is six feet under the ground.' She winked a lashless violet eye at Yasmin and grinned. Her false teeth were preposterously large and white.

'You've not touched your lunch again,' said Yasmin, pointing to the tray on the bedside cabinet. 'You're not on hunger strike, are you?'

'Tcha!' She clicked her tongue the way she did when Yasmin was being more stupid than usual. 'These days my stomach rebels unless I give it only what it wants. That's tea and biscuits. A little yogurt and stewed fruit. I used to have a very strong constitution, you know. I could eat anything and everything, and I did! Very strong stomach I had.'

'You must be hungry,' said Yasmin. 'I'll try to find you something.' She looked over at the pantry, a white cubicle with a glass door, next to the linen shelves. No chance of liberating a digestive or custard cream. Not without the help of a Cotillion employee.

Zlata waved a clawed hand. 'The way my mother fed us it was essential to develop an iron stomach. She served up strips of cow tongue boiled in milk and called it stroganoff. We were penniless but proud! My mother was a princess, so she claimed, and when I found out it wasn't true she was already dead and—' She broke off as Julie arrived.

'When you have a moment,' said Julie. She nodded and walked away towards her office.

'I'm coming,' said Yasmin. 'Sorry,' she said to Zlata.

'Go! Go! You go and do your work. Don't forget the whisky next time. The sun will shine and we will sit outside together for a little farewell drink.' She sounded cheerful about the prospect of attending her own wake. 'You promised, pumpkin, so don't forget.'

'I won't,' said Yasmin, though she knew she couldn't do it. It was definitely against the rules.

'And have you set a date yet?' Zlata leaned in conspiratorially.

'I'll have to see . . . but as soon as possible I'll take you outside for a bit of fresh air.'

'The wedding! Have you set a date for the wedding?'

'Oh! Well ... actually ...' It was too difficult to explain everything.

'You've had another row? Don't worry, pumpkin, so it goes. The course of true love never did run smooth. When I married Dimitri it was nearly three months before I let him into my bed. Of course I didn't want to marry him because he was so much older and it was to pay a debt my father owed, you see ... Well, he turned out to be the love of my life ... Now what are you crying for?'

'Nothing,' said Yasmin. 'I mean, I'm not. Sorry. I'm fine.' She stood up. 'Sorry, I do have to go. Shall I set up your book for you?'

Mrs Antonova grunted and put on her reading glasses. Behind the thick lenses her eyes were disturbingly large. 'Take a tissue, pumpkin. And yes, I'd like to read, thank you. Grab that book there – under the tray.'

Yasmin set up the book on the fold-down table that hung over the bed. The table stayed in place for barely two seconds before it began to droop. She pushed it back into place. Julie was waiting to see her, she had to prepare for the stroke clinic, chase up results from haematology, write care plans for two new admissions ... but Mrs Antonova wouldn't be able to read if the damn table didn't stay put.

Yasmin looked round for help.

'Go!' Mrs Antonova tried to flap her away. 'I can manage.' The book, a hardback, most likely another of her well-overdue library books, toppled to the floor, opening and landing with its pages splayed.

Yasmin picked it up and tried again. The table stayed high this time but listed to the side. Yasmin held the book in place.

'Harrison!' she called out as Harrison trundled into view pushing his yellow bucket-on-wheels. Two bottles of disinfectant spray hung like handguns at his hips. For once he wasn't singing.

'How're you, Doc?'

'I know it's not your job, but is there anything you could do about this table? It won't hold still.'

'Loose screw,' said Mrs Antonova.

'No problem.' Harrison unearthed a screwdriver from somewhere about his person.

'You deserve a pay rise,' purred Mrs Antonova. 'Tell me, have you ever read *Lady Chatterley's Lover*?'

Harrison shook his head. 'Tell me about it, Mrs A.'

'Anxiety and depression?' Yasmin was stunned.

Julie held out the card for her to sign. *Get Well Soon*, it said on the front in shiny pink capital letters. Inside, the words *Thinking of You* were printed in sober black and surrounded by expressions of support and signatures from everyone in the department. *You are amazing and we miss you! Love from Niamh. PS Don't hurry back though, take all the time you need!*

'I'm ordering a bouquet to go with the card,' said Julie. 'If you want to put a couple of pounds in?'

'Of course,' said Yasmin. 'But Catherine? She seemed fine, didn't she?'

'Dr Arnott's been having panic attacks for a while now. She's been signed off for two weeks but I think it'll be longer than that before she's well enough to come back.'

Catherine, with her muscled calves and music recitals, her Head-Girl-in-heels walk and Latin phrases, so confident and capable. Catherine was having panic attacks? 'I didn't notice anything,' said Yasmin. 'Did you?'

Julie didn't reply. She never gossiped and she wasn't about to start now.

Wishing you a speedy recovery, wrote Yasmin, and instantly regretted writing something so lame.

'Thanks,' said Julie as Yasmin put the card back on her desk.

'I'm leaving this box here for the flower money until the end of the day.'

'Right. Will do. Oh, if there's any chance of getting the pantry opened and finding a few biscuits for Mrs Antonova . . . she's not had any lunch. Says the food doesn't agree.'

'No one's turned up today from Cotillion,' said Julie. 'I mean, for the pantry. The cleaners have come but they don't have a pantry key.'

'It's ridiculous,' said Yasmin. 'Why does it have to be so difficult?'

'It saves money, apparently. Privatising the custard creams.'

'Right! The vending machine is broken again.'

'I know,' said Julie. She reached for her handbag. 'I have an emergency supply. I'll give Mrs Antonova a few digestives and a cup of tea.'

She was in the departmental office, putting on her coat, when Professor Shah bowled in.

'Dr Ghorami! Still gracing us with your presence after all?'

'After all?' she said. Professor Shah's hair was extra bouffant today. His lips were fat and too shiny. 'I've just finished a shift.' She'd managed to dodge him earlier on the dementia ward. The ward was always quieter when he was around, as if the patients were awed by his presence.

'James tells me you're quitting medicine. Decided it's not right for you. Or you're not right for it!' He gave a forced little laugh.

Pepperdine had been talking about her behind her back? Telling Professor Shah things about her that he had no right to tell. 'No, I've not. I've not decided.'

'If I may be permitted an observation?'

Yasmin was silent, knowing Professor Shah didn't really want her permission, but he waited until eventually she was forced to say, 'Yes, of course.'

383

'In my experience, it's not uncommon for girls – young women – such as yourself to go into medicine because they feel pressurised. It's a suitable profession, aspirational, secure . . . or they come from a medical family. These girls can find themselves struggling.'

'Which girls? The brown ones?' She didn't care how rude she sounded. He couldn't get away with saying things like that.

Professor Shah smiled unctuously. 'I know whereof I speak. I've seen it in my own family. When the girl finds a suitable husband she drops out of medicine. Is your father a doctor, by any chance?'

'No,' said Yasmin. 'He's not.'

SEGREGATION

'It wasn't like that,' said Pepperdine. 'I mentioned it only to illustrate a point. About Catherine Arnott. Darius and I were discussing how much pressure junior doctors are under and I remembered what you'd said to me – that you'd thought about quitting.'

'Well, it's obvious he thinks I should, so thanks a lot!'

He got up and closed the office door. 'Yasmin, he doesn't. He has his faults but he knows you're a good doctor. You bruised his ego, that's all, and he's making you pay. Don't take it so seriously.'

She had walked in here so angry she could hardly see straight, and now she was simply exhausted. She wilted onto the desk. 'He asked if my father's a doctor. And I said no!'

Pepperdine laughed. 'So what? It's none of his business anyway. Look, I don't want to make excuses for him but they're keeping us waiting on the announcement – the Centre of Excellence thing – and Darius affects nonchalance but he's anxious as hell. Though that doesn't mean he should be picking on you. Or anyone. Do you want me to . . . have a word with him?'

Yasmin shook her head. If she reached out a hand she could touch him. He had a light blue shirt on as usual, a new one that still bore fold marks from the packaging. She wished he'd look at her properly.

'And how are you?' He looked down at the floor as he spoke. 'Aside from . . . ah, here. How are things at . . . at home?'

Since Christmas she'd been waiting, and he hadn't said anything. She'd made such a fool of herself that night.

'Oh, you know,' she said, and laughed.

'Not really. I don't.'

'Fine. Well, *things* aren't, but I am. Fine.'

'Ah, good,' he said. 'Good.' He lifted his eyes and gazed somewhere over her shoulder, distracted by all the important things he had to plan and do.

'My father has been having affairs.' That got his attention. 'Not recently, but in the past he had affairs with several women.'

'I'm sorry to hear it.'

He did look sad. Or maybe he didn't. It was difficult to tell with him.

She said: 'I think the truth is most men are unfaithful. Maybe most women too. That's just how people are, I think. When it comes down to it.'

'Yasmin,' said Pepperdine, 'I . . . um . . .'

'You're busy, right. That's okay, I'm going.'

'No, that's not . . . I was wondering if . . . on the subject of, ah, infidelity . . . not to put too . . .'

'What?' She held her breath. She desperately wanted him to say something. Anything!

'You were going to tell your . . . did you tell him? You don't have to tell me, of course, if you did or you didn't.'

'Not yet.' If he acted like it had nothing to do with him then she would too.

'I see.'

'No, you don't! I haven't told Joe because I'm ashamed. I'm so ashamed.' She looked at him, shifting his weight uncomfortably, and the desire arose in her to hurt him. 'I don't ever want anyone to know I ever slept with you!' She burst into tears.

He tried to put his arm around her but she pushed him away. He sat on the desk next to her.

'Sorry,' she said. Her nose was running. She wiped it on her coat sleeve and it left a silvery mark on the black wool.

'It's okay.'

'You've hardly said anything to me since Christmas. And there are other things going on . . . my brother's girlfriend is having a baby any day, and my mother . . . It doesn't matter . . . There's just been a lot.'

'Maybe,' he said, 'maybe we could go out for dinner and talk about it. Since there's a lot to talk about.'

'That would be nice. But I can't because . . . someone might . . . I could come round to yours?'

He put a hand on hers and despite the hotter-than-hell radiator and her boiled-wool coat, she shivered.

'I don't think that's a good idea.' He took his hand away.

'Why not?'

'Because it's not right. You know it's not.'

'I'm going to tell him. I am. I have to do it at the right time in the right way or it'll . . . And everyone cheats on everyone, even . . . Well, just . . . people do, all the time.' *Even Ma.* But she couldn't bring herself to tell him. Though she'd exposed herself to this man in every conceivable way (and in some ways she still found inconceivable), she couldn't tell him her mother had become a lesbian. Or not a lesbian, exactly, but had a woman as a lover. *Your father has kept me tied up here like a goat.* They'd been harvesting the marrows and the onions and Ma had said that. Tied up here like a goat. Segregation. Something about segregation. Baba keeping Ma apart from . . . the community? Whatever that was. He didn't *know*, did he, about Ma liking women?

'Not everyone,' said Pepperdine.

'Not everyone what?' She put a hand against his cheek.

'You said everyone cheats.' Very gently, he peeled her hand from his face. 'But it's not everyone. I haven't. I've never been unfaithful.'

'Really?'

He laughed. 'Yes, really.'

'I'm going to tell him.'

'Not on my account, I hope. I wasn't trying to pressure you into anything . . .'

'No,' said Yasmin stiffly, getting up. Again she had the feeling that he'd played a game and outwitted her. 'Not on your account. Not at all.' She squeezed a smile from her lips. 'By the way, do you think Shah overmedicates patients on the dementia ward on a regular basis?'

It took him a moment to catch up with her change of gear. 'Ah, because of Mr Babangida? You think he overprescribes because of what happened in that particular case?'

'Well, that wasn't great, was it? Poor man had a broken bone and he's being silenced with antipsychotics. But actually, I've been noticing how quiet that ward is whenever Professor Shah's been there.'

Pepperdine massaged his jaw. 'Do you have any evidence? Have you *looked* for any evidence?'

'No. I was just wondering if you'd noticed anything.'

'I haven't. And I think it's highly unlikely.'

'Okay.' She tried to sound breezy. She opened the door. 'I'll take you up on that offer of dinner one day!' She gave him the benefit of her best happy face, because she knew she had no right to feel hurt by him.

'Yasmin,' he said, and turned up his palms.

She went back to the ward because she remembered about the money for Catherine's flowers. Niamh was in Julie's office counting up notes and coins.

'What's wrong?' said Niamh. 'You look terrible.'

'Nothing. I'm just in a hurry.' She fumbled in her bag, trying to find her purse. 'Hope I'm not too late to put something in for . . . '

'Julie asked me to do the order. Look, I'm not trying to be nosy but you're obviously upset about something.' Niamh had nail varnish on. Bright red, which was a mistake because it made her coppery hair look orange. It was also against the rules.

'Here,' said Yasmin, handing over a ten-pound note. 'I signed the card already.'

'Poor Catherine,' said Niamh. 'She was obviously one for bottling it up. It's important to talk to someone, isn't it? About problems.' She tilted her head, performing sympathy.

'You've got nail varnish on,' said Yasmin.

Niamh inspected her fingers. 'Oh, I forgot! I've been off sick for three days. My back's been terrible, the sciatica, and I could hardly walk the first day, I swear, it was that bad.'

'Okay,' said Yasmin. 'Bye.'

'It's much better now,' said Niamh, 'thanks for asking. Thanks for your concern, it's so nice to know you care about your colleagues and don't treat us all like we're beneath your notice or anything.' She pursed her pretty mouth.

Yasmin stood there and took a deep breath. She put her hands on her hips and blinked. Niamh was unbelievable! *I'm not trying to be nosy, but* . . . If she hadn't stuck her nose in in the first place and told her about Joe going home with that nurse. Not that she was to blame. But . . . she enjoyed it. She milked it. She wouldn't shut up about it. *You're obviously upset about something.* Seriously! Unbelievable!

'I'm sorry,' said Yasmin. 'It's been hard to keep track of all your ailments. I'm so glad you weren't in such bad pain that you couldn't lie around painting your nails.'

'You know what, Yasmin, I give up! I've gone out of my way to be nice to you and all you do is throw it back in my face.'

You know what, Yasmin, he's not bad looking. Honestly, I'd do it. I'd fuck him. Niamh was always trying to flirt with Pepperdine. And he never even noticed. Yasmin had fucked him. How about *that* as something to throw in her face!

'Take that nail varnish off,' she said. 'It's a breach of the hygiene rules. The rules are there for a reason, Niamh, and they apply to you as well.'

FISH OUT OF WATER

They had gathered in the snug (as Harriet called it) to watch Rania on television. *You say women who adopt Islamic dress aren't truly free because we've been conditioned.* She looked remarkably relaxed, as though taking part in a televised debate was nothing out of the ordinary. *But do you say the same about the women on* Love Island? *They choose to show their bodies. Do you raise concerns about whether they've been conditioned by the culture? Do you criticise* them *for imagining they are free?* She wore spike-heeled ankle boots, black jeans with a tiger-print blouse. And a black ninja underscarf with criss-cross peak, fitted tightly at the neck. She'd normally wear it only as a base layer for a chiffon hijab, but the way she'd styled it was cool.

'Bravo!' said Harriet, who was missing her Sunday-morning yoga class.

'Rania is Yasmin's very-very good friend,' said Anisah, not for the first time. 'At the school and now also.'

Yasmin put a finger to her lips. 'Shh!' She had so much to tell Rania. Although she wasn't sure she *would* tell. The prospect of divulging her parents' infidelities to anyone, even Rania, was not one she relished.

Flame, who had chosen to lie belly-down on the floor, made

a noise like an old-fashioned kettle about to come to the boil. 'Patriarchy,' she said. It sounded like a sneeze. She sniffed and rubbed her nose. Perhaps it was a sneeze.

The camera cut away to another guest, a middle-aged woman in a blue skirt suit and red and white striped blouse who responded to Rania's question: *I would, actually. I find that show distasteful and unchristian.* The 'panel' consisted of four guests, two on either side of the presenter, their chairs arranged in a semicircle on a stage in front of the studio audience.

The presenter was a man whose handsome features had been curdled by age and other disappointments. He turned to Rania. *What do you say to that? Linda is saying it's not about discriminating against Muslim women. She'd question the choices of women who uncover more or less everything in the same way she'd question those who chose to cover it all.*

Applause from the audience.

Flame shifted about on the rug. One bare foot came to rest between Ma's socked-and-sandalled feet. Yasmin tried not to stare. Ma sat in the wingback chair, sewing basket on her lap, seemingly oblivious to Flame's naked heel against her ankle.

What I say to that is British society does not, in fact, question the agency of those young women who choose to wear miniskirts or low-cut tops. Linda might dislike their choices but society as a whole doesn't view those women as incapable of deciding for themselves what to wear. It's not a crime to be immersed in one's culture. Western culture is no less immersive than any other, but when it's pervasive it becomes invisible – it's hegemonic. You don't know you're submerged in it any more than a fish knows it's in water, it's simply what is.

'Very powerful,' said Harriet. She had managed to insert herself between Yasmin and Joe on the sofa. 'Amazing eyes!'

'Shush,' said Joe. 'We don't need your running commentary.'

He always seemed irritable with Harriet now. Harriet had

blamed Yasmin for that, but Yasmin had always been so careful – too careful? – about not criticising Harriet.

The presenter tried to say something but Rania powered on. *We who choose to wear hijab – or niqab or burka – are the ones who make active choices. It's we who are fish out of water. And when you criticise our choices you're criticising many of the people who are already vulnerable, already targets, already experiencing discrimination and hate crime.*

'She's fabulous,' said Harriet.

The presenter selected a woman from the audience to put a question to the panel. *My question is to the imam. Why does your religion say that a woman should cover herself up so she won't be subject to men's uncontrollable desires? Men should be able to control themselves!*

The imam was seated next to Rania to make up the pro-hijab team. He seemed amiable enough and had so far stuck to pronouncements of Islam as a religion of peace. The imam agreed heartily with the audience member and just as heartily contradicted himself. A woman should dress modestly. This was common sense. It was better never to be alone with a man to preserve a woman's safety and reputation.

'Well, here's some breaking news,' said Flame, her upper torso rising cobra-like from the rug, 'women have desires too. We are not simply receptacles for male desire.'

Yasmin had a sudden urge to grab the pinking shears from Ma's sewing basket. Transgress, transform, transcend. That was Flame's motto. Printed in columns of Chinese letters down her back. If Yasmin transgressed by stabbing her in the thigh, Flame would transform it into a performance piece and Anisah would transcend it all by failing to notice anything.

'A woman's desire,' Flame continued, 'is a dangerous phenomenon. That's why men try to close it down. Don't you agree, Yasmin?'

'Mm,' said Yasmin. She found it hard to look at Flame. She

found it hard to agree with anything Flame said, especially this. Though there was much truth in it. Joe had misunderstood her when she talked to him about Flame and Ma. She wasn't homophobic. She wasn't prejudiced at all. It's the way she tries to speak on Ma's behalf as though Ma's some kind of halfwit. She's got Ma imagining she's going to make a living selling her stupid pickles that she could hardly give away in Tatton Hill. Imagine it was your mother, she said, and they both laughed. Okay, she said, but it's my mother and you see how that's a bit of a shock. You should be happy for her, he said, and she was trying, she honestly was.

'Your friend has guts,' said Harriet. 'She's marvellous. The pressure towards deracination in this country is profound, and I salute her for refusing to bow to it – for retaining her authenticity.'

'What do you mean?' said Yasmin. 'What do you mean by authenticity?'

'It's fairly self-explanatory,' said Harriet, 'but it means living her own truth, writing her own story, being true to her Muslim identity. Are you suggesting she's inauthentic in some way?'

'No, I'm saying you don't know her so you're not in a position to judge. You don't know what her truth is, you don't know the essence of her at all.'

Ma started to cluck but Harriet waved her complaint away. 'It's quite all right. Why don't you enlighten me then, Yasmin?'

She didn't know if she could explain it. They were all waiting, looking at her. It riled her the way Harriet declared Rania to be authentic. It implied that Yasmin wasn't. Or maybe it didn't. But it was a pernicious standard in any case. What about Ma? Was she being untrue to her Muslim identity by having a girl-friend? Allah sees what's in your heart, Ma would say, and if she was wrong about that then there'd be no room for her in her own religion. Why was wearing a hijab about living the truth?

Rania had many truths and they weren't all on display in a piece of cloth wrapped round her head.

Flame turned the television off. Ma fussed with a length of mauve fabric.

'I'll make coffee,' said Joe.

'Not for me,' said Flame. 'Got to go.'

'Oh, yes,' said Harriet, 'the Dutch theatre chap. *Bonne chance!* Though he'd be lucky to stage your show, of course.'

'If Rania lived in Iran,' said Yasmin, 'she'd be part of the anti-hijab movement that's starting up. She'd be leading it. She'd be taking her headscarf off. She'd be driving with the wind in her hair and posting it on social media.'

Everyone laughed. A text alert sounded and Ma scrabbled in her sewing basket. She stared at it for a moment then held the phone aloft.

'Alhamdulillah! She is born! The baby is born! The coolness of my eyes! She is here!'

Ma's eyes indeed brimmed with cool tears of joy, the blessing from one of her favourite stories.

COCO

The baby lay on her back, helpless as an overturned beetle, waving her crooked limbs. Her skull was elongated from the forceps delivery, circled with scanty black drifts of hair and perfectly bald on top. Above the ill-fitting nappy the umbilical cord stump poked angry and red. Her eyes were drilled tightly as Rawlplugs and her skin was yellow and wrinkled, as though she'd been lightly fried in sunflower oil.

'Oh,' gasped Anisah, 'she is too-too beautiful!'

'Gorgeous,' said Yasmin, as Arif slipped his little finger inside his daughter's miniature fist.

Harriet stood over the cot and made her pronouncement. 'Darlings, you must be so very proud. Now, Lucy, I have something for you, because everyone brings presents for baby so I come bearing gifts for mum.' She swept around to the other side of the bed.

'Beautiful face,' said Anisah, holding onto Arif as if she might pass out with joy, 'beautiful toes, fingers, hair ... even colour is beautiful like mango. Everything perfect, no need for worrying.'

'She's just a bit jaundiced, Ma,' said Arif.

'Very common in newborns,' said Joe. 'Nothing to worry about.'

Arif wrapped an arm around his mother and kissed the top of her head. He wore a blue-check flannel shirt with a clean pair of chinos. He looked taller and broader, even his neck had thickened so that the Adam's apple no longer resembled a golf ball stuck in his throat. Where was the scrawny kid, the lank-haired, screwed-up, guitar-strumming waster? Was he still inside that all-of-a-sudden manly frame? Was he lurking somewhere behind this grown-up-Arif-in-grown-up-clothes, with his trousers falling down and pants on show? Beneath the beaming, confident face was there another more familiar face, her little brother's, sulking and scowling? Yasmin looked closely at Arif and he smiled at her so warmly that her heart swelled and her voice cracked a little when she spoke. 'Have you decided on a name?'

'Coco,' said Lucy. She lay propped up on a barrage of pillows strewn with hand-knitted baby clothes, muslin squares, burping cloths, washcloths and wash gloves, and a jar of baby bottom butter. 'Coco Tallulah,' crooned Lucy. 'Don't you love it? We love it, don't we, Bun Buns?'

'Yes, we do,' said Arif, in a high-pitch sing-song to his daughter.

It struck Yasmin as some kind of miracle: even a raw recruit like Arif knew, without being taught, that babies prefer high-frequency tones. She stroked Coco's feathery hair with her fingertips. 'Coco,' she whispered, 'Coco Tallulah, I'm your Auntie Yasmin.' The baby turned her head towards the touch of Yasmin's hand, and her eyes opened suddenly. They were beautiful, nutmeg brown, and the yellow sclera around the iris didn't matter, Ma was right: she was perfect anyway. Coco gurgled and gulped and a bubble grew and burst on her lips. They laughed and cooed, the three of them, Yasmin and Arif and Anisah, in raptures at such precocity.

'Don't let her get cold,' said Lucy. 'Can you swaddle her? Do you remember how to do it? Not too tight.' She sounded exhausted. 'Not too loose,' she added.

'We should go and let you get some rest,' said Yasmin. Lucy had dark circles around her eyes and her face was pale and puffy.

'Don't go yet,' said Lucy, 'Mum and La-La would be gutted. They've only gone to get a bite. Be back in a minute, so don't go yet, there's only supposed to be three visitors at a time but we're lucky we got this side room and only one other bed and she went home two hours ago so there won't be any problem, it's only about not making too much noise, you know, being inconsiderate. Look what Harriet brought me! It's lovely, isn't it?' She held up a frothy white negligée and started to cry.

Arif went to her and she wept into his neck.

The baby, getting hungry or cold, or sensing she was no longer centre of the universe, screamed and paddled her feet and fists. She turned from yellow to pink then mauve. Anisah bowed over the cot and, with a palm on her granddaughter's rigid stomach, tried to appease her with words. Coco, Coco-sona! Dulali! But it made the baby angrier. Coco was tiny and helpless but her fury was enormous, it filled the room.

'Good set of lungs,' said Joe, smiling. 'She'll be an opera singer. Or maybe punk will be more her style.'

Yasmin stood spellbound. The baby was angry and her anger was absolute: free from fear, or guilt or doubt. She wasn't imprisoned by self-consciousness. She laid claim to her birthright of simply being herself. Yasmin smiled in wonder and envy. Enjoy it, little one, enjoy it while it lasts.

Anisah swaddled Coco in a pale blue cellular blanket, and delivered her gift-wrapped and quieted to her mother, who stopped crying and looked instantly and deliriously happy despite her red eyes and blotched cheeks.

Hormones, thought Yasmin.

'You're a mother now,' said Harriet, her eyes fixed on Lucy and the blue bundle. 'It is the sweetest privilege in life. The sweetest! May she bring peace to your heart! May she give comfort! May she bring joy! May she . . . '

Harriet couldn't continue because she was the one weeping now. Joe grimaced and walked to the other side of the room. He sat down on the vacant, unmade bed. The others looked on in astonishment. Who knew Harriet Sangster could cry? And over a baby of all things!

Anisah went to put an arm around her, but Harriet shrugged her off. 'Excuse me, I'm sorry . . . I'm going to the Ladies . . . no, I don't need accompanying. I'm fine. I just got a little carried away.'

Janine and La-La returned bearing an outlandishly large bar of milk chocolate and the whiff of cigarettes. Lucy fended them off Coco. 'She's just gone to sleep. This chocolate's amazing but I shouldn't be eating it . . . do you think I'll ever get into this?' She held up the negligée and sighed.

'Course you will,' said Janine. 'But what's the rush? Ignore all that post-baby-body Instagram rubbish.' She sank into the chair.

Anisah watched anxiously as Lucy devoured more chocolate. 'Oh, why I didn't bring food?'

'Don't fret,' said Janine. 'There's fruit in the basket, and they bring the dinner round. Long as you're not starving, count your blessings, that's what I say.' Janine, it seemed, had a talent for accepting things as they were.

La-La wore pink jeans and a fluffy grey jumper. She'd dyed her hair to match the jeans. 'Supplements,' she said, dancing around, tidying gifts, folding cloths and blankets, finding a vase in a cupboard for the flowers Harriet had brought. 'Can't go wrong if you take an iron supplement and vitamins. Where's my handbag? I want to take photos.'

The handbag was swiftly located and everyone whipped out their phones. Lucy smiled valiantly and rotated the baby in her arms so that Coco's face was visible, tiny and golden atop the stiff blue sarcophagus.

'Coo-coo, Coco!' Janine snapped her fingers, trying to make the baby open her eyes.

'Mum, don't,' said Lucy. Her voice was mild as usual but – coming from her – the brevity of the sentence was severe.

Lucy rolled the bundle up her chest, almost to her chin, presenting the back of the baby's head with its glowering forceps mark. She addressed Joe: 'Will that go away? Because the doctor said it would but it's not.'

'It's absolutely fine,' he said. 'It's nothing, the bruise will go and the shape is only temporary . . . because of the fontanelle, the soft spots on her skull – you probably remember from any baby books you read?'

Lucy nodded. 'I know, it's just different when it's not, you know, in a book any more.'

'I will send photos for my sisters.' Anisah smiled maniacally as she snapped away.

'To Amina-auntie?' Yasmin had met Ma's eldest sister only twice. She lived in small-town America with her dentist husband and their three now grown children and her religiosity was compounded by a siege mentality. Amina was so devout she had no choice but to criticise everything and everyone on the earth. And Ma was proposing to send her evidence of her unwed nephew with his infidel girlfriend and their illegitimate child?

'Amina and Rashida, both,' said Ma.

Rashida was different. She lived in Mumbai and taught chemistry. When Yasmin was fourteen, Rashida had come to stay for a whole week in Tatton Hill while attending an academic conference. Ma was delirious with excitement before, but the visit had been blighted by Baba, who treated Rashida like an intruder, perhaps as Ma's family had treated him. Still, Rashida and Anisah corresponded more frequently after the visit and Rashida – because she lived in cosmopolitan Mumbai – was far more open-minded and liberal than Amina.

'Really?' said Yasmin. 'You're sending to Amina?'

'Amina and Rashida, both,' repeated Ma.

Arif sat on the bedside cabinet, cradling his daughter, who had woken and was attempting to wriggle out of her bindings. Thus far she'd succeeded in liberating one arm. 'Want to hold her, Apa? You haven't held her yet.'

'I'd love to!'

Arif handed Coco over and Yasmin inhaled that ineffable sweet baby smell. She ran her fingers lightly over the warm, misshapen, precious skull.

'See how long the fingernails!' Ma lifted her granddaughter's tiny fist. 'It will be okay,' Ma whispered in Yasmin's ear. 'You will have a baby also.'

'You take her,' said Yasmin. She'd confided in Ma about Joe's infidelity but Ma had never asked her about it since. Did she just assume the wedding would go ahead? Had she forgotten about it? Didn't she care because now all she cared about was showing off Arif's baby? And doing whatever it was she did with her girlfriend. It will be okay. That's what she always said, regardless of the facts.

'My friends, my dear, dear friends, here you are. What an utterly gorgeous delight.' Harriet made an entrance with arms outstretched. Janine and La-La grabbed her hands, one apiece, and all but kissed the rings.

Harriet regaled them with an anecdote about Joe's birth, how she'd planned on having him at home in a birthing pool with homeopathic pain relief and then eating the placenta, and had ended up screaming to be taken to hospital.

She had everyone under her spell. All but Joe.

Yasmin looked from Joe to Harriet and back again. What had happened? What had Harriet done to piss him off so much?

'Well, you must come to the exhibition of course,' said Harriet. 'I'm hoping the book will be printed by then too.'

Janine said: 'Men talking about their tackle! It'll be educational really. I've never asked any man what he thinks about his. Well, you don't, do you?'

'No,' said La-La, 'but I've known a few fellas who've asked me what I thought of their cocks!'

'Mum!' said Janine.

Harriet winked at La-La to show she didn't object at all. No need for fancy language as far as she was concerned.

Harriet didn't belong here and yet she had them all eating from the palm of her hand. Baba should be here, not her. Why did Baba have to be so snobbish? Yes, Arif was right. If they weren't too 'common' for Harriet, why did Baba assume they weren't good enough for his son? Harriet Sangster was a million times posher than Shaokat Ghorami. He talked about Lucy as if she was lower class but what class was he? He came from nothing. He was an immigrant. He was a doctor. Perhaps he was afraid that the rungs he'd climbed were slippery.

Arif had sent a message to Baba at the same time as Ma, but Baba had stayed away. Whatever his reasoning, whatever his fears, it was unforgivable. Someone had to tell him, and that someone could only be Yasmin.

THE OLD FEAR

'No, I don't want to see it. If this is the reason for your visit you have had a wasted journey.' He turned and shuffled away into the sitting room. The backs of his slippers had become crushed beneath his heels.

'Baba,' she said, following, 'I was going to come today anyway.' Before she turned the key in the lock she'd steeled herself. She'd give it to him straight. She wouldn't plead or apologise. But already she'd tried to soothe him with a lie.

'Well? Why are you here?'

'Okay. I *am* here because of the baby – she's called Coco Tallulah, by the way – and I did want to show you the photo of her because she's here, she's real, and you've got to start accepting it. I don't care if you look at the picture, but please go and see her. *Please.*' She was pleading, but what else could she do?

He didn't move or speak. Barely twitched a single face muscle. Yet she could see it: the anger inside him like a big black wave, swelling, sucking, gathering, until it had to come crashing down.

Finally, he said: 'That girl has already finished him. Arif is finished. We will not speak about this again.'

'But he's working,' she said, 'and he's still making his film, and he's going to be a good dad, I know he will. And Lucy's going to be . . . ' She trailed off, suddenly filled with despair.

Was Baba still drinking? He rocked silently back and forth on his broken-down heels. She breathed in deeply but couldn't smell whisky on him.

He didn't say anything.

She braced herself for what was coming, the old fear stirring inside. Arif was right, she had always appeased him, because she was frightened . . . of what she wasn't sure . . . He never beat her, never slapped her . . . he hit Arif though, and if he was angry with her he hit Arif harder, she was sure about that . . . Come near me, he said, and she went, though she didn't want to . . . No, she went and listened to him talk about anatomy and penicillin . . . and she combed his hair without protest, plucked the white hairs from his head and hid her feelings so deeply she could hardly feel them at all.

Baba was tight-lipped and silent; he wielded the silence like a weapon.

'She's your granddaughter,' she said. 'Arif has a daughter and you should be happy for him. He's working, earning money, and he's doing something he cares about too, on top of that. It's not what *you* wanted, but it's his life. It's *his* life, for God's sake.'

'Something he cares about? What is that?' He spoke the words slowly, restraining himself, it seemed, from shouting them.

'His documentary,' said Yasmin, 'Islamophobia. Injustice.' When Baba was angry with her, she always looked down. Not this time. She held his gaze.

'In India,' he said, 'there is injustice. In this country, there are only excuses. Someone didn't speak to you nicely? Will it kill you? Will it keep you down? Only if you allow yourself to be so weak!'

'But she's your granddaughter! You say family's the most important thing, and she's your family. You can't pretend she doesn't exist. You've got to accept what's happened. If you don't—'

He walked towards her. The veins in his neck stood proud. 'Stop this! Enough!' He backed away from her again as if he didn't trust himself to get too close. He turned and, still standing, bent his head to a journal and read aloud: 'An 84-year-old man presented with fever, malaise and blue-black discoloration of the fingers and toes—'

'If you don't . . .' she repeated, talking over him for the first time in her life.

He raised his voice and kept reading. 'The patient was a nonsmoker. On examination he was found to be afebrile—'

'Listen to me, Baba! If you don't . . .' She groped for a consequence big enough. Something that would shake him, make him realise the magnitude of his mistake.

' . . . palpable radial dorsalis pedis pulses on both sides . . .'

' . . . you'll die alone!' she yelled.

He moved swiftly towards her and in his hand he held a club. He held it upright, like a truncheon. Her heart beat in her throat.

'You'll die alone,' she said again. Her voice was a low croak but she got the words out, she would not yield. She closed her eyes and waited for the blow.

When it did not come she opened her eyes again. Baba, the club raised above his head, looked murderous. But he was angled away from her, poised to strike the onyx coffee table. As she watched, his face crumpled and the fight drained out of him. Inch by inch, he folded, sinking by painful increments to his knees. Finally he let the club fall.

He opened his mouth but seemed incapable of speech. It occurred to her that he might be having a heart attack. Despite this she didn't move.

'Go!' he said, eventually.

'Are you okay?' But she'd already decided that he was. He wouldn't bend, so he would break. But he hadn't broken yet.

He didn't answer. 'Bye,' she said, walking towards the door. 'Wait!'

She zipped her coat and turned up the collar.

'Wait,' he said again. 'Listen to me, Mini—'

'No,' said Yasmin. 'I'm sick of listening to you.' She marched into the hallway and, on an impulse, ran upstairs to Ma and Baba's bedroom. The wedding jewellery. It didn't belong here. She opened the drawer, fished out the velvet bag and stuffed it into her pocket. Her coat hung lopsidedly and pulled against her neck. Baba had turned his bedside cabinet into a bar. His ruby-red crystal tumbler stood next to an empty ice bucket and a pair of tongs. Behind them stood rows of miniatures: Ballantine, Bell's, Cutty Sark, Dewar's ... He'd put them in alphabetical order ... Famous Grouse, Glenfiddich, Haig, Johnnie Walker, McCallum's, Talisker. Yasmin ran her fingers along the little bottles. Her hand closed around the Talisker. She dropped it into her other pocket. She added another bottle, and another and another, until both sides of her coat felt weighed down equally.

The curtains were open. Yasmin looked down into the back garden. Ma's garden. It took a while before she could make anything out through the dark. A polythene shroud over some long-withered crop flapped brazenly. Ma would never weight it down. The bony branches of the dead cherry tree, like an X-ray against the whitish panes of the greenhouse. Between scrubby patches of vegetation, bare earth, like the mounds of freshly filled graves.

Ma would never come back to this house.

'Your mother's family,' said Shaokat. He blocked her way when she ran back downstairs. 'They treated me like a cockroach.

If I ate more than one spoonful of rice and lentils your naani complained about the expense.'

'I have to go,' said Yasmin.

'There are things you don't understand,' said Shaokat. 'There are things you don't know.'

'I know more than you think. I know about your *home visits*. What you were really up to.' She'd promised Ma she wouldn't confront him. But what did it matter now?

'If there was some spot of dirt somewhere, your naani said, Oh, look how filthy – well, if you take in rubbish from the street, it is difficult to keep the house clean.'

'Did you hear me? I said, I know about your affairs.' How anxious she'd been before that first family dinner with her parents and Harriet. First and last, as it turned out. But not for the reason she'd feared. Harriet threatened to bring sex into the Ghorami household. The chaste and cardamom-scented home. Well, it smelled of mildew and dust and vegetables boiled with turmeric now. And it wasn't chaste. It never had been. They were all at it. Deceiving each other. Deceiving themselves.

'There are things you don't understand. I am not an animal. There are reasons, and you don't know the history, how things happened.'

'Well, go on then! Tell me!' He was pathetic. And what she'd said was true: he would die alone.

'I am trying to tell you. Your grandfather, your naana . . .' He cleared his throat, 'He was not like your naani. He had done the deal and he knew the deal was the best he would get. Maybe the only one. He was a businessman. He paid for my education, my board and lodgings, and I married his daughter. He thought like a businessman: always there is capital deterioration and when the deterioration reaches a certain point, there is no option but to invest. Your grandfather invested in me. And I tell you: he saw a good return.'

He held himself upright and proud. His brown suit trousers were shiny at the knee.

'I'm going,' she said. She'd heard enough. The past was the past and it didn't justify anything.

'Mini,' he said softly, 'I have never betrayed her. Your mother.'

She shook her head. There was no point staying here any longer. No point arguing with him. 'I have to go.'

He reached a hand towards her and she shrank back. He gave her a wounded look. 'But you haven't told me about the MRCP exam. You passed? Of course you did, but I have looked for a letter and nothing has arrived. Perhaps they don't send letters these days?'

'I didn't do it,' she said. 'I didn't do the exam.'

'You . . . you failed?'

'Are you deaf? I said I didn't do it. If I'd taken it, I would have failed because I didn't study. But I didn't take the exam. Is that clear now?' It was exhilarating to speak so freely. The revolutionary thrill of blowing up the old order, asserting freedom by any means necessary . . . and some that were unnecessary but pleasurable.

He moved away from the front door, no longer blocking her way.

'I never wanted to be a doctor,' said Yasmin. 'I only did it for you.'

'No,' he said. She heard the fear in his voice.

'Yes! I only did it for you!'

'No,' he said again. 'It was I who did everything for you. Mini, I—'

'I'm not Mini! Stop calling me that.' She marched past him, flung the door open and went out without closing it. The first thing she saw was his hump-backed bug-eyed car.

She stamped back up the path and yelled into the house. 'And your car! It's embarrassing! Get rid of it!' This time she slammed the door and ran.

ESCAPADE

Mrs Antonova kept sliding down in the wheelchair and this time her wig snagged on the back. 'Ouch! Take it off, will you, angel? I don't care who sees.'

Without the exotic purplish creature lounging across her scalp, Mrs Antonova would look even more frail and vulnerable. And already Yasmin was wondering if she'd made a mistake by bringing her outside. 'But I don't want your head to get cold,' she said, adjusting the curls. She lifted Zlata to sit a little higher. Zlata was so light, just scraps of skin and bone. And she kept slipping down like an under-stuffed ragdoll. Maybe there was a good reason why doctors weren't supposed to push patients around in wheelchairs.

'Cold! I'm frying like a knish inside all these blankets. I'll thank you to lift my arms free.'

Yasmin obeyed. 'Comfortable now?' She'd parked the wheelchair in the middle of the 'village green', that pitiless vale of concrete in the centre of the hospital grounds.

'Lovely,' said Zlata. 'What an adventure! An escapade! Heavenly. The sun on my arms!'

Yasmin sat down on a low wall to the side of the wheelchair. The sun wasn't, in fact, shining. Her phone pinged.

Another anxious-new-parent message from Arif. *Take her to the GP if you and Lucy are worried*, she texted back. *But if she's feeding, peeing and pooing and doesn't have a fever then I'm sure she's fine.*

Zlata said something but the words got lost beneath the wail of an ambulance. In the distance, shoals of nurses swam in and out of the automatic glass doors of the main entrance.

Yasmin leaned in close to catch the words as Zlata tried again. 'I hope I haven't got you in trouble, pumpkin.'

'Not at all. And if you had it would be worth it.' To hell with the insurance issue. Nobody was going to sue her for pushing a wheelchair. There was no specific rule about not breaking into the pantry on a smash-and-grab raid for biscuits but it probably came under some general heading about unprofessional conduct.

'Will Harrison be all right? That nurse was very angry with him.'

'He was only helping me, and I asked him. So don't worry, I'll take the blame.'

Yet again Mrs Antonova had gone hungry because there'd been no tea trolley and all she wanted to eat was digestives. Not the most healthy of diets but as Mrs Antonova pointed out she was capable of deciding for herself what she would and wouldn't eat. The Cotillion workers didn't turn up because the company was in financial difficulty and the staff, none on monthly salaries, worried about working shifts for which they might not get paid. Harrison was trying to do the work of three people but he stopped to help Yasmin.

She was hammering on the pantry window with an extra-wide bariatric rolling stool. The door, of course, was locked, and in a moment of insanity she'd picked up the stool and whacked it against the window. She couldn't stand it any more. In that moment she had sincerely believed it was the system that was insane and that she was being rational. The glass seemed to be bulletproof. Out of sheer frustration she hammered it again and again.

The ward had gone awfully quiet. Everyone stood around and watched – nurses, student nurses, health care assistants, the podiatrist who had been attending to ingrowing toenails and fungal infections, the locum doctor, the new senior registrar. Those who couldn't stand watched from their beds. Julie would have intervened for sure but Julie wasn't there.

'Want help, Doc?' Harrison held out his hands and she nodded dumbly and handed the stool over to him.

Harrison put the stool on the floor. He inspected the window. She thought he wasn't going to help her after all.

Then, with a single powerful boot he kicked in the pantry door.

'Thanks,' said Yasmin.

'Need anything else?'

'A wheelchair. Do you think you could find me one?'

'Sure thing,' he said.

Niamh came over. 'What's going on?'

Yasmin ignored her but Zlata cheerfully revealed that Yasmin was taking her outside for a breath of fresh air and a nip of Scotch.

'There are rules, Yasmin,' said Niamh. 'Or don't they apply to you as well?'

Harrison sang his tuneless song as he lifted Mrs Antonova into the wheelchair. She was tiny in his big arms and her ankles, protruding from her nightdress, looked like chicken bones. Her gums had bits of mashed digestive sticking to them when she smiled, but her eyes were radiant, triumphant and grateful, and when Harrison bent over to strap her in she puckered up for a kiss.

'There you are, princess,' said Harrison. 'Now put it here.'

He offered his cheek and she kissed it. 'You made my day,' he said.

'Glenfiddich,' said Zlata, admiring Baba's collection of miniatures as Yasmin opened her bag. 'Lovely. Let's make a toast.'

Yasmin hesitated. The Trust had a total alcohol ban. She was putting a patient at risk, that's what they'd say.

'Ready?' Zlata warbled something in Russian and raised a mottled arm.

Yasmin clinked bottles. If she denied Mrs Antonova now it wouldn't be about putting the patient's interests first. It would be out of sheer cowardice. She said: 'What did that mean?'

'May we always have a reason for a party! My mother's favourite toast. She always found a reason for a party, even if there were no guests and nothing to eat but kasha and nothing to drink but moonshine.'

Yasmin took a sip from the miniature and grimaced as it went down. Mrs Antonova chuckled. She seemed much revived by the mixture of adventure, fresh air and alcohol. At ninety-six years old it was possible her heart could fail any time, or go on beating until she was one hundred, one hundred and one . . .

No, she was frailer now than she'd been a month ago. But there was no point measuring her grip strength or mobility. Zlata had more or less stopped eating. She refused to be weighed. She said quite plainly she was ready to die.

'I think about her all the time now, my mother. For my thirteenth birthday she . . . '

Mrs Antonova recounted a number of stories Yasmin had heard before. Baba would know she'd stolen his whisky collection, but if he knew what she was doing with it right now . . . She should have told him she was quitting medicine, just to see the look on his face. Not that she was going to – what else could she do? If she wasn't a doctor, she'd be . . . she wouldn't

412

be anything. *Your grandfather invested in me.* What Baba was really saying was, *I invested in you. Capital deterioration,* he'd said. What did that mean? Was he talking about Ma? Did he mean me? A depreciating asset, is that what he thinks?

'And pride is a very expensive commodity,' said Zlata, not for the first time.

'When you found out your mother's stories weren't true,' said Yasmin, 'were you angry? She said she was a princess – I guess that made you royalty too. And then you weren't.'

'To tell you the truth, I don't remember. It's quite possible.' She took another sip of Scotch, and Yasmin wiped her chin with a tissue. 'Now, tell me – have you made up with your fiancé? I do hope so, because you make such a lovely couple. He reminds me, you know, of Dimitri, my first husband. A very strong jaw.'

'Oh, I don't think you've met him,' said Yasmin.

'Not met him! I'm his favourite, didn't you know?'

Perhaps she'd downed too much whisky. Or her mental faculties were going. She was certainly confused. 'You're mine too.'

'Had a lovely chat with him this morning on his ward round. I told him, don't worry about the age gap, pumpkin. Well, he knows all about Dimitri already.'

She meant Pepperdine. 'He's not . . . we're not . . .'

'Got yourself a good one, so forget about it. The tiff, whatever it was. I always like a strong jaw in a . . .' She yawned. 'In a man. Dimitri was my first husband and I was only . . .' She closed her eyes.

HARRISON

Ma had been thrilled by Harrison's chivalry when Yasmin told her the story, leaving out, of course, the details about the alcohol. She wanted Yasmin to give him six jars of chutney, the full range, as a token of appreciation. Yasmin kept meaning to take them in but forgetting because she was always in a rush. Today she'd remembered. But she couldn't find Harrison.

She had these six jars of Anisah's Achaars: Authentic Bengal Pickles and she needed to get rid of them.

'Julie,' said Yasmin, 'have you seen Harrison anywhere?'

'That would be unlikely.'

'So, you haven't?'

'Not since he got sacked.'

'What?'

'Not since he got sacked,' Julie repeated. She wasn't in the habit of leaking her opinions or emotions but it was clear she thought Yasmin was to blame. 'Pepperdine was looking for you, by the way.'

He was in his office, eating a very late breakfast at his desk. A croissant flake was stuck to the corner of his mouth and it didn't budge when he wiped the coffee foam from his top lip.

'I don't think there's any point speculating,' he said.

'It was Niamh, wasn't it?' Nobody else would have made a formal complaint. It had to be Niamh.

'Look,' he said, 'it doesn't matter. We are where we are.'

'It does matter! She's got him sacked and it wasn't his fault.'

'Who?' He rubbed the corner of his mouth with a thumb. It made her stomach lurch and she didn't know what she was feeling: disgust or desire.

'Harrison. The cleaner, you know the one who's always—'

'Singing, yes, I know who he is but I didn't know he'd been fired.'

'Well, you know now. And if anyone should be fired it should be me! I'm the one responsible.'

He nodded. 'That's what I need to talk to you about.'

'Oh,' she said.

'Darius was, um, keen to go down the disciplinary road, let's say. But he agreed in the end that I'd give you an informal . . .' He grimaced. 'An informal reprimand. And remind you to undertake the sensitivity training course.'

'Okay. Go on then.' His hair was grey at the temples. He had trouble looking her in the eye. His jaw was too heavy. Blood on the carpet. Blood on the wall. He was old. Too old.

'That's it,' he said. 'Done. Consider yourself reprimanded. For what it's worth . . .' He reached his hand across the desk and placed it on hers. 'Yasmin, could we—'

She didn't let him finish. 'I don't think that's a good idea.' His line. It felt good to throw it back at him. She pulled her hand away. 'And I can fight my own battles with Shah. I'm not expecting any special treatment.'

He sighed. 'Yasmin, why don't we go out for dinner and we can at least clear the air?'

Clear the air! It was nearly the end of February, and he'd humiliated her on Boxing Day. Told her she had a mean streak.

Told her to stop acting like a child. And for two months he says nothing and now he wants to clear the air! She was speechless. All she could do was glare at him.

'I don't want things to be awkward and I'm sure you don't either, so maybe we could eat a meal together and talk? There'd be no harm in that, would there?'

He was so measured, so calm, so distant – it was infuriating. A feeling had been building inside her and she hadn't known what it was but now it was obvious. He smiled at her and she saw fondness, she saw sadness, and she *hated* him. She hated him for being sad and fond, because he had no right to feel that way. Did he think she had no pride?

'Of course we could,' she said evenly. 'But I'm only here for another few weeks before I move on. I'm sure we'll get along well enough until we never have to see each other again.'

CENTRE OF EXCELLENCE

Professor Shah's door was closed as always. Yasmin knocked and marched in without waiting.

Professor Shah was on the phone. 'I'll call you back,' he said and hung up.

'I'm here about Harrison.' She glanced around at the shelves, covered in framed awards, certificates and prize cups for achievements in the fields of medicine and golf. A photograph of three young children with a blank-faced large-breasted blonde woman. Another of Shah at the wheel of a red sports car.

'I suggest you make an appointment through my secretary,' he said smoothly. He laced his hairy hands together on top of his stomach.

'But I'm already here.'

He assessed her for a while. Eventually he said: 'What can I do for you, Dr Ghorami?'

'Harrison. I'm here about Harrison.'

'A patient, I presume?'

'A cleaner in the department. He was fired.'

Professor Shah shook his head. His hair, well lacquered, didn't move. 'What has that got to do with me? I confess I'm at a loss.'

'I want you to get him his job back. He didn't deserve the

sack. He was helping me with Mrs Antonova, that's all. He just did what I asked him to do.'

'Oh, I see! Perhaps we should get him back and fire you?' He twinkled at her as though it was all good clean fun. He had begun to enjoy himself.

'As long as you get him back.'

'That sort of thing is way above my pay grade,' he said airily. But she saw he was irked by the flatness of her response. No rise from her meant less fun for him. 'As you know, cleaning is done by a private firm and you'd have to speak to . . . I don't know. Someone in purchasing?'

'He was kept on as staff. He's the father of your wife's trainer. When the cleaning was contracted out he was the only one who kept his job.'

'My wife's trainer? She's probably got through several personal trainers since then. You know how women can be.' He chuckled and his hands moved up and down as his belly rose and fell.

Yasmin stared at the fleshy webs between the fingers, the hairy knuckles, the neatly clipped fingernails.

'Okay, let's wrap this up,' he said. 'I'm busy. There's nothing I can do for your cleaner friend. If you're so concerned for him perhaps you should have thought about his best interests before you dragged him into whatever the hell it was you were doing. As for you – if James hadn't put in a word, you'd be gone as well. Because you're out of chances, and I have the reputation of the department to consider. Now – off you go!' He slapped his hands down hard on the desk, and it made her jump. He laughed as though she was a silly little thing and the last thing he'd meant to do was intimidate.

'Yes, you do. The department's reputation is very important. You have to consider it.' She took a seat.

He looked at her incredulously. 'I beg your pardon?'

'There's a lot at stake, isn't there?'

He glowered. 'Who the hell do you think you are?' And there it was. The smokescreen of joviality lifted and there was the bully, stripped bare.

'They'll be making the announcement soon, won't they, about the Centre of Excellence. Millions in funding. Huge expansion. You as the figurehead.'

'What do you *want*, Dr Ghorami?'

'Me? I don't want anything. It would be a shame, though, if . . . ' She gave him a sorrowful smile. 'You wouldn't want it to go to another hospital just because of a story. Maybe one about patients being unsafe here, let's say because of some rogue doctor wheeling them about and giving them alcohol.'

He snorted. 'You wouldn't be that stupid. I'll refer you to the GMC myself if that's the game you intend to play. You'll lose. Now get out!'

'But I am that stupid,' said Yasmin, 'because I'm quitting medicine.' It was a lie. Baba wanted her to be a doctor, but that didn't mean she didn't want it too. It had taken a while for her to see that. Professor Shah, though, would swallow the lie, because of what Pepperdine had told him. 'No skin off my nose. But yours . . . ' She knew by the look on his face that it wasn't enough. 'And that's not all, is it? Remember Mr Babangida, with the broken arm? Remember him? How's *that* going to play?'

'If you think you are going to blackmail me you are stupider than I thought.' He slammed his hands on the desk again but this time she was ready and she did not flinch. She was calm.

'I'm so stupid,' she said, 'that I'm going public about it. My concerns. Little things like how quiet the dementia ward is when you've been in there.'

'You are cracked in the head. You can't be a whistleblower when there's nothing going on!'

'Isn't there? Over-sedation of patients is pretty serious.'

'That doesn't happen.'

'What about Mr Babangida?'

'It would have healed anyway!' His nostrils dilated with rage. 'He wouldn't have known the fucking difference. It's immaterial!'

She had started to waver but Shah's attitude, his arrogance, his indifference to his patient, gave her resolve. 'Gosport,' she said. She let the word dangle. The inquiry was on-going and it was looking into hundreds of deaths in the Department of Medicine for Elderly People at Gosport Hospital.

'It's difficult to imagine how that went on for so long,' she said, 'even though some staff raised concerns about over-medication for several years. And some relatives. Nobody listened then, did they? But they'd listen now, don't you think?'

'You little bitch. There's nothing like that going on here and you know it.'

'Well, it would have to be investigated. The Centre of Excellence will still be built, but it will be built elsewhere and you won't have your name on it. Is that a risk you're willing to take? That's what you've got to decide.'

'What do you *want*?'

She looked at him. He seemed genuinely to have forgotten. 'Harrison gets his job back. I'm sure you can make it happen if you put your mind to it.'

'That's all? That's it? Are you fucking kidding? All this bullshit for a cleaner? You really are cracked in the head.'

'Would it be better if I asked for money?'

'Get out of my sight.' He stood up and loomed over her.

'When you've given me your answer.'

'He'll get his job back. But you . . . ' His face contorted. A vein on the side of his skull bulged and throbbed. 'Wherever you go from here I have contacts. I know people in every Trust across the country and I promise you I will never forget about this.'

'Aw, that's sweet,' said Yasmin. 'I'll always remember it too.'

VIRAL

The video clip lasted all of seventeen seconds and it played over and over on a loop. Rania, swaying on her feet, holding a shot glass. *You can all watch if you want.* A long dark curl of hair springs licentiously from her hijab. A hand appears and tugs at Rania's sleeve. The image blurs and momentarily blackens then Yasmin appears in the frame next to Rania, who is seated now. Yasmin says something indistinct and subtitles appear: *You need to sober up.* Rania looks straight into the lens and chants: *One more drink! One more drink!* Then she is on her feet with a shot glass and the scene plays out again.

'Oh, shit,' said Yasmin.

'I know.' Rania turned her phone over to lie face down on the table. 'It was posted months and months ago, but it's only just gone viral.'

'Because you were on telly?'

Rania shrugged. 'Guess so. It took a while, but somebody put the clips together eventually – and I look like the biggest hypocrite.'

'Oh, shit. How awful! But just don't look. Don't go on social media right now.'

'I'm getting lots of hate. Hey, this pub's not that bad – you made it sound like a dive.'

They were in The Crosskeys and it was pretty empty for a Thursday evening. The after-office crowd had either gone or never shown up. A few solitary men gazed into their pint glasses, a line of young women – maybe nurses – plaited along the bar, and a group of medics in the far corner sat round a table, picking at a pile of tortilla chips topped with radioactive goo. It was a pub that served a function rather than the kind of place anyone really wanted to be. Rania had called Yasmin at work and asked to see her. It sounded urgent. In an hour Yasmin was meeting Joe here. They were going out for dinner, just the two of them. Less than an hour now, and Yasmin had a lot to think about, but Rania had never needed help, never asked for advice, before today.

'If I'd known what this was about,' said Yasmin, 'I wouldn't have said to meet me in a *pub*.' She looked around as if someone might be surreptitiously filming Rania sipping her orange juice. Nobody was paying the slightest attention.

'To be fair to the Islamophobes,' said Rania, 'they're moderate compared to some of the Muslims. Or maybe just less inventive about the ways in which they'd like me to die.'

'That's horrible,' said Yasmin. 'I'm sorry.'

'It's actually quite funny how they're all so keen to tell me *I* should be ashamed of myself but *they're* not ashamed of themselves for telling a woman she deserves to be raped or disembowelled or whatever. Like they truly think they've got the upper hand morally. Read this one, for example.' She picked up her phone and scrolled. 'Here you go. What should I reply to that?'

Yasmin read the message. 'You shouldn't. Stay off Twitter! It's vile.'

Rania took the phone back and scrolled some more. 'Some new ones here . . .'

'Rania,' said Yasmin.

'Okay, you're right. I've stopped.'

'Doesn't matter what those people say, they don't know you. They have no right to judge.'

Rania chewed her bottom lip. For a moment she looked as if she might burst into tears. Yasmin had never seen her cry. 'Thanks,' said Rania eventually. 'Thank you. It's not a good feeling, you know. You think it wouldn't affect you but it does.' She rolled her eyes. 'You know what would cheer me up? Show me some photos of Coco. You've got some on your phone, right?'

Coco was seven weeks old and Yasmin had seen her a few times and Arif kept sending photographs. Coco, wrapped in a fluffy pink towel, cocooned in a rabbit-pattern sleeping bag, wearing a multicoloured cardigan knitted by Ma with one sleeve longer than the other, dressed up as a strawberry with black tights, red dress and green hat.

'And this one,' said Yasmin, 'is my favourite.' She had five missed calls from Arif and voicemail. He could wait until tomorrow. Tonight she had enough on her plate. He'd turned into such a fusspot, calling or messaging every time Coco so much as sneezed.

'Gorgeous,' said Rania. 'She's adorable! What's it like to be an aunt? Is it making you broody?'

'I love it. She's changed so much already. She's not yellow any more, for a start.'

'What about Joe? Does he want to have kids straight away, or wait?'

'We . . . I don't . . . I can't . . . ' She shook her head. She was going to tell him tonight that she couldn't marry him. She was going to tell him about Pepperdine.

'You can't have children?'

'No,' she said. 'It's not that.' It was the middle of March and nothing had changed. Ma was still hawking her wares at farmers' markets or running around with Flame. Although, thank God, at the moment Flame was in Holland with her stupid show. Baba was living in unsplendid isolation from the rest of the family. And she'd tried to talk to Joe because they couldn't go on like this for ever, sharing a bed but never touching each other, endlessly pushing back the wedding date. Pretending everything was fine. They'd been so in love. They couldn't admit to each other they'd used up all the love so fast. What's wrong, she'd ask him, and he'd say, Nothing's wrong, and look utterly terrified.

'What is it?'

'Nothing.'

'Nothing? How long have we known each other?'

'It's *everything*,' she said.

It came out quick and garbled but she didn't gloss over any parts. When she'd finished she felt lighter. It wasn't what she expected. She felt lighter, but also guilty for not feeling worse. 'I'm a terrible person,' she said. 'He deserves better than me. You must think I'm terrible.'

'Ya Allah,' said Rania. 'Trust me, after all the judgements I received these last twenty-four hours, I'm in no mood to judge anyone.' She took Yasmin's hand and squeezed it. 'All these things going on and you didn't say a word? You've been suffering alone.'

'I guess so,' she said, and the sadness surged up inside her. 'But it's all my own fault, anyway.'

'All these things,' repeated Rania.

'He'll be here in five minutes.'

'I'll go now.'

Yasmin kept a tight grip on her hand. 'Don't.'

'Want me to come for dinner and do the talking for you?' She stood up. 'Will you tell him everything? Like you told me?'

'I think so.' There was one thing she hadn't told Rania about: Ma and Flame. She'd told her about Baba's 'home visits', that wasn't unspeakable. Maybe Joe was right and she was prejudiced after all. She didn't want to be. She didn't want to be that kind of person. She hoped she wasn't, but hoping – she knew – wasn't good enough.

'Be brave,' said Rania.

He was late. Only five minutes, but by the time she saw him come through the door she felt anything but brave. The dread had built quickly. She was sick to her stomach. How stupid to think she could tell him in a restaurant! She wouldn't be able to eat. If the tables were close together everyone would hear. She was bound to cry. Oh my God! He would cry too. He'd walk out. He'd turn the table over and smash the crockery. She'd thought it would be best to speak in public, in a neutral space, with dignity and restraint. It was the worst idea she'd ever had. She must have been out of her mind.

'Let's go,' he said, and picked up her coat from the back of the chair.

'Hello,' she said. He looked at her so earnestly that she felt every fraudulent molecule of her heart.

'Haven't you spoken to him?'

'Who?'

'Let's go,' he said. 'Come on. It's Arif. He's been trying to reach you. I mean, it's Coco – she's in hospital.'

MOTTINGHAM DISTRICT AND GENERAL

The baby was sick. Coco Tallulah was very sick, and if she died it would be Yasmin's fault. In the waiting area at Mottingham District and General Hospital, Ma fingered her prayer beads and recited her prayers while Janine wept into her tea from the vending machine and La-La accosted every passing member of staff for information they weren't able to provide. But Baba was here now. He'd come this morning, as soon as he knew. He wouldn't let Coco die.

But if she did, it would be Yasmin's fault. She traced back her failures and crimes.

She hadn't returned Arif's calls. Joe had been the one to respond, and then he'd driven Yasmin to the hospital. They hadn't been able to see Coco or Lucy but they'd sat with Arif and he hadn't blamed Yasmin for anything.

She should have taken him seriously instead of thinking he was fussing. She should have consulted Joe, but she was too caught up in her own selfishness. Would Joe have said anything different? She wished he could be here now instead of at work.

But Baba was here. Though how could he assess Coco properly now she was in hospital and he was trying to look over the shoulders of medics who were no doubt trying to keep him out of their way?

Take her to the GP if you and Lucy are worried. They took her to the surgery and the GP diagnosed a cold. Arif sent a photo of Coco asleep in a Moses basket with a caption: *Back to the usual hectic round!* A day later they went back to the surgery and Coco was running a little fever. Arif messaged: *Doc says give Calpol but bottle says only for over 2 months old.* She reassured him. *They give paracetamol in the neonatal unit, just got to work out the dose on weight. Did the GP do that for you?* Arif confirmed it. *Okay,* she said, *let me know how she is. Calm,* wrote Arif. *Noblem.* She had to ask what noblem meant.

Two days later she texted: *How's Coco?* They'd taken her a third time to see the GP and this time she'd prescribed anti-biotics. Just to make them go away, thought Yasmin. Arif sent photographs of Coco at Lucy's breast, on Janine's lap, held aloft by La-La. *Seems better,* he wrote. *Got eczema or something on her hands. Take to doc for that?*

She told him there was no rush. She told him to get E45 lotion from the chemist in the meantime.

If she'd been paying more attention . . . Then what? What would she have diagnosed?

Ma dropped her beads. She sat there in the plastic bucket seat that was screwed to the ground and she seemed as incapable of moving as the chair.

Yasmin reached across and picked them up. She left them on Ma's lap, and a few seconds later the clacking began again.

Arif walked into the waiting area. His hair was greasy, his face glazed with worry and exhaustion.

'What are they saying now?' Janine jumped to her feet.

Yasmin hugged him. 'Sorry,' she whispered. 'I'm so sorry.'

His arms hung limply round her shoulders. 'They still don't know what's wrong with her.'

'How's Lucy coping?' Yasmin let him go.

'Not good.' He slumped down next to Ma and hid his face on her shoulder.

'It will be okay,' said Ma.

'You don't know.' His voice was muffled in her sari.

No, you don't, Yasmin echoed silently. It's what Ma always said.

'Haven't they got *anything* to tell us?' La-La was constantly on the move with nothing to do and nowhere to go. 'There's got to be *something* to tell. More blood test results? What they're giving her now? What they're doing next?' Her pink hair had faded from cotton candy to pink champagne. She looked at Arif, who remained inert and unresponsive. 'Hey, you,' she called as a porter walked through the waiting room, 'yes, you, hold on a minute, I want to speak to you.' She raced after him.

Yasmin let her go. La-La needed the activity, and if it meant chasing nurses, health care assistants and porters – anyone in a uniform – down corridors that was fine. She might even hazard upon a doctor eventually, but unless it was one of Coco's doctors, a porter would do just as well.

There was nothing to be done but sit here and count up her sins. The rift with Baba – she should have healed it rather than made it worse. He would have been on the case straight away, but Yasmin had fucked things up by going to Beechwood Drive and insulting him. *Who the hell do you think you are?* Professor Shah was right. She was out of control.

She had sinned and sinned. Blood on the sheets. Blood on the pillow. A bloody handprint on the wall.

She'd done so many things wrong.

How nasty she'd been to Niamh.

Niamh had tried to be nice to her, and she'd *thrown it back in her face.* That's what Niamh said. *I've gone out of my way to be nice to you.* Niamh had a point.

'Wish I could *do* something,' said Janine. 'I feel so useless. Sat here like scrap at a junkyard. No use to anyone.' She began to cry again.

'You're here,' said Arif, sitting up, 'that's all that matters. We need you here, and you're here.'

'I am. I'm here,' said Janine, looking at him with boundless gratitude for recognition of the vital role she played.

'Fruitcake,' announced Ma, putting her prayer beads down. She wore one of her good saris, indigo blue with tiny silver stars and a plain cream border. Her hair was smoothed into a tidy bun. Of all of them she was the least agitated. 'We will have cake now.' She reached down for one of the carrier bags at her feet. Even in an emergency she never left the house without several shopping bags of various kinds.

'I'll have some, Ma,' said Yasmin.

'Yes, I could manage a bit,' said Janine.

Arif mumbled that he couldn't eat anything.

'It is your duty,' said Ma, 'to keep up strength for our Coco Tallulah. You will eat.'

Arif ate. He asked for a second slice.

'When can I see her?' Yasmin had held the question as long as she could. She'd hoped Arif coming out meant she could go in.

Arif shook his head. 'They don't want more people in there. They've been trying to get rid of Baba. But you know what he's like. I think they're a bit scared of him.'

She was desperate to talk to Baba. She'd got as much information out of Arif as she could when he'd come out to see her first thing this morning. Coco was floppy and barely responsive, her temperature was high (he didn't remember the number, only that she was burning up), she'd been dehydrated but they were getting fluids into her now. They were giving her antibiotics intravenously but nothing was making any difference, it felt like they were all just watching her die. Eighteen hours they'd been here. They'd done some kind of scan and it didn't show anything. They stuck a massive fucking needle in her spine. It's not meningitis. It might be a viral infection. It might be a bacterial infection. It might be a parasitic infection. They wanted to know if Coco Tallulah had come into contact with any cats. *As if we'd let a cat sit on our baby's face! Her lips have swollen up. What has Coco done to deserve this? She hasn't done anything wrong.*

She needed to talk to Baba.

'Could you go and get him? Ask Baba to come out and give me an update.'

Arif nodded. He tried to smile. 'Two doctors in this family! Not bad, Apa! Knew I'd appreciate it one day.'

Baba delivered his report to the four women, hands clasped behind his back, which was ramrod straight. The doctors were running through a battery of tests, and by this means of elimination a diagnosis would be secured. They were doing everything possible with all due urgency, and Coco was in the best of hands. If they wanted to go home and get some rest they should. Any news would be conveyed to them with the utmost haste.

Ma took his big bony hand and held it between her two soft palms. Her Tasbih, ninety-nine silver beads, dangled from her wrist. How many times today had she cycled through them? Thirty-three beads for each part of the dhikr, and Yasmin recited each one silently: Subhan Allah, Alhamdulillah, and Allahu Akbar.

'They will find the answer,' said Anisah.

Yasmin envied her certainty. Her faith.

'They will find,' repeated Anisah, looking up at her husband.

She meant Baba would find the answer. That was what she was telling him.

Shaokat placed his other hand over Ma's two hands. The

tendons flexed as he gave a gentle squeeze. 'You will pray for our granddaughter,' he said. 'Allah will hear you. I will do whatever I can.'

Yasmin turned her head away and wiped a tear from her cheek.

CASE CHALLENGE

'They do not know what to do,' said Baba when they had left the waiting room to talk in private. 'I suggested acute adenoviral infection. They looked at me as if I were mad.'

'Have they ruled it out?' The doctors wouldn't like being told what to do by a family member. And Baba probably rubbed them up the wrong way.

'No,' said Baba. 'Let's walk. It is better for thinking.'

She walked the corridor with him. He strode and she had to trot to keep up. The corridor was painted lavender. It had the reliable hospital smell of boiled veg mixed with bleach.

'The test for it is simple,' said Baba. 'Rapid DFA – the result can be obtained within six hours. If they had ordered the test when I suggested it, we could have known by now. You're aware of it – rapid direct fluorescent antigen. Yes, rapid DFA. But they are moving too slowly. Counting on the antibiotics. In my view this is a mistake. The fever has already lasted five days.'

'Is there a rash?' At the end of the corridor Baba turned on his heel, and again she trotted after him. 'What's the white blood cell count? The platelet count? Haemoglobin? Tell me what they know so far.'

They walked up and down together, sidestepping the

occasional shuffling patient, and he gave her the facts and figures. Sometimes he paused to refer to the notepad on which
he'd made copious notes. Transaminases were normal. GGT
was high, and C-Reactive Protein was very high. Abdominal
ultrasonography showed a focal bowel wall thickening, mild
oedema around the gallbladder, mild hepatosplenomegaly and a
lymphadenomegaly near the hepatic hilum. Resin blood culture
and serology for Epstein Barr Virus, Mycoplasma pneumoniae,
Chlamydia pneumoniae, type 1 and 2 Herpes simplex virus,
Parvovirus B19, Coxsackie viruses and Toxoplasma Gondii
were all in process. Tomorrow, he felt sure, they would all be
ruled out.

'Why do you think so, Baba? Is there anything you're not
telling me?'

He halted and turned to face her. 'Of course not! We will
work it out together. We will solve the case challenge together.
Isn't that what we did for so many years?'

BAGGAGE

The next three days passed agonisingly slowly and painfully fast. The intravenous antibiotics brought the fever down but the respite proved fleeting and Coco's temperature shot back up. Lucy scarcely left her daughter's side. Yasmin was finally allowed in to see her niece. Coco appeared to be shrinking and curling, as if she'd had second thoughts about coming into this world and wanted to get back in the womb.

Joe came whenever he could. Janine and La-La fell in love with him. He's gorgeous! Such a gentleman! He can take my pulse any day! It was a gift he had, of paying attention, making you feel special, the very centre of the world. It was a gift he shared with Janine and La-La, and Yasmin watched as their spirits rose when he came and crashed when he left again.

She walked outside to the car park with him. 'Yasmin,' he said, 'can't you get her into Great Ormond Street? I'm sure they're doing their best, but a local hospital . . .'

'How do I do that, exactly? Grab her and run?' She hadn't meant to sound so angry. 'Sorry. If I'd paid more attention earlier, I might have been able to—'

'Stop! You know that's not true.' He put a hand under her chin and tipped it up so she had to look at him. Those eyes. So pale and mild and ardent all at the same time. The first time she'd looked into them was the first time in her life she had felt seen.

'Your mum was here yesterday,' she said.

'What did she say?'

'Nothing. She came, that's all. It was nice of her. Does she have a thing about hospitals? A phobia?'

'No. Why?'

'She was upset.' Harriet wept in the waiting area; it set Janine off again. 'And she got upset in the maternity ward.'

He shrugged. 'Don't know. Don't think so. So she didn't say anything?'

'What would she say?' The wind lifted her skirt and she smoothed it down. The sky was clean chlorine blue above the expanse of black tarmac and the bright metal roofs. The wind whistled around the cars. 'Joe,' she said, 'have you and Harriet . . . has something happened? Have you had a row?'

His face whitened. It was the way patients looked when they stood up too quickly after an injection or having blood drawn. It was a sign that they might faint. 'We need to talk,' he said. 'But not now.'

'Yes,' she said. 'Not here.'

'I . . . the thing is . . .' He struggled with some emotion she couldn't distinguish. 'The therapy, it's been . . . it's been a lot harder than I thought and . . . it's brought up a lot of . . . You see, I talked to Harry . . . about . . . some of the things it brought up. And it was hard. Really hard for her to hear. I'm sorry, I shouldn't be loading this onto you now.'

'It's fine. You can tell me. It's about your dad?'

'Sort of. I'll tell you, but it's a long story so . . . Turns out I've got a whole lot of baggage I never even realised.'

'I'm sorry.'

'It's not your fault.'

If he hadn't gone to therapy that baggage would still be stowed out of sight and out of mind. It was better, supposedly, to talk about everything, but was it really? It had never been that way in Yasmin's family. They kept each other in the dark. Only when the light got in did the Ghoramis start falling apart.

'Joe,' she said, 'that dinner we didn't get to have? I wanted to talk to you about us.'

'Sounds serious. Were you going to break up with me?' He brushed a strand of hair from her face. He was smiling but she felt a tremor in his hand. Perhaps it was only the wind making his eyes water, but it was unbearable to look at them.

'No, of course not,' she said.

SANDOR

Sandor sat at the desk reading through the talk he'd written: *On Clinical Wisdom: Guidance for Practice, Training and Research.* He turned over and saw Melissa's elegant scrawl in the margin. *So very true,* she'd written, *and when you've finished healing the world would you be interested in going out to dinner with your wife? PS I love you.*

He'd make a reservation for dinner at that place she liked, the Italian with the burrata she couldn't get enough of.

Sandor read on: *Why do we return so often to such figures as Freud, Jung, Rogers, Minuchin and Satir? We do so because deep in our hearts we know we must pay attention to so much more than empirical studies, therapeutic techniques, cost-benefit analyses. We turn to them for their penetrating insights into the human condition. What really matters. How can one guide a client along a path to well-being and a rich and purposeful life without considering what those things mean?* He hadn't said enough – anywhere in the talk – about connection. Perhaps he could find a suitable place to drop in his favourite quote from Albert Einstein. He wrote, at the foot of the page: *A human being is a part of the whole, called by us, 'Universe', a part limited in time and space. He experiences himself, his thoughts and feelings as something separated from the rest – a kind of delusion of his consciousness. AE, letter, 1950.*

The doorbell rang. Sandor put down his pen, poured a glass of water from the cut-glass decanter, and went to greet his last patient of the day.

'She wanted to come,' said Joe. 'You're lucky I didn't let her.'

'She's angry with me?' Joe had talked to his mother; he'd done it exactly as planned.

'Just a bit.'

'And you? How are you feeling?'

'Honestly, I'm not quite sure. There's so much going on.'

There was another sick baby, Joe had told him on the phone. A relative of the fiancée.

'But I think I feel good. Does it make sense to say I feel kind of *purged*? You know when adults get baptised and they're immersed in water and it supposedly washes their sins away? I think it's *that* kind of feeling, of possibility. Does that sound insane?'

'Not at all.'

'I feel bad for Harry. But not as bad as I imagined. Once I started, it had to come out. I thought, This is *my* life and I want it back, I'm claiming it.'

'No regrets?'

'I don't think so. I wasn't going to say the words covert incest. But I did. I don't think I regret it.'

'It must have been difficult for your mother to hear.' He could see her now. Harriet Sangster gazing back at him – scrutinising, sceptical – from his computer screen.

'Yes. Difficult to hear. Harder to live with as a helpless kid.'

It was a rebirth of sorts. 'I'm so glad you've been able to come this far this fast.'

'Thanks. If I hadn't come to you . . .' He shook his head at the thought. 'Harry's pretty devastated. Do you think we'll get past it in the end?'

'Hard to predict. Sometimes a breach occurs, often when the parent refuses to acknowledge the truth of the situation.'

'That's her. That's Harry.'

'Give it time. One thing that's helpful to remember is parents frequently replicate the family systems in which they themselves grew up. And do so without knowing it. You told me your grandparents died before you were born and you don't know a lot about them. You might want to ask some questions.'

'She didn't like her mother much and she was close to her father.'

'Yes, I remember you saying and that's interesting as far as it goes.'

'Which isn't far.'

'Exactly.'

'I'm going to see my dad. On my way to the interview in Edinburgh.'

'How are you feeling about that?'

'Okay. Anxious about talking to Yasmin. Can't do it now because her niece is in hospital. It'd be totally wrong to lay anything else on Yasmin right now.'

'And if the niece recovers?'

'When I get back from Edinburgh.'

'You're resolved on that?' He had a new energy about him.

'One hundred per cent.' He grinned. 'That's the ballpark.'

'How's your impulse control been faring? There's been a lot of stress. Any flare-ups?'

'Not at all. Haven't been fighting it.'

'Don't be surprised if it returns. In fact, it would be a miracle if it doesn't.'

'I'll expect it then. I'll be ready.'

'A support group might not be a bad idea.'

'I'll find one.'

He's ready to fly, thought Sandor, ready to move on. And that was the aim. 'I'm proud of you,' he said.

'I'm proud of me too,' said Joe. 'So, you never told me if you're available for Skype sessions. In case I do end up moving to Edinburgh.'

'For you,' said Sandor, 'I am.'

The restaurant was booked and Melissa was upstairs putting on her face. Sandor sat in the kitchen, waiting with a glass of wine. His arm ached. He was out of shape and he had to do something about it. Adam was moving to London. Sandor was thrilled, all three of them were. Melissa said in future he shouldn't work so much. He should make time for his loved ones.

His mind came back to Einstein. *This delusion is a kind of prison for us, restricting us to our personal desires and affection for a few persons nearest to us.* You see, Melissa? You see? He couldn't cut himself off from patients who needed him. *Our task must be to free ourselves from this prison by widening our circles of compassion to embrace all living creatures and the whole of nature in its beauty. Nobody is able to achieve this completely, but the striving for such achievement is in itself a part of the liberation and a foundation for inner security.*

And that was all the wisdom, clinical or otherwise, that was ever needed. The essence of Sandor's learning: compassion and connection. His breath was short. He was going to start exercising. He was definitely going to get in shape.

THE SIXTH DAY

On the sixth day at Mottingham District and General, Baba walked the corridor with Yasmin.

'I was too hard on him,' said Baba. 'I have not been a good father to Arif.'

'Baba . . .' said Yasmin.

'No, you were aware of it. We won't pretend otherwise, will we? Not now.' He raised his tangled eyebrows above the black frame of his bifocals. 'I feared for him too much. I thought his life would be harder than yours. That business with the police . . . I was harsh. Unforgiving. But a young Muslim man is seen as a threat. If you are seen as a threat, you yourself are not safe. Do you understand? I wanted him to be safe.'

'We can talk about it another time. It's not important now.'

'I went about things the wrong way. Naturally, he hid the pregnancy from me. He'd expected only condemnation, and that's exactly what I gave him.'

'But let's focus on Coco. That's what Arif would want.'

'Exactly so,' said Baba. 'Let's continue.'

But after only one more lap of the corridor Baba said he felt tired. He sat in the waiting room with the women. He asked for the wall-mounted television that played incessantly but silently to be turned off because nobody was watching it, and because he couldn't concentrate with all that flickering going on. But he didn't look as though he was concentrating on anything. He kept looking around for other distractions. He offered to sort out Ma's voluminous bags of wool.

Ma and Janine and La-La now spent most of their time knitting. They knitted jumpers for Coco, hats for Coco, socks, cardigans. If they knitted enough tiny garments then Coco would live. Yasmin didn't know how to knit but Ma taught her the simplest stitch and over the last three days she had managed a wobbly pink scarf.

Baba toyed with a skein of pale blue mohair. He picked a ball of white wool out of a carrier bag and put it in a different bag.

'Come on, Baba!' Yasmin said under her breath. There had to be another angle to consider, another test that could be run. Baba couldn't give up like this.

They must have walked miles together, up and down the corridor, systematically going through the possibilities. The blood cultures had all come back negative. No mucosal or lymph nodes changes had been observed. A second ultrasound had shown improvement in the bowel thickening and oedema and the baby was passing normal stools, the brief period of diarrhoea having resolved. He had considered infantile parotitis with an unusual presentation but the ineffectiveness of the antibiotics ruled that out. At his insistence a test had been run for early-onset inflammatory bowel disease, but the faecal calprotectin and faecal occult blood were both negative.

Yasmin asked as many questions as she could think of, some of them stupid, some irrelevant, some that made him halt for a moment before resuming his long march towards a diagnosis. How had she ever decided his case challenges were a waste of time? He'd had a lifetime's preparation for this. It had to pay off. It had to. It would be okay, Ma was right.

Arif came in and Janine went scurrying off to see Lucy and Coco. They were strict about having no more than two visitors at the bedside.

'I've got to make Lucy eat,' said Arif. 'All she's eaten in two days is half a sandwich.'

Ma rummaged for tasty morsels in a stack of tiffin tins. 'Will she like this pakora?' She offered one to her son. 'Not spicy, but tasty.'

Arif sat down and ate the pakora. He offered no opinion on its suitability. He rested his elbows on his knees and covered his face with his hands.

'She's going to die,' he said.

La-La and Ma stopped knitting. Yasmin hadn't realised how much noise the needles made until they stopped.

'No,' said Yasmin. 'She's going to be fine.' She glared at Baba but he said nothing. He carried on fiddling with balls of yarn.

'That's right,' said La-La. 'Isn't that right, Shaokat?' For the last couple of days she had stopped bouncing and bounding. She barely spoke. She knitted feverishly.

'Most certainly,' said Baba, still winding wool. 'You are correct.'

Baba would save Coco, and Ma would go back home. Yasmin had told herself this over and over. The past few months would vanish in a haze of obscurity because they'd never talk about it, any of them, because they were that kind of family and Yasmin was glad. It looked like Baba had given up, but he wouldn't. He wouldn't concede defeat on the case challenge of his life.

'Allah does not burden a soul beyond that it can bear.' Ma spoke with the fervour she reserved for quoting from the Surahs or learned theologians, or Imam Siddiq. 'Our Coco Tallulah will not be taken because we could not bear. And my husband will not allow.' If she had a trace of doubt in her it was well hidden. She put her trust in Allah and she had total faith in her husband.

443

Arif lifted his head from his hands and looked at Shaokat, but Shaokat didn't return his gaze. When Baba had turned up at the hospital Arif had put his arms around his neck and cried. Lucy wanted him next to Coco almost as much as she wanted to be there herself. Baba hadn't apologised for his behaviour. He would do better than that. He would save their daughter's life. But he hadn't saved her, and now he could not look his son in the eye.

Ma stood up and kissed the top of Arif's head. 'I will go for namaz. We will pray together, no?' She held out her hand to Yasmin.

Yasmin took Ma's hand but stayed seated. She had accompanied Ma to the multi-faith room several times but the more she went through the motions the less it all meant. All the trappings and rituals and rules only made the whole thing feel fake. 'You go,' she said. 'I'll pray in my own way.'

She watched Ma go. At least Ma seemed to have forgotten all about her special friend. What would have happened if Flame hadn't left to tour her show in the Netherlands, Spain and Denmark? If Flame had turned up at the hospital with Ma day after day? Imagine how terrible . . . No, don't imagine it!

La-La resumed her knitting.

Arif changed seats to sit next to Yasmin. He looked haggard and bewildered. He had thick stubble on his chin and cheeks. Whenever he'd tried to grow a beard it was scanty, it made him look young. He didn't look young any longer. He'd aged a decade in a week. 'I can't pray,' he said. 'I've tried, but I can't.'

'It's okay,' said Yasmin.

'Is it? Thing is . . . ' For a few moments he was mesmerised by the click-clack of La-La's knitting needles. 'Thing is I'm definitely Muslim. But I don't really believe in God. Do you? I mean, I know you've been praying with Ma and everything, so . . . '

444

Yasmin thought for a while. 'I think I do,' she said. 'Maybe.'

'You're a better Muslim than me.'

She shook her head. 'No. I'm definitely not.'

'It is finished,' said Baba, finally putting the wool bags aside. 'Much untangling but now it is done.' He slapped his hands together. 'This task has cleared my head and something has become apparent to me.' He ran his tongue around his lips. 'I must go home and rest. A tired brain is no use to anyone.' He stood up and performed one of his stiff little bows before walking away.

'Baba!' Yasmin jumped up to run after him.

Arif pulled her back. 'He's right. Let him go.'

THE SEVENTH DAY

On the seventh day at Mottingham District and General, Baba returned to the fray. He arrived in his best suit and tie and walked ceaselessly up and down the corridor. His brogues squeaked loudly on the tiled floor.

'The baby's hands are peeling,' he said to Yasmin, 'this indicates what?'

'Eczema? Psoriasis?'

'Not a chance. The hands are not swollen, but they are telling us something. What is it?'

'I don't know.' Come on, Baba, come on!

They walked for two hours and went through everything again but it was no use. They didn't get anywhere.

'Baba,' said Yasmin, 'I've got to sit down.'

'Go,' he said. 'I will walk.' He was sweating. The fabric of his best suit was so thick it could probably stand on its own.

'Sit with me. You're exhausting yourself again. We can carry on sitting down.' She thought he wouldn't agree but he nodded and strode ahead to the waiting room.

Everyone had given up on the knitting. Ma worked her prayer beads. Janine was catatonic. La-La laced and unlaced her fingers endlessly. Shaokat disinterred a handkerchief from the depths of his too-long jacket and mopped his face. 'Shall we start from the beginning again?' He frowned. 'No. We must approach from another direction.'

Yasmin waited and waited but Baba had lapsed into silence. She waited longer. He was thinking. Give him a chance to think.

When she went back to work she'd apologise to Pepperdine. He was right when he said she should stop acting like a child. She'd been so unreasonable. She was going to be a much better person after all this. Let Coco live. I've learned my lesson. I'm sorry and I will be humble for the rest of my life.

And is it humble to think this is all about you?

'No,' she said, aloud. 'No, it's not.'

'I don't understand,' said Baba.

She stared at him and was frightened. He wasn't ruminating; he was blank.

'Look at these photos of Coco.' They had to snap out of it, both of them, and remember what was at stake.

Baba sighed and adjusted his bifocals. Yasmin slid over the intervening plastic seat and sat next to him. The waiting area, with its plastic seats and plastic ferns in plastic pots, its carpet stained with tea and threadbare from all the pacing relatives, its mute and fuzzy television screen and filthy barred windows, was a place designed to make you give up hope. But she would not. Ma and Janine and La-La sat in a row opposite. They all stared vacantly ahead. She wouldn't let Baba slide into their collective coma with them.

'There she is!' She held the phone under Baba's nose. 'Arif sent all these. She looks sweet there, just after her bath. That Babygro is very silly, with the dinosaur spikes, but I think she gets away with it.' She scrolled a bit. 'What else – oh, Ma knitted that. And here she is as a strawberry. Ridiculous. And gorgeous.' She was wittering but she'd caught his attention.

447

'Strawberry . . . She is dressed as a strawberry.'

'Cute, isn't it?'

'No,' said Baba. 'Yes. Let me think.'

'Baba?'

'Atypical. It could be. It's not impossible.' He stood and began to pace.

'Baba?'

Ma held a finger to her lips and smiled.

'One of the symptoms,' said Baba, 'is strawberry tongue.'

'Is her tongue really red?'

'No,' said Baba. 'But for infants under six months there is lower incidence of several symptoms including mucosal and lymph node changes, strawberry tongue and indurative oedema of the palms and the soles of the feet. Her hands have been affected in this case.'

He couldn't pace any longer. They were all crowding round him now.

'What it is?' said Ma.

'Is it curable?' said Janine.

'Tell us!' said La-La. She began to cry, though she had not cried before.

'It's not certain yet,' said Baba. 'The only way will be to administer the treatment. If it works, we will know the diagnosis is correct. There may be resistance. We will fight for it. She is very young to develop this condition. It would be a very rare occurrence but that does not mean it should be ruled out. There have been neonatal cases, it is not entirely unknown. I read a paper some years ago. Obscure clinical manifestation is more common in the infantile version. It is a disease that affects more males than females. But children of Asian ancestry are known to be at higher risk.'

'What is it?' Yasmin, Janine and La-La spoke as one.

'What it is?' said Ma.

Baba straightened his back. His feet were in ten-to-two position as though he was about to take up his clubs. 'If I am not very much mistaken, it is Kawasaki Disease.'

READY TO GO

She's still there, but they say they'll discharge her tomorrow.' It was Yasmin's first day back at work.

'Kawasaki,' said Julie. 'I've heard of it but that's about all.'

'It's pretty rare. Probably an autoimmune disease but even that's not entirely certain.'

'So your dad's a clever guy,' said Julie. She wore a new uniform, royal blue with a pinstripe. While Yasmin was keeping vigil at Mottingham District and General the announcement had been made about Barney's becoming a Centre of Excellence for Elderly Care. Julie had to attend the press conference in her new dress and if they didn't make her matron now she'd be leaving, because she'd been doing a matron's job for years on a ward sister's salary.

'I guess so.' Baba had kicked up an almighty fuss. Coco's doctors were – unsurprisingly – sceptical. But they were thrilled when Coco responded so rapidly to the intravenous immunoglobulin. As Baba predicted, the treatment proved the diagnosis correct.

'And there's no long-term damage?'

'We think not. She's got a tiny aneurysm in her left arm, we're not too worried by that. She'll be on aspirin for a few weeks to thin her blood. And she'll have to have regular scans.' There was a possibility that delayed diagnosis had inflicted coronary artery abnormalities, but none had shown up as yet. 'By the way, is Niamh in today?'

'She's in the falls clinic this morning. Should be finishing around now. But is it something I can help you with?'

'No, it's okay, thanks.' She was going to apologise to Niamh. The prospect was as appealing as administering an enema but it had to be done. It was difficult to imagine Niamh receiving an apology with good grace.

'Well, it's good to have you back.' Julie meant she had to be getting on.

'One thing,' said Yasmin. It was a question she'd been avoiding all morning. Mrs Antonova had gone. It was possible that a place had finally been found for her in a nursing home. It was possible. 'Mrs Antonova?'

'I know you were fond of her.' Julie put a hand on Yasmin's arm.

'When?' Zlata was ready. She was ready. It wasn't a tragedy.

'The first day you were off. I'm sorry,' she said. 'I was with her. She was very peaceful. It wasn't a struggle. I think she was ready to go.'

'Yes,' said Yasmin. 'I think so too.'

She sat down on the toilet lid and wept. She haemorrhaged tears. Yanked more sheets of toilet tissue from the roll and wet them through in seconds. Dark splodges formed on her skirt. She used her sleeve to wipe her face. Zlata had been ready, but Yasmin – though she had been expecting it – was totally unprepared.

At last she balled the tissues, threw them in the toilet and flushed them down. She washed her hands and face and stood there examining her reflection in the chipped and occluded mirror above the basin. Her lashes were spiked. Her cheeks were blotched and her skin sallow, as though it hadn't seen daylight in months.

The bathroom door opened and Yasmin tried to arrange her face to look normal.

Niamh walked in. She looked radiant. 'So you're back,' she said. 'Heard your niece is better now.'

Yasmin nodded. Since the day of Mrs Antonova's escapade they'd barely spoken to each other. She had rehearsed the apology many times in her head and now she braced herself because it was obvious from the set of Niamh's prettily glossed lips that the apology would be rejected.

'Niamh,' she said, and she couldn't speak because she was crying again. If she opened her mouth she would howl.

Niamh came towards her. She didn't say anything. She put her arms around Yasmin. Yasmin wept on Niamh's shoulder.

'I know,' said Niamh. 'I know.'

He wasn't going to let her in. The realisation came like the dawn: gradually then all at once.

'I'm sorry I was rude to you,' she said. It was the second time she'd turned up at his house unannounced. This time he'd found her on the doorstep rather than crouching behind the bins, and this had seemed like a distinct improvement until he failed to invite her inside.

'Forget it,' he said. 'Doesn't matter.' He had his shirtsleeves rolled and wore a blue and white striped apron. His hands and wrists were tanned. All the running he did through the winter. His arms would darken now spring had arrived.

'I thought we could . . . you know, make up with each other.' She tried to sound light-hearted, but in truth she felt desperate. Not for him. She just wanted to lose herself for a while.

He looked at her fondly, as if she was some kind of charity case. 'There's nothing to make up. Really.'

What if she kissed him? Would he relent and let her in? She studied his face for signs. His forehead was lined and scattered with faint freckles that would come out in the sun. He'd weather like a statue left out through the seasons. If she pressed her lips on his it wouldn't make him feel anything.

'And don't imagine I'm turning you away,' he said.

'But you are!' She bleated it. Behind her a passer-by laughed, as if he'd heard.

'Now's not a good time,' said Pepperdine. 'Why don't we organise something?'

'Joe had to go away for a few days, to see his dad. But as soon as he gets back . . .' What was she pleading for? Forgiveness? 'And my niece has been in hospital for a week, as you already know, so I've not . . . but I will . . . I was about to . . . not because of us, obviously because—'

'Yasmin,' he said gently. 'I'm sorry, but it's not a good time.'

'James?' A woman's voice from down the hallway.

'Oh,' said Yasmin. 'You should have said.'

He smiled. Another apology. 'I'm making dinner.'

'Right. Well, have a nice evening.' To her horror she giggled like a silly schoolgirl. 'And apologies for interrupting.' She turned and walked down a couple of steps, holding onto the wrought-iron handrail because all of a sudden her legs felt wobbly.

'Have you got an umbrella? Wait a moment,' he called. 'I can lend you one. Looks like it's going to bucket down.'

She stopped and looked back at him. She got a hold of herself. 'For the record,' she said, 'you were wrong.'

'About?'

'When you said I wanted something more than sex. You were wrong.' She stumbled as she reached the bottom step but she didn't look back when she heard him call out to her again.

HARRIET

The bathwater, ragingly hot when she forced her body into it, is cold. She lifts a hand and examines the shrivelled skin on her fingertips. Her stomach undulates beneath the water until the disturbance subsides. With the same hand she explores the contours of her belly, then her breasts, and the strangely soft feel of her ribs. I am dissolving, she thinks. Even my bones.

She is thinner than she has ever been. Eating has become another chore which she no longer cares about. Not since . . .

How could you believe it? She begged him. How could you think such a thing?

Because it's true, he said. That's how.

Cool and calm and dry-eyed. Brainwashed. Indoctrinated.

She howled with frustration. Sandor Bartok. If her courage had not failed her that day, when she sat outside Bartok's house. If she'd confronted him . . . but it was too late, he'd done his work, and she was ignorant and defenceless. Too late. Too late.

Darling, she said, you realise Americans can be strangely puritanical about sex? Despite being a nation hooked on pornography. It strikes me that you only discovered your supposed sex addiction when you began therapy. Fully-informed and consensual casual sex is nothing to feel ashamed of. Don't you see how your therapist may have twisted everything?

No, Mother, he said.

He only called her Mother to hurt her.

It's not really an addiction, she said, it's freedom, it's self-expression.

She thought: That's what this is, a bid for freedom, a reason not to shackle himself in matrimonial chains. She said: You don't have to marry this girl. You don't need to invent a reason to get out of it. You don't have to prostrate yourself in front of her and say, sorry, I'm a sex addict. It's truly preposterous. You can see that, can't you, darling? My darling boy. Joe. Joseph. My love. Just talk to me. Please. What did I do to deserve this? I've always put you first, haven't I? Haven't I?

She'd get him struck off. The American. There was a professional body and she would have him removed from it. She'd sue him. That's what Americans understand: money. She knew where he lived. Watch your back, Bartok! I'm coming for you. Me. Harriet Sangster. You think I'm nothing? I'll destroy you. I'll see you in Hell where you've put me!

It did not last long. A few days, and then she was weak and helpless. What could she do? How could she even complain about this Bartok? She had to keep it to herself because how could she even give utterance to that vilest of words. She'd drown in shame. It would kill her. Revenge was impossible.

Joseph went to stay with his father, and that felt like the final insult, until he told her he was applying for a job in Edinburgh. One phone call per week. That is all she will be allowed. Boundaries, Mother. Down she went, further down into the hole. The days in bed, Anisah's soft, unanswered knock at the door; a slice of toast, half-eaten; a book, soon abandoned; a crocus, plucked and crushed between the fingers.

The water is freezing. She has to stir herself. He will be on the train now, on his way back to London. But he has insisted he spend the afternoon with Yasmin, before she, who gave him life, gets to set eyes on him.

What does she know? What does Yasmin know?

I'll tell her, Mother. But when I'm ready, and not before.

He used that word again. Mother. Does he know how much it hurts her? She has done everything in her power not to be like Mother. She has loved her child, loves him still, with all her heart, the entirety of her being. Mother wasn't merely distant. She was cruel. Only loved Hector. Wanted Harriet to be the one who died. She said it, only once, but she said it. I wanted a son, not a daughter.

Mother doesn't mean it, Daddy said. She's just angry.

Why did she say it then? Harriet wailed.

When Joseph first confronted her she sobbed and sobbed, but never in front of him. Never let him see or hear. She was careful. She protected him as always. She hid her rage from those around her. It wasn't difficult. The sick baby took all of everyone's attention. Of course, they all know now that *something* is wrong. Poor Rosalita, in deep distress, has made peace with Anisah, and is practically in mourning. She must try to seem normal before Rosalita calls the undertaker. Or – worse – a priest.

Harriet climbs out of the bath, shivering, and wraps herself in a virgin white towel.

THE SUMMERHOUSE

The door to the summerhouse was padlocked. From the veranda she looked back at the house through the rain-needled garden. The house seemed insubstantial, hastily sketched behind the pastel washes of lilacs and witch hazel, the bronze thicket of flowering quince. Down here the stone path was lost to nettles and thistles. A maple tree rustled overhead. Bluebells, long-necked and weary, huddled around the veranda. An hour ago they'd endured a hailstorm.

Rosalita would have a key. But she might want to know why Yasmin needed it. Nobody went in the summerhouse. It was built of soft yellow bricks and the cedar shingles on the roof were beginning to flake and curl. Through the window Yasmin had seen a pair of wooden loungers, a padded bench, a kitchenette with flower-sprigged curtains half-drawn across the under-shelves. And a table laid with teapot and cups and saucers as if a tea party had been abandoned during some long-ago emergency.

The plan had been to meet on the Heath. His train from Berwick-upon-Tweed arrived at King's Cross around noon and he'd go straight there from the station. Yesterday the forecast had promised sunshine, at worst a shower or two.

She'd have to go back to the house and ask Rosalita for the key because she wanted to settle herself down before Joe came. Rosalita wouldn't ask questions: her attention was solely on Harriet.

What's wrong with Harriet? Yasmin asked Joe on the phone. *It couldn't be* only *what he'd told her about therapy. Surely, she reasoned to herself, Harriet would be over that by now. Whatever the criticisms of her parenting skills it wouldn't be so devastating. Harriet had said it herself: the mother always gets the blame.*

Nothing's wrong with her, Joe said.

She was drunk at two o'clock in the afternoon.

She's been wearing her kimono all day.

She shuts herself in her bedroom and cries.

Don't worry about it, he said. She's okay.

She doesn't eat.

She hasn't brushed her hair.

She hasn't spoken a sentence longer than five words.

Joe said: I can't talk about it on the phone.

So there *is* something else. Just tell me, is she ill?

No, he said, nothing like that.

You'll understand when . . . Listen, let's meet on the Heath. I'm going to tell you but it's too difficult on the phone. The Heath or somewhere else, but not in the house.

Joe, she said, is it all because you've gone to your dad's?

If it rains, he said, we should find somewhere else. Somewhere private.

Sunshine tomorrow, she said. That's the forecast.

But if it rains.

Okay.

I have to tell you something tomorrow.

Me too. *There was no reason to delay any longer. There'd never been a reason that was good enough. And she was glad – so very glad – that Pepperdine turned her away, because this had nothing*

458

to do with him. Pepperdine had done her a favour. He was with someone. A woman. That was good because it made things clearer. This was only between the two of them: Yasmin and Joe.

It's pretty big.

Mine too.

If it rains . . .

Somewhere private. I know. Let's meet in the summerhouse.

She left the door open to get some air inside. Her fingers were flecked with oil and rust from wrestling the key into the padlock and there was a cut on her thumb from forcing back the bolt. The floor was thick with dust and mouse droppings. Cobwebs coated the roof joists. She hadn't realised, peering through the window, how filthy it was. The water dripping from her jacket turned the dirt to mud.

It couldn't end here.

It had to. *See you in fifteen minutes*, he'd texted.

That was ten minutes ago.

She took off her jacket, tossed it on one of the loungers and sat down to wait at the table laid with fine china dredged with grime. She sucked the blood off her thumb.

He slung his rucksack on top of her jacket and bent to kiss her forehead. 'How's Coco?'

'Back on the breast. Putting on weight. Bringing joy like you said she would.'

'Thank God.' His hair was dark from the rain. He wore a navy hoodie, unzipped over a white T-shirt. The lower part of the T-shirt was dry. Black circles around his eyes. He looked as if he hadn't slept for days.

'You're knackered. Was it intense?'

'You know what the weirdest thing was? Neil's got a beard. I wasn't expecting it. For some reason it really pissed me off.' He laughed. 'I worked it out in the end. It's because of the thing with my chin?' He pressed a thumb into the dimple. 'Always said it was the only thing he'd ever given me. And I guess I wanted to see it. So dumb, the way these things work! But if you figure them out . . .' He trailed off.

'What did you talk about? Must have been hard to know where to start.' Now he was here in front of her she didn't know if she could do it. It would be the hardest thing she'd ever done in her life.

'He's got beehives,' said Joe. 'And *chickens*. He bakes his own bread, fancy bread in plaits and coils with seeds and stuff. His wife grows veg. She's got rough hands and red cheeks. She doesn't even dye her hair.'

'And you liked her.' He'd told her so on the phone. 'Did you like him too?'

'I don't know. Maybe. In a way I felt a bit cheated. Like I'd gone all the way up there to see my dad and he wasn't there – the man I thought was my dad wasn't there. Does that make sense?'

'I think so.'

'I thought I'd confront him about everything and then either we'd make up or I'd storm off. We talked about his grandchildren instead. Two step-grandkids, Lily and Ethan. He showed me how to collect honey from the hives. We walked the dog.' He widened his eyes, as though recounting mysterious rites.

'Did you *try* to have it all out with him?'

He shook his head. 'He talked about how he handled everything so badly when Harry got pregnant. What a selfish bastard he was. The regrets he's had ever since . . . about me.' Joe's cheeks grew pink. He smiled to himself about his little boast. 'He keeps a box of photos of me in his bedroom. There's a framed one by his bed.'

'Joe,' she said, 'I'm happy for you.'

'Well, he's hardly the perfect father.'

'No. Mine's not either.'

'But he's the only one I've got.'

'Exactly,' she said.

The sun came out and printed maple leaves across the wall. The room shimmered gold, all the dust and dirt alchemised. She had to say it now. She looked in his eyes and it tugged at her guts. When he delivered a baby by caesarean section and put his hands inside to pull the baby out, the mother could feel it despite the epidural. *It feels like someone doing the washing up in her belly.* He told her that soon after they met. It was how she felt when he looked at her. As if he'd slit her open and slid his hands inside. It felt like fear. And love.

'I used to sleep in here sometimes,' he said. 'When I was a kid. I'd bring a blanket and pillow and lie on that bench. I'd bring a torch and read comics.'

'Sounds fun.'

'Not really. I was scared of the spiders. All the strange noises. And I used to roll over and fall on the floor. I remember screaming and screaming once but nobody heard.'

'Why did you keep coming? When you had that whole big beautiful house?' *I have to tell you something tomorrow. It's pretty big.* He meant something about Harriet. He wanted to be out of the house, away from her.

'Harry had parties.'

'Right. You came for a bit of peace and quiet. Joe, I've got to—'

'That's not it,' he interrupted. 'No. I'd come because I'd seen her with someone. I spied on her sometimes. Of course I got upset. Then I'd run down here with my blanket and hope she'd go crazy when she realised I was missing. But she never did.'

'She never went crazy?'

'She never realised.'

'That must have hurt.'

461

'I was stupid. I went back to the house for breakfast and she didn't get up until lunch.'

'She loves you, though. You know that.' There was nothing big he could tell her about Harriet. She was an erratic, eccentric, overbearing mother. She exaggerated the sins of the father to wash away her own shortcomings.

'I do,' he said. 'I know.' He fiddled with a teacup and rubbed the dust from his fingers. The china shone white where he'd handled it.

'There must be a rainbow,' she said. The rain made splintery sounds on the cedar shingles.

'You've got something to tell me,' he said. The sunlight vanished and his face lost colour. It was grey and white like the teacup.

'You have too.' Maybe he was going to break up with her. And she wouldn't have to tell him anything.

'Ladies first.' He smiled but he looked grim.

'Joe, just say it. Please!'

'Okay. Right.' He took a deep breath and blew out hard. 'Oh, fuck. Okay. This is so fucking hard.' He laced his hands together behind his head and screwed up his face. It was going to take strength – physical strength – to get the words out. He was limbering up.

'It'll be okay,' she said. 'Honestly. Just say it.'

'Oh, fuck. Okay. This is it.' He took two long breaths. 'You know I've been seeing a therapist. About my dad. Right. The thing is, he uncovered . . . no, that's the wrong word. It turned into being more about Harry. I mean my relationship with Harry, which has been . . .'

'Dysfunctional,' said Yasmin. He wasn't breaking up with her. That was wishful thinking. He really did want to talk about Harriet.

'I understand certain things now about her, which means I understand some things about myself and—'

'I slept with someone,' she said, talking over him. She repeated it so there could be no confusion. No doubt about what she'd said. 'I slept with someone. More than once. I've been unfaithful. Several times.'

He gaped at her. 'What?' He leaned in across the table to check she wasn't some imposter.

'I'm truly sorry. I'm so, so sorry.'

'You *slept* with someone? Who? Who is it?' He looked at her in disbelief. He wasn't angry yet.

'Does it matter who he is?'

He couldn't look more stunned. He closed his mouth and opened it again. 'I guess it doesn't,' he said eventually.

'I really am sorry.'

'Wow!'

'I should have told you before. But there was . . . no, there's no excuse.'

'You slept with someone. You.'

'Yes, me,' she snapped. 'I did.' He was like a cartoon character bashed on the skull with little birds and stars flying round his head. Did he think she wasn't capable?

'How many times?' He blinked at her. He smiled. For a moment she thought he was about to laugh.

She'd prepared for him to be angry. She'd determined she would not justify herself by bringing up his infidelity. She'd run through every permutation and how she'd respond, even to unlikely scenarios such as Joe forgiving her and begging her to marry him still. But she hadn't prepared for this. He was acting as if she'd told him she could walk on water.

'I lost count,' she said.

'Really?'

'No.'

'I'm pissing you off. I didn't mean to,' he added with sudden and tremendous fervour. 'I don't want to piss you off.'

'I'm a horrible person!' She had fooled him so thoroughly. She'd fooled herself. 'I'm a terrible, awful person. That's the truth.'

'No, no,' he said. 'No, you're . . . '

He was quiet.

'You're not a terrible person,' he said.

'Things haven't been right between us, have they? I mean, this is supposed to be the honeymoon period where everything is perfect. And it hasn't been.'

'The honeymoon is after the wedding.'

'You know what I mean.'

He nodded.

'I think we should break up,' she said.

'Because you're with someone else?'

'I'm not with him.'

'But you don't want to be with me.'

'It's not working, Joe, is it? It's not how it's supposed to be. We can't just carry on and pretend everything's fine, because it's not. Don't you care that I've been sleeping with someone else?'

'I care,' he said.

'I haven't found the ring. I've looked everywhere. I'll pay you back for it.'

'Don't,' he said. There were tears in his eyes. 'So this is it, then? It's over. You've made up your mind.'

She couldn't speak any more so she nodded.

'Oh, God,' he said. His shoulders heaved and then he sobbed with his face in his hands. She got up and when she went to him he grabbed hold of her and wept on her chest. She didn't know she was crying until she saw her tears fall on the back of his neck.

'I'm sorry. I'm sorry.' She kept repeating it and he kept saying it back to her although he had nothing to apologise for. The rain beat down on the shingle roof and the door swung on its creaky hinge and somewhere a crow called out in alarm, and they held each other and swayed together like two survivors on a life raft.

Later, when the rain had finally stopped, and they'd shared a shop-bought prawn mayo sandwich and crisps from his ruck-sack, they took the chairs out to the veranda and watched the snails suck-and-slide across the boards. They watched the sag-and-spring of the dripping maple leaves. The crows fighting over some dainty morsel in the tall flowering grass.

Joe went into the summerhouse and came out with a blanket. He pushed his chair closer to hers so the arms touched. They sat with the blanket across their laps. He sneezed. Then she sneezed, and then they both laughed.

This is how it would be, she thought, if we'd been married for fifty years.

'Okay?' he said. 'Warm enough?'

'Yes,' she said. 'Thanks.'

He held out his hand for hers and she gave it. 'Are you in love? With him. Whoever he is.'

'Definitely not,' she said.

'Just "no" would be more convincing.'

'Just no, then. No.'

'You're allowed to say yes. Don't tell me who he is, though. Not yet.'

'What were you going to tell me? You said it was big.'

'It was,' he said. 'But now it's not.'

'But what was it?' She shivered though she wasn't cold. She was tired. Spent. It was the build-up, the tensing of every sinew and muscle, the climax, the relief.

'I haven't been completely honest with you,' he said.

'Oh,' she said. 'That makes two of us.'

'I went to see Neil. But only for two nights. I've been to Edinburgh as well, for a job interview.'

'Oh! And?'

'They offered it to me. I accepted.'

'Congratulations!'

'Thanks.'

'Why didn't you tell me?'

'Sorry,' he said. 'I was worried about telling you. The job starts right away and . . . running off when . . . then Coco and everything. I kept putting it off.'

'But Harriet knows?'

He looked away. 'Yes.'

'Is that why she's so upset?'

'She's upset because she knows. Yes.'

'You told her but you didn't tell me.' Of course Harriet would be distraught. She didn't want to let go of him. It was astonishing but there it was again, that little flare of jealousy.

He looked right at her. 'I'm sorry,' he said. 'For everything.'

'Me too,' she said. 'Is it too soon to say let's be friends?'

'I think the small print stipulates some kind of cooling-off period. But fuck it! Let's break the rules.'

'What are we going to say to everyone?'

'Whatever you want. I don't care.'

'We'll say it was mutual. Amicable.'

'Fine.'

'Ma will go home with me. But I haven't packed yet.'

'No rush. No one's kicking you out.'

'Flame's coming back in a couple of days.'

'How's *that* going to go?'

'It's not. It can't. Ma will go home with me.'

Joe yawned and shuddered. He took hold of her hand again and closed his eyes. 'You've knackered me out,' he said, and the way he said it made it sound pleasurable.

They sat there, hand in hand, and sometimes they talked and sometimes they didn't. She squeezed his hand. He squeezed hers. The sun came and went, flinging shadows across the grass. She closed her eyes and the lilacs smelled good, even the smell of the wet earth, the wet leaves, was good. They smelled like decay. Like spring. Like life.

Dusk came. Above the steaming rooftops, above the city jotted faintly in mauve the moon hung pale and patient. Soon it would be its turn to shine.

She had to ask. At last, she did. 'Were you going to break up with me?'

'What?'

'You're moving to Edinburgh. Were you going to ask me to go with you?' He'd cried when she said it was over but that didn't mean anything. She'd cried too. Maybe his tears were tears of relief.

'Of course.'

'We were still going to get married?'

'I love you,' he said.

'To be honest, sometimes I felt like you thought of me more as a friend.'

He shook his head.

'Tell me really and truly: were you going to break up with me?'

'I didn't want to break up with you,' he said. She believed it. She believed he didn't want to hurt her. He didn't want to tell her there would be no wedding, no marriage, no happily ever after.

'Fine,' she said. 'Make me the villain.'

'I'll try,' he said. 'But no promises. It's a pretty big ask.'

'I used to think I was a good person.'

'You are. You're not a bad person.'

'Sometimes I'm horrible.'

'You mean you're human?'

'I'm going to miss you.' Suddenly she was desolate. She'd had everything and she'd thrown it all away. And now she'd be alone. They could have made it work. He didn't want to break up with her. She'd thrown it all away and for what?

'I'll miss you too. I'll write to you. Will you write to me?'

'Letters?'

'Letters would be great. I don't think I've ever written a real one. Or got one.'

'But I won't have anything to write about!'

'You won't? Then you'll have to make something up.' It was dark now and he stood and held out his hand. 'Good people do bad things sometimes. Quite a lot of the time. It cost me a lot to learn that in therapy. But I'm letting you in on it for free.'

'Thanks,' she said. She kissed him, and he kissed her back, on the lips. It was a tender kiss. It was chaste.

DO YOU MISS HIM?

Ma was finally coming home. Four whole weeks after Yasmin packed her bags and moved back in with Baba. The whole time she'd been making excuses. I am having time for me, she said. I am still thinking. Yasmin said, You can think at home, Ma! Ma and Baba had reconciled at the hospital. Yasmin had seen them hold hands. She'd watched Ma forgive him. He'd saved the life of their grandchild and what else would he have to do before Ma said enough was enough and left the past in the past where it belonged?

Harriet is sick, said Ma. She needs me to take care of her. Yasmin said, She's got Rosalita for that. You can't stay there for ever.

Ma didn't mention Flame so Yasmin didn't either.

Yasmin said, You'll be closer to Coco. A *lot* closer. You'll hardly see her if you stay in North London. Ma snuffled into the phone. I will be ready. Just two more days.

But when Yasmin arrived after work, at 7 p.m., there was no sign of Anisah. Harriet's sharp-heeled ankle boots clicked across the hall and into the library.

'You take the armchair.' Harriet cleared a space for herself on the teal velvet sofa. It was covered in books. 'I thought we could talk in here,' she said.

The room was in tumult, the shelves ravaged, books scattered everywhere. White lilies filled the tall blue vase, their scent thickening the air, but they were past their prime, the petals thinning and browning, in a state of decay that should have ended their tenure in any room in the house.

'What happened?' said Yasmin.

'Can't find a book,' said Harriet brightly. 'You know how it is.'

'Which book were you looking for?'

'The right one,' said Harriet. 'Why don't you sit there, Yasmin?' She wore a sand-coloured ribbed-knit turtle-neck dress and she looked very elegant and very thin.

'Where's Ma? Is she packed? I've ordered a taxi for seven thirty, a big one because I'm not sure how much stuff she has to take.'

'Cancel it,' said Harriet. 'Please,' she added. 'She won't be ready. Please do sit, Yasmin.'

She sat and took out her phone. Before the call connected, she said, 'If I go upstairs and help her pack maybe we don't have to cancel.'

Harriet shook her head and Yasmin went ahead with the call.

'How are you?' said Harriet.

'Fine, but what's going on?'

'You've heard from him?' Harriet's lips stretched a little as if reaching for a smile that remained beyond them.

'We've exchanged emails a couple of times but we both need some space at the moment.' So that's what the interview was about. Of course! Harriet missed Joe so badly, she'd made herself ill, and of course she was desperate to hear any tiny crumb about him. In his email Joe said he was so busy at work he was managing to speak to Harriet once a week at most. 'How are you?' said Yasmin. 'How are you feeling?'

'I'm well, thank you,' said Harriet.

'You look it,' said Yasmin. But Harriet, despite her immaculate grooming, still looked worn. 'You look like you've recovered.'

'Do I? I miss him. Do you miss him?'

'Yes, I do.' She had known she would. It was natural for it to be painful for a while. 'But it was for the best that we split up. I don't think it was a mistake and I don't think he does either.' She was careful not to make it sound like a question, but she watched Harriet's face for signs, for a flicker of contradiction. Nothing. Yasmin experienced a stab of disappointment, as if she wanted Joe to regret breaking up. Which she didn't, of course. 'I'm very fond of him,' she said, stressing the crucial word. 'I think I always will be.'

'Yes,' said Harriet. 'Fond.'

They sat quietly for a few moments, as if observing a respectful silence for the death of the engagement. The death of love. Vanquished so easily. So easily replaced by something so weak. *Fond.*

'Oh, I almost forgot! I have to give you this.' She dug into her handbag and pulled out a crumpled polythene sandwich bag. 'Sorry, I don't know where the box is, it might be here. It's the ring, I found it at home, left it in the soap dish on the kitchen windowsill at Christmas.'

Harriet accepted the bag but put it down on the coffee table without comment.

'We don't use the soap dish because we have a liquid soap dispenser, but the dish is still there for some reason, and it has a lid and the lid was on. I don't know if I put the lid on or my father did, but I must have taken it off – the ring, I mean – to wash something up and then it's been hidden until now, well, a few days ago, but . . . ' She was babbling. She was overwhelmed by the certainty that Harriet was about to tell her something she did not want to hear. Not about Joe. It wouldn't be about Joe because that was over. Ma wasn't here. She wasn't coming home. She'd eloped with her girlfriend.

'Where's Ma? Where is she?'

'Anisah has asked me to talk to you about something.'

'Oh, God,' said Yasmin.

'You know the story of how your parents came to be married.'

'What's that got to do with anything?'

'The version you know isn't true. Anisah has decided the time has come for you to know.'

'She can tell me herself,' said Yasmin, getting up. 'Is she upstairs?'

'Yasmin, please sit down. Not for my sake, for your mother's. Thank you.' Harriet paused. 'Anisah will tell you herself. But she asked me to speak to you first so you're prepared, and so that you give her the space and time to speak. So that you are ready to listen.'

'Ha! Ready?' She snorted. 'I've been asking for the details since I was ... since forever, really. Right, okay. I'll go up and get her. She can tell me in the car on the way home.'

'Yasmin,' said Harriet sharply, 'Anisah was afraid you would be in a rush. That you'd try to bundle her away without giving her a chance to speak to you.'

'That's ridiculous,' said Yasmin. 'Nobody is *bundling* anyone anywhere.'

Harriet looked at her archly. 'Are you sure about that? You seem to be in a dreadful hurry.'

'We'll talk in the car. My father's waiting.'

'No,' said Harriet, in her most commanding voice. 'You won't. She will not do that. You will go upstairs to her and you will sit down and hear what she has to tell you. She will talk and you will listen. Is that clear?'

Yasmin, speechless with anger, got to her feet. She glared at

Harriet. How dare she! As if Yasmin didn't know how to behave with her own mother!

'She's a brave woman,' said Harriet as Yasmin reached the library door. 'Honour that, Yasmin. Honour her.'

LOVE MARRIAGE

'It was my first time walking alone but it was not far and I knew the way. I had a feeling of excitement. I was feeling like – now I am a free spirit!' Ma smiled. They were sitting together on the end of her bed. The packed bags were arranged neatly by the door, a suitcase, two holdalls, three boxes and six nylon laundry bags.

Yasmin was still bristling. *Honour her.* Of course she honoured her mother! She couldn't wait to get out of this house. 'Ma,' she said. She held it in. She would let Ma take her time, if it was suddenly so important to her to fill in the blanks, although she could scarcely have chosen a more inopportune moment.

'Yes?'

'Nothing, Ma. Go on, I'm listening.' So far Ma had talked about her first term as a student, how thrilled she had been to be allowed to attend university. One evening she went to the cinema with a girlfriend, a fellow student, who was picked up afterwards by her brother. He was supposed to give Anisah a ride home too. But Anisah said goodbye to her friend in the foyer, saying she wanted to walk home alone, which was forbidden, and swearing the friend to secrecy.

'I thought I knew the way, but when I came to the place

where Naana's office should be – our house was close to it – I did not recognise anything. Somewhere I took a wrong turn. I turned around and tried to walk back the way I came. I thought if only I get back to the cinema I will start again and all will be well this time. But I could not find my way. And I was so, so worried. Your naana would be angry with me because I was forbidden to walk alone.'

'Were you scared? Being out alone after dark.'

'So far, no. Only I was worrying about my father. All my money was gone at the cinema so I did not take a rickshaw. I did not want to go in the house and ask for money to pay the driver. I was not allowed to take a rickshaw alone, this was forbidden also. For some time I kept walking, thinking soon I will find the way.'

Ma rustled the folds of her sari up and to one side so she could sit cross-legged, as she continued to describe – in quite unnecessary detail – her perambulations. She wandered into an area without pavements, where the roads doubled as sewers and there were no streetlights, no shops except for the hole-in-a-wall kind. The houses looked on the verge of collapse. They had crazy rooftop extensions that jutted out so if you leaned out of a top-floor window you could reach your hand to the building opposite. Yasmin fought her impatience as best she could, surreptitiously surveying the bedroom for items Ma might have forgotten to pack. The wardrobe doors were open, the rack empty, but some items of clothing had fallen to the floor and been overlooked. A hairbrush lay on the dressing table.

'Then I was running,' said Ma. 'Panicking. It was a bad area and I ran away from it. I was scared what would happen to me.'

Yasmin took Ma's hand and squeezed it. Her mother had lived a sheltered life. But I would have panicked too, she thought. Lost in a dicey part of London, in my teens.

'By chance I took a better road and I came into a more

respectable area. I saw a man who looked respectable. I asked this man for directions.'

'Oh!' said Yasmin. Finally, she thought, we are getting to it. So that's how they met. That's the big secret! She'd asked her parents so many times how they met and all they said was vague things about libraries. What was so wrong about meeting your future husband in the street? 'It was Baba!'

'No! No!' cried Ma, as if Yasmin had suggested something scurrilous.

'Oh! I thought . . . Then, what's this story?'

'I am trying to tell.'

'Sorry, Ma.'

Anisah continued. The man she asked for directions was middle-aged and looked respectable. He was shocked to learn that this young girl was out at night all by herself and that not a soul in the city had any idea where she had gone. This is a dangerous situation, he said, for an innocent girl like you. In fact, he told her off, much as her own father would. Follow me, he said, and he turned and walked away and he didn't even look behind to check she was still with him.

When he went into the house, she stayed outside because she knew better than to go into a house with a man who was not her relative. But he was impatient, even a little angry. Come inside, he said, my wife will give you something to drink, something to eat, and when my driver returns, he will take you home. Could I use your telephone to call my parents please? She was reassured by the mention of his wife. Yes, he said, I will place the call and you will tell them that you are sorry and also that you are safe.

'Are you okay?' said Ma.

Yasmin nodded, though her stomach was starting to writhe. How did it end, this story? It could not end happily.

'I went inside with him but then he remembered the telephone was out of order. His wife had gone to stay with her sister.

I was thinking, thinking. What to do now? I said to him, Will your cook be kind enough to give me something to eat? I was not hungry, but I wanted to know we were not alone together.'

'Smart move,' said Yasmin. So, she has a scare but escapes because she keeps her wits about her. Was Baba the cook? Mystery solved *at last*.

'Smart move,' Yasmin repeated, with added gusto. She grinned at Anisah, but Anisah stared straight ahead and she was not smiling.

'He laughed, this man,' said Ma. 'Cook is sleeping, he said. But you look good enough to eat. I think I will have you for a snack.'

'Ma?' said Yasmin, because Anisah had grown still and silent. 'Ma?'

At last, Ma turned her head to look at Yasmin. 'I will tell you what happened next. I am ready to tell you, if you are ready to hear.'

'Tell me,' said Yasmin.

Anisah told the rest of her story. She tried to fight this man but he was much bigger, much stronger, and she was afraid he would kill her. When she tried to push him off, he punched her face. He dragged her upstairs afterwards, threw her in a bedroom and locked her inside. Some time passed, she didn't know how long. The window was barred or she would have thrown herself out of it. Anisah paused at this point to wipe the tears from Yasmin's cheeks. Anisah remained dry-eyed. Yasmin determined to control herself so her mother could speak freely. Whenever the bile rose in her throat, she choked it down as quietly as possible.

'He came back, maybe one hour later. I don't know how long. He came with another man, middle-aged and respectable-looking like him. They came in the room and he locked the door and put the key in his pocket. He said, You go first. He pushed his friend towards me.' Anisah's voice caught in her throat and she swallowed. But when she resumed, she spoke her words clearly and she held her head high. 'Then he laughed. He said, I mean second, I already had a go.'

Just before dawn they carried her downstairs and into the street and pushed her onto the back seat of a car. He drove her home, dragged her out so she fell on the road. She crawled the last few feet to the house.

What she'd done, her parents told her, was unforgivable. But what she did a few days later was worse. She was still in pain, still recovering from her injuries, when she went to the police. She went without her parents' permission. They'd threatened to lock her in the house if she even thought about reporting what had happened to her. Nobody must know. It was early in the morning when the man delivered her torn and bleeding and only servants and nobodies were awake. Servants could be controlled with bribes and threats, but if others got to hear about it, her life would be over. She was damaged goods. Nobody would want her.

She feigned compliance, even remorse. Tried to take care of the abrasions and lacerations. And when she got a chance she ran from the house and got a rickshaw to a police station. She had memorised the licence plate. She'd found a letter in the bedroom drawer that proved the man's identity, and hidden it in her clothes. She'd heard them call each other by name, that's how little they thought they had to fear from her.

Arrests were made. There was a scandal. The man was a local politician and protests were organised. It was some kind of plot to discredit him, a plot made by Muslims against a respectable Hindu, the newspapers reported. Your naani, said Anisah, promised to drink bleach and die. But your naana was a businessman and he settled the matter. He paid the men. They demanded a large amount of money. He knew, if he did not pay, the protests would continue and destroy his business.

She was kept under lock and key. It was the end of her education and as her parents saw it the end of her life, the rest would be all housework and waiting to die.

'Oh, Ma!' said Yasmin, choking. 'How ... awful ... terrible. How ... ' She had kept quiet to allow Ma to speak but now she had no words.

'Yes,' said Ma. She rustled her sari. 'But let me tell the rest. I will sit over there, because my back is aching now.'

Ma pushed Yasmin gently. Yasmin sat up. She hadn't realised she was leaning so heavily on Ma.

Anisah lowered herself into the chesterfield armchair. She sighed. 'I will finish the story of how I met your baba.'

Yasmin stared at her mother. Her pink and yellow sari, the bangles on her softly padded wrist, the messy crown of hair, the round nose that twitched when she was emotional. It was twitching now. 'Ma,' said Yasmin, 'what you've just told me, it's so ... I mean, you don't have to tell me now about meeting Baba. You could tell me another day. This is just so ... *big* ... maybe you and Baba is another story for another day.'

'It is the same story,' said Ma. She patted the scrolled arms of the chair, as if she knew it would miss her when she had gone.

Yasmin's grandfather, Anisah explained, had a friend who was a professor of some kind of medical science. He was moving to Bombay for a new job. My driver will be unemployed, he said, and he is a bright boy, very keen to improve himself. I have two drivers, Anisah's father said.

I was thinking of your daughter's troubles. It will be difficult for you to find the kind of husband for her that you would have selected so easily before. Anisah's father said, No, I will not give her to a driver. Better to have a spinster daughter than a driver as son-in-law.

The professor didn't give up. I agree, he said. But this boy has something, he has determination, he works like an ox but he is no dumb animal. He finished high school and dreams of becoming a doctor. Half the night he reads my science journals, sometimes I quiz him on a topic and he is better than most of my postgraduate students. If you invest in this boy you settle the matter of your daughter's future and you will have a doctor for a son-in-law.

And is he willing? Anisah's father, though he valued his family's status highly, suspected even a servant would not want a woman who in his own eyes had been so publicly devalued, humiliated, who had brought shame on all their heads. Even a poor man has his pride.

I'll speak to him, the professor promised. In two days, I will return with his answer.

'Go on,' said Yasmin, because Ma had stopped speaking.

'You know the rest,' said Anisah.

RESCUE ME

'Oh, Ma!' she said, between sobs, sitting at her mother's feet. 'Ma!' She wept into Anisah's lap.

'Don't cry,' said Ma. 'It is okay.'

Yasmin hiccuped. All that sobbing. She looked up at Ma.

Ma was still dry-eyed, but she looked worried. 'I am sorry,' she said. 'I am sorry for upsetting you like this.'

'Oh, Ma!' said Yasmin, and succumbed to another weeping jag.

Ma waited patiently. She held Yasmin's hand and when the tears finally stopped coming, she used the end of her sari to dry Yasmin's face.

'Why didn't you tell me before?' said Yasmin.

'It was long ago,' said Anisah. 'And your father did not want to. I also did not think it was a suitable story for telling to children.'

'But I've not been a child for years,' said Yasmin.

'You are always my child.'

'I wish you'd told me before.'

'You think these are easy things for me to say? You think it is easy to tell? To tell to my child?'

'I'm sorry ... sorry, Ma. It's so awful. I'm so sorry that happened to you. You were so brave and I'm proud of you.'

'Now you understand about your father. Some things you will understand now?'

Yasmin's mind raced to catch up. 'You mean, why Baba had to pay back the money for his education? It was a business arrangement, so he had to pay the money back. I didn't even know about that until Baba told me, just months ago. I always thought Naana supported your choice and you chose a poor boy, so Naana paid for everything.'

'He always made hard bargains. He was a businessman, always. But what I mean is, you understand now why Baba does not mix with other Bengalis, other Muslims, Indians. Why he has kept so separate. It is the shame.'

'Shame? Ashamed of you? I don't think that's true at all.'

'No. Shame is for himself only. This I believe.'

'But why? It doesn't make sense.' Baba? Ashamed? Baba was upright and dignified and proud. 'Oh! The home visits! The other women . . .'

'No. That is separate.'

'Then I don't understand. Baba is so proud of everything he's achieved, how far he's come, and—'

'Yes,' said Ma, 'your father has pride and also he has shame. These two are two sides of same penny, isn't it?'

'The same—' Yasmin stopped herself from correcting Ma. 'Are they?'

'Yes, they belong to each other. It is so.'

'Okay,' said Yasmin, 'but what is he ashamed of?'

'He is not ashamed of his wife,' said Ma. 'Always from the start he is telling her how she is good and brave and he is proud of her. In his heart he is proud of his wife . . .' Ma smiled. Though she'd distanced herself from the accolade she still seemed a little bashful. 'But in his heart, he is ashamed of the arrangement. This business arrangement with my father. He takes the girl, who does not want to marry. He takes her for money.'

482

'He loves you, though, Ma,' said Yasmin, the tears once again welling. 'He does love you. I know he does.'

'I know,' said Ma. 'Your father is a good man. For one year after we married, he did not come near me. In that way. Always apologising. Apologising for being my husband. He knew everything what has happened to me and he was unhappy how my misfortune was his good fortune. You understand?'

'I think so,' said Yasmin. 'I don't know. But also, he rescued you, didn't he? In a way.'

Ma acknowledged it. 'Rescue me, yes.'

'And you rescued him.'

'These things also are true. But I am explaining your father's shame to you. About the arrangement. He took it but he was ashamed of himself because he took it.'

'And now?'

'We have discussed all. On the telephone.'

'Did he know you were going to tell me tonight?'

'He knows.'

'Oh,' said Yasmin. That was why Baba changed his mind about coming to collect Ma this evening. 'And who else knows?'

Ma was lost in thought. She didn't answer.

'Does Arif know?'

'No. I will tell, but not now. He is busy with Coco.'

'Does Flame know?'

'She knows.'

Try telling that to a woman who's been raped. That morning in the kitchen, Yasmin had assumed Flame was talking about herself. But Harriet had gone straight to Ma. I was so blind, thought Yasmin.

'Does Flame know you're going home tonight?' But maybe Ma wasn't going. She looked so wistful. Maybe she was thinking about staying, waiting for Flame to return from her latest trip to Brussels or Paris or wherever it was she was performing. 'You're coming with me, aren't you? Ma?' Yasmin struggled to her feet, and held out her hands to help her mother up.

'Yes. I am coming.' But Ma didn't move.

'What about Flame?' said Yasmin, letting her hands drop. 'Are you still …? I mean … is …?' She didn't know how to phrase it.

'She is my special friend,' said Ma. 'You are against her. But she is good.'

'I'm not *against* her. I don't know her, really.'

'You do not like because she is a woman.'

'Because she's a woman?' Yasmin repeated dumbly. Was Ma accusing her of prejudice?

'She is lesbian.'

'I *know*, Ma! I don't care. But what about Baba?'

'He is my husband.'

'I don't understand. Are you and Flame going to …?' Her head was spinning. She smoothed the skirt of her navy shift, looked down at her ballet flats, trying to anchor herself to reality, to ordinariness. 'I suppose,' she said, struggling to make sense of it, 'he had his home visits, his other women … I suppose it's fair.'

'Fair?' said Ma. 'No. It is not like this.'

'How is it, then?'

'What do you want to know?'

Yasmin sighed and shook her head. She didn't know what she wanted to know. 'Baba said you agreed to him having affairs.'

'Your father is a good man, but I did not want that side of things. I did my duty only and after I have children I did not want to any more. He knew. He did not try to force anything. The opposite. And I told him, It is okay – go, go and find a way. This is what he did.'

Yasmin stared down at this woman, her mother. Ma was exactly the same as ever and completely different. A sheltered life. Yasmin hadn't understood anything. She was the one who was naïve. She was the one who had been sheltered.

'He's bought new spider plants for the kitchen,' said Yasmin. 'He's painted the gate. He's so excited you're coming back. Mr Hartley as well. He keeps asking about you.'

'We will go now,' said Ma.

They moved the bags downstairs. Harriet had gone to bed; she and Ma had already said their farewells. Yasmin felt sorry for Harriet, in that big house all alone.

They sat in the kitchen to wait for the taxi.

'My angel,' said Ma, 'are you okay? You are very sad, no?'

'Yes, it's awful what you went through.' Yasmin's eyes were still sore.

'No, you have broken the engagement. You are suffering.'

'I'm not.' She chewed her bottom lip. 'Really, I'm not. I'm okay. It had to end and the end wasn't as bad as I thought it would be.' Joe had taken it so well. Too well. Which proved they weren't meant to be together.

'Maybe after some time apart your mind will change. Love will grow again.'

'No, it won't.' She was so busy with the new job, the longer journey, the insane hours, and she'd started studying again – she thought about Joe, she missed him, but they were not in love with each other and that was that.

'I have taken time away,' said Ma, 'now I am going back to your father. You see? Life is not simple. You do not know what will happen with Joe.'

'Okay, Ma.' She wouldn't argue, because Ma had used her best stubborn voice. She wasn't in love with Joe. And she had decided she didn't believe in love. Love was as phoney as the story she wrote at school about Baba and Ma. What was love anyway, except a biological trick? It was larger doses of hormones like oxytocin and dopamine, which delivered a euphoric rush. It was lower levels of serotonin, which induced anxiety and made you focus obsessively on the object of your 'love'. It was elevated levels of adrenalin and norepinephrine making your heart flutter and your palms sweat. She liked Joe and he liked her. The rest was a temporary chemical imbalance.

'Oh! I must take the labels,' said Ma, getting up. She hurried towards the utility room. 'There is a little box I must take.'

'Anisah's Achaars: Authentic Bengal Pickles, made in my own kitchen,' Yasmin said, reading off a label when Ma returned. 'I like it! The new labels look great.' They would also become true after Ma went home.

'Carrot, lime and ginger has been my bestseller. Only two left. All stock is low. Tomorrow I will make more.'

'Fantastic! Ma, I'm proud of you!'

Ma beamed.

'I'll take the wedding jewellery and sell it at the weekend.'

'No, I will do this. I will sell for a good price.'

'I'm sure you will. Arif will be happy. He deserves it, and they need to have their own place.'

Ma took Yasmin's hand. 'Your brother asked me to tell you something. He does not want you to be upset.'

'Oh, God,' said Yasmin, 'what now?'

'He is getting married.'

'To Lucy?'

Ma laughed. 'To Lucy. Who else should he marry?'

'But why would I be upset?'

'Because you were supposed to marry. You are the oldest. You work, you find the right boy and make the plan to settle down. Arif has jumped ahead. You do not mind about it? He is worried for you.'

'Mind! No, I don't mind. I'm delighted.'

Ma patted Yasmin's hand. 'I told him. I told him, Arif, your sister will be pleased for you.' But she looked relieved, as if she too had doubted it.

They heard the sound of tyres and gravel and then the car horn.

'Let's load up,' said Yasmin.

'You remember,' said Ma, 'the first time I was coming here? How nervous. About dress. About food. And about Mrs Sangster.'

Yasmin nodded.

Ma looked around and got up slowly. 'Things have changed,' she said. 'So many things have changed.'

SIX MONTHS LATER

POSSIBILITY

The doorbell rang again. Yasmin raised the sash window, leaned out into the cool crispness of the autumn air, and surveyed the sleepy Sunday-morning street. A clubber, stripped to the waist, hoodie tied around his hips, lifted his arms and hugged himself as he stumbled homeward. A dogwalker steered her inquisitive black Lab away from him. The delivery van was parked in the middle of the road.

'Hello? Up here!' Yasmin called down. 'Is it signed for? Do I have to sign for it?'

The driver stepped back, shook his head and held up the package as if to prove it.

'Then I'll buzz the door open and you can just leave it in the hall. Thank you!'

She'd already run down once this morning to receive a package for Rania, and she was trying to concentrate on something important. Rania was writing for a new magazine aimed at Muslim women. She wrote on beauty, fashion and halal dating, and companies had started sending her samples of clothes or make-up. It was only a sideline to her work as a lawyer but she approached it with the same energy and rigour that she brought to her day job. Right now, she would be returning from

Bradford where she had gone to see for herself how a modest-fashion brand produced its goods. She wanted to find out if the clothes were made in sweatshop conditions. If so, it was something she would not condone and promote.

Yasmin sat down at her desk. She was writing a letter back to Joe and although she was three pages in, she hadn't even begun to reply. She'd told him about this flat that she and Rania were renting on the top floor of a divided Georgian house in a genteel street in Camberwell, with a gastropub on the corner. They'd been here five months now. When you turned past the pub onto the main road you breathed in traffic fumes, the aroma of fried food and freshly baked daktyla bread, and the essence of city, which was petrol and steel, money, poverty, possibility, friction and rubbing-along. She'd written about Rania's new part-time incarnation as fashion-guru-cum-agony-aunt. As Rania put it, there had been a 'backlash to the backlash' after the viral video incident.

Yasmin's fingers hovered over the laptop keyboard. Perhaps she should delete everything she had written so far and get straight to the point. But what did she want to say? She'd received his letter, an actual letter waiting for her in the communal hallway on the communal shelf above the radiator, with a real stamp, and her name and address handwritten on the front, though the pages inside were typed and printed out ... she'd received his letter three weeks ago.

A few days later she sent him a holding email, to let him know she would be writing a proper letter.

She'd written about Ma. Anisah's Achaars were selling well at farmers' markets across London. Ma and Baba loaded up the Fiat Multipla and on weekends he drove her to wherever she needed to go. Often, he stayed to help her serve customers, or hand out samples. Sometimes Flame went too. *Don't ask me,* Yasmin had written, *how that works.* All Ma would say about

Flame was that everyone in Tatton Hill minded their own business, meaning Yasmin should as well.

Yasmin needed another coffee. She needed a break, although this morning she had added only one sentence to the letter, and then deleted it.

While the coffee brewed, she leaned against the sink and thought about what Ma had said about wearing a sari from now on for all the market days. It increased sales. It did not make the pickles authentic but if people believed it then what else should she do? She could make English-style chutneys just as well, and jams too, but the apple or fresh fig chutneys and the gooseberry jams and orange marmalades hardly sold at all, whatever she wore.

In his letter, Joe had asked if 'anything more had happened' with Pepperdine. He didn't name him, of course, because he didn't know a name. 'The guy', he wrote. 'I was wondering if anything more had happened between you and the guy. You don't have to tell me, obviously, but I find myself wondering.'

Yasmin opened the fridge. No milk. She'd forgotten she'd used the last of it on her cereal. She'd have to drink the coffee black.

She hadn't thought about Pepperdine for ages. When she did what she remembered most of all was how unhappy she had been. That savage desire. The need she had to escape. The way she blamed him for not falling into line with whatever fantasy she had been writing for herself. Pepperdine didn't play his role according to her script. But she hadn't shared that script with him, and now she couldn't even recall what it had contained. Except for the fact she was cast as the lead. No, nothing more had happened. She still owed him an apology.

Yasmin took her coffee back to her bedroom and sat down in front of her laptop again. She scrolled up to the top of the letter.

Dear Joe,

I'm glad you told me everything and I want to start by saying I'm not angry at all. It must have been very difficult for you to write it all down.

Well, you asked for news about everyone, so I'll tell you, starting with Arif. He and Lucy and Coco are all doing well. Coco is crawling now! You've probably seen on Facebook? If so, you know how gorgeous she is. Arif has started his first proper job, at a TV production company as a researcher, and Baba is pretending he knew all along that his son would 'enter the media', as he puts it. Arif's film has been shown at a couple of local documentary film festivals, so that's another feather in his cap. Lucy's still on maternity leave from the orthodontic practice. They haven't got their own place yet because Arif is determined to save up himself and not take any handouts. Looks like he's finally growing up!

She'd written about her work, the department, the new colleagues, and an entire paragraph on the daily commute to Brighton. She'd written about Rania, about the flat and how much trouble the removal men had getting Rania's sandstone coffee table up four flights of stairs, and about Ma and Baba and Flame. She'd told him everything without saying anything.

In his letter Joe said he was attending a support group in Glasgow called Sex and Love Addicts Anonymous. He said there wasn't a group in Edinburgh, so he had to travel. Joe said apologising to the people you've hurt because of your addiction was part of the twelve-step recovery process. He wrote that she should not feel any pressure to absolve him of anything. She thought long and hard about this. What was there to absolve? He'd told her from the beginning he was sick of dating around. He hadn't been clear about what that meant exactly but she

494

hadn't asked. Once he had tried to tell her but she stopped him. She didn't want to know.

He mentioned that his therapist, whom he had been seeing for online sessions, had died suddenly of a heart attack. Joe regretted not thanking him properly while he had the chance. *In a way, though it may sound a bit dramatic, Sandor saved my life. Perhaps a better way to put it would be, he saved me from a life I didn't want, and gave me the possibility of a better one. I wish I had told him that, though I think he probably knew.*

Without Sandor, he went on to explain, he would never have come to understand the root cause of his addiction. And without that understanding, he'd only been able to suppress it, as he had during the time when they were together – barring once, though he didn't mean to minimise the transgression – and what Sandor had given him was the means to overcome the addiction rather than contain it.

Harriet had been devastated. Blindsided. Enraged. Terrified. She was, above all, in denial. At first, she refused to accept there could be even a grain of truth in the notion that she had nurtured her son in any way that could conceivably have been a little unhealthy, let alone outright destructive.

She's come out of the other end now, Joe wrote. *It was a long, dark tunnel but she's come through it as I knew she would. (Sometimes I doubted it, but not often.) It took her a while to understand that I'm not blaming her but I am holding her responsible. There's a difference. Once she got it, she could start hearing me properly. We could have real conversations. And here's the biggie – she's worked out something incredibly important about her own childhood.*

Yasmin took a sip of the coffee. Without milk it was too bitter and she went back to the kitchen to add a teaspoon of sugar.

She stood at the counter and stirred the spoon in the mug, round and round, scrape-and-clank, scrape-and-clank, bubbles on the surface, tidemarks around the rim. She'd been wrong about so many things. Looking back, she'd understood so little. She'd been wrong about Arif and Lucy. She hadn't understood Baba. She'd made all sorts of misjudgements and assumptions. She'd taken Ma for granted, thought of her as just Ma, and not a person. Certainly not as the impressive person that she was. Also, she'd misjudged Ma's relationship with Harriet. As if Harriet could only have been interested in her as a temporary exhibit, or pet to be fondled and discarded. She'd underestimated Ma and she'd underestimated Harriet. She'd force-fitted false narratives onto Pepperdine who had always been straightforward with her. He was kind and available. She was neither. Yet she managed to blame him for failing to provide a miracle cure for her tangle of miseries. She had even been wrong about Rania, her best friend, whom she castigated for always being right, for being invulnerable.

And Joe.

It's me, she thought, watching the spoon go round and round, it's me who had to be right all the time. And mostly I was wrong.

But there was one thing she had been right about, the thing she kept telling herself was stupid. There was something off about Harriet and Joe's relationship. She didn't understand it, thought she was weirdly jealous. Or insecure. Or prudish. Told herself to get over it when Harriet went to talk to Joe while he was in the shower.

I didn't understand it, but I felt it. Should she write that – something like that – in her letter? How would it make him feel if she did? Or if she didn't?

She took a sip of the coffee. Too sweet. She poured the rest into the sink.

*

496

Harriet had gone back to writing her childhood memoir. She had said so when she came to dinner at Beechwood Drive.

But it was Joe who had explained why. She'd found her story, at last: the covertly incestuous relationship between her and her father. She had promised, without any prompting from Joe, that the memoir would be confined to her own childhood and she wouldn't write a word about Joe. She was learning to respect his boundaries and was eager to prove it. *It's progress*, wrote Joe. *I can safely say that we are both making progress.*

Harriet and Ma were still friends. A week ago Ma had called to tell her to put the radio on because Harriet was being interviewed about sexual harassment in the workplace. How a whole new wave of feminism was being mobilised. The interviewer introduced her as 'Harriet Sangster, feminist activist and commentator', and she said, 'Activist, writer and intellectual, darling. Do try to be accurate.'

Joe wanted to know if she would come to Edinburgh for a weekend. She could stay at his flat or he'd book her a room somewhere if that would be better. They'd said they would stay friends, but maybe she wouldn't want that now she knew the truth about him. He'd understand if that's how she felt.

Maybe after some time apart your mind will change. Love will grow again.

She didn't believe in love. She reminded herself of this fact.

Her palms were clammy and her pulse was elevated.

He wanted her to go to Edinburgh and every time she thought about it, which was often, there was a chemical reaction in her body. How had he phrased it exactly? The letter lay on her bed. She read it over every day as soon as she woke up.

She threw herself onto the duvet and snatched the letter up and searched for the page. Here. This part. Right here.

It's probably too much to hope for, but I'd love it if you came up for a weekend. I'd love to see you. Stay here or I'll book you a room. There's a hotel close by. I wouldn't blame you if I never hear from you again. But I'd be incredibly sad, because I miss you. I wish everything was different. I wish I'd done everything differently. Told you from the very beginning. I can't undo the past and I can't know the future, except for one thing: I'll never make the same mistakes again. I will probably make different ones. I won't start pleading my case because I don't feel I have any right to, and I've probably pushed it already, for which I can only apologise. Don't answer straight away. Or not at all if you don't want to.

Yasmin curled herself into a ball.

She hugged her knees into her chest and closed her eyes and her smile was so big it was like her whole body was smiling.

Oxytocin. Dopamine. Norepinephrine. The release of hormones. That's what was happening. That's all it was. Physiology. Simple physiology.

Life is not simple. You do not know what will happen with Joe.

She lay, curling into the feeling, enjoying the warmth of the sunlight that suddenly fell on her, the backs of her eyelids tingled pleasantly in the glow; and she could sense the rich honey tones of the light that drenched the bed, the room, the flat, the whole of the city. It felt beautiful.

She opened her eyes. There was no sun. The day was steadily blue, grey and white. *Life is not simple.*

Still, she felt joyous. Full of irrational hope and nonsensical joy. She felt like shouting. Or singing. Or dancing. Due to a temporary chemical imbalance. For no reason.

She jumped off the bed and opened the wardrobe door to look at herself in the full-length mirror. Her hair was a little wild. Her eyes were wide and her cheeks flushed, her lips looked full. Physiology. Basic physiology. She hugged herself as the half-naked clubber had hugged himself walking down the street, coming off whatever high he'd been on.

The question was: were they causes or were they symptoms?

That's what she should be asking herself. Which came first? It was chicken and egg. Egg and chicken. Love and hormones. Hormones. Love. Egg. Chicken. Egg. She was giddy. That was a symptom. Or was it a cause?

I wish I'd done everything differently. That makes two of us!

She flung the sash window open and leaned out into the street that was waking up. A woman walking by with a giant loaf of Greek bread in her hand, covered in nigella and sesame seeds. An old man dressed for Siberia, beetling along at an impressive pace. Two boys kicking a football across the road from one pavement to the other. A silver Audi slowing and then speeding off. A family in beautiful white robes making their way as they did every Sunday to the Eritrean Orthodox church.

'Good morning,' called Yasmin, to everyone and no one.

The white-robed man looked up. 'Good morning,' he said. He patted his two children on the shoulder and they looked up and smiled and repeated the greeting.

'Life is not simple,' said Yasmin.

The man regarded her seriously. He nodded as if he understood her point perfectly. As if it was a good idea to shout it out of a window. As if Ma's words were worth repeating. As if they were worth something in this world.

CREDITS

Page 8: Meridale V. Baggett, M.D., Sarah E. Turbett, M.D., Shmuel S. Schwartzenberg, M.D., and James R. Stone, M.D., Ph.D., 'A 59-Year-Old Man with Fever, Confusion, Thrombocytopenia, Rash, and Renal Failure', *The New England Journal of Medicine*, 2014, 370:651-660
DOI: 10.1056/NEJMcpc1310004. Excerpt reproduced with the permission of *The New England Journal of Medicine*.

Page 405: Image Challenge, 20 December 2018, in *The New England Journal of Medicine* (https://www.nejm.org/image-challenge?ci=20181220)/. Excerpt reproduced with the permission of *The New England Journal of Medicine*.

Page 437: Excerpt from *The Collected Papers of Albert Einstein* reproduced with the permission of Princeton University Press.

ACKNOWLEDGEMENTS

Many publications were helpful to me in the research and writing of this novel. I mention the main ones here, and I would like to express my thanks to their authors. In the world of doctors and patients: *Elderhood: Redefining Aging, Transforming Medicine, Reimagining Life*, by Louise Aronson; *Also Human: The Inner Lives of Doctors*, by Caroline Elton; *In Stitches: The Highs and Lows of Being an A&E Doctor*, by Dr Nick Edwards; *Your Life in My Hands: A Junior Doctor's Story*, by Rachel Clarke; *The Language of Kindness: A Nurse's Story*, by Christie Watson; and *The Doctor Will See You Now*, by Max Pemberton. In the field of psychotherapy, I am indebted to the works of Gabor Maté, in particular *In the Realm of Hungry Ghosts: Close Encounters with Addiction*; to Kenneth M. Adams, author of *Silently Seduced*; to Richard Schwartz and Martha Sweezy, authors of *Internal Family Systems Therapy*; and to Susan Cheever for *Desire: Where Sex Meets Addiction*. I have also found inspiration in the following texts: *Tales from the Quran and Hadith* by Rana Safvi; *It's Not About the Burqa*, edited by Mariam Khan; *Love, InshAllah: The Secret Love Lives of American Muslim Women* by Ayesha Mattu & Nura Maznavi; and *The Things I Would Tell You: British Muslim Women Write*, edited by Sabrina Mahfouz.

Thank you to Neel Mukherjee, for saying, 'Let it be there.' I am grateful beyond words.

I'd also like to thank Grant and Wendy Bardsley, Michelle Byford, Santi Pathak, John Mullan and Bran Nicol for reading the manuscript and giving such helpful feedback; Adam Kay for including the chapter *Mrs Antonova* in *Dear NHS: 100 Stories to Say Thank You*; Beatrice Monti della Corte Rezzori and the Santa Maddalena Foundation for providing my first writing retreat: six weeks of exceptional hospitality, glorious views from the 'Bruce Chatwin tower', and the most luxurious gift a writer can receive – time; Ailah Ahmed for sterling editorial advice; Sarah Savitt for being a brilliant editor and publisher; Nico Taylor for the beautiful cover; Hayley Camis, Zoe Hood, Celeste Ward-Best, Nithya Rae and the whole Virago team for being such a joy to work with; Nan Graham (as ever and always!), Sabrina Pyun, and Katie Monaghan at Scribner; Jonny Geller and Binky Urban, for unstinting support and guidance; Viola Hayden, Ciara Finan, Kate Cooper, Katie Battock, Nick Marston, Camilla Young, and all the wonderful denizens of Curtis Brown; and thank you to Helen Brice for the great unlocking.

Thank you to Simon Torrance for living with this book (and me) for so many years. And to Felix and Shumi, for being yourselves.